W9-CFQ-629

THE FLOATING
FELDMANS

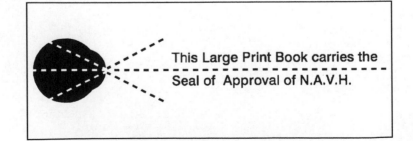

This Large Print Book carries the
Seal of Approval of N.A.V.H.

THE FLOATING
FELDMANS

ELYSSA FRIEDLAND

THORNDIKE PRESS
A part of Gale, a Cengage Company

Farmington Hills, Mich • San Francisco • New York • Waterville, Maine
Meriden, Conn • Mason, Ohio • Chicago

LIBRARY OF CONGRESS CIP DATA ON FILE.
CATALOGUING IN PUBLICATION FOR THIS BOOK
IS AVAILABLE FROM THE LIBRARY OF CONGRESS

ISBN-13: 978-1-4328-7023-2 (hardcover alk. paper)

Published in 2019 by arrangement with Berkley, an imprint of Penguin Publishing Group, a division of Penguin Random House, LLC

Printed in Mexico
1 2 3 4 5 6 7 23 22 21 20 19

For Charlie, Lila, and Sam,
my Floating Friedlings

It started with a shriek. Then a series of gasps. Finally, from somewhere deep in the room, came a chorus of "Fight, fight, fight!" The chant quickly grew in volume, and suddenly it seemed like everyone was shouting for blood.

"Ladies and gentlemen, may I *please* have your attention!" Julian Masterino attempted to calm the chaos for a third time, but he was no match for the angry rabble. From his perch on the bandstand, they looked like a swarm of flies, circling and buzzing in a cacophonous roar. Normally Julian's uniform, a fitted white sailor's jumper and his ever-present megaphone, was enough to will a hush over a rambunctious crowd. But tonight, in a black tuxedo, he blended in with everyone else on the ship. To make matters worse, the volume lever on his megaphone was broken. Meanwhile, babies wailed in high chairs, the elderly guests

7

whined from motorized scooters, and the able-bodied adults dashed about in their formal wear vying for a better look at the crime scene. The leader of the barbershop quartet, the evening's opening act, gazed desperately at Julian from under his bowler hat and plucked a few helpless chords in C on his banjo. Julian gave him the universal symbol for "not now," a quick slash to the neck, and he quieted down.

The paramedic team skidded onto the dance floor, propelled into the scrum of people by the weight of equipment they probably wouldn't need. To Julian's practiced eye, the two gentlemen who had, moments earlier, been throwing punches at each other were not the sort of people for whom violence was a preferred method of conflict resolution. They were amateurs at best — and the injuries they had sustained were undoubtedly more to their psyches than physical. Still, the older guy was on the ground, blood running from his nose. It was time to clear the room.

But how could it be done? Julian was a seasoned pro, but even he had never tried a last-minute relocation of three thousand hungry diners. Short of an iceberg, he'd never envisioned a scenario that would require such a thing. And now, faced with a

8

ship full of guests determined to ignore his instructions, there weren't a lot of good options left. Julian could think of only one surefire way to regain command of his people. Throwing caution to the wind, he reached for his megaphone and pressed firmly on the talk button.

"Attention, all guests aboard the *Ocean Queen.* The main buffet and all-night ice cream bar on the Starboard Deck will be closed until further notice."

A shocked hush immediately dropped over the crowd, and Julian smiled to himself.

"That's not fair," complained an anguished mother of three. "My kids are still hungry!"

Hungry? On average, passengers aboard the *Ocean Queen* consumed six thousand calories per day, sitting down to no less than five full meals. The midmorning "snack" consisted of pastries, a full salad bar, and a taco station. Afternoon tea was the least dainty meal Julian had ever laid eyes on. Instead of finger sandwiches and bite-size lemon tarts, the kitchen staff put out twelve-foot loaves of streusel from which the guests could hack off as much as they liked. And, as far as Julian could tell, they liked a lot of streusel.

"This is an all-inclusive ship," barked a

burly fellow who stood to the left of the bandstand. He had accessorized his tuxedo with a bolo tie and cowboy hat and was already working his way through a plate piled high with meat. "And we all know you save the best food for the formal night!"

Julian was prepared to promise an impromptu chocolate fountain and make-your-own-sushi opportunity, if only everyone would exit in an orderly fashion. But before he could position his megaphone, an attractive older woman stood up and addressed the crowd. She had been crouching on the floor, tending to the more senior of the two bloodied combatants — the sad-faced man who was now cradling his knee. Julian couldn't help but admire the way the woman presented herself: She wore a beautiful blue satin gown that stretched forgivingly across her wide hips and her hair was swept into a precise chignon.

"What is wrong with you people?" she shouted, her voice impressive and thunderous. "From the minute you woke up this morning, you've been stuffing your faces, pushing and shoving in the buffet lines like you've never seen a croissant before. Get a grip on yourselves. My husband was just punched in the face by my son-in-law, who has apparently hated our family for the past twenty years."

"That's not true," said the other erstwhile combatant in a breathy voice as he was lifted onto a stretcher by the paramedics. This second, younger man was obviously the bitter son-in-law. "It's just . . . you guys . . . acting juvenile . . . and I . . ."

"You do not need to defend yourself!" belted a younger woman in a pink dress who stood beside the man's stretcher. She stared daggers at the ballsy lady in the blue satin and said, "Mitch has *nothing* to apologize for, *Mother.*"

Holy hell. A dueling mother-daughter ensemble was certainly not needed on the night that was meant to be the crescendo of the trip, the black-tie party known as An Enchanted Evening, which would set the tone for how generous the guests would be when parceling out gratuities. And if they weren't opening their wallets widely, Julian would be hearing about it from everyone on the staff, from the lifeguards down to the porters, the whole crew blaming him for not keeping the guests happy.

"Everyone, listen to the cruise director, and get off of this deck *now,*" yelled the mother. Then the daughter chimed in: "You will be fed. You will have your formal night. You will be 'enchanted,' for heaven's sake.

11

Just let the doctors attend to my husband in peace."

"Mom? Elise? What the hell is going on?" asked a middle-aged man as he pushed through the crowd. The newcomer had graying hair tied in a bun, and, as Julian couldn't help noticing, his outfit did not conform to the night's dress code require-ment. He was tugging on the hand of a hu-man Barbie doll teetering along in four-inch heels. Julian blinked twice. This overly made-up girl wearing a dress that could have doubled as an Ace bandage was none other than the amazing yogini he'd met in Ashtanga class earlier that day.

A picture was forming in Julian's mind. This was the Feldman family. He vaguely remembered chatting with them at the around-the-world dinner the night before, and he'd seen the daughter — her name was Elise — just hours earlier in the coffee shop. They were all on board to celebrate a big birthday. If memory served him correctly, they were vacationing together in honor of the matriarch in blue.

Julian hated to see things like this happen on one of his trips, and not just because it meant reduced gratuities and filing extra paperwork with the corporate office. It truly broke his heart when a family with grand

12

plans to bond and share quality time was reduced to blows and name-calling. This wasn't the first time it had happened. And it wouldn't be the last. Maybe it was the fact that passengers on cruise vacations were sequestered from the outside world — and that submerged feelings were bound to surface whenever people volunteered to isolate themselves. Or maybe it was the consistent low-level nausea they experienced at sea that activated bad behavior. Julian had one theory, originally espoused by the ship's previous captain, that involved those motion sickness patches everyone stuck behind their ears: He posited that they actually worked like hearing aids, amplifying all the irritations that normally went unnoticed.

Julian's assistant, Lindsay, approached him from behind and whispered something in his ear. He smiled, knowing the immediate crisis had been solved.

"Attention, all passengers," Julian said, clearing his throat for emphasis and raising his megaphone once again. "A free drink will be provided to all guests who relocate to the Mariposa Ballroom on the Discovery Deck."

It was like shouting "fire" in a crowded room. The adults grabbed their children by the wrists, gave their elder counterparts a firm push at the back of their wheelchairs, and set out dutifully to secure their complimentary cocktail. The *Ocean Queen* was an all-inclusive ship when it came to food and most onboard activities, but alcohol was strictly pay-to-play.

Once the room was cleared of everyone except himself, the Feldmans, and a few overzealous paramedics, it was terribly quiet.

"Is there anything I can do?" Julian asked. He approached the family cautiously, stationing himself directly in between the two stretchers. His role in these situations could vary greatly. He could be anything from therapist to ice pack bearer, arbitrator, or bouncer. Sometimes all he needed was to present a voucher for a complimentary land excursion, and the entire family was able to put aside their squabbling in deference to the freebie.

It was hard to read the Feldmans, though. The older woman was tough. He could tell from her rant. The daughter, Elise, was just as voluble but far less confident — she fell a little more on the hysterical side of the spectrum. The rest of the family? Julian couldn't make heads or tails of the dynamic there.

"We're sorry for the trouble," the elder

Mrs. Feldman said to Julian, looking mortified as she tended to her husband's busted nose.

"You and Dad started it," Elise snapped.

"Let's not worry about blame now," Julian said. "I just want to make sure everyone is feeling well enough to enjoy the remainder of the trip." *And that I don't need to throw anyone in the brig,* he thought to himself.

The teenage girl bent over Mitch on stretcher #2, and Julian was relieved to see signs of life in her vacant face.

"Sweetie," Mitch said, rolling with great effort onto his side to access the wallet in his pocket. "Take a few twenties and go with your brother to the arcade."

The girl started combing through a wad of bills.

"No! No money!" Elise roared, grabbing the wallet away from her. "We have *no* money to spare. Zero. And honestly, Rachel, your father probably dislocated his shoulder and is clearly in agony. Your grandfather is also in serious pain. How can you be so selfish?"

Man-Bun stepped forward gallantly.

"Rachel, here's two hundred. Take Darius and go." The blonde on stilts looked at him like he was Jesus and Mother Teresa rolled

15

into one.

"Take it, Rachel," the grandfather said firmly from stretcher #1. "You kids need to clear out of here."

"Over my dead body!" said Elise. "No one wants your drug money, Freddy!"

Drug money? Julian stared at Freddy, imagining bags of cocaine hidden all over the ship. He felt a prickle of nervous sweat beginning to form at his hairline and debated asking one of the paramedics to take his blood pressure. But no, he needed to stay in command.

Who was this family? The *Ocean Queen* regularly attracted a motley crew, but its passengers' foibles were, for the most part, the extremely visible kind. Like with the BDSMers — everyone basically knew who they were, especially Housekeeping, who had to step over the gags and harnesses on the cabin floor every morning. The Feldmans, on the other hand, were outfitted like schoolteachers chaperoning the prom. All except Freddy, but that didn't make him any less of an enigma. He had an aging Jimmy Buffett sort of vibe; he looked far more like a goofy beer snob with a trophy girlfriend than a drug dealer.

"Let's not get excited again," Julian said, slipping into the therapist role. "Why don't we let the paramedics finish their job, and then I'm sure you can all calmly discuss everything in a more intimate setting. I'd be happy to offer you one of our private dining rooms — we can set up a cheese plate and a few bottles of good burgundy, absolutely free of charge." Julian couldn't have these crazy people airing their (potentially criminal) dirty laundry all over the *Ocean Queen.* He'd get crushed on TripAdvisor.

"I think it's probably best if you just leave us alone now," said Freddy's too-young girlfriend. As the words left the girl's pillow lips, Elise's face contorted in rage.

"And I think that *you* don't get to have an opinion," Elise shouted at the younger woman. "You aren't even a member of this family!"

Julian could tell that, for Mrs. Feldman, this exchange was the last straw. She stepped in between Freddy and Elise, who were obviously about to go a few rounds themselves, and said, "Everyone: *Cut it out.* This is my birthday celebration. We will all get along for the next twenty-four hours or else."

Mrs. Feldman hadn't actually raised her voice during this little speech, but the intensity of feeling behind her words was clear. A seam in her blue gown had ripped

17

from the sheer force of her heaving bosom.

Julian took a sudden step back. Shouting, blood, threats, raised fists. It wasn't what he'd call a successful night aboard ship. And he'd done all he could to simmer things down. If free food and alcohol couldn't help the Feldman clan, they were perhaps beyond repair. He quietly slipped out of the room and headed toward his own cabin on the staff floor, which was below sea level, leaving the warring family members on deck to berate each other until sunrise.

Boat life was a matter of simple rinse and repeat. Eat, argue, bingo. Eat, argue, show. Eat, argue, excursion. And then eat some more. If he didn't see the Feldmans at breakfast the next morning — if the feud was enough to overtake their appetites — he'd know they were in real trouble.

■ ■ ■ ■

Part I
The Call

■ ■ ■ ■

ONE

When the call came for Elise Feldman Connelly, she was in Costco.

Elise — mother, wife, friend, shopper — eyed the checkout lines from her spot in the outdoor furniture aisle, which were growing even longer as she studied them. She hated queuing in stores, all that extra time to ponder the contents of her cart with the twin forces of desire and guilt. She should know better than to go to Costco on a Sunday, when the lines were always eternal. Maybe she'd put her cart aside, ask her favorite store manager, Jeff, to watch her stuff, and then return tomorrow when she could swipe and dash. But no, then the thrill would be gone.

How Elise craved that soaring spike in adrenaline that shot pins and needles to her extremities and sent butterflies to her stomach. She sighed and looked back at her cart, fighting off the urge to calculate. The total couldn't be much. She had tossed in maybe eight or nine hardcovers at most, three frozen cakes, a few packages of T-shirts for Darius, and a bunch of sports bras she'd need now that she'd signed up for Class-Pass. Underneath, reading glasses, an electric screwdriver, a terry cloth robe, rubber flip-flops for the whole family (they appeared to run small so she'd chosen two sizes for everyone), new cutting boards, a set of knives, a Magic Bullet, a yoga mat, a George Foreman that looked more advanced than her current George Foreman, and a delicate fourteen-karat gold necklace for Rachel. Plus the faux ficus tree that was being held for her at the register.

"Elise," came a familiar voice barreling toward her. She felt her pulse quicken, that brief pleasant feeling of being recognized in a crowded place. She turned around to find Jeff, her Costco bestie, driving a flatbed down the wide aisle.

"You look like you found some good stuff today," he said, throwing an approving nod toward her cart.

"Not sure I'm going to take it all," she responded, watching Jeff's smile slide into a droop. "I probably will, though." And like that, his expression lit up again. He didn't work on commission. No Costco employees did — she'd once looked it up. Perhaps she and Jeff just shared something, a special satisfaction from knowing items were going to be purchased, bagged, put into a trunk, and taken to a new home. It was like a form of adoption — making things into possessions.

She was probably the first person to wax poetic in a discount big-box store. But she had a million dizzying thoughts tunneling through her mind that needed expression or she'd have a stroke. And these thoughts, they were like dough going through a pasta maker (she owned three), coming out in ribbons. There. She'd managed two euphemisms in one breath, putting a pretty face on both her crippling addiction and her runaway mind.

"Elise." Jeff's voice again. While she was lost in her reverie, he'd come off his perch and was standing rather close to her. She wanted to ask him to let her sit in the truck so she could see the aisles from a different vantage point, but she hadn't worked up the nerve yet. "I'm not supposed to tell anybody, but the mesh shorts you buy for your son are going ninety-seven cents this afternoon."

Prices at Costco ending in ninety-seven cents. It was the holy grail of shopping at the big-box retailer. It meant a product was getting discontinued and therefore going on sale. Elise felt an actual shiver running down her spine, forcing her to twitch with nervous energy. Had they just cranked the air? Or was that simply her body's visceral reaction to commerce, her raison d'être of the past year? She glanced at her watch, an irresistible Apple with a white band for which she'd waited in line for nearly six hours like a teenager staking out concert tickets.

"It's only another two hours," Jeff said, sensing her hesitation. "We're about to set up a frozen pizza station. You could eat lunch here while you wait." It was thoughtful of Jeff to consider that it was lunchtime. When was the last time her husband had checked to see if she'd eaten? She was so used to being the caretaker that the very suggestion from another human that she do something for herself made her eyes sting with tears.

Elise considered what waited for her at home. Her son, Darius, was out with friends, so she couldn't harass him about the college stuff, and Mitch was at work, like he was every Sunday. Rachel, though. Smart, social, and oh-so-distant Rachel. She was home for another month before going back to school, but her daughter was acting like she'd rather hang out with a rotting jellyfish than her mother. Supposedly that was how all kids were on their college breaks. Or so her friends assured her to make her feel better. But they all told white lies sometimes to spare each other's feelings. Hadn't she recently assured Kate Willing, the bake sale coordinator, that her monkey bread was outstanding and promised her neighbor Susan Shifter that the sleeveless dress she wore to the July Fourth barbecue was quite à la mode?

Who could be sure of anything? Life in the suburbs was so mottled with artifice and carefully concocted stories, so busy with get-togethers and fund-raisers and board meetings, that actually knowing what went on behind the picket fences was impossible. Nobody she'd ever met in the flesh, not her husband, her best friend, or her rabbi, knew her dirty secret. Only an anonymous "doctor" (air quotes necessary since she hadn't been able to validate Dr. Margaret's credentials) in an unknown location knew the depths of her current plight, and even with Dr. Margaret (the use of first name being the primary reason Elise questioned whether an actual advanced degree had been obtained) she wasn't totally honest. Not about how she'd gone and ruined everything for her son. Not about how she'd maybe even capsized her marriage as well. Elise headed in the direction of the frozen food aisle, following the scent of the pepperoni warming on a hot plate.

Twenty minutes after Elise had settled herself into a vinyl chair with a half dozen pizza bites arranged in muffin tin liners on her lap, her mother's face appeared on her watch along with an appropriately shrill ring. Last time the Feldman clan was together, Yom Kippur nearly a year ago, Darius had taken pictures of everyone and uploaded them to her phone so that when her family members called, their faces announced themselves before their voices. It was a warning, their mug shots reminding you why you might be better off letting the call go to voice mail.

Her mother was all done up in the picture, reddish bob hair-sprayed to withstand a tornado, face lacquered like an expensive piece of furniture. Annette Feldman was a decidedly attractive woman. Even now, with the deep ravines around her eyes and the gentle curve of sagging flesh under her chin, she still fit into the category of women deemed pretty, which meant an inordinate amount to her. Elise had her mother's broad

26

cheekbones, the same auburn hair that looked vaguely on fire in certain lighting, even the slanted nose, a combination that for whatever strange reason worked. Perhaps it was the favorable ratio of eyebrow to forehead or the color wheel compatibility of skin and hair tone. Scientists were forever trying to explain what makes someone appealing to look at. Elise couldn't figure it out, but she and her mother both had it, a possession that couldn't be bought, unlike everything else around her.

It had to be said that Annette did much more to enhance her natural beauty than Elise, with weekly hair appointments maintained with Velcro rollers nightly and consultations with makeup artists who swore they could erase a decade with the sweep of a contouring brush. Elise's father, David Feldman, a respected Long Island obstetrician who had delivered several thousand babies over the course of his four-decade career, strongly opposed plastic surgery, so Annette was forced to make do within the limits of powders, dyes, and creams.

Annette always tried to share her beauty tips with Elise, who would humor her mother by listening, and then never try any of them at home. She'd yet to show up at her mother's doorstep wearing that shade of lipstick Annette swore was flattering for their shared complexion or text a picture of herself wearing the denim blazer from the Gap that supposedly would do wonders to minimize the birthing hips that were the female Feldmans' calling card. Poor Rachel already had them, and while she attacked the spin bike with ferocity, they didn't whittle down even so much as a centimeter. And she didn't yet have children upon whom she could blame their girth. It made Elise reflect on the curse of motherhood: to feel your children's shortcomings so much more acutely than the children themselves felt them. A needle in the heart of a child is a dagger to the parent. Maybe that was why Annette was so relentless with her tips. If Elise gained five pounds, it was as though Annette had gained twenty.

The Feldmans had been on their way to synagogue in Elise's hometown of Great Neck, the Long Island setting of many a privileged rat race, when the photo appearing on her phone was taken. And they were all fasting, or at least Elise, Rachel, and the senior Feldmans were, so everyone was crankier than usual. On full stomachs, the Feldman family was known to clash over matters as small as whether the day's weather was "mild" or "temperate," but without even water to drink or a morsel of food since sundown the night before, all bets were off.

Mitch, her Irish Catholic husband, had downed a granola bar, mercifully in the bathroom so nobody with an empty stomach would have to ogle him, but Darius — her thoughtless teenage son — had marched right into his grandparents' kitchen that morning and filled his cereal bowl so high it might have reached heaven faster than their prayers. Such chutzpah, Elise had thought. Just like his uncle Freddy, who was, of course, a few thousand miles from Temple Beth-Am that day, not living up to a single family obligation.

"Who chooses Yom Kippur to visit?" Annette had whined en route to services. "The entire holiday is only twenty-five hours long. And you're not even staying for break-the-fast at the Goldfutters'."

"It's the Day of Atonement, Grandma," Darius said. "You can tell us what you think we need to atone for."

"Darius, keep quiet," Elise said. "Mom, this was the best we could do this time around. Junior year is critical for Darius. And Rachel has midterms. Plus Mitch needs to work." *And me? Well, I just can't bear to be back home for longer than a day,*

29

Elise continued in her head. *Negotiating with your self-absorption and little "suggestions." Facing Dad's disappointment head-on, which is not unlike staring directly into the barrel of a flashlight first thing in the morning.* "Besides, we're together. Not every holiday has to be about a meal." But as with many families, the Feldmans' currency was comestible, and being together without generous platters of gefilte fish, eggplant spreads, and deli meats arranged on the good china was like entering a mall without your wallet, the feeling of pointlessness rising to the absurd. Chewing kept the Feldmans' mouths occupied, which saved them from myriad arguments, misunderstandings, and offenses. Perhaps Annette was right and Yom Kippur wasn't the best time to visit.

Elise swallowed her second pizza bite before answering the phone. Jeff hadn't been wrong about the mesh shorts. The powers that be were walking down the aisle at that very moment with their omnipotent price guns, and Elise felt a flutter of excitement that nearly eclipsed her fear of answering her mother's call.

"Hi, Mom," she said in a deliberate clip.

"How are you, honey?" Annette asked in a purr, which immediately made Elise suspicious. Her mother wasn't much of a question asker, unless it was self-referential, the most frequent being "Does this make me look fat?"

If Annette was another kind of mother, the nonjudgmental, anything-goes type, Elise might have considered opening up to her, though not right then in the aisles of Costco. Dr. Margaret said there was no such thing as a nonjudgy, relaxed mother and Elise felt at once that she wasn't conveying the essence of Annette convincingly through the written word. Their sessions were timed to exactly fifty minutes and since Elise wasn't the fastest typist, she was essentially communicating her problems in Twitter-like shorthand. Their next session was going to be devoted to Elise's father and she thought she ought to book a double. Dr. Margaret was undoubtedly a Freudian.

"I'm fine. Just doing some errands. I think Darius grew three —"

"Anyway." Annette cut her off in mid-sentence. "I'm calling because I have exciting news to tell you. As you know, I've got something big coming up next month."

Shit, thought Elise, feeling the kick of the pepperoni rise in the back of her throat. What had she forgotten? A medical procedure, possibly, though she couldn't recall hearing anything of the sort. It was probably another award getting bestowed upon her parents. The Feldmans' synagogue was often feting its long-standing members with vaguely named honorariums, like the leadership, charity, and fellowship awards. These types of events, whether at the temple, the hospital, or the Rotary Club, always involved a crash diet for her mother, a frantic search for the perfect dress, and then, after the fact, complaints about the seating. One year it was being placed too close to the booming speakers, then, after letting her dissatisfaction be known, it was being put too far away from these very same offending instruments of amplification.

Sometimes, if the occasion warranted, it meant Elise and Mitch had to fly across the country to be there, as they had done when her father had received a lifetime achievement award from the hospital upon his retirement two years ago. Mitch had a smile on his face the whole evening, legitimately happy to see his father-in-law presented with a bronze plaque and a crystal paperweight in the shape of a baby (which Darius and Rachel found exceptionally creepy). And why shouldn't he be? Mitch, with his inquisitive mind and endless questions, was always eager to learn the workings of another profession or partake in the rituals of other cultures. He was a born journalist, a student of human nature, gifted with an open mind. And, more to the point, he didn't have to endure having David whisper in his ear, as Elise had after she'd wished her father hearty congratulations, "This could have been you."

"Dad, you, or both this time?" Elise didn't mean to sound so callous, but a horde of people was crowding around the shorts and Elise recognized one of them as the father of a tall, lanky boy in Darius's class. Which meant he might be competing for the same size. It would be nearly impossible to maneuver the cell phone and her cart and to rifle through the pile at the same time. Elise had fancy footwork in retail outlets, but she wasn't an acrobat.

"What are you talking about?" Annette asked, already exasperated. "I'm referring to my seventieth birthday." And here she dropped her voice to a stage whisper, Norma Desmond announcing she was back at last. Elise would bet the entire stack of size larges in front of her that her mother was alone, the theatrics simply because she couldn't help herself. Annette conducted herself as though there was an audience around at all times, her performance carefully crafted to please adoring fans who, as far as Elise could tell, lived inside her own mind.

"You know how I detest birthdays, of course," Annette added without a trace of irony.

Her mother was the epitome of etiquette when it came to discussing age in public. Growing up, Elise and Freddy were strictly forbidden from telling any of their friends how old she was. It was another miscalculation of Annette's, wasting her parenting capital to impress this upon her children. To anyone eighteen years of age and under, anyone forty-plus falls into the unspecific category of ancient. Any age differences between Annette and other mothers in their neighborhood were indistinguishable to the students at their high school, who saw all they needed to know in the mom jeans and dorky pocketbooks. Freddy and his friends would have been too stoned to even remember, had they actually learned the closely guarded secret that was Annette Feldman's age. And she, Elise, had more important things on her mind in high school than her mother's vintage. At the time, Ivy League acceptance loomed ahead of her, and it seemed every A she garnered was as necessary as a vital organ.

"Ah, yes," Elise said, realizing that in fact

August did mean another birthday in the Feldman family. The four nuclear Feldmans had their birthdays dispersed across the seasons, as though God had spread it out that way to ensure they communicated at least once a quarter. She hadn't given the matter of her mother's milestone birthday much thought, other than considering it was a legitimate occasion for her to be shopping. Once Rachel's college layette was fulfilled and Darius was chock-full of boxers and deodorant, Elise would get a little desperate to find things she or her family "needed." Thankfully need was a subjective conceit, though she wouldn't relish having to defend some of her purchases in front of a jury.

For Elise the upcoming month meant a serious return to dealing with Darius and his college applications. So little had gotten done over the summer. Every time she went to nag him to write his personal essay, or even start the far less daunting task of filling out the basic information on the common application, she stopped herself, unable to force her son to work on something that she might have rendered moot.

The irony was that Darius's leaving for college had triggered all the turmoil, the shot heard round the world. Dr. Margaret had helped her see that, though she was unwilling to let the matter of Elise's problems freeze at the proximate cause, hence the sessions devoted to the senior Feldmans. Together, in the safe space of their private internet chat, they revisited that fateful day when all the parents of high school juniors had gathered in the cafeteria, reduced to sitting on those backless benches and sipping bitter coffee, to learn about . . . *the college admission process, dun dun dun.* She'd attended the very same meeting when Rachel was a junior, quite calmly, but the finality of her youngest leaving the nest had affected her in ways she couldn't have foreseen. Mitch's face, which she kept stealing glances at, was mostly blank during the talk. He took some notes in the reporter pad he always carried in his back pocket, but generally looked glazed over, clearly not experiencing the combustion of emotions that was making her heart feel like an egg cracked into a sizzling pan. Mitch had gone back to work afterward, taking his own car, but she'd gotten behind the wheel of her minivan and sobbed for nearly an hour.

Once her tears ceased, but with her cheeks bearing the telltale stains, she'd driven to the mall — anything to avoid returning home, where life would be all but silent before she knew it. She found herself in the dressing room of a midpriced dress shop and tried on a black sheath just for the hell of it. When Elise emerged from the dressing room, the salespeople predictably gushed, but even she had to admit the cut *was* very flattering and the hemline hit in the perfect spot (generous thighs hidden and slender calves on display, such that she felt like she was carrying a secret beneath her dress). She'd swiped her credit card and left with the weight of the folded garment bag over her arm, but paradoxically feeling lighter. Then she'd gone next door and chosen a pair of matching heels.

By the time she was done, closing time at the mall (she'd never been there when a voice came on the loudspeaker to tell shoppers it was time to wrap it up — how depressing that sound was), she had five bags divided between two hands and a spring in her step. If Darius's leaving for college was the catalyst for her addiction, then the purchase of that black dress was her first taste. What difference was there really between white powder and black thread when the end result was that the buyer couldn't get enough of it?

Unable to look herself in the mirror anymore without crippling guilt, which was especially difficult given how often she was in a dressing room, last week she did what she should have done back in June. She called the school guidance counselor, a smug little thing named Janice who talked to her in code about "reach schools" and "safety schools." Darius was a solid B-minus/C-plus student, with a B or B plus sprinkled in here and there, typically in his English classes. And his SATs were in line with his grades, even though she and Mitch held out hope that his natural ability would shine through on a standardized test. Fortunately he was doing a retest this fall.

Privately, they thought Darius might even be smarter than the self-motivated Rachel, but what difference did it make if he never applied himself? The guidance counselor and she cobbled together a list of places where Darius stood a fighting chance and agreed to meet again in late September, with Mitch and Darius as well.

Elise knew it was fruitless to ask herself the age-old question that parents with disparate children ask themselves. Elise and her own brother were diametrical opposites, so why should she be surprised that Darius was unmotivated and Rachel the golden child in spite of receiving the same love and nurturing, both of them seeds tended to with equal diligence and care? Her children's dissimilarity was the slap in the face she deserved for ever questioning why her own parents couldn't get it right with Freddy. Still, she held firm to an optimism that Darius would not turn into her brother.

"Anyway, you know me, I don't like to be the center of attention," Annette went on, snapping Elise back to the present. She had to smile, even as she noticed the dwindling pile of mesh shorts left for the taking. *I know you*, Elise thought. *It seems* you *don't know you.* "But, well, given the circumstances, I thought it would be really nice if we all got together to celebrate."

Elise felt her face grow hot. How did her mother know about her circumstances? And why would getting together help? Unless . . . unless Mitch had in fact found out what was going on with her and reached out to her parents. And this birthday celebration was just a ruse to do some kind of intervention, like on reality TV where everyone sits on a couch looking very serious and the unsuspecting target walks into the room to find their loved ones terribly disappointed in them. But no, it couldn't be. Mitch may have been onto her, but he'd never tell her parents without confronting her first. Even if she'd squandered so much of what they'd built together, treating their bank account like it was a toy funnel, he owed her at least that much. Not to make her a fool in front of her parents, especially her father, the esteemed David Feldman, M.D.

"What did you have in mind?" Elise said, tallying a list of ready excuses why the trip home to celebrate the milestone birthday couldn't be longer than a day or two. Moving Rachel back into the dorms. An appendectomy. A crisis at work for Mitch. She'd let her husband, the writer, select the final story line and together they'd flesh out the details.

"A five-day, four-night cruise to the Caribbean. We leave in three weeks."

Elise felt a hole in her stomach so cavernous a thousand shopping bags couldn't fill it.

"And Freddy agreed to this?"

"He's my next call. So I've got to go."

She pictured her brother, cell phone tucked in the back pocket of tattered jeans slung low around his hips, so unprepared for what was coming. Nobody ever does see the Mack truck before impact, do they?

TWO

When the call came for Freddy Feldman, he was lighting a joint, thinking (as he was prone to do whenever he lit up) that if his family could picture him at this very moment, they'd have the entirely wrong impression. He was forty-eight years old, hadn't lived under the same roof as his parents or sister since he was a teenager, and yet their exasperated faces, distorted like Picasso portraits, appeared to him way more often than he'd like. Sometimes even during sex, when the nubile Natasha with her deer-like eyes and musky scent lay panting beneath him.

He exhaled that familiar cloud into which he'd disappeared many times over since his first puff at age fourteen, and — as though she'd read his mind — his mother's phone number appeared as an incoming call on his cell phone. It showed up as Annette, not Mom, because he thought the formality more fitting for the woman who'd lost faith in him when he was barely a college sophomore, though admittedly a Deadhead decimating his brain cells at least twice a day.

Technically, he was *leaving* college at the time, packing up his dorm room midsemester after the disciplinary board had said there could be no more chances. He'd even been forced to watch as his mother gussied herself up and flirted with the dean, a neatly mustachioed academic who was more than likely gay, to plead his case. It was pointless. The school, a third-tier liberal arts college in Vermont, had had enough of Freddy Feldman. As they walked out of the dean's office, Freddy could sense it was the defining moment when his mother believed he wasn't worth the trouble any longer. He saw it in the way she threw his clothes into a duffel without folding them. The fact that she never once asked him if he was hungry, though he'd not had a bite since they'd started gathering his belongings early that morning. She even came back from the commissary with a frozen yogurt for herself, nothing for him. Years later, stoned on the couch watching *Dr. Phil,* he remembered some head shrink saying that "food didn't equal love," addressing a couch overflowing with obese talk show guests. Well, for his family, it was a pretty close approximation, the offer of a piece of cake the equivalent of a kiss on the forehead.

Worst of all that day — way beyond the offense of the fro yo — was the way his mother avoided eye contact with him. She looked more carefully at his mix tapes, dirty boxers, and unopened textbooks, even the garbage that overflowed from his waste-basket, than she looked at him the entire day. The downcast eyes said it all. Like her lids, his stock was going down.

Now his mother only called him on his cell, though he'd provided her with his of-fice number several times. It was as though she simply couldn't accept that he was now a businessman making an honest day's liv-ing. Though to be fair, he'd been scant with the details, telling his parents that he was involved in a local farming venture and of-fering nothing more. What he really did wasn't the kind of thing his parents could ever understand or respect, even if it was legitimate and damn lucrative. Because all of his ventures were obscured by ambigu-ously named LLCs, he was unsearchable to them.

He pressed decline on the call because he had a roomful of men waiting for his re-action. Because he wasn't ready. Not then, with a lit joint in his hand and all its attendant feelings.

"I like it," he said finally, and he observed that the crowd gathered around his desk let out a collective sigh of relief. He'd been running his own company for nearly six years, and still he couldn't believe that he had the power to make someone nervous, let alone have an effect on anyone's livelihood. "It's very smooth. Not much aftertaste."

"So glad you like it. The soil was very cooperative this season," said Mike Green Hand. He was a genius of the earth, a Native American who worked some of the best acres of marijuana lands in the region. Like Freddy, he didn't have a college degree. He might not have finished high school — or if he did, it was a nonaccredited one on the reservation, but he had more knowledge of chemistry and biology in his thumb than any science teacher Freddy ever had.

A lawyer produced paperwork and all the gathered men, dressed in T-shirts and ripped jeans that took business casual to a new low, put their signatures on documents that would govern a deal worth four million dollars. Freddy thought about doing the thing that seemed appropriate for the moment. To take the bottle of Macallan off the

44

shelf and pass out glasses for everyone to toast the closing. But he was antsy to phone his mother back and find out what she wanted. It wasn't exactly every day she called.

If he had a normal relationship with his sister, he'd call her first for intelligence. But she'd never once come to his rescue, always happy to play the foil. Freddy the fuckup, Elise the excellent. His sister's stock went up whenever his went down, as though they were competing companies and there was limited market share. It was a rather cold way of looking at his family, thinking of his parents' love as a scarce resource, but he'd always had a hard time believing anyone who said parents couldn't have a favorite after what he'd endured. Though if anyone would be sensitive to treating children fairly, it would be him, after feeling the nefarious effects of ranking.

It was hard to know if children were on the horizon for him and Natasha. She was so young, a kid herself in many ways, all squeaky laughs and skinny limbs. Even his niece, Rachel, the only Feldman with whom he felt any real kinship, had awkwardly asked him how old Natasha was when she'd visited last spring with her college friends. He could tell Rachel was embarrassed by the situation, worried her stuck-up pals from Stanford would think he was some kind of pervert. He'd rounded up Natasha's age, only to be outed when his girlfriend announced after a few glasses of wine that she was twenty-nine and "one-quarter." At least he knew Rachel wasn't going to report anything back to his sister and brother-in-law, considering she was visiting him when they thought she was in Guatemala building huts with Habitat for Humanity.

"Gentlemen, I've got to make some calls," he announced. Once alone, he reached for his office phone, tugging at his leather rope necklace nervously with his other hand. His mother may not call him on his work number, but that didn't mean he wouldn't use it to call her back. She'd recognize the Colorado exchange. They weren't *that* estranged.

"Annette Feldman," his mother's voice sounded in a haughty purr after three long rings. Annette had mastered the art of the professional greeting after thirty years managing his father's medical office. "Dr. Feldman's office," she'd practice at home when they were younger, sometimes coming dangerously close to a British accent — Annette Feldman (née Schwartz), the insurance salesman's daughter from the Bronx, sounding like the chair umpire at Wimbledon. He shook his head at the memory, remembering how he and Elise used to imitate their mother, sometimes going Cockney, other times Scottish.

"It's Freddy," he said. "This is my office phone."

"Ahh, Freddy!" she said, sounding positively giddy to hear from him. Now he really wondered what was up, feeling his insides roiling. It had to be one of his vital organs she was after or else she'd never sound so damn excited to hear his voice. "I have some good news."

It was a sign of how little he knew them anymore, a metaphorical ocean between them, that he could barely imagine what it was. His best guess was that it was something related to Elise and Mitch and his little sister couldn't be bothered to tell him herself. Perhaps they'd bought a new house because Mitch got promoted. Or maybe his nephew, whom he barely knew, had gotten into college. Yes — it was something Connelly related for sure.

He felt agitated at Rachel for not mentioning anything to him. She'd emailed him just yesterday and mentioned nothing of the sort, just said something about having a new boyfriend and the relationship being "complicated." She didn't bold the word, but he

47

sensed the complication wasn't of the "he's too into beer pong" variety and that he ought to give her a call to probe. Other than that, her email contained the usual complaints about her mother's hawk-eyed vigilance and her father's didactic rules — the way he raised her like a dad on a TV show, with his "young lady" this and "back in my day" that. Freddy bet that she couldn't wait to return to college in a few weeks, to break free of the shackles created by the four walls and roof of a family home. He knew the feeling well, how you could be in the place you supposedly belonged most in the world and yet feel like an interloper.

"What is it?" he asked, relaxing his grip on the phone when he felt his hand cramping.

"You know what next month is, right?" He heard his mother's voice take on an unexpected lilt, which made her sound less resolute than normal.

The coming month was a lot of things for Freddy. It signified a year of being with Natasha. It was when he was set to close on another eight hundred thousand square feet of grow houses. It was his best buddy Nick's bachelor party in Tahoe. None of these things had the slightest bearing on his mother, unless Natasha had gone and done some crazy girl shit and introduced herself to his mother over email. She'd pestered him only once or twice about meeting his family, so that was unlikely. Still, he could never be certain. He didn't think his previous girlfriend would burn all his underwear on the front porch either and post the video on Facebook. He was in the midst of hazarding a guess when his mother continued.

"My seventieth, of course. And I really want to celebrate with you and Elise and Rachel and Darius."

He couldn't help noticing that his mother didn't mention Mitch, which doused him with the slightest feeling of satisfaction. His righteous sister had nearly fallen out of their parents' good graces when she'd chosen to marry an Irish Catholic, and not the Kennedy type either. Freddy's brother-in-law was from a blue-collar family in Pittsburgh and his mother wore a big fat cross around her neck at all times, the kind with Jesus splayed across it. The message of forgiveness went right over Annette's head. Elise's mother-in-law did take it off for the wedding after Annette pleaded for days that it would insult their rabbi. He was proud of his sister for having the balls to do something unexpected, to risk pissing off Annette, and by extension David, who was willing to take up any cause of his wife's rather than disagree.

Shortly after the wedding, defeated by Annette's and David's outrage at his lack of being born Jewish, Mitch had briefly flirted with conversion. "So long as they don't need to do anything to me down there, I figure why not," his brother-in-law had said to him after a few beers once, gesturing toward his fly. In that moment, Freddy kind of liked Mitch, even if he was a bit spineless. Though, to Mitch's credit, when he found out they would in fact have to do something to him "down there," the conversion issue was off the table.

"And Mitch too, of course," Annette added, before Freddy could do the pedantic thing and remind her of his existence. In the end, Mitch had proven to be the most malleable man on earth, and after only a few years of marriage to Elise, he was participating in the family seder and professing his love for matzo ball soup, even with his foreskin intact. There was little for his parents to do but accept him into the fold.

Freddy took a moment to process what Annette had said, squeezing the stress ball on his desk, which was shaped like a marijuana leaf. Hard to believe his mother was seventy. Seeing her as rarely as he did, she was frozen in time, stuck somewhere in the abyss of middle age. Now that was where *he* was and his parents had moved firmly into the next phase of aging: the golden years. He imagined their days passed with eighteen holes at the club, doctor checkups, and stereotypical kvetching. It didn't sound golden to him, not that he really had a clue what they were up to.

The tradition of the Feldman family getting together for the holidays had fallen by the wayside, at least for him, and he never felt he was all that much missed. One time, it had to be seven or eight years ago already, his mother told him — a fully grown adult — that he couldn't go to synagogue with his long hair. The way she looked at him, it was as if she expected him to drive over to Supercuts that very moment. But he wouldn't give her the satisfaction, even though he'd been planning on lopping off four inches anyway.

"What'd you have in mind?" he asked, surprised that his mother would want to make any sort of occasion out of her birthday. She wasn't one to shy away from the spotlight (the Feldman bookcase was lined with VHS videos of her yearly performances at the country club talent show), but an occasion where her age was the cause for celebration seemed incomprehensible. It was almost a reason to call Elise, so they could ponder it together. He often wondered if his sister ever thought back to their childhood the way he did . . . the times they would roll their eyes at each other in the back of their parents' Volvo as they listened to their father complain about his medical partners — especially the dreaded Dr. Shoreham always trying to steal his patients — or how they used to hide in the pantry during dinner parties and gasp at the way their parents' friends talked when they thought no children were in earshot. That camaraderie had all stopped by the time Freddy reached the end of middle school. He remembered hearing Elise whine to his mother one day after finding out she'd have the same math teacher he'd had in seventh grade. "I hope he knows I'm nothing like Freddy. He'll probably hate me when he realizes I'm his sister." "No, no," his mother had gently soothed her favorite. "You two are nothing alike and Mr. Mackay will realize it immediately."

"A family trip, as a matter of fact," his mother said now, tunneling him back to the present. "A cruise to the Caribbean."

Somewhere, the biggest mic he could picture dropped.

Three months earlier, Natasha and the girls she worked with had gotten a hookup to tag along on some rich guy's sailboat that was leaving from Big Sur for a four-night pleasure cruise. She'd begged him to come along and he thought it was a good idea, pretty sure he didn't want his leggy girlfriend, who favored string bikinis, suntanning on the bow of a ship without him around. So he'd gone, totally unsure what to pack for the trip. He hadn't been in a bathing suit since overnight camp, and even then his belly was softer and paler than the lean torsos on his friends. His legs were nearly hairless, a phenomenon he couldn't understand, considering his chest had dense wiry patches and even his nose would be a thick brush if he didn't trim regularly. Natasha never complained, goggling him with her adoring eyes, even though his body looked like a weathered newspaper next to her glossy magazine.

From the moment he stepped on the boat, he instantly regretted it. Before they'd even left shore, the gentle rocking of the Pacific set his stomach into fits of rolls, cramps, and angry gurgles. By the first evening, even the admiring Natasha said he looked ghoulishly green. The boat was impressive, everything mahogany and stainless steel, with a crew-to-passenger ratio of three to one. And still their cabin was a shoe box and he couldn't dress or brush his teeth without bumping an elbow or a knee, so that his greenish face was complemented by black-and-blue marks on his appendages by the end of the trip. But worst of all was the feeling of captivity, harkening back to those few lone nights he'd spent in jail cells. And this was in the best of circumstances, where he had a girl in his bed every night and a French Culinary Institute–trained chef preparing his meals three times a day. Five days of lockup with his family? Inconceivable. Water torture would be more pleasurable, he thought not hyperbolically. *Water torture.* How perfectly fitting.

"Are you there, Freddy? I think we got disconnected. Freddy? Freddy?" His mother always yelled into her cell phone, as though rising octaves could repair spotty service.

"I'm here. Mom — that sounds really nice, but I just don't think I can get away from work for a week. I have a lot going on here."

"I'm sure you do," she said without any perceivable sarcasm or probes for specifics. Perhaps she'd just given up. Not surprising after he'd delivered nothing but one-word answers about his job in the past: *farming, land, investing, fine, good.* One time just for kicks (or a more deep-seated desire to come clean) he'd said that his business was "grass related" and his mother had actually said: *I hope you are putting on sunscreen before sitting on that lawn mower all day.* "But this means a lot to me. And your father."

"Did Elise say she was going?"

"Funny," Annette said, sounding like she'd just figured out the answer to a riddle she'd been contemplating all morning. "She asked me the same question about you."

"How was your day, baby?"

Natasha was sprawled on the couch in the living room when he got home from work, watching one of those ridiculous Bravo shows she couldn't seem to get enough of. Even though she'd formally moved into his place two months earlier, each time he came home and found her there — whether she was cooking dinner or relaxing in the bath — he felt like she'd snuck in, having taken the key from his back pocket when he wasn't looking. It wasn't that she was particularly overbearing or trying to steer their relationship into the fast lane, it was more that Freddy, despite his age, felt like an imposter playing house.

"Not bad," he said, coming up behind her

to kiss her earlobe, something he knew she loved. "We signed the papers."

"That's great," she said, popping up to give him a proper hug. "We should celebrate."

He followed Natasha as she ambled gracefully into the kitchen, going on tiptoe to reach two champagne glasses. Her T-shirt rose when she lifted her arm and he inhaled sharply at the sight of her smooth back, tawny and tight. He, the stoner weirdo that the popular girls used to thumb their noses at, had a *hot* girlfriend, a yellow-haired chick who smiled all the time and rubbed his shoulders after a long day. It almost made him want to attend his thirtieth high school reunion, to walk the hallways with his hand resting on that gorgeous back, displaying Natasha like a tempting tray of hors d'oeuvres.

"Oh, shoot, we don't have any champagne. Beer?" She turned around, two sweating Amstels in her hands. "What's wrong? You don't look like a guy who wants to celebrate." She walked toward where he'd seated himself at the kitchen table and draped herself like a throw blanket on his lap.

"No, I'm good," he said.

"Tell me," she said, cupping his chin like

he was a little boy. Natasha was young enough to believe that most problems had solutions; it was just a matter of devoting sufficient hours to talking it through. She watched a lot of *Oprah.*

"I got a call from my mother today. She's turning seventy next month and she wants all of us to go on a cruise together to celebrate." He panicked the minute the words were out of his mouth. What if Natasha thought "all of us" meant her too? Freddy had been so overwhelmed with the prospect of a family reunion that he hadn't even considered whether Natasha should come along.

"That's really fun," she said. Natasha obviously didn't share his same fears about being trapped on Gilligan's Island with her family. He had never given much thought to her parents, as if Natasha had simply manifested without a family or a background. Now he was intrigued by her folks: people so well-meaning and without agendas that she desired a week at sea with them.

"I guess," he said, scratching his head. "It's just weird of my mom to celebrate her birthday in such a big way. We used to be forbidden from even mentioning it. Me and Elise, that is — my sister." He realized he never spoke about Elise to Natasha. He wondered if they would like each other. One of them had a stick up her ass and the other didn't, but if he remembered correctly, Elise had a sharp sense of humor and Natasha was quick with a laugh, so there was a chance at compatibility.

"Maybe she's changing as she's getting older," Natasha ventured, swiveling her torso so she faced him squarely. She was much more than just a pretty face, but what a face it was. He really liked the glow of the dewy skin on her cheeks, even if it was a bit too smooth and radiant for someone his age to be stroking.

A few weeks ago he'd seen Elise's pictures on Facebook from some deadly suburban barbecue and was shocked by her wrinkles and sunspots, visible even in the grainy photo taken in weak afternoon light. That was his *little* sister looking positively haggard. Mitch, also in the frame of the photo, was similarly showing signs of his age — thinning hair, a paunch that would probably extend past Freddy's own if they stood in profile, dad socks hiked to midcalf. Even if Natasha laughed at all of Elise's jokes until she was hiccuping and her stomach hurt, his sister might still hate his girlfriend just because of her buoyant breasts and washboard abs.

"Maybe," he acknowledged, thinking how much he'd changed in his life. He should be the last person to go around accusing anyone of being static. "But it's more than that. I just can't really see myself on a family vacation at this point in my life. My parents still think of me as the same screwup they constantly had to fish out of the principal's office. And my sister — though she's done nothing more in her life than join the PTA — is treated like royalty. I'd come away feeling like shit about myself."

"I could go with you," she said. "Talk you up." Now she straddled him, kissed him firmly on the lips. "You're no screwup to me." When she ran her fingers through his hair, he noticed she was wearing the Cartier Love bracelet he'd given her for her birthday. He wasn't a materialistic guy, but he had all this money suddenly and felt like he ought to use it. He didn't derive much pleasure from shopping, but it seemed logical to do something with the cash in his bank account other than let it collect de minimis interest. Freddy didn't know a whit about investing in the financial markets. He knew land, he knew pot, and he knew stoners. And, most important, he knew he was better off buying himself a few expensive treats than to risk losing it all in the Nasdaq.

What he really ought to buy was a house, something ski-in, ski-out, but he was comfortable in his one-bedroom apartment. When Rachel and her friends had visited, they'd been perfectly happy sharing air mattresses that he'd arranged in the living room. He felt a kinship with the college kids, having never really reached that inevitable-for-most place where he desired a fancy kitchen with a Wolf range or a marble bathroom with a steam shower like other "adults." How he wished he could just buy his mother an extravagant gift and dispense with his birthday responsibilities that way. Annette was more classically materialistic, a keeping-up-with-the-Goldmans type, but he could tell this time was different. His mother was thinking bigger than a store-bought good. She was thinking *quality time.*

"I'm not sure that would be a good idea," he said, but when he saw Natasha's face fall he reconsidered, first for her benefit, then his own. "You know what, why not?" He figured the whole trip was going to be a shit show anyway, so why not bring along his jailbait girlfriend to throw another log on the fire? Give his family something else for which to judge him. Especially Elise, who, for all her humor and propensity to defuse

60

an uncomfortable situation with a joke, never cut him any slack. If only she knew what her own daughter was up to and the trouble he'd bailed her out of last year. He'd never rat out Rachel, though. No matter how many high-handed digs Elise threw his way.

What was he thinking? There was no way he could leave his business now. Not with the big deal in Nevada so close to getting approved and the cover story in *High Times* coming out in a few weeks, which could set off a storm of business opportunities. If only he could use work to bow out gracefully. After all, his father had worked six days a week until the day he retired, never showing a trace of remorse about having to miss an obligation. For David Feldman, a vacation meant an extra day tacked on to an otherwise necessary trip — like when they stayed over another day to see Alcatraz after a cousin's wedding in San Francisco or drove to Newport after Elise's graduation from Dartmouth. But then again, delivering babies, performing hysterectomies, blasting ovarian cysts — these were indisputably more worthwhile endeavors than supplying Mary Jane to the blurry-eyed college kids on spring break or the hedge-funders looking to spice up après-ski. Though there was his palliative clientele, those cancer patients for whom what he was peddling was more comforting than anything made by Glaxo-SmithKline. Or so the patients told him when he had occasion to meet them in one of his shops.

His parents — especially his father, the sort of doctor who rolled his eyes at homeopathic remedies and simply humored women who credited their fertility to meditation — would doubt anything *he* was a part of could be of use to the sickly. He still remembered what his dad had said to him at the sixth-grade science fair after he'd proudly displayed his invention, a flavor contraption for kids to change the taste of their medicine at home to bubble gum, blue raspberry, or minty chocolate: "That would never work because pharmacists wouldn't let children tamper with their medication." As if Freddy had been planning to apply for a patent at age twelve. All Freddy had wanted was a big pat on the back and to see a look of pleasure in his father's eyes. After all, the whole invention was clearly a nod to his father's profession. Feeling crushed in the middle of the school auditorium and fighting back tears, Freddy wished he'd made a homework machine like so many of the other kids, all of whom were getting swallowed up by hugs and kisses.

"So, am I packing my bags?" Natasha teased, putting a suggestive finger on Freddy's chest. "I am very anxious to meet this family of yours. If they're anything like your niece, I think we'll have a great time."

"They're not," he said, though he realized he didn't know his nephew at all. Rachel complained about Darius a bit, but in a generic "my little brother is annoying" kind of way. The trip could be a nice way to get to know him, if Elise would let him hang out with the "black sheep" of the family, as even he'd taken to describing himself when anyone inquired about his upbringing. *Some black sheep,* an investor of his — a big shot from New York City — had recently joked at a closing lunch celebrating a major import deal. *You're more like a cash cow.* Rachel had mentioned that Darius wasn't the superstar student that she was and that her parents didn't like the kids he hung around with. Maybe he and Darius could compare notes on what it felt like to disappoint people just by being yourself. He could show Darius that not all genetic Feldmans were as uptight as his mother. There. Now he had another reason to go on the trip. He found that he was arguing against himself, half of his brain mounting more reasons to present to the other side of him that knew going on a ship with his family, where the only way off was to plunge into the freezing morass of the Atlantic, was a very bad idea.

"Yes, I think you should pack your bags," he said, giving Natasha's waist a gentle squeeze.

"Yippee!" She bounded off his lap.

Natasha looked so elated, obviously thrilled to be moving their relationship to the meet-the-parents level, that even Freddy caught himself smiling. How bad could it be? He'd spend time with Rachel. Get to know Darius. Make his mother and girl-friend happy. And, over the course of five days and four nights, make sure every member of his family realized he was no longer Freddy the Fuckup. He was success-ful, living the life he wanted in spite of them, and he'd be damned if after a week on the high seas every Feldman didn't see it that way.

THREE

Was there anything more ironic than being forced to buy a new wallet because all the credit cards you ordered and maxed out and paid down and reordered didn't fit into your original wallet anymore? If there was, Elise couldn't think of it.

If everything wasn't such a big secret, she'd have loved to share that observation with Mitch, who always found her very clever and quick — a "keen observer of daily life," he'd proudly described her. She was quite taken with any compliment that reinforced that she still had a brain in working order, especially from her wordsmith husband. Once upon a time, in another life, she used to memorize peptide chains and chemistry formulas with relative ease. Now she rarely remembered a complete grocery list without writing it down.

She was at the mall for the fourth time that week, ringing up a black leather wallet priced at nearly three hundred dollars. Maybe the exorbitant cost would make her hesitant to wear it out and she'd stop reaching all day long to play eeny-meeny-miny-mo from her lineup of credit cards and hope the selection wouldn't be declined. By that logic, she should buy an even fancier wallet — a real brand name like Gucci or Prada. If one were clever enough, it was possible to rationalize just about anything.

Three days, punctuated cruelly by three restless nights, had passed since her mother called about the trip. Since then, a peppy travel agent named Marlene had reached out to retrieve everybody's passport numbers and arrange flights to Miami. This vacation had to be costing her parents a fortune. She'd been on the website of the company operating the cruise, Paradise International, and studied the boat's impressive features. The *Ocean Queen,* the ship they would be taking, was truly a floating city. It had eighteen floors (*decks,* to be precise), twelve restaurants, an ice-skating rink, a bowling alley, a thousand-seat live theater, and an IMAX cinema.

When she got lost in the pictures (the travel agent had also overnighted a forty-page glossy brochure), inserting herself side by side with the middle-aged models, silver foxes, and wrinkle-free ladies in white linen getting "pampered," "spoiled," and "indulged," it was possible to imagine that she could actually have a good time. More than a good time, really. An amazing time.

The people in the catalog were better versions of her and Mitch: throwing dice, dancing the salsa, laughing with smiles so wide it seemed toothpicks were holding up the corners of their mouths. When had she last seen a live show? (The *Ocean Queen* brought Tony-winning performers to serenade the passengers.) When had she last sat by a pool with a good book, even though she and Mitch lived in California? (The *Ocean Queen* had six different swimming destinations to choose from, with dreamy names like the Serenity pool, Festive pool, Tropical pool, Lounge pool, and Lazy River pool.) She wondered if Rachel and Darius would avail themselves of the Teen Scene pool, with its twenty-four/seven DJ and waterslides so "thrilling" you were guaranteed not to miss your PlayStation (the brochure's words, not hers). Both her children could use some vitamin D and time away from their devices. If she were in medical school today, Elise would choose to study neuroscience instead of endocrinology. She worried

67

about how all that constant connectivity was altering the way the brain's neurons fired. In forty years, when she'd need her children to care for her, she suspected their minds would functionally be mashed potatoes. They already barely looked her in the eye. Maybe it was because she couldn't be filtered or swiped right or left.

She hadn't told Rachel or Darius about the trip yet and she could barely guess how they would react. They were mysteries to her, these teenagers of her own flesh and blood, who shared her eye color, high-pitched laugh, and protuberant lips. She'd only mentioned the trip to Mitch yesterday, carrying it around with her for two days like a shopping bag she needed to keep hidden. Her husband had only two weeks' paid vacation from the *Sacramento Bee* and she was shocked when he didn't grumble about wasting his precious time off on a trip with her parents. Instead, he'd looked at the brochure with a glazed expression, doing the same mental calculations she had done, and said simply, "Love it." The marketing materials that Paradise International produced really were extraordinary, as vivid as virtual reality glasses. If you stared at the pictures long enough, you could feel the fluffy bathrobe envelop you, taste the lobster dinner, smell the therapeutic sea air. And best of all? Her parents were footing the bill for the all-inclusive trip and she would have no need to spend a cent on board. Just a little shopping before the trip for essentials only: seasickness patches and sensible boat shoes. And maybe a few new bathing suits, since with her new ClassPass membership, she'd probably shed a few pounds before departure.

She wondered whether Freddy had consented to the trip. Even she hadn't given her mother the official green light yet, telling the travel agent not to make any arrangements until she was sure Mitch could get off work. It was a lie, but she needed a few more days to consider whether the prospect of sandy beaches, five-course dinners, and something called a "towel concierge" was worth the mental anguish of being under the thumb of her parents. Freddy had to be making a similar judgment call, although he wouldn't have the extra burden of worrying about how his children would perform. "Behave" was probably a better word. Rachel and Darius weren't circus animals!

The last time she'd heard from her brother was probably about six months ago. He had called her while she was on safety patrol outside the high school and she could barely focus on a word he was saying while the aggressive car pool moms were gunning for position and a newly licensed junior nearly impaled her despite the neon orange vest. It had almost sounded like Freddy said he was selling pot, but she knew that was ridiculous. One — he would never cop to that. Two — why in the world would he have called her to tell her a thing like that? However he was scraping by, she was pretty sure he would be hard-pressed to turn down a fully paid vacation, even if it meant scrutiny, criticism, and all-around stress from the parental units.

Elise headed toward the parking lot, feeling like if she didn't leave the mall within the next ten minutes, she would break her solemn vow to treat her new wallet as though it was Krazy-Glued shut. As she neared the exit, dangerously close to an easy detour into Bloomingdale's, her cell phone rang. It was her banker from Wells Fargo, Michelle Shapiro, the mom of a girl in Darius's class whom she'd been forced to ask recently if there was such a thing as banker-client confidentiality. There wasn't, not in a strictly legal sense, but Michelle had assured her she wouldn't breathe a word of what she knew about Elise's situation. Still, Elise avoided meeting Michelle's gaze at the PTA meetings and in the school parking lot, whereas at the bank, squeezed into Michelle's small office midway down a long, soulless corporate hallway, she did the opposite — looked into her banker's heavily made-up eyes and pleaded for a lifeline.

"Hi, Michelle," Elise said, dashing outside. She feared some announcement over the mall loudspeaker that would reveal her whereabouts and didn't need to give any more reasons to Michelle to be unsympathetic to her plight. "How's everything? I saw in the *Teen Bee* that Caroline was awarded a scholarship from the mayor's office." Michelle was a single mother with one child, Caroline, who was a star student, a superb athlete, and the recipient of more awards and accolades than any single child's bedroom could hold. Elise had never been to Michelle's home, but she imagined the line of trophies started outside the front door, next to an unsightly garden gnome, and snaked its way through the kitchen sliders and out to the backyard. Caroline would have countless offers from colleges thrusting academic scholarships at her, but even if she didn't, it wouldn't matter. Michelle had scrimped and saved and invested and done all the things responsible parents do to safeguard their child's future. She hadn't tapped into her child's fortressed college fund to buy closets' worth (correction: closets *plus* a cage at U-Store 4-Less in Folsom) of things to fill the bottomless void cratering inside her. *Things.* They were everywhere. Always available for purchase, sating her in the short term, their long-term benefit leaving her in a slow ooze.

"Yes, I'm so proud of her. Is this a good time to talk?"

Why did people ask that before they told you something that you didn't want to hear? As if there could be such a thing as a "good" time for upsetting news. She and Mitch used to talk about similar mundane aggravations: waiters refusing to write down complicated orders, limp handshakes, pedestrians with zero umbrella etiquette. Now everything Elise thought about had to do with shopping: frustration when the UPS guy showed up late, getting home with packages and seeing the salesperson never removed the antitheft sensor, being forced to pay twenty-five cents for a shopping bag because California was a state of die-hard environmentalists with clearly no sympathy for shopaholics. These observations, a trough of petty grievances, were all related to her private world, so deeply connected to her shame that she feared that sharing even a single anecdote — like when the Home Depot clerk forgot to ring her up for two packages of tulip seeds so she got one free — would give her away. So instead, around her husband she vacillated between uncharacteristic silence — treating his questions of "What did you do today?" as accusations to which she'd defensively respond, "Nothing!" all the while picturing the trunkload of goods in her car that she'd later transfer to the attic — and creating elaborate alternative versions of her day, like the car nearly running out of gas or badly tripping on the steps outside Darius's school. No wonder she sometimes found Mitch looking at her like a stranger.

What would become of them when (if!) Darius left for college and it was just the two of them padding around the house? Creaky steps and whistling appliances the only audible sounds after twenty years of tears, laughter, bickering, and all the other ambient noise created by children? Dr. Margaret said the first year would be tough for both of the new empty nesters, with both her and Mitch trying to find a satisfying equilibrium after so much chaos. They would need to relearn who they were to each other when they weren't just coparents. But what the hell did Dr. Margaret know anyway? It wasn't as though she came via recommendation from Elise's general practitioner. No, no. Elise had latched onto Dr. Margaret while her body was slicked in cold sweat and she had four shopping bags digging into the crooks of her elbows. She had been at Walmart twenty minutes earlier and run into Vicki Lancaster, her next-door neighbor.

"You got a cat?" Vicki had asked innocently enough.

"Huh?" Elise had responded, genuinely confused. "Mitch is allergic. No cat for us." A dog was a possibility. Elise had already considered whether a Goldendoodle might be just the thing to ease the pain of Darius leaving home.

"Oh. You have a massive bag of Fancy Feast in your cart," Vicki said, looking worried.

Elise glanced down at her cart.

"Ah, that. Checking in on a friend's Persian while she's away," she said, recovering quickly. "Anyway, Vic, I've got to run. So good to see you."

Elise had dashed into the next aisle and nearly collapsed. She had zero recollection of lifting the seven-pound bag of cat food off of the shelf and loading it into her cart.

It was like it must have happened in a blackout state. It was the first time she said out loud to herself: *I HAVE A PROBLEM.* Back home, still shaken and with Mitch watching the 49ers in the next room, Elise quietly Googled "online therapist" and was matched with Dr. Margaret within minutes.

"Sure, it's a good time," Elise now lied to Michelle, as carefree shoppers tumbled past her toward their cars. She sat down on the steps of the parking lot, cradling her cell phone closely as if to keep the conversation from leaking into the universe, making it real, a fact to be reckoned with. If the particles of her secret spilled out, it would become something with mass that Mitch could hold in his hand and consider from every angle, and that was simply terrifying.

"I'm afraid I don't have great news for you."

Michelle cleared her throat in that way meant to humanize her. She was about to let Elise know that she couldn't help her because the favor well had run dry. So she did that throat-clearing thing to convey that she was just another tired mother, dealing with a sore throat or a bit of food stuck in her windpipe. They could relate to each other over these small irritations even if they didn't share Elise's tremendous financial plight. She pictured Michelle bent over a microwaved thermos filled with leftovers, because she was a frugal parent who didn't waste money on dining out.

"I can't extend you another line of credit. And given the state of the local real estate market, I'm not sure efforts to take out a second mortgage would be at all fruitful. I'm afraid as far as the bank is concerned, there's nothing more we can do. Regarding Darius, there are many community colleges in the area that might suit him. Or perhaps you want to think about applying for a scholarship? I remember he was the most talented writer when he was little."

Many moons ago, Darius Connelly had won a literature prize in a competition sponsored by the local library. Mitch had encouraged their little third grader to enter, claiming he saw in Darius the same creative spark he'd had as a child, the very one that led him to his career in journalism. Darius had written the most wonderful story about a brother and sister trapped in their elementary school after hours, and how the wily kids had used what they'd learned in their math, science, and physical education classes to break out. He'd been motivated primarily by the cash prize (twenty-five dollars), but when Darius stood up on a footstool to have his picture taken with the mayor and school principal, wearing his medal around his neck, there wasn't a prouder child on the West Coast. For the rest of the school year, Elise practically crowed when she went into the school for pickup. But in June, when she and Mitch attended the final parent-teacher conference with their feathers in full plumage, the teachers barely mentioned their boy's achievement. Instead they focused on him roughhousing at recess and routinely failing to turn in his homework on time. Hearing what Michelle just said about Darius's writing ability, well, it only proved what Elise had been thinking for the past decade. That when people looked at her underachieving son, especially compared to Rachel, they wondered what went wrong, trying to trace Darius's failings to a particular misstep they themselves could avoid.

"Considering I can't even get him to write his college personal statement, I don't see him tackling any scholarship essays." She didn't mean to take out her anger on Michelle, who couldn't help that her daughter was a regular Tracy Flick and that Elise was a PTA mom gone off the rails.

"I'm sorry, Elise. I really am."

"I know," Elise said. "And I'm sorry that I

avoid you at school."

"You'd be surprised by how many others do the same," Michelle said, with a guffaw. It was as though the banker had suddenly handed Elise a life buoy, she took that much comfort knowing there were other parents lurking the halls of Sacramento High with clandestine problems, possibly more salacious than hers. Gambling, prostitution, second families. The sky was the limit when you pondered other people's depravity. Maybe that was how Elise had let things get so bad. Because she knew it could always be worse if she let her imagination truly roam.

"I know community college doesn't sound that appealing to you and Mitch," Michelle continued and Elise felt her pulse quickening. Did Michelle think she was an academic snob? Or know that she was at the top of her class at Columbia Medical School? Was Michelle also aware how Elise felt that moment during her third year of med school when she saw the double pink lines on the stick and was so thrilled that she could no longer focus on peptides and amino acids and molecular bonding because there was a person growing inside her? And did Michelle know that when Rachel was born at thirty-three weeks, she was only four pounds, would have fit in the palm of Elise's hand if the NICU nurses would have let her hold her? That going back to school, leaving this true peanut of a child in day care, was unthinkable, and that by the time Rachel caught up in all her physical and intellectual milestones (and then some), Elise was already pregnant with Darius? Michelle couldn't possibly know all of these pieces of her, things she rarely spoke about, even with Mitch.

Elise had never questioned the choices she'd made in life, not until Rachel started talking nonstop about choosing a major at Stanford and Darius readied himself to move out of the house. When she was raising her young children, she felt exhausted and busy and important, like she was running a small country from her kitchen, her laptop and the driver's seat of their minivan portals to a world as complex as an investment bank or an emergency room as far as she was concerned. Now that she wasn't in the thick of it anymore, she was starting to see that coordinating Rachel's ballet with Darius's T-ball wasn't the Herculean feat it had once seemed and that there was a very large, unused part of her brain gathering dust. And the hours, there were so many of them. As a lunch-making soccer mom, the day felt too short, the grips of daylight always slipping away from her. But with teenagers who needed her less and less, the day stretched into a vast continuum, so that after she finished her coffee, read the paper, and took a quick shower, the hour hand wasn't even close to meeting the nine.

"True," Elise consented. "Community college is not our first choice."

"Do you have any family that can help out? At least to cover part of tuition?"

Did she have family? Ha! Boy, did she. Family that she was about to be trapped with on a giant sea monster. A group of people for whom Mercury was permanently in retrograde when they were together. There was no way she would ask the senior Feldmans for money. Not when they pooh-poohed Mitch's high-minded but low-paying career choice. Not when they depended on her to be their one responsible child so they wouldn't feel like total failures. Two opposing reasons not to ask them for the money, one driven by resentment and the other driven by compassion. How Feldman was that? To be so utterly conflicted by feelings that you decide just not to engage.

Unless . . .

She could pretend she needed the money

for something else. An idea was fomenting at rapid speed and her heart was racing faster than if she was first in line to enter Best Buy on Black Friday. She'd tell her parents that she was planning to start her own business. That she had decided, with Darius leaving for school, that she could use what she'd learned in medical school to go back to work even if it was too late to become a doctor. She was toying with starting a home nursing business. No, an app! Everyone was doing an app. She was working on an app for diabetics to monitor their daily food intake and blood sugar levels, which would automatically generate a report for their doctor that could be transmitted electronically. Eureka! She would call it Di-Count. No, Dia-*Beat*. What a double meaning! Her father, a Luddite who'd never quite mastered the hospital's online prescription system, would be proud of her for doing something with her education but way too intimidated by the mere mention of the app store to offer any involvement.

The only remaining glitch was explaining why it was a secret from Mitch. She needed to make sure her new "business" wasn't going to be the main topic at mealtime aboard the *Ocean Queen*. The answer came to her quickly. Mitch was a respected newspaperman who oversaw the science and pharma beats at the *Bee*. He couldn't risk accusations of conflict of interest, not when he was covering area hospitals and drug companies. So she'd tell her parents that she couldn't involve Mitch or discuss the business in front of him. When her app never surfaced, she'd be three thousand miles from her parents. She'd explain to them, over the phone, that someone else beat her to it or that it was too difficult to secure a patent. By that point, she'd have nipped her addiction in the bud, used the loan to pay for Darius's first year of college, and would be working her way toward paying back her parents.

Doing what? Of that she wasn't sure, but as a double Ivy Leaguer, how hard could it be to find gainful employment? She could always get a job in retail, be the oldest cashier at the Gap. On second thought, maybe retail wasn't the best environment for her to work in, though didn't they say anorexics often choose to work around food to prove they can restrain themselves? She'd tell Mitch she was bored without the kids at home and needed something to occupy her days. It wasn't as though her parents were going to beat down her door to get the money back promptly. Decades of working as a doctor in private practice, back before the insurance companies cannibalized the profits, had to have netted her parents a hefty nest egg. If they could pay for the entire family to board this luxury liner, surely their coffers were flush.

And Darius! Clever Michelle (clearly the apple didn't fall far from the tree in that family) had planted the most magnificent seed when she'd brought up her son's former glory. When Annette first talked about the boat, all Elise could think about was the feeling of being confined by her parents. What she hadn't considered was that she could also do the trapping. For five days she would have Darius locked up, without his friends or his car. Without Wi-Fi! She'd make sure by the time the ship returned to port in Miami, that kid would have the best damn personal essay UC San Diego — wait . . . no . . . even better . . . UCLA had ever seen. Darius and Rachel were sharing a stateroom on the trip, square footage totaling two hundred and twenty. If that didn't echo what he'd written about in third grade, Elise didn't know what did. She couldn't imagine his creative juices wouldn't flow with the sensory overload on board.

"That," she said to Michelle, trying to smother her excitement, "is not a bad idea."

83

When she hung up the phone, a text message from Darius appeared saying he wasn't going to make it home for dinner. It probably meant he was up to no good, but all Elise could take away was that she suddenly had an extra hour. She rose from the parking lot steps and made a hundred-eighty-degree turn. A green sweater dress had caught her eye on the way out of the mall and now she had the time to try it on. It would be her one last hurrah.

FOUR

When the call came for Mitch Connelly, he was in the midst of thinking that now would be the perfect time for a family vacation. Somewhere warm. Somewhere nice. Hell, he'd even thought of the word "pamper" before Elise read it to him from the brochure.

His wife had sounded positively shaken when she first told him about the family trip. She had sent an urgent text message, while he was in the midst of an editorial meeting, that read: Feldman drama . . . CALL ME. He had slipped out of the meeting, worried about illness, a fight, an accident. The last thing he expected to hear was that his in-laws wanted to take them on an all-expenses-paid cruise to the Caribbean. He knew his wife got uptight around her parents, but a free vacation was hardly a catastrophe. Besides, those massive ships had so many activities and forms of entertainment — the commercials made cruising seem like Las Vegas at sea — that he could imagine not even seeing the other Feldmans except at mealtimes. It was hard to picture Annette and David at the craps table or at the late-night jazz bar, where he and Elise might retire after a family dinner.

More to the point, the Feldmans weren't nearly as bad as his wife made them out to be. His father-in-law, the standoffish sort, read medical journals and watched crime shows for his primary entertainment. He was one of those guys who lived to work instead of working to live. And he, Mitch, could appreciate that, though he tried to be a more modern and involved parent than David or his own father had been. He felt awful for David when a hand tremor abruptly cut his four-decade-long career short. For Mitch, he analogized it to sitting in front of his computer one day and being at a loss for words, his brain simply unable to recall the perfect turn of phrase or adjective, letters swimming in incomprehensible groupings in his mind. It would be a nightmare to not be able to do what he loved and he didn't understand why his wife was so unsympathetic.

His mother-in-law was in perpetual motion, spring-cleaning across seasons, plan-

86

ning charity dinners, and gossiping about the neighbors with a frenetic energy. But Annette was a loyal wife to David, even when he wasn't the easiest to live with, and a devoted mother to Elise and Freddy. From the line of framed pictures in the hallway of their home on Long Island, Mitch could deduce those two never lacked for anything. Piano lessons, ski instruction, overnight summer camp where they dressed in tennis whites. For all their griping, his wife and brother-in-law had had it pretty damn good. Mitch was similarly baffled by Elise's lingering disdain for Freddy. He had his issues, but he was pleasant enough to spend time with and, to be honest, Freddy's shortcomings only served to elevate Elise's position in the family hierarchy. As one of eight children, six of them boys, Mitch would have gladly enjoyed the chance to stand out. Sometimes Mitch visualized his own sibling dynamics as Olympians standing on that three-level podium, except with everyone beating the crap out of each other. But not for Elise. All she had to do was not be a screwup and the gold medal was hers. But she acted put out and disappointed by Freddy, as though she were his third parent.

"We either have to go or come up with some rock-solid excuse for why we can't make it. It's not like my mother gave us a lot of notice, so it shouldn't be too difficult. What do you have going on at work that we can use?" Elise had asked. She was paranoid about being found out, so whenever they used his work as an excuse to avoid Feldman gatherings, it always had to have some origin in truth in case her parents did a little digging. The four-part series on Northern California's transit system they used to dodge a cousin's bar mitzvah did come out a month later, but it was already complete and logged for fact-checking when they said Mitch was working on it twenty-four/seven. Considering how irritating Elise found her parents, he couldn't understand why she went to such great lengths not to upset them. That was another Feldman puzzle he couldn't crack.

His wife didn't even realize the significance of the timing — how this trip was coming at exactly the perfect moment for him. How could she, when he'd kept his plans tightly under wrap for the past six months? He hadn't wanted to tell Elise until he had firmly made up his mind and negotiated his departure package with the publisher. Perhaps that was manipulative and unfair, but he just couldn't handle another voice interfering with what was already a difficult decision. Besides, he came from a family that didn't "discuss" every last thing ad nauseam. Still, he knew there would be hell to pay once Elise found out how long he'd known about leaving the *Bee* before telling her.

Now he was ready. At this point, he was just waiting for Darius to turn in his college applications to break the news, since Elise seemed too fixated on that endeavor to handle anything else at the moment that would portend a life change. The sight of a burned-out lightbulb was enough to send her over the edge lately. A minor domestic issue, like Darius and Rachel fighting over who finished the Cinnamon Life, and Elise was in the car within fifteen minutes claiming she needed some air. And he got it, having dodged so much of the child-rearing pains because he was always at work. After nearly twenty years grinding away at the thankless and unpaid job of motherhood, he could see why she needed a little "fresh air" lately. But with his excitement mounting and his last day at the *Bee* approaching, he couldn't wait much longer to clue her in.

"And if we do go, can you handle the passports?" Elise had continued. "I think the kids still have another year on theirs since we renewed right before we went to

Israel for Darius's bar mitzvah, but ours likely need renewing."

What a mess that trip had been. Darius wasn't the kind of kid that could get up on the temple stage and recite passages in front of a crowd, let alone ancient Hebrew prayers he didn't understand, so they'd decided to take a trip to Israel, just the four of them. Mitch hadn't converted when he married Elise, but he'd agreed to raise the kids Jewish without much argument. Anything had to be better than the nuns, so he hadn't even done much research into the matter. Had he given thought to the absurdity of lavishly celebrating a punk thirteen-year-old, as they'd done with Rachel (who knew flowers could cost that much?), he might have objected. Annette had hit the roof when she found out the grandparents weren't being included in the Israel trip (she wasn't remotely mollified knowing his parents weren't invited either) and had sent passive-aggressive emails the entire time they were away. The truth was that they couldn't afford to take Elise's parents with them and he felt uncomfortable asking them to pay their own way. He knew — even if he tried not to let it bother him — that the Feldmans (they of the pair of white BMWs in the garage and the perfect suburban house set on a bucolic two acres with a paid-off mortgage) were disappointed that he didn't make more money. Notwithstanding that he was a Fulbright scholar when he met their daughter. The bottom line was that he didn't provide their precious Elise with more of life's luxuries, and his in-laws were old school in that way.

What they didn't get was that Elise wasn't the materialistic type. The lasers radiating from the other suburban moms wearing designer clothing and flashy jewelry seemed to bounce off his wife like she was Teflon, though he had noticed more shopping bags around the house lately. But with Elise, he never had to worry. She was whip-smart and handled their family finances astutely, applying all that precision with which she'd once attacked her medical books to the management of their home. He could focus at work knowing that his wife could balance a checkbook with one eye closed, find the best value for internet and phone service, and know exactly how to invest what little they had remaining so that even if it didn't grow exponentially, it modestly increased to the point where the idea of him and Elise putting their children through college, taking a trip around the world, and finally paying off their mortgage was actually feasible.

And most important . . .

The thought bubble into which Mitch had disappeared the last few months danced over his head again. All this living safely within their means and putting off trips and a golf club membership and a fancy car was going to allow him to take the leap he was about to take. Those coworkers of his, stretching their dollar beyond where it could go without tearing, couldn't dream of doing what he planned next. It was all he could think about day and night, at the gym jogging off his protruding gut, at work while he slurped the cafeteria tomato soup, even at night when Elise stripped to her nightgown in front of him. All he could see were words, fonts, bylines, and typesets, those ingredients that would amount to his dream: an online literary journal with a focus on satire. Material was everywhere around him: the high-strung parents at the local high school chewing their nails from the football field sidelines; the suburban McMansions sprouting around them like weeds; the composting stations at every corner that people pretended not to notice. A fight in line at the bagel store on a Sunday morning could make him feel like he was living in a present-day *Lord of the Flies.* And he felt an urge to channel his observations and musings in a way that he couldn't do in his current job. There was humor everywhere he looked if he remembered to step back an extra ten feet, to see the panorama; and his need to put it out in the world, repackaged as entertainment, felt almost suffocating. He just needed a good name, and that was where telling Elise would come in. Literary journals always had the oddest names, like *Ploughshares* or *Salt Hill,* and there was satire even in that. Elise would help him come up with a name that was equally highbrow and self-effacing.

The financial implications of his career shift were not to be trifled about. The entire publishing industry was falling through quicksand and the chances of successfully launching a new journal online were slim. He just felt grateful that he and Elise were at a place where they could manage it: Both kids had college funds and Rachel's four years at Stanford had been prepaid through a marvelous incentive plan that guaranteed a tuition lock. Elise successfully refinanced their mortgage a few years ago so the payments were even more manageable. And now, a free trip, coming at just the right time. He was planning to take a few weeks off after his last day at the *Bee* to help Rachel move back into the dorms and to breathe some life into Darius's nonexistent college search. The office space he'd chosen in which to set up his new venture wasn't going to be vacant for another month, so he'd enjoy the Caribbean with his family and then work a few weeks from home, spending time with Elise in a way they hadn't since before having children.

The trip itinerary listed a black-tie dinner on the third night of the trip, with an elaborate nine-course tasting menu. He'd gotten the Feldmans into the habit of toasting before a meal and since then, they'd taken to toasting just about everything: Rachel's soccer team, the installation of a new refrigerator, the birth of every baby his father-in-law delivered. Mitch decided he'd kick off the toasts at the cruise's formal dinner with his big announcement. His in-laws might not be terribly impressed, but he really didn't care. He was nearly fifty years old and he'd toast what he felt like toasting, even if it meant receiving only a few half-hearted clinks and a "hear! hear!" or two in return. The only reaction that mattered was Elise's — especially after he'd waited so long to loop her in. He hoped and prayed the majestic setting and the lubrication of champagne would help.

"I want to go," he had said to Elise while

the two of them sorted through the travel agent's promotional materials together. He noticed a softness in his wife's face while she ogled the pictures and he wanted more than anything to freeze her in that moment, where her worry lines blurred and her lower lip hung open in wonder. He'd never bought himself a fancy car or sat in first class. But for one week, he'd be the guy in the pool float with a drink in his hand, living like a boss, his wife splayed on a nearby chaise lounge sipping a piña colada.

FIVE

Annette Feldman hated that when she had to make the calls, she was nervous. She'd birthed, raised, and loved those children to within an inch of her life and yet she had heart palpitations just thinking how much Elise and Freddy wouldn't want to go on a trip with her and David.

Things with the children, well, really with her entire life, had been better when David was working. She was his office manager for nearly forty years, dealing with the insurance companies, maintaining the schedules, keeping the nurses and support staff happy. She fielded the calls from the pharmaceutical reps and managed the equipment servicing. She foisted lunch on David when he was too busy to take a break and remembered everybody's birthday and their favorite kind of cake, including the building janitor and the UPS guy. So busy were her days that by the time she came home from work, prepared dinner, and watched one TV show to unwind, she was too exhausted to do any thinking beyond how many syringes and plastic pee cups to reorder. But two years ago, David scrubbed in for the last time, brought the last life into the world that he would, and drank his last cup of coffee outside the operating room.

Now the two of them were home all day, looking at each other like strangers, doing that dangerous thing older people were prone to do: taking stock of their lives. This feeling of utter uselessness, a void that snowballed daily, it was the real reason she sided with David's disappointment about Elise not having a career. It wasn't that she cared about the expense of the Ivy League schooling or what she said to her friends in the card room at Fresh Meadow Country Club after listening to them brag endlessly about their progeny's successes. *Ruthie bought a country house . . . Peter made partner . . . Daniel's hedge fund had a banner year.* All that gloating made her want to vomit. What got her in the gut was that her daughter had nothing of her own, no slice of the world — however infinitesimal — that would nourish her and fulfill her when her children grew up and Mitch turned into a roommate instead of a lover, if he hadn't

97

already. She'd had it until recently, a territory she ruled, a place where she was needed. Even if her job was at David's office, she controlled every inch of that twenty-square-foot space behind the reception desk. Now she was a seventy-year-old woman with children and grandchildren who lived nowhere near her and her office job had been filled by a twenty-three-year-old graduate of some internet university.

Elise and Freddy both had their reasons for moving away, she knew that, but it still hurt when she saw her neighbors' driveways filled with SUVs every weekend and her friends had to cut short lunches because of grandparent responsibilities. Once or twice on the phone she'd hinted as much to Elise, who'd said something like, "Oh, please, you're saying you want to watch Darius play video games or listen to Rachel be a total bitch?" It was true she had no more desire to stand in the heat watching teenagers play baseball than she had had to sit on the floor at a baby class while a bunch of toddlers shook maracas mindlessly. But now her grandchildren were older — a spontaneous matriculation into adulthood — and she was ready to get to know them.

Annette had David, for now, but what were the two of them to each other at this point in their lives? Wrinkled, arthritic has-beens. David was stooped over so that he no longer topped six feet and she was wider and dimpled despite eating the same number of Weight Watchers points for the past thirty years. They were half-people without their children. Everything they had done, every decision they had made, was for what they hoped had been in their children's best interests. The working nonstop, David rising before the sun and seeing more patients than his throbbing lower back could handle, was so that Elise had the best piano teacher and could travel to France for a tennis program and Freddy could have SAT tutors and the name-brand sneakers. Even the moms' nights out to the movies that Annette went to were in service of being a better, more patient parent the next day (the parenting books actually said so!). She volunteered at the school so that the principal would look more favorably on Freddy. She and David piled into the car with Elise and Freddy to visit the grandparents often enough so their children learned the meaning of respecting their elders. They took them to museums and watched documentaries with them so they would be well-rounded citizens of the world. Annette cooked for them every night so their bones would grow and their tissue would be nourished with herb-crusted chicken and energy-boosting rice pilaf when so many of her friends were popping TV dinners into the microwave. And yet. What had she sowed?

Her kids barely called. Everyone told her when she had Elise how lucky she was to have a daughter, chanting that saying: A son is a son until he takes a wife; a daughter's a daughter for the rest of your life. Well, her daughter looked at her like she was nothing more than a silly woman with silly concerns, because caring about one's appearance was somehow a crime. Lately Annette felt herself taking on a burdensome quality vis-à-vis Elise, like she was a houseplant that just wouldn't die. Well, she never asked anything of Elise. They lived on opposite coasts, the give-and-take between them embodied in that very fact of geography. And her son, going back to that little ditty, well, he hadn't yet taken a wife, but he'd never been the devoted boy to begin with. She and David had given these children everything, so why did they hate her? She cringed thinking of that word. They didn't *hate* her. She chastised herself for even thinking it. They loved her, in that biological torrent that eclipses anything environmental. But did they like her? No, they probably did not.

Still, the cruise. If her group of friends was any indication, these milestone birthdays warranted some type of fanfare. David probably didn't even realize how much it was costing. She didn't care, which was uncharacteristic for her, a woman who reused tea bags until the water barely took the color of the leaves. They'd worked their whole lives, David on call for most holiday weekends, waking up at all hours of the night to bring parents their greatest joy. She put in overtime investigating cheap printing services, negotiating cut-rate leases for the medical equipment, arranging for David to give pharmaceutical talks for extra money. They had a decent nest egg, even if it had taken an unexpected hit, and they could afford to take their children and grandchildren away for the week. If they didn't pay for everything, there was no chance the trip would ever happen. Mitch made peanuts and Freddy, well, she didn't quite understand how her son scraped by. He had no wife and children, so his expenses were minimal, but she wondered if he even owned a car or had health insurance. It was true she could ask, but that was patronizing. Her firstborn was nearly half a century in age! Boy, if that didn't make her feel past her expiration date.

The trip, of course, was really about David. He was sick, though they never talked about it, treating his illness as taboo a topic as an extramarital affair. His hand tremor that put an end to his career had put them in a tizzy for weeks while he got tested for Parkinson's, multiple sclerosis, and a brain tumor. Everything was negative and they rejoiced upon hearing it was simply a symptom of old age, too many years of overuse as a surgeon, holding his digits perfectly still to stitch a level-four tear or grasping a scalpel tightly to perform a hysterectomy. His muscles had simply given out. But eight months later, totally unrelated to the tremor, David was back at the doctor. He'd been feeling tired, dizzy, short of breath. Annette was sure it was anxiety. They both knew how nerves could be more exhausting than working a full day on your feet, and the transition to retirement had been stressful for both of them.

It was leukemia. Cancer was knocking on the door of too many of their friends, as though getting to seventy was like sending a personalized invitation for abnormal cells to come on over and reproduce in any of your vital organs. Now it was here for them. The doctors said he had a sixty percent chance of survival. David had demanded to know the statistics, but it made Annette ill to think in such cold, hard facts. One day when David was out running errands, she'd actually filled a small candy dish in their home with six red marbles and four black ones. Closing her eyes, she drew marbles for almost an hour, trying to get a feel for the odds by rubbing the stones blindly.

David insisted on not telling the children. He was a practical man and he knew Elise and Freddy wouldn't be able to help him — not from California and not from Colorado, and not even from up close. What would help him would be sticking strictly to the care plan crafted by his team of doctors at Mount Sinai, eating the right diet, and taking his meds. Annette was in agreement that they shouldn't tell the kids either, but for different reasons. She honestly didn't know if they'd be crushed and come running to their father's side, in which case she'd feel guilty for burdening them, or if they'd gravely disappoint by sending only the perfunctory flowers and calling once every few weeks. Strange that she couldn't predict how her own children would behave. Even sadder that she was too afraid to find out.

One month ago, Annette was in the waiting room at the hospital while David was receiving one of his weekly radiation treatments. She'd brought along her knitting (she was in the process of making a sweater for the child of one of David's nurses), but she couldn't focus. Her stitches were sloppy and she wouldn't think of handing over a gift that wasn't perfect, especially to Marie, Annette's favorite of David's caretakers. Instead she focused on the TV, trying to follow a soap opera in which a family was at war, this brother suing that brother, this mother in therapy because of her daughter, that grandparent cutting this grandchild out of his will. It was ugly to watch, even though everyone had a pretty face. But then a captivating commercial came on for Paradise cruises, and an alternate world was depicted. Grandparents riding paddleboards with grandchildren, husbands and wives holding hands on the dance floor, families celebrating around large tables filled with towers of seafood and bottles of champagne. And she made up her mind. Both versions of family were absurd, the *Days of Our Lives* and the Paradise International, but if she were to choose one for inspiration she would go with the latter.

The Feldmans, all seven of them, were going to take a cruise. Everyone would be a captive. *Her* captives. Nobody could claim they had friends to visit or that they needed to cut the trip short for work. They would be stranded together on the high seas and she, as the one footing the bill, would be in charge of making sure it was all smooth sailing. Life was too short to behave like they were on daytime television. She looked back down at her knitting and took it up with renewed energy, fixing the sloppy stiches, tightening the pattern, admiring the beauty.

SIX

When the call came for Darius, he was staring at Marcy Lungstrom's breasts, round, fleshy, heavy as honeydews, and listening to her laugh at a stupid joke. Her giggle was the exact opposite of what she carried on her chest. It was light and fluffy and Darius wanted nothing more than for Marcy to be balanced on his lap now, giggling away, rather than comfortably splayed on Jesse Traynor's lap, his hands gripping her waist just mere inches below those gorgeous, overflowing boobs. They weren't a couple, Jesse and Marcy, and thank God for that. It was just that Jesse had a way of being in the right place when Marcy needed a seat, always had his hand on the fridge when Marcy wanted a beer. Darius was really starting to hate his best friend with his perfect timing.

Darius, Marcy, and Jesse, along with Jesse's older brother Jasper and some of his buddies from the car dealership and Marcy's lackey Elin, were sitting in Jasper's poorly lit, run-down condo, drinking and passing a joint around. Darius casually skipped the bud each time it came to him. He wondered if anyone noticed, or if the rest of them — including Elin — were too engrossed in Marcy's every movement, the way her curves cut through space, to even look his way. The girl had an ass like a peach on steroids. Why he had to think of Marcy's body as the parts of a fruit salad he couldn't comprehend. He hated fruit, but she was a chick that called to mind fresh produce. Their crew had been meeting up like this every day after work and Darius felt himself sliding off a precipice, spending time with Jasper and his cronies, versions of himself in a few years if he didn't get his act together. Even desiring the fleshy, bawdy Marcy, a bad girl in training, was symbolic of his poor choices. He ought to break away, even thought to ask Rachel for some big-sister advice, but every time he saw Marcy's name on the group text confirming plans, he found himself back on Jasper's ratty green couch with the ketchup stains just to be in her presence.

He felt a ringing in his pocket and knew it was probably his mother calling. All his friends texted, using shorthand and abbreviations and emojis to communicate, sometimes when they were in the same room. For some reason, it was easier to ask what everyone wanted to do after school over text than to call, fishing for the right words while on the other end of the phone you could hear your friend's bored impatience. Darius stepped a few feet away from his friends to take the call, happy for the interruption since a bulge was forming in his pants and there was nothing like his mother's shriek to cool his engine.

"What's up?" he asked, trying to sound nonchalant in case Marcy was in earshot. He knew he was in hot water at home, having not touched any of the college crap his mother piled on his desk or cracked open his SAT prep book (a fall retake was definitely in order after he earned a score hovering near 1000 in the spring). And he hadn't even told his parents that he'd lost his job lifeguarding at the town pool after getting caught on his cell phone from the chair. He'd pulled it from his bathing suit thinking the vibration might be a text from Marcy, but it was a damn CNN alert about a forest fire. His parents would freak out when they found out he'd been canned, which wouldn't be long, considering his father was the editor of the local paper and knew every crumb of homegrown gossip.

"Hi, honey. I'm calling with exciting news," his mother said, uncharacteristically not inquiring about his whereabouts. Their conversations typically started with an inquisition: Where are you? What are you doing? Who are you with? His father had certainly schooled his mother well in the five Ws. "I think you will be excited to hear that we're all going on a family trip. With Grandma and Grandpa Feldman."

"We are?" he asked, surprised by his mother's enthusiasm. His parents thought he couldn't hear them muttering to each other from the front seat of the car or from behind the closed door of their bathroom, but he had ears like a hound dog, especially when it came to family intrigue.

"Yes. We're taking a cruise to the Caribbean and it leaves next week. So you'll need to tell your boss you can't work the last week of summer. I hope he won't be too upset. Just blame it on me if he is."

Darius felt the familiar pit materializing in his stomach, the three vodka cranberries he'd downed (only because Marcy had mixed them) now working their way back up his intestines. He never wanted the lifeguarding job to begin with. He wanted to work at the skate shop, next door to where Marcy worked at the ice cream store, but couldn't even get an interview. He was a clown on a board. The only things skater about him were his haircut, his clothes, and the music he listened to — all things that could be bought. Attempting any trick on the half-pipe, he was as ungraceful and heavy on his feet as a sumo wrestler walking a tightrope. Instead, Jesse got the job, which paid much better than the lifeguarding gig and afforded him the chance to time his breaks with Marcy's.

"Um, okay," he choked out, wondering if he could somehow cover up his firing by burying it under the early departure. "And I promise to work on my college stuff tonight."

"You know what? Don't even worry about that for now. We'll figure it out."

Darius shook his head involuntarily, his mother's laissez-faire attitude conversely making him anxious. He wanted her to lay off him most of the time, but now he just wished she would act like herself, even if that meant being overbearing and nosy. Something was definitely off with her, which was why he'd answered her call to begin with. Just a few weeks earlier, Darius had invited over some of his high school friends to hang out on a Sunday. His father was at work and his mother said she was spending the day at their neighbor's country club. Rachel was at work, even though it was a weekend, because she was treating her internship at the law firm as though she was Ruth Bader Ginsburg and the place couldn't run without her. Still, Darius was nervous that any one of his family members might show up unexpectedly, so he'd led the crew up to the attic where they could drink their gin and Cokes with impunity. He hadn't been to the cobwebbed, dank room since his days of playing hide-and-seek with Rachel and he couldn't fathom that anyone else had been up there recently either. He took a flashlight with him, doubtful that the ancient bulb on a string had any juice left, and was the first to enter the room, his friends laughing like goofballs behind him. He nearly dropped the flashlight when the light spilled into the room.

There had to be nearly a hundred shopping bags of different sizes, shapes, and colors covering every inch of free space in the attic. Mountains of packages, piles of crap, all in this clandestine location with its sloped ceiling six feet tall at the highest point, smelling of mothballs and mildew. He inched closer, no longer hearing the voices and cackles of his friends and even — as had never happened to him before — forgetting that Marcy was mere inches behind him. He peeked inside a few of the bags, lifted contents, fished out receipts. His mother's name was on the first one, then the second, then the third. Quickly he went rabid, tearing through all the bags while his friends looked on in confusion until he told them all to just start drinking without him, knowing in a few minutes they would be draped in the blur of heavy-duty buzzes and wouldn't question what he was doing and why his attic looked like a cross between a garage sale and Santa's workshop. The bags were filled with the most motley assortment of stuff he'd ever seen — clothing, appliances, sneakers in all sizes, journals, cookbooks, gardening tools, camera equipment, costumes. He studied the receipts more closely. They were all dated within the past year. They all said "Elise Connelly." The only differences were the last four digits of the credit card numbers printed on the white slips. There must have been twenty different numerical combinations, meaning his mother had a hell of a lot of plastic to swipe.

His first thought was to drive over to Rachel's office and tell her what he'd uncovered. But she'd brush him off if he showed up unannounced, embarrassed by her unshorn, sloppy brother with the dirty Vans and chin pubes, as she called his attempt at a goatee. She had been such a bitch to him all summer.

So instead of running to his sister, Darius had sunk into the weight of one of the shopping bags, this one filled with a football-themed comforter. It was the type of thing his father might have gotten for him when he was eight and still thought his boy would be a jock like his old man. He decided the best course of action was to do nothing and say nothing. Notwithstanding his decision to stay quiet for the time being, he knew with total certainty that he had stumbled upon an ugly secret of his mother's. He just wasn't sure how bad it was. Didn't want to know either. His mind was cloudy enough just navigating his social life, remembering to take his lifeguard tank top every day so his parents wouldn't be suspicious, and memorizing different sixteen-letter words he'd never think about again after he retook the SATs.

Now, a month later, his mother was telling him, all rosy and bright, that they were going on a trip with the grandparents he knew she had issues with. And that he

shouldn't bother working on the college applications that both his parents had been
dogging him about since June. Strange
things were afoot in the Connelly household. Even his father, the straightest arrow,
was being dodgy. He'd closed his office door
several times when he'd heard Darius approaching. He assumed his dad was looking
at porn — Jesse's dad was an addict — but
maybe it was something more nefarious.
Perhaps he'd find out on the boat. There'd
be nothing else to do and he needed some
way to distract himself while he endured
five Marcyless days.

"All right," he said to his mother, looking
over at his friends. The joint was smoked by
now to the bit and he relaxed a little. For
some reason he had it in his head that once
he took a puff of marijuana, he'd no longer
be standing on the precipice, he'd be firmly
planted on the dark side. Maybe it was all
the stories he'd heard growing up about
Uncle Freddy. "That sounds cool."

"You're going to share a cabin with Rachel," his mom added. "Should be fun."

"Sharing with Rachel?" he said, forcing a
groan. The truth was that he didn't mind at
all. He wanted the face time with his sister,
to put himself so squarely in front of her
that she couldn't pretend he didn't exist.

She'd see that he did in fact need to shave, that he could be considerate in close quarters, that he read every night before bed — real stuff, like Vonnegut and Kerouac. He wanted her to observe his neatness and his rigorous personal hygiene regimen, because earlier in the summer she'd walked into the bathroom and caught him sniffing his belly button lint. She made a huge fuss about it and of course he'd denied it, even though it had been true, but it was only to make sure he was cleaning in there thoroughly enough.

"Well, you two will just have to deal. Grandma and Grandpa are paying for this trip and I can't very well demand you have separate rooms. I hope and expect you will both be on your best behavior on this trip."

"Whatever," he said, noticing Marcy staring intently at Jesse as he regaled the group with some idiotic story that was probably made up. "I gotta go."

"Darius?" his mother said, sounding like she didn't want to let him go.

"Yeah?"

"I bought you some new socks and shorts. Also school supplies."

"Okay, Mom," he said, feeling a sickness he was certain was unrelated to the vodka come over him.

115

SEVEN

2200 hours. 10 miles from Port of Miami.

Feldman, David, M.D.
Age 72. Great Neck, New York. Special requests: None. Interests: Rest.

Feldman, Annette
Age 69. Great Neck, New York. Special requests: (1) Low-sodium, high-fiber meals for David Feldman. (2) Feldman and Connelly parties must be seated together at every meal. (3) Feldman and Connelly cabins should be near each other. Interests: Family. Knitting. Mah-jongg. Entertaining.

Connelly, Mitchell
Age 47. Sacramento, California. Special requests: Couples massage billed to separate account for myself and Elise Feldman Connelly. Interests: Writing. Reading. My

116

family. Comedy.

Feldman Connelly, Elise

Age 44. Sacramento, California. Special requests: Make sure my family has fun. Are there boutiques on board and are traveler's checks accepted? Interests: Finding rare objects. Collecting. Gift selection.

Connelly, Rachel

Age 19. Stanford, California. Special requests: Can the spin bike be reserved? Interests: Spinning. Not being forced into the teen club.

Connelly, Darius

Age 17. Sacramento, California. Special requests: None. Interests: ~~Boarding.~~ None.

Feldman, Frederick

Age 48. Aspen, Colorado. Special requests: Please transfer from standard stateroom to Deluxe Royal Suite on separate deck away from rest of Feldman and Connelly parties and bill the difference to my account. Put flowers in room with card for Natasha Kuznetsov. Deliver a tray of cookies and candy to room of Darius and Rachel Connelly and sign "From Uncle

Freddy" along with gift cards to use in the arcade and at the teen pool. Interests: Depends what is legal in international waters. Kidding! In earnest, surviving this trip.

Kuznetsov, Natasha
Age 29. Aspen, Colorado. Special requests: Is there Wi-Fi? If no Wi-Fi in room, how do I get Wi-Fi? Please be in touch with me regarding Wi-Fi. Interests: Yoga. Getting a tan. Relaxing. Getting to know my boyfriend's family.

Julian Masterino looked over the ship's manifest for the last time before he was due to set sail aboard the *Ocean Queen* the next day. Next to him in bed, his partner of three years, Roger Alistair, was palming the latest James Patterson. Their French bulldog, Takai, panted between them.

"Anything interesting?" Roger asked, stifling a yawn. They had done this routine at least fifty times, Julian reviewing the passenger questionnaires the night before embarkation, Roger asking questions about the newest crop of travelers.

"Standard fare. A family celebrating a birthday and nobody wants to be on the trip."

118

"You should have been a therapist, not a cruise director. You'd make more money and wouldn't have to leave me all the time." Julian rolled his eyes.

"Boring! I couldn't stand to listen to the same people's problems for years on end. With the cruises, you get the dysfunctional families, the hopeful couples, the depressed old people, the irritated kids, and you get to make a difference for them in a week, sometimes less. You'd be surprised how effective an all-you-can-eat buffet is in boosting serotonin."

"Yes, I've heard the omelet station is very therapeutic," Roger said, turning on his side. Though he clearly considered Julian's job pure fluff compared to his position as general counsel for the Miami Dolphins, every time his partner returned home bleary-eyed and still adjusting to terra firma, Roger would insist on a full recounting: Craziest complaint at Guest Services? Drunkest person at karaoke? Roger demanded it all.

Julian turned off his bedside lamp. He needed a full eight hours before he set sail with three thousand strangers that he had to transform into friends, trusting travelers, and satisfied customers. Complicated people with thorny relations, much like the Feldmans of the manifest.

"Good night, Roger," Julian said softly, already feeling himself melting into the mattress. It was already 2230 hours. His time for shut-eye was ticking away.

"I gotta come with you on one of these cruises someday," Roger said, closing his book with a thud. "We'd have a great time. The captain can marry us. You know you can't avoid talking about us getting hitched forever."

"Uh-huh. Tonight I can. You know I need sleep before I ship out," Julian mumbled. "Good night, Rog."

■ ■ ■ ■

PART II
SEA LEGS

■ ■ ■ ■

EIGHT

When Freddy saw the *Ocean Queen* in all her glory, nine hundred feet of hulking iron, steel, and wood, he decided his mother had accomplished her goal. He felt small and inconsequential and that he couldn't measure up. All morning he'd been puffing out his own chest, reminding himself of everything he'd accomplished, looking at Natasha for reinforcement, but when their taxi pulled into the parking lot and he had to roll down his window and crane his head to see the ocean liner's full height, once again he felt unimportant. Like a blip on a radar or a single ant in a colony. It was like the ship was his family and he was the little dinghy clinging onto the back.

"That's one of the lifesaving boats," Natasha said when he expressed the metaphor to her. She smiled in triumph, satisfied that she'd prevented him from self-pity at least just this once.

123

They stepped out of the taxi and squinted at the scene before them. The whiteness of the boat reflected in the sunlight made staring at it directly almost impossible, so they were forced to take in the throngs of their fellow passengers. This is America, Freddy thought, taking in the masses in their Hawaiian shirts and floppy hats, already reeking of coconut sunscreen. The selfie sticks were out and proud, even though the scenery was nothing more than a ship too large to fit into the frame of any photo and a few thousand passengers juggling unwieldy suitcases and children. He took a sharp breath as a look of fear spread across his girlfriend's face.

"It's going to be fine," he said and put a protective arm around Natasha. "Let's find my sister. She said she'd meet me by the character stand, whatever the hell that means."

After an inquiry to one of the numerous greeters scattered in the loading zone, they were informed that the character stand was about a hundred yards to the left of the registration desk. Natasha and Freddy headed in the direction of the mile-long rectangular table where sailor-suit-clad attendants were checking in passengers. The sign above the table read WELCOME, OCEAN

QUEENS: FROM THIS POINT ON, YOU ARE NOW CONSIDERED ROYALTY.

Freddy nudged Natasha. "They might want to work on their marketing. Unless my mother inadvertently booked us on a gay cruise."

Natasha laughed and Freddy felt himself swing to the other side of the pendulum again. How dependent on praise was he that a little giggle sated him? Perhaps if his reservoir of adulation as a young man hadn't been so depleted he'd be less needy. Or was it just his nature to seek even the smallest forms of adoration, much like his mother, with her insistence on arriving late to dinners so she could receive compliments on her outfit?

"It's cheesy," Natasha said. "But I don't care. I'm excited to meet your family. Glad your mom and dad were cool with me coming."

Freddy stared in wonder at this young bird who let him sleep with her, and fondle her breasts whenever he wanted, and who laughed at his jokes no matter how terrible. She was so lacking in suspicion and angst that he couldn't help picturing her childhood as a leisurely stroll through a field of cotton candy. He felt guilty subjecting her to his own family, but at least it would give

125

her some *context.*

As they hung a left toward where Elise and her family were meant to be waiting, Freddy wondered how the initial meet-up would go. He was surprised when Elise had texted him a few days earlier. So I guess we're doing this? she wrote to him and inserted a boat emoji. Seems so, he responded, simultaneously pleased and irritated by her overture. He was the older brother. He should have reached out first. His sister was always beating him, in school, in parent approval, and now in kindness. She had suggested they meet up before boarding and he couldn't think of a good reason to say no.

It made him cringe to imagine the forced distance his niece would put between them, Rachel waving at him limply instead of him sweeping her into a bear hug. As if Elise would ever have an inkling that he'd bailed her daughter out of Santa Clara County Jail four months earlier and hosted her and her pals for a week over spring break. Freddy had looked the other way while they drank themselves silly after shredding the slopes, but his product? — he didn't let them touch it, not that Elise would ever believe him.

"I think I found the character stand," Natasha said, suddenly wide-eyed and looking like she might break into a run in the opposite direction.

"Holy sh—" he started to say as he took in the cast of court jesters on stilts placing paper crowns on the passengers' heads and handing out light-up wands. He turned suddenly to Natasha, cupped her by the chin firmly, and said, "Thank you so much for coming. I will make this up to you."

As they drew closer, Freddy spotted his sister. She looked better than she had in the Facebook photo. Her hair was tied up in a high ponytail, the way she used to wear it when they were kids, and she appeared fit and well-groomed. He'd forgotten how short she was. She was going to hate standing next to the leggy Natasha, who was merely two inches shy of a modeling career. Freddy was pleased that Elise was looking nothing like the tired, overwhelmed housewife she'd seemed to be on his computer screen. He saw his niece and nephew a few feet away from their mother, both glued to their phones, their heads rounded forward like Neanderthals. Darius was a clone of Mitch, with his dark blond hair and lanky frame, though Mitch kept his hair short with a tidy side part and Darius's was hanging in long, loose clumps. He knew his sister must hate it, along with the baggy jeans and wallet chain. Rachel, as usual, had her innocent veneer intact, and Freddy smiled to himself thinking about how deceiving appearances can be. He still chuckled when he pictured her slumped into the corner of the holding cell, desperately trying to achieve modesty with the scant fabric of what he hoped was a costume. Beyond Rachel, Freddy spotted the back of Mitch's head. The poor guy was righting two suitcases that had toppled over and had a bulky camera dangling off his arm.

"That's them," Freddy said, gesturing toward the Connelly clan.

"Why are they all wearing yellow?" Natasha asked.

Freddy looked back. His sister and her family were, in fact, all wearing sweatshirts in a particularly bright shade of chartreuse. Elise could be haughty and condescending, but at least she'd never been the type of woman to dress her family in matching outfits.

"I have no idea," Freddy said, shaking his head dubiously. "That doesn't seem like my sister."

He rarely thought much about Elise's life in California, probably because he was largely cut out of the family canvas by the time she moved west, but now he found himself pondering it. Had his sister become a matching-outfit soccer mom automaton? Once upon a time she'd almost been cool, with a secret belly button ring his parents never found out about.

Freddy and Natasha wheeled their suitcases over to where his sister was standing. Thankfully as they ambled over he noticed Elise decline a photo opportunity with the *Ocean Queen* mascot, a whale wearing a crown. So she wasn't completely certifiable.

"I feel like we're all going to be whales after this trip," Natasha said, eyeballing the mascot with trepidation. "I read they have mini buffets to tide people over between the regular mealtimes. And dinner is typically five courses."

"You don't need to worry," he said. Freddy let Natasha gain a few steps on him and he admired her body for the thousandth time. She was a perfect hourglass, her tiny midsection visible on account of her midriff-baring shirt and low-slung jean shorts from which the string of her thong protruded. How was his family going to react to his girlfriend of one year that he'd never told them about, young enough to be his daughter? Who worked as a masseuse at one of the nicer Aspen hotels but still his parents would assume was a hooker?

At forty-eight years old, Freddy had never once introduced a girlfriend to his family. For starters, there had been none in high school to bring around. He'd spent those four years sickly pining for one girl after another, several of whom were Elise's friends. If she'd only thought to put in a good word for him with Amy Simon or Jenny Baron, maybe he wouldn't have turned into a twenty-two-year-old virgin who finally gave it up to a weathered fifty-something housewife supposedly "at the spa" while her husband and children skied all day. In college, his luck was slightly better than in high school, the war zone of acne on his face finally declaring a ceasefire, but still it was tame hookups when he was high as a kite and the girl, usually a stoner with ratty hair and a Phish T-shirt, was too. And then he was kicked out of school and things went really downhill. So this was technically the first time that Freddy Feldman was introducing his parents and sister to a bona fide girlfriend.

"Elise," Freddy called out and gave his sister a friendly wave. At least he was the first to shatter the silence between them.

"Hi there," she said, offering up a sheepish grin. He couldn't tell what was behind his sister's somewhat embarrassed look. Was it shame at how distant the two of them had grown and a feeling that it was more her fault than his? Or was it just because of their surroundings, the realization that they were two middle-aged travelers who wanted to stand out in this crowd for being more chic, sophisticated, and worldly, but who more likely than not blended right in?

He bent down to hug her, hoping the warmth would set the right tone for the trip. He didn't want to give his family the cold shoulder, which could make them think he was still the insecure guy who as a child would flee the dinner table if he thought he was being teased. Besides, he was a pot peddler, and stoners were nothing if not friendly.

"You look great," he said to Elise after releasing her from the hug. His sister waved off the compliment.

"I'm old," she said. She raised her eyebrows and her forehead indeed had more lanes than a superhighway.

"How are you guys doing?" he asked his niece and nephew. He couldn't believe how tall Darius had become. The last time they'd all been together as a family was at Rachel's bat mitzvah — a ridiculous party where she'd been bounced around on a chair in a sequined dress. That would have been about

131

six years ago. Freddy looked again at Darius and couldn't remember for the life of him attending or even being invited to his bar mitzvah. Could Elise and Mitch have cut him from the guest list? He hadn't behaved badly at Rachel's. He didn't toke the whole day and he'd put on the yarmulke in temple, which was the perfect size for his bald spot anyway. He'd have to ask Rachel if Darius had had a party when he was alone with her. He needed face time with his niece anyway, to ask about the "complicated" boyfriend and to make sure she was staying out of trouble.

"Great," Rachel said, a sly smile spreading across her face. When she leaned in to give him a kiss on the cheek, Freddy noticed she was wearing her tiny diamond stud earrings. They were the same pair she'd asked him to hold on to when she'd spent the night in jail, worried some thug in the county pen would rip them from her ears. He'd highly doubted it, seeing that the other inmates were mostly sorority girls in short skirts who'd done one too many vodka shots before committing some Class D misdemeanor. He blinked twice as the earrings twinkled in the sunlight.

"You look so grown-up," Freddy said to Rachel, making a big show of looking her up and down and giving his sister a look that said, "Has it been this long?" Was he overdoing it? Probably. In actuality Rachel looked much younger than the last time he'd seen her in the holding pen, wearing black leather ankle boots and gobs of dark eye makeup.

"It's been a while," Elise said.

"Where'd Mitch go?" Freddy asked.

"Let me see," Elise said, turning around.

"What the — ?" Freddy asked, his jaw dropping at the sight of his sister's back. His mother's face, blown up, was airbrushed onto the bright yellow sweatshirt. Underneath her picture, written in jumbo font, it said: *Happy Birthday, Annette . . . 70 Years Young!* He quickly glanced back at Rachel and Darius. His nephew was closest. Freddy spun him around and saw the identical image on the back of his sweatshirt. Rachel turned herself around to save him the trouble.

"Elise!" he exclaimed.

"Mom's going to hate them, huh? I have one for you too, by the way. I didn't know about her," Elise said, shifting her gaze to Natasha.

Shit. Freddy realized that he had actually forgotten his girlfriend was even standing there.

133

"I was just about to introduce you to my girlfriend," Freddy said, putting a gallant arm around her waist. "This is Natasha Kuznetsov." He thought perhaps her multisyllabic, Slavic surname might add a bit of gravitas, summoning Dostoyevsky.

Natasha extended her hand toward Elise, who seemed to take it rather reluctantly.

"It's so great to meet you," Natasha peeped. "Freddy has told me so much about you."

Freddy shuddered. His girlfriend's favorite word was "so" and she liked to drag it out unnecessarily.

Elise raised her right eyebrow dramatically, a talent she'd had since childhood that Freddy had always envied. He could form his tongue into a clover, but there was so much more practical use for a well-timed single eyebrow raise. It immediately put the other person on the defensive, questioning what the quizzical look meant. Though this time Freddy knew immediately. *She's. So. Young.* That's what his sister was thinking when she floated up her eyebrow. And though it wasn't her habit, he was sure Elise was dragging out the "so" in her mind.

"Has he, now?" Elise said, looking back at Freddy. She knew it couldn't be true. He and Elise were more like second cousins at this point than siblings. His girlfriend's comment made it obvious she was trying to ingratiate herself with his family. She'd promised to make him look good, but this wasn't the way he'd expected. He'd rather she dangle her bracelet in their faces and gush about how Freddy couldn't resist buying it for her.

"You must be Freddy's niece," Natasha said, looking at Rachel.

His niece looked at Natasha with fresh, appraising eyes even though they'd already spent nearly a week together giggling on the couch and watching *Real Housewives.* Why did it look to Freddy as if she was taken aback by her age for the first time? Maybe he was just being paranoid, though he wasn't even stoned.

"I'm Rachel," she said, pointing to the place on her sweatshirt where her name had been embroidered in red thread. What the hell was wrong with his sister? Elise had to have lost her mind ordering this cheesy swag. Plastering their mother's face on the back of a sweatshirt and expecting them to wear them at the same time like they were hillbillies at a family reunion?

"And you must be Darius," Natasha said, touching his nephew on the arm gently.

Freddy's nephew looked like someone had

135

cut out his tongue. His eyes darted from here to there, unable to settle comfortably anywhere on Natasha. At least *somebody* was impressed, even if it was only a hormonally inflated teenage boy.

"I — I — Yes, I am," he finally stammered.

"What's wrong with you?" Rachel said, elbowing her brother in the ribs. "You didn't shut up on the car ride over here and now you're mute."

Freddy seized up, feeling Darius's discomfort and embarrassment so acutely his heart actually skipped a beat. He liked to think that his niece was nothing like her mother, but seeing the meanness cross between the siblings made Freddy question his instincts.

"Rachel — stop that," he said, despite knowing it wasn't his business to intervene.

Natasha offered Darius her warm honey smile, the one where her doe eyes crinkled, seeming unfazed by the kid's inability to utter a coherent sentence in her presence.

"Elise, seriously, what's the deal with the sweatshirts?" Freddy asked.

"Mitch has yours in his bag," she said by way of explanation. "Look, there he is."

Freddy's brother-in-law was stationed at one of the dozen or so information booths. He appeared to be deep in conversation with a group of tourists. People, Freddy corrected himself. They were all tourists now.

"I wasn't asking where mine was. I was asking why in the world you made them. We aren't *those* kind of people."

"Well, maybe we should be," Elise snapped at him. "I suppose you don't even want your tote bag. Mitch! Come back. Freddy is here!"

Freddy watched Mitch's head snap around and break into a smile when he saw him. A potential ally, Freddy thought, making a mental note to be extremely nice to his brother-in-law from the get-go. He would definitely need a friend if he were going to stay afloat.

NINE

I'm. So. Old.

It was the first thought that went through Elise's head when she saw the tall, bronzed, wrinkle-free woman — no, girl — beside her brother. Not that this Natasha person wasn't age-appropriate for Freddy. Not that she looked like someone who could be a companion for Rachel on the trip. No. The first thing to run through Elise's mind was a high-speed movie of everything about her that was deteriorating with age: her skin, her body, her sex drive, her patience. What a soul-crushing thing it was to stand next to a sexy young thing with genetic blessings to spare.

Elise hadn't been feeling particularly bad about herself when she woke up that morning and stared at her reflection in the medicine cabinet. Instead of slogging through her face care routine half-asleep, she had rubbed the cream into her temples for an extra beat and bothered to slick on primer before her foundation. When she headed to the kitchen for coffee, she noticed a spring in her gait that she hadn't felt in ages, like the tile floor was a rubber gymnastics mat. She was a step closer to solving her major financial crisis, which, if she was successful, *would* be like barreling over a pommel horse. Not far behind that victory would be Darius returning to shore with a fully written essay and a complete list of colleges where he would apply.

After draining her caffeine without rinsing the mug (might as well practice the feeling of being waited on in anticipation of the boat), Elise even returned to her makeup vanity to add mascara and eyebrow pencil, noticing that taking the time to brush on powder and roll out the liner really did make a difference, not that she'd ever admit it to her mother. But then she came face-to-face with Natasha (more like face-to-shoulder, actually) and felt immediately like a fossil, a relic from the species *Elderatius motherenza*. This was a classic Feldman failing: They were all guilty of constantly measuring themselves against other people, too often each other. All the Feldmans lived in a comparative world. Even her father, with his numerous awards and accolades from the hospital — his shelves had sterling silver stethoscopes and wooden plaques to spare — wouldn't consider his year a success if he didn't deliver more babies than his partner, even if just by one. So no matter how content Elise was feeling earlier that day as she pulled together the last-minute contents of her beach bag (a new one because her old one really was on its last leg), learning that she'd have to keep company with a woman at least two decades her junior, essentially a fetus in jean shorts, was quite the pin in her balloon. A little warning from Annette would have been nice.

Worse, though, was the audacity of this barely legal, nubile girl to pluck the sweatshirt Mitch handed to Freddy right out of his hands and throw it on over her shrunken tank top. Elise had not worked so hard to create this personalized swag to celebrate her mother's birthday to have it fall into the hands of a non-family-member she'd never met before. She'd spent hours trolling Etsy to find the right vendor who could airbrush Annette's photo on the back and embroider everyone's names on the front. Elise shivered thinking about how much it had cost. Seven sweatshirts, which once she added on the bells and whistles — the personalization, the fleece lining, the organic cotton —

140

had come to over a thousand dollars. And then the vendor had sweet-talked her into matching tote bags. Over text, Elise had told DezinedwLuv about the upcoming cruise and was all too easily talked into adding convenient bags they could lug around the boat to hold their sunscreen, motion sickness tablets, and hand sanitizer. Elise consoled herself into thinking it would be her last hurrah, although those were fast becoming famous last words. At least this was a selfless act. Instead of ending Shopapalooza by running to Bloomingdale's for cashmere sweaters, she'd decided to make her last spending binge about her mother. And not just Annette, but the entire family.

Now this complete stranger — the same one giving her son impure thoughts, no less — was wearing one of the sweatshirts she'd labored over. It had ruined everything. Elise would need to seek a different final shopping binge. She prayed the boat had some decent stores. It would be tragic if her last go-to-town splurge was on travel-size Advil packets and flip-flop magnets in the sundries shop.

As much as Elise wanted to be fuming at her brother for toting along an interloper, a part of her was grateful to have Natasha on board. In the presence of a stranger, the

141

Feldmans would undoubtedly be better behaved. During her childhood, her parents had never fought when she had a friend over — a foreign body forced an automatic détente. Of course, it would have been preferable if said stranger in their midst now was a college friend of Rachel's or, even better, a sycophantic boat staffer assigned to attend to the Feldmans from sunrise to sundown.

As a rule the Feldmans, even Freddy (anyone could see that the trendy man-bun and his platinum arm candy were an obvious bid for approval), cared what other people thought about them. They wouldn't cause a scene on the boat. They wouldn't "make waves." Nautical puns were invading her brain and she wanted to repeat them to Mitch, who appreciated good wordplay in an adorably nerdy fashion. But this particular pun made her think of the store where she'd gotten a bunch of new bathing suits for the trip, a boutique called Wave Maker at their local mall, and she worried her face would betray guilt if she even said the words out loud.

"So, Natasha, how did you and my brother meet?" Elise asked, waiting for Mitch to finally make his way back over. She'd sent him to find out what time their luggage would get to their rooms and he'd gotten himself entangled in a conversation with a lively group of Japanese travelers measuring selfie sticks.

"It's a great story," she said, giggling as only a person under forty was wont to do. "We met on the massage table. I'm a masseuse at the St. Regis Hotel in Aspen."

Freddy looked embarrassed. "Natasha has amazing hands," he stammered.

Natasha lifted her hands and rotated her wrists as if to prove their worth. They were rather lovely, Elise had to admit. Like, nail polish advertisement nice.

"Thanks, babe," she said, standing on tiptoe to kiss Freddy. Elise noticed she was wearing one of those iconic Cartier Love bracelets. They were a staple among the wealthier housewives in her community, usually received as a birthday present or for an anniversary. Obviously Natasha's was a fake. So tacky. Still, Elise wondered where she got it. It was a rather good copy.

"Anyway, Freddy always used the same masseuse at the hotel. My coworker Alexis, who is really awesome at hot stone and Swedish. But Alexis went to Coachella — she's so lucky — so I took over her clients and got Freddy. We got to talking after the massage was over. His scapula was really

143

tight, so I gave him some pointers. Over the next few months, Freddy must have gotten like a million massages before he finally asked me out. Now here we are, one year later," she said, reaching her arm around Freddy's waist.

So many questions pulsed through Elise's mind. One year with this girl?! What was her brother doing getting weekly massages at an expensive hotel? What did Natasha see in Freddy? Was Elise supposed to know what Coachella was? And, seriously, where did her brother's girlfriend get that Cartier knockoff? It was nearly perfect!

"That's so nice," Rachel said, smiling genuinely. Elise didn't even realize she had been listening. Her children were permanently glued to their smartphones and Elise had long since given up competing with the tweets, posts, and texts. Just her luck that while Rachel and Darius tuned out everything she had said for the past five years, they perked up to listen to Natasha.

"I really want to go to Coachella," Darius chimed in. Now Elise was flabbergasted. Darius was actually making conversation with an adult (assuming Natasha could be considered one). She couldn't remember the last time he'd mustered anything more than a grunt or a "Fine, Mom." She supposed that was what having double D breasts and being utterly beautiful could do: get the attention of a lazy, distracted seventeen-year-old boy who otherwise preferred to play Fortnite.

Finally Mitch appeared.

"Freddy, good to see you!" he exclaimed, slapping Freddy on the back good-naturedly. What was up with Mitch? First, he was over the moon to go on this cruise and second, he hadn't mentioned work since they left home, when he typically called his desk editors every twenty minutes. Now he was acting far too simpatico with Freddy — like her brother was an old college mate and not the source of her parents' angina. Something was afoot with her husband, of that Elise was certain. The kids were leaving the nest, and he didn't seem remotely concerned about all the extra square footage in their house and the cavernous spaces in which they would feel their emptiness. On the career front, even though there was credible chatter that the *Bee* was going to be purchased by a media conglomerate from Chicago, Mitch was nonplussed about the changes that might portend. And, from what she could see now, he wasn't even fazed by the perky, sky-high tits that were protruding into his personal

145

space, shooting off Natasha's body like twin rockets. If Elise wasn't harboring such a big secret, she might have probed her husband to get to the root of his overwhelming complacency. But she didn't dare. It was hardly the time to open up a chorus of "Anything you want to tell me?"

Freddy returned the back slap with vigor. She wasn't surprised that her brother liked Mitch. Everybody did. Even her tough-to-please parents could only complain about his religion, which they acknowledged was an accident of birth, and the fact that he didn't take home a Silicon Valley salary.

"So great to see you, buddy," Freddy said to Mitch. "You're looking good! I'd like to introduce you to my girlfriend, Natasha."

Mitch extended his hand but didn't give her more than a one-second glance. Elise smiled to herself with satisfaction. If Freddy was hoping to show off Natasha to Mitch, well — Mitch wasn't taking the bait. She wished her son would take a page from his father, but it was too much to expect a dopey teenager to realize that breasts eventually sag and looks fade and if you can't make decent conversation with your partner, marriage will feel like the seventh circle of hell. Was it wrong to assume Natasha didn't have much to say for herself? Probably, but Elise was lacking the patience not to judge a book by its cover at the moment. They would be trapped on a boat together for the better part of a week and they'd learn soon enough what Natasha was all about.

Speaking of boarding, where in the world were her parents? Her mother and father were typically prompt and yet they hadn't made their way over to the predetermined meeting point. She'd expected her mother to have arrived at least an hour before the rest of them in order to scope out the best of everything — the shortest lines, the best table in the dining room, the priority seating for the shows — dragging her father along as though he cared just as much as she did about outdoing everyone else on the boat. Both her parents were spineless when it came to handling the other. Maybe it was generational. She and Mitch helped form each other, two potters constantly switching wheels, while her parents left each other alone to pursue their idiosyncrasies unfettered.

Elise wanted to spot her mother coming so she could pop out her lipstick for a fresh coat. The color in her bag was a matte pink called Fabulous Fuchsia — Annette had pressed three tubes into her hand the last time they were together, claiming she got them as free samples. Elise was resolved to start this trip off right, to give her mother the fewest possible reasons to criticize. After all, she was planning to ask for a fifty-thousand-dollar loan. A simple gracious overture toward her mother, like paying extra attention to her appearance, was hardly a sacrifice. It was like when Darius would approach her about staying out past curfew or for extra spending money and Elise would wonder why he hadn't at least pulled up his pants first. Rachel was clever enough to present the best side of herself before making any requests. She'd say something like, "Yum, I love when you make lasagna, Mom!" before broaching the idea of going to Cabo with her friends for senior week. And even though Elise saw through it every time, it still worked. Darius perhaps had a higher IQ than Rachel, but her emotional intelligence smoked him every time.

"Take those off," rang a shrill voice through the general pandemonium.

Elise spun around and came face-to-face with her mother, who, if she had smoke coming out of her mouth, couldn't have looked more like a dragon.

"Mom, I didn't see you coming," Elise said, flushing. So much for her cosmetic touch-up.

"That's because you're in the wrong place. You told me to meet at the welcome center and this is the photo booth. Your father and I spent the last twenty minutes looking for you. We are exhausted and have been dragging around our luggage. Finally, I spotted Darius and we pushed our way over here. What are these awful sweatshirts you are all wearing? I will not have my age on display. Rachel — did you make these?"

Rachel looked up from her phone. "Me? No way. I hate them."

"Good. You?" Annette addressed Darius, who offered a resounding head shake.

"You did this?" she asked, turning back to Elise. "Why in the world would you think I would be happy having everyone on this ship know that I'm" — she dropped her voice in the way that people spoke about cancer — "seventy?"

"This entire boat is full of people your age celebrating milestone birthdays. You're much younger than that person over there." Elise pointed out a man confined to a wheelchair who had two giant number balloons attached to his armrest. "He's eighty-five."

"Well, at least when the wind blows he looks fifty-eight," Annette cleverly retorted.

"You should be proud of your age, Mom. Plus I thought you'd like having a memento from the trip. Look around at all the matching shirts. It's a thing." She pointed toward a group of young Indian women wearing tank tops that said *Raja's Mates of Honor* and then to a multigenerational group of black men with hats that said *The Baker Buoys.*

"We aren't those kinds of people," Annette hissed.

"Grandma!" Rachel said, snapping to attention.

"I didn't mean *that.* I mean we Feldmans aren't the kind of people who wear ridiculous matching clothing. With my picture, no less!"

Elise realized how badly she'd miscalculated. She'd never get that money back. It wasn't like all the other stuff she bought that she told herself she could, at least theoretically, return. There was no resale market for Annette sweatshirts. Her mother actually looked scary in the picture — the image Elise emailed to the vendor had to be stretched to fill out the backs and so all of Annette's most striking features were magnified: the tented eyebrows, the streaks of rouge, the witchy, closemouthed smile. Not even the hipsters who dumpster-dived at

Andy's Cheapies would be comfortable wearing it ironically.

"David — can you believe this?" Annette asked, looking at her husband. He shrugged.

"Take 'em off, kids," Elise said.

"Thank God," Darius said, slipping out of his and crumpling it into a ball.

"And by the way, Mom, *you* went to the wrong place. If you look back at your text messages, you'll see this is exactly where I said to meet."

"Don't text me, Elise. I can barely see the screen. You know about my floaters."

"That's ridiculous. You text me," Elise argued. "Besides, we'd already agreed on this spot when we spoke on the phone."

"Mom," Freddy cut in, and Elise suddenly realized he and Annette had yet to greet each other. "Happy birthday."

Annette took a noticeable step back to appraise him. An uncomfortable amount of silence passed before she spoke. Elise found she was holding her breath.

"Thank you," she said, and Elise heard the stiffness in her mother's voice as if it were a freshly starched shirt. "This must be Nina?"

"It's Natasha," Freddy's girlfriend purred sweetly. If she was put out about the name mix-up, it didn't show. "It's an honor to meet you, Mrs. Feldman."

"An honor?" David chimed in, cocking his head quizzically.

Elise shuddered. Why would her father need to ridicule Natasha and Annette in one breath, all before he'd even greeted his own grandchildren?

"It's just a real pleasure," Natasha rephrased, straightening her back to its full dancer-like potential. Good girl, thought Elise, sensing suddenly that Natasha was shifting from foil to friend. They could gossip about celebrities poolside, develop inside jokes over martinis, and — Elise chided herself at the thought even as she felt herself getting giddy — shop together. At least she could watch Natasha shop. It would be like viewing performance art, seeing someone with a perfectly proportioned body try on clothes, fastening buttons over sculpted abs and revealing the absolute lack of need for a bra. Maybe, just maybe, someone would confuse them for sisters over the course of the week.

"Shouldn't we head for the gangway?" Elise said to her mother, unable to watch this introduction unfold for another minute.

Annette looked at her watch and cast a look of panic.

"Oh, yes, we'd better. Since you told your

father and me to meet in the wrong place, we are way behind schedule. We can forget priority seats for tonight's cabaret."

"Try to ignore it, babe," Mitch whispered, squeezing Elise's elbow gently. "It's almost happy hour." Connellys coped with each other by knocking back Jameson shots. The Feldmans, it seemed, were still looking for their salvo.

TEN

Annette had eyes on her children for a full five minutes before she went over to them. David didn't see them. He was too busy looking at the ship. Her husband was difficult to impress, but she could see the boat literally took his breath away. They had been married for forty-eight years and so she knew when she saw David's eyes darting back and forth that he was counting the portholes and the levels, calculating how many rooms the ship had, the amount of gas it required to glide across the ocean, how many pounds of bread sat in the kitchen waiting to be devoured. He was a numbers guy, a chemistry major in college, the perfect candidate for a career in medicine. Her husband prayed at the altar of facts and figures, even when it came to family. For example, Elise had studied for nineteen years straight (assuming the real learning started in kindergarten) and they

154

had expended three hundred and eighteen thousand dollars on her education (a staggering sum, Annette conceded). How many times had she heard David repeat those numbers to her? What could she respond in the face of the cold, hard evidence that their investment had not produced dividends — at least not the kind David anticipated, a child to hang up her shingle next to his?

From a distance, Annette made out Elise and Freddy hugging. Her heart should have been surging with joy at the sight of her grown children embracing, and yet it made her nervous. What did that embrace mean? Was it commiseration over having to be on this trip? Were they whispering to each other about her? All children seemed to have complaints about Mom and Dad. It was what kept therapists in business. She considered that if her children were united on the trip, it would be impossible to play one off against the other. Maybe the two of them had come to the same conclusion and they were forging an early alliance. Suddenly, embarking on the cruise felt less like starting a vacation than signing a waiver to compete on *Survivor.*

Her grandchildren too loomed in the distance, fuzzy outlines of young adults she ought to know better. She wondered if Rachel and Darius were excited for the trip. They were staring down at their phones, like all the other young people Annette came across, studying their devices while crossing the street or holding up the line at the supermarket. Given their attachment to the internet, she imagined her grandchildren had used at least a few minutes of their nonstop time online to Google the ship and see everything it had to offer for their age group. Discos with DJs they supposedly would have heard of. A teen pool where they wouldn't have to see flesh that was riper than eighteen years of age. A bouldering excursion specifically for young people.

That was what those little devices were for, wasn't it? Looking up information. Finding things out in advance so nothing was left as a surprise anymore. It had been so much easier to buy off Rachel and Freddy when they were sheltered little kids who hadn't seen and done every last thing on earth. A lollipop was received with a goggle-eyed smile and a pillowy kiss. A twenty-dollar bill for a birthday was treated like precious gold. Now these teenagers were inaccessible. Certainly to her, an old lady, but also probably to Elise and Mitch. She wondered if Mitch's parents had anything to do with their grandchildren now that they were grown up. How Annette had hated to hear little Darius sing the praises of his other grandmother's fruitcake when he was a small boy. Couldn't that woman serve these children anything else besides a Christmas treat? Annette wasn't even ashamed of her base competitiveness. Grandparents inherently came in rival pairs. To pretend otherwise was just for show.

Elise and Freddy pulled apart and Annette heard herself exhale, the breath leaving her body in a sharp cloud of anxiety.

"You okay?" David asked, taking notice of her for the first time since he'd seen the ship.

"Yes, yes. I should be asking you that," she said, offering him a bottled water from her bag, which he accepted. "You should be wearing your baseball hat, by the way. The sun is very strong." She pointed at his bald head to make the point. He wasn't hairless as a result of his drug therapy. David Feldman and his hair had parted company when he was in his early forties, but Annette never minded. Who needed him walking around the hospital with those gorgeous dark curls when any one of the young nurses, cute and pert in their starchy whites, would gladly take her place?

"I'm fine," he said curtly. "Odds are low

that I will develop a second form of cancer. Remember, we agreed not to discuss anything on the boat, so I don't want you fussing over me."

"But the children aren't even around," Annette protested. "They're over . . ." She was about to point them out to David but realized she still wasn't ready to approach. She had so many misgivings about this trip and couldn't remember what had made her so damn determined to take it just a month ago. There was little room for upside here. Even if miraculously they all got along reasonably well for the week and shared a few laughs, the minute the boat docked upon return they would all retreat to their own lives, like tenants in an apartment building who briefly interact in the elevator. Elise would be sucked back into her life in California, tending to Darius and visiting Rachel at school. They'd have their weekly call, typically on Sundays when Mitch was at the office and the kids were busy with friends. It rarely skidded below the superficial. Elise would update her on the goings-on of the children and Annette would tell Elise about some local intrigue, like a shop owner arrested for tax fraud or a neighbor caught cheating. They both feigned mild interest, and it was obvious to Annette that Elise was always doing something else on the phone. She could hear the click clack of the laptop's keyboard or the buzz of the laundry machine. She was no better. While Elise told story after story about the progress of Darius's plantar fasciitis, Annette would be flipping through a magazine or, more recently, rereading articles on drug trials.

Freddy would go back to doing whatever the hell it was he was doing in Colorado. She feared pressing him for the specifics, only noting with relief that he hadn't asked her and David for money even once in six years — this after years of cash mysteriously walking off from her wallet when he was still under their roof. Which meant he'd somehow landed on his feet. Sometimes he described himself as a financier. Other times he mentioned the farming industry. It made little sense and Google was of no use. The latest theory she and David had devised was that he was leasing farm equipment and they just hoped he hadn't gotten sucked into another pyramid scheme. About a decade ago, Freddy had been selling juicers door to door which were supposed to retain the vitamin content of the produce during the blending process. He took payment for a few hundred orders, which he turned over to his boss, and then the equipment and his cut of the sales never arrived. Who had to cover the losses? You guessed it. If there was a harebrained scheme around, Freddy Feldman had a nose for it. For what it was worth, no matter what either of her children were doing to occupy their time in California and Colorado, it didn't involve her.

Elise had never needed Annette, even from day one. She'd tried in earnest to breastfeed her, but no matter what, Elise would simply not latch. After a week of this, Elise sucking for a moment or two before spitting out the nipple as if it was rotten, Annette moved to formula. And then anyone could give the bottle to Elise — the nanny, David, any friends who came over to visit — and so Annette became simply part of a cycle, no more important than the next cog in the wheel. In fact, David seemed to have a more natural touch with the placement of the rubber nipple in Elise's mouth. Nothing changed as Elise grew. She was content to be left with any babysitter, poured her own cereal from the time most children were first forming syllables, and never once asked for help with homework. It was like raising a ticking time bomb, Annette dreadfully waiting for that final dose of self-sufficiency to kick in before being put out to pasture.

But Freddy? He was needier than a week-old puppy as a child, which made Elise's independence all the more startling. He'd come first and so Annette expected all her babies to be wailing, colicky messes demanding to be held at all hours of the night. As he grew, he required her help with everything. His meat had to be cut into infinitesimal bites or he'd reject them. She had to read to him for hours in the evening or he couldn't fall asleep, and by middle school she was color-coding his folders so he wouldn't misplace his homework (though he still often did). It was only in high school that Annette felt herself getting eclipsed by the increasing role of friends in her son's life. And what friends they were! He didn't seek out the varsity letter wearers or the brainiacs like his little sister. No, Freddy gravitated to the misfits, the ones with the blue hair that made people wonder, *Where are the parents?* I'm right here, she wanted to shout when she felt someone judging her son. This is not my fault. Do you know how many times I had to read *Harold and the Purple Crayon* each night? *After he had sailed long enough, Harold made land without much trouble.* She could still recite the entire book by heart.

161

What did it matter, though, how much these children had needed her back then? Now they *both* found her useless, an extra piece of baggage. If they thought of her at all. She asked herself for what had to be the hundredth time why she had planned this trip. To prove that she was still a mother as she steeled her way into a new decade and her ovaries hadn't released eggs in twenty years? To know that the Feldmans were still a unit, even if only for a week, like a piece of Ikea furniture that you know won't last forever, though you still screw in the last bolt with optimism? Her mind was operating like a runaway train since David's diagnosis. And what do you do with a runaway train? Apparently, redirect it to a slow-moving boat.

"Let's go," she said to David, pretzeling an arm through his and guiding him toward the children. For her marriage she was eternally grateful, but also painfully afraid as she knew now more than ever how precious their time together was. When she had found herself drowning in a pity bath thinking about the distance between herself and her grown children over the years, Annette took solace in the partnership she had with David. And while she loved her children more than her husband — in that

162

fierce, nature over nurture, primal kind of way — she had to admit the volume of hours she spent with her husband far exceeded the time with her children. Nobody she knew — and she did comb through her mental Rolodex in consideration of the issue — seemed to have equally close and fulfilling relationships with both their spouse and their children. So if she had to choose with whom to have a more natural and comfortable rapport, it wasn't so terrible it was the person she was growing old with. Or rather *hoping* to grow older with. She pictured the rows of pill bottles that now lined their vanity, the dull amber slapped with all those extra warnings in pastels making her nauseated within seconds. But she shouldn't complain. She wasn't the one swallowing a dozen horse pills three times a day, feeling her body ravaged from the inside out.

As they inched closer to the throngs of passengers amidst which stood her children, Annette stopped dead in her tracks. She was suddenly confronted with a grouping of funhouse mirrors and in them she saw her face, prismatically distorted, with comically big hair and stripes of rouge on her cheeks. But it wasn't a mirror. Her face, a caricature-like version of it, was staring at her from the backs of a half dozen sweatshirts. Annette squinted to make out the writing. *Happy Birthday, Annette . . . 70 Years Young!*

How could her children — or was it her grandchildren — be so cruel? Were they deliberately trying to embarrass her with that absurd picture Photoshopped onto a sweatshirt in a garish shade of yellow? Could it possibly be retribution for her making them come on this trip? But she hadn't forced it! Yes, she had strongly intimated how much it meant to her that the family be together to celebrate this milestone. And her children knew that historically she preferred to bury her birthday in a biographical footnote. But still, Elise and Freddy were hardly dangling from yo-yo strings, ready to jump at her beck and call. Quite the contrary. How many holidays had she and David celebrated alone, the two of them quietly slicing a turkey on Thanksgiving while listening to David's favorite jazz musicians, because their children were "just too busy to get away"? Too many to count. And yet on this occasion, her children had accepted the invitation without much prodding. So the sweatshirt meant something else. Somebody — a blood relative of hers — thought it would make her happy. And that was even worse. She was a stranger to her own kin.

She hadn't intended to start squabbling with Elise the minute she saw her. If anything, she'd committed to plastering a smile on her face no matter what slights slipped from either of her children's mouths or the rudeness she faced in her grandchildren. But she was so rattled by the sweatshirts, so frighteningly unnerved by the sight of Elise and Freddy hugging like old friends, that she found herself yelling at her daughter for giving her the wrong place to meet, which wasn't true, but as she thrust herself into the argument, the veracity of what she was saying felt irrelevant. All Annette had wanted was for everyone to get along on the boat and yet she was instigating. She thought about the stash of Ativan mixed in with David's drugs. He was supposed to take them if he felt himself getting nauseated on the boat or anxious in general about being away from his regular doctors. He would hardly notice if she filched one or two.

And what was up with Freddy's girlfriend? She was a bigger surprise than the sweatshirts. Natasha, the interloper with whom they were stuck eating the next fifteen meals with, looked no older than a college coed. A beauty she was, of that there could be no

165

doubt. And nothing seemed patently wrong with her either — at least not off the bat. She had a pretty smile, shook hands with both Annette and David confidently, and, notwithstanding her cheesy and totally inappropriate choice of outfit, was poised and well-spoken. Perhaps she needed a green card. She had an eastern European look to her. How awful for a mother to think this way of her own son. To believe that a looker like Natasha wouldn't want anything to do with Freddy unless there was something to be gained. Annette decided not to share her suspicions with David just yet, curious to hear his initial reaction before she infected it with her own.

It had been some time since she and David had had their last heart-to-heart about Freddy and what would become of him. Both of them acknowledged it was pointless to try to help him out now — it wasn't as though they had a family business he could join like so many of their neighbors' children had enviably done. The less capable sons and daughters (usually it was the sons) took on roles with big titles and little responsibility. It was the ultimate gift a parent could give a child who needed support, but it wasn't like David could magically bestow a medical degree upon their son. And what else could they have done for him? She hardly needed any help with the office management. A few years ago, Annette had made David join Facebook under an assumed name (she'd picked up that tip from a similarly situated friend) so they could spy on him. Freddy didn't post much and, when he did, it was usually banal pictures of him rafting or barbecuing with friends, yokels dressed in ridiculous sleeveless tank tops and ratty cargo shorts, a criminal focal point with all those gorgeous aspen trees and snow-capped mountains in the background. The point was, Freddy was fine. He wasn't a surgeon or a lawyer, he didn't check the boxes they'd drawn for him, but he was happy and healthy as far as they could see. Annette reminded herself she shouldn't be asking for more. They knew families who'd suffered tragedies far greater than children not earning college degrees. Privately, after he'd eaten a good dinner and situated himself in his beloved recliner in the family room, she would remind David of this indisputable fact from time to time and he wouldn't disagree.

Now that the whole family had grouped together on the dock, Annette spearheaded the effort to board the boat.

"Elise and Mitch, I booked you in a lovely

stateroom on the seventh floor, not far from ours. With a balcony," Annette said, hoping they realized that she and David had splurged for this extra amenity. "Rachel and Darius, you are a few decks below in an interior room."

Rachel rolled her eyes visibly. Annette hoped Elise would scold her daughter for the unappreciative attitude, but she said nothing. In fact, from what Annette could tell, Elise was in another world. She certainly seemed nervous. Annette regretted their scuffle and hoped it wasn't the source of whatever was bugging Elise.

"Sounds wonderful," Mitch said while Elise was apparently too distracted to respond. "We really appreciate this trip, Annette. You too, David."

Annette looked Mitch up and down. He might really be the most normal of the lot of them. A hardworking family man, even-tempered, good to Elise. Sure, he wasn't a member of the tribe, but she'd long since gotten over that. It had bothered her so much in the beginning that she'd firmly decided not to suggest that Mitch call her "Mom." Now she regretted it. He was the only one to say thank you so far for the trip. The only one whose face wasn't painted with abject fear, like her children's, or pure jadedness, like her grandchildren's. It was too late now, though. Elise and Mitch had been married for over twenty years. It was hardly the time to make the "call me Mom" overture.

"You're very welcome, Mitch. And I must say you are looking extremely well," she said, patting him on the cheek. At the very least she could be overly gracious to him.

"Freddy," she said, turning to her son. "You and" — Annette struggled to pick out his girlfriend's name from the word stew in her brain — "Natasha are in a cabin just a few doors down from Elise and Mitch. Also with a balcony." Heaven forbid she didn't treat Elise and Freddy perfectly equal on the trip, Annette thought. She'd never hear the end of it. Annette had even made the travel agent triple-check the square footage of the rooms to make sure they were the same. "Yes, Mrs. Feldman," the always chipper agent had reassured her. "Both your daughter and son are in staterooms that are two hundred and eighty square feet." That sounded frightfully small and Annette imagined Murphy beds and airplane bathrooms. She said as much to the agent, who assured her the boat was a feat of engineering and the rooms would be perfectly adequate. She worried for David, who needed a comfortable bed and a tub. The agent had laughed when she asked about the latter. "First cruise?" she had said.

"Actually, Mom, Natasha and I changed rooms," Freddy said, not meeting her gaze.

"Honestly, Freddy, would it bother you that much to be next to us for a few lousy nights?" Annette snapped. She just knew one of her children would move to another part of the ship seeking privacy. They barely ever saw each other as it was.

"It's not that," Freddy said, and damn if Annette didn't notice something of a faint smirk creep across his face. "Natasha and I are staying on Deck Sixteen."

Deck Sixteen? But that was the Suites Only level. How in the world was her son paying for that? She hoped he wasn't so desperate to impress this pretty, young thing that he was going into debt for it. Further debt, most likely.

Elise, for the first time, seemed to come to attention.

"But Deck Sixteen is where the suites are. That's the club level."

Apparently both her children had done their homework. She'd insisted the travel agent overnight the glossy brochures to them, since the pictures and amenities listed would be far more persuasive than anything

170

Annette had to say.

"Correct," Freddy said, putting an arm around Natasha. "We thought we might like a little extra space."

Natasha smiled and this time her expression wasn't full of sweetness and charm. It was haughty. "Freddy and his hotels," she chimed in. "I always tell him we don't need a huge room, but he does it every time."

Annette had nothing to do but accept what was happening. The room she'd reserved for her son wasn't good enough. Elise would be seething with jealousy, not to mention eaten alive by curiosity as to how Freddy was paying for all this. And David — well, he just looked tired watching the whole turn of events unfold.

"Fine. Whatever," she muttered. "Let's just go check in." She pointed toward the registration desk and nudged Darius and Rachel along.

"Actually, we're already checked in," Freddy said. "The club level has priority service. They took our bags from the cab and already gave us the room key. See everyone at dinner?" he asked, the corners of his mouth turning up again.

Annette was fuming. She looked to Elise for a sympathetic eye, but her daughter had slinked away and appeared to be trying on a

171

pair of cat-eye sunglasses from a pushcart.

"Let's go," she said firmly to David and at least someone listened to her.

As they moved across the gangway, a peppy girl appeared before them with a Purell dispenser in hand. "Washy, washy!" she chirped, dropping dollops of the clear gel into both David's and Annette's hands. Annette felt the force of David's sharp exhalation on the hairs along the back of her neck.

ELEVEN

Darius wished he hadn't called her. If he could do it all over again, maybe a simple text message saying good-bye. Or even a tag on Instagram, where he could mention in a comment that he was going on a cruise. But no, he had to pick up the phone like a total loser and say, "Hi, Marcy? It's Darius," as though they both didn't have caller ID! She'd giggled when she heard his voice. Was it that obvious he was in love with her? Apparently so. Her giddy, high-pitched laugh upon hearing his voice made that fact painfully clear.

The minute Darius heard about the trip from his mother, his first concern was the Wi-Fi. He, Marcy, Jesse, Jesse's brother, and some others were in constant group-text communication. If he didn't respond for a few days, they'd probably just forget he existed. He'd miss out on all the inside jokes over the course of a week and by the time he reached land again, they'd all have a new hangout and a new lingo and he'd be back on the outside clawing his way back in. Which he wouldn't care that much about if it weren't for Marcy. She was perfect. There was no one else in school as beautiful, as cool, as sexy as she was. He felt like a loser announcing on the group text that he was getting on a cruise ship with his grandparents and wouldn't be in touch for a week. He figured everyone would just ignore it and his contribution to the conversation would be dangling like a spider from a web, the eyesore in an otherwise well-knitted conversation.

So he called Marcy.

At least he wasn't so moronic as to say he was calling to say good-bye. No, he took the time to fabricate a cover story. She'd recommended a band to the group the last time they'd all been hanging out — Lata Skata — and he'd of course run home and downloaded all of their music and listened to it well into the night. When he dialed her number, he planned to start off by saying thank you for the excellent recommendation. It was a lie. The only thing he liked about the cacophonous sound of Lata Skata was that it made him think of Marcy. Then Darius could casually mention that he was "heading out of town for a week" without getting into specifics. This way she might take notice of his absence on the group texts — not that he ever managed to spearhead plans like the older guys or crack jokes like Jesse. No, all he managed to intersperse were bland iterations of "cool" and "ha-ha."

Her laugh had taken him aback so much that he failed to stick to the script. Instead he blurted out: "I'm going away on a cruise to the Caribbean with my nana." *Nana!* He'd never once called Grandma Annette "nana" and yet somehow that was what he said. After the moment passed, he knew with certainty he would never lay a hand on her boobs. Never. He'd probably never touch *any* breast because Marcy would tell all the girls in school what a loser he was. The best he could hope for was a fresh start in college, if he could get himself in.

"That's sweet," she said and he didn't know what kind of sweet she meant. Sweet like cool that he was going to the Caribbean and might surf and snorkel? Or sweet like cute that he was spending time with his grandmother? Correction. His *nana.*

He decided not to assume anything and just responded, "Yeah." Collecting himself, he added something more coherent. "Anyway, I just wanted to tell you that I listened to Lata Skata."

"And?" she said, growing animated, her excitement seeping through the phone in an audible gush.

"Sick. Thanks for the recommendation."

"Anytime, Darius. Anytime."

She'd used his name when she didn't have to. Surely that meant something. His father used people's names when he wanted them to open up more. It was a way to establish familiarity and was a convenient trick of journalists. It was stupid of him to read so much into it, but he couldn't help it.

"Well, I'll see you when I get back," he said.

"Yep," she said, now sounding a million miles away, like she was scrolling through Snap or watching TV.

He'd hung up, discouraged all over again.

That was three days ago. Now he stood with his family waiting to embark, praying that by the time he returned to shore Marcy would have forgotten all about that pitiful call. Maybe his acne would also clear up by the time he returned. Supposedly the sun could dry out whiteheads.

Mostly, Darius hoped the time away from Marcy would help him focus on other things, like college applications and figuring out why he was so afraid of the triple pike.

It wasn't likely, though. Even as he packed for the cruise, he wondered if Marcy would like the bathing suits he chose and if she would think his Ray-Bans were too mainstream. Rationally, he knew it didn't matter. But he couldn't stop imagining scenarios where they'd encounter each other on the boat. At the teen pool. In the arcade. And he wanted to look just right. His mother had made some offhand comment to him that with the boat having three thousand people, there were sure to be some pretty girls on board. It was one of her desperate attempts to bond with him. But he just shrugged noncommittally when she'd said it. After what he'd uncovered hiding in their attic, Darius was certain he was hardly the one in the family who needed confession.

Other than being apart from Marcy for longer than he could stand, Darius found himself excited for the trip. He wanted to get to know his uncle Freddy. Rachel had said he was really cool, but when he'd pressed her on how she knew, she just said she did and to leave her alone, a dismissive response typical of his snooty sister. And while his mind was filled with the gruesome possibility of Marcy and Jesse getting together in his absence — she'd once told Jesse that he had great hair and now Darius couldn't stop seeing her fingers, skinny twigs with nails always painted in venomous colors, running through it — he was still looking forward to a break from the group. It was exhausting having to be on all the time. To worry about saying the right thing, laughing at the appropriate time — but never too much, because that was lame — and constantly maintaining an aura of cool.

Cool.

What did it mean? Darius didn't know if it meant legitimately not caring (and if so, he had no shot) or just being really good at seeming like he didn't care. He longed to speak to Rachel about these things. After all, his sister had managed the impossible in high school. She was popular and had made honor roll, was respected by the nerds on the chess team and welcomed by the pretty cheerleaders at their lunch table. The boat was his chance. He wouldn't be so naive as to ask for a formal tête-à-tête. But ultimately they'd be forced into a lot of time together — the interior rooms (where he knew they'd get stuck) were only one hundred and fifty square feet. They were going to be sharing a bunk bed. At night, when he could avoid eye contact, he would gently broach the topic of how he could better navigate the tortures of high school social pressure.

There were only so many nights in a row his sister could pretend to be sleeping when he started talking to her.

But after laying eyes on Freddy and his girlfriend — a creature who literally forced his eyes to bulge from his head (thank goodness for the maybe-cool-maybe-not Ray-Bans) — he decided perhaps his uncle might be a better source of advice. To hell with Rachel. Her high school boyfriend, a bencher on the lacrosse team, was nobody that spectacular in Darius's estimation. And she was way too obsessed with her stupid summer job, an unpaid internship at a local law firm that advertised on phone booths. And, if he wasn't mistaken, Freddy actually seemed interested in him, even reaching over to give him a combination back pat and head rub as a greeting. It was a glorified noogie, but somehow when Freddy did it, it wasn't lame.

There was another reason Darius was hoping to get some face time alone with his uncle. He wanted to discuss his mother. It felt like a betrayal to talk to his dad about it, and Darius didn't want to be the cause of friction between his parents. That was supposing his father didn't already know. Based on his father's lighthearted jokes about the electric bill being high on account of their menopausal mother (major TMI, in Darius's opinion), he didn't seem overly concerned about the household spending and was likely in the dark, much like the shopping bags.

Even if Uncle Freddy was useless, it would be a relief to unburden himself to an adult. This was the sort of thing Darius might have told his high school guidance counselor — Ms. Green was always saying she would offer a nonjudgmental ear to anyone who knocked on her door — but he was dodging her because of college applications, not to mention that rumor had it she was sleeping with the assistant principal and therefore Darius wasn't eager to come a-knocking. Darius was pretty impressed when his uncle mentioned he'd moved up to the club level suites. If nothing else, he wanted to check out Freddy's room.

"Move, Darius," Rachel said, shoving him in the direction of their room as he walked with his sister down an interminable hallway. Somehow he'd gotten saddled with carrying her hand luggage and his own so that Rachel could use her precious last few minutes on land to do who knows what on her phone. She was constantly on Instagram and Snapchat and email, but when he tried to sneak a peek at her screen she'd move it out of his field of vision. They weren't even "friends" on social media, a fact that astounded him. They were each other's closest blood relatives, shared more DNA between the two of them than anyone else, and yet in the world of social media they were perfect strangers. The two of them had coexisted under the same roof for seventeen years and yet he was hesitant to try to follow her on her social channels. Fearful he'd get a rejection.

Should he be surprised, though, by his sister's coldness and utter disinterest in his existence? How many times had he heard his parents gleefully telling the story of waking up one morning to find that Rachel had packed all of his baby things into her Polly Pocket suitcase and suggested to his parents at breakfast that he might be happier living with their next-door neighbors, a family with three grown boys who might like to have a little one again? "Because I still a baby," she had cooed, climbing into their mother's lap. "So we don't need another one." Why were his parents so joyful every time they repeated that story to someone? They seemed to revel in how bright it made Rachel seem, so capable of taking matters into her own hands. Nobody ever focused on the rejection element.

"What did you put in this bag, ten hair dryers?" Darius moaned, looking forlornly at his gangly arms. Maybe if he had muscles like Jesse's brother, with bold tattoos that undulated around the curve of the biceps like snakes, then Marcy would like him. Darius had never seen the inside of a gym. At his high school, the weight room was the domain of the jocks. He could only imagine the snickering if all one hundred forty pounds of his skinny flesh went inside the weight room on the ship, which looked from the pictures like training ground for the Marine Corps. Maybe he could convince his father to buy one of those multipurpose machines that ran infomercials in the middle of the night so he could exercise at home. They were expensive but always came with some kind of payment plan. Though he was probably better off going to his mother nowadays, Darius thought, with a sizable helping of irony. Clearly she was up for buying pretty much anything. That realization nauseated him, even when he considered using it to his advantage.

"I don't blow-dry my hair, idiot," Rachel said. "These are beach waves." She reached for a clump of her hair as if he was supposed to know what that meant. "I packed books. They're those rectangular things with pages inside."

He was about to say, "I know what books are," but decided against it. Acting defensive would only let his sister know that she was successfully getting under his skin, like a mosquito bite that gets itchier the more it's scratched. So he stayed quiet but dropped her bag flat on the floor, leaving Rachel to drag it the rest of the way to their room, scraping it along the dizzying geometric pattern of the carpet. Darius couldn't figure out the décor on the ship just yet. It was like wannabe fancy: chandeliers, marble, and streaked mirrors that were supposed to look important. But it was the kind of place he knew would have one-ply toilet paper. Though, to be fair, there were a lot of butts to wipe on board.

"This is it," he said when he finally reached cabin 2122. Producing the key card from his back pocket, he slid it through the slot in the door handle, but the red light didn't go green. Darius turned it over and tried again, even though the diagram above the handle clearly indicated the magnetic stripe side should be down. His heart started racing. He heard Rachel's footsteps padding behind him, along with the thumping of her bag, and he tried the key on both sides several more times. At one point, the

183

light shifted from red to green, but by the time he went to pull the handle down it was back to red again.

"Uck, let me do it," Rachel said, reaching for her own key. Naturally, Rachel's worked perfectly. She pushed open the door with a smug smile. Though, once she stepped inside, Darius saw her face darken immediately.

"You've got to be kidding me," she said. "This is worse than sleeping in a tent."

Darius pushed past her. He expected bunk beds, like in the brochure, but instead there were two beds side by side, each narrower than a standard twin. In between was a wooden table in the up position, like the tray on an airplane, which was meant to be a shared night table. He immediately questioned where he would put his night guard case. Rachel would freak if he put it there, but he always kept it right next to the bed in case he wanted to yank out his orthodonture in the middle of the night.

"Where's the bathroom?" she asked, spinning around in a panic. "Phew, I found it." She yanked open a door that couldn't be more than twenty inches wide.

"Rachel, look," Darius said, noticing a small basket with an envelope taped to it sitting on the dollhouse-scale desk. "There's something here for us. It's a present. Must be from Grandma and Grandpa."

Rachel climbed over a luggage rack and bumped her hip on a chair as she headed over to see what was inside. Darius watched her wince in pain and bit back an instinctive, "You okay?"

"There's candy in the basket," Darius said. "Let me open the envelope." He saw Rachel move to grab it out of his hand so he quickly ripped it open. "We each got a hundred-dollar gift card to use in the teen lounge and at the arcade!"

"Grandma and Grandpa are so cheap," Rachel said. "I can't believe they would do this. Grandma, like, rinses out Ziploc bags to reuse them."

Darius held the little card that came inside the envelope in Rachel's face. "It's not from Grandma. It's from Uncle Freddy." He caught a mysterious glint in Rachel's eye. "We should tell Mom. I feel like she thinks her brother is a bum."

"Uncle Freddy is not a bum," Rachel said definitively.

"How do you know?" Darius pressed, now more curious than ever. His family had almost no contact with Freddy. Perhaps Rachel was just saying that to be contrary. Even Darius had noticed how much his sister disagreed with everything the rest of them had to say, something his parents had complained about all summer.

"Because I —" she started then stopped. "I just know. I can tell. Mom whines that Grandpa is disappointed in her and doesn't even realize she judges her brother for not having some lame corporate job. It's hypo-critical."

Darius had to agree.

"I gotta get out of here," Rachel said, plucking her gift card from his hand. "This room is suffocating. There's not even a window! I'm going to explore the boat. See you later, D."

When she was gone, Darius lay down on the bed with his feet dangling off the edge. He found he was smiling. Freddy was proving full of surprises. He and Rachel had actually talked — like, shared a moment of real discussion. And he hadn't pictured or thought about Marcy for a full ten minutes.

TWELVE

It was Death Day when Mitch made up his mind about leaving the newspaper.

Every Wednesday at the *Bee,* the reporters tackled writing obituaries for people who were still alive, healthy mortals who were drinking their morning coffee and paying their bills while simultaneously a journalist they'd never met sat summarizing their accomplishments in approximately four hundred words. This was standard practice for newspapers. Unlike other events the reporters covered, gas explosions and weather events and political scandals, the obits were predictable pieces of reporting. It was a fact that everyone would eventually die, so in the newspaper world, it paid to be prepared. Sundays and Mondays were devoted to breaking news and features; Tuesdays were for follow-ups and analysis. Thursdays and Fridays were spent covering the local weekend events, mostly cultural activities. So Wednesdays were for the deaths. In his career, Mitch had edited hundreds of obituaries, so he was an expert at distilling a life into bullet points. It was only natural for him to imagine his own obituary, even down to the adjectives that would be chosen.

Sacramento — Mitchell Joseph Connelly, 99, died peacefully at home surrounded by his family on Tuesday. (*He figured he might as well be optimistic about his longevity.*) He leaves behind a wife of 70 years, Elise Feldman Connelly, two children, Rachel and Darius, and six grandchildren (*why not?*). Mr. Connelly, a graduate of Notre Dame University and the Columbia University School of Journalism, spent his entire career at the *Sacramento Bee,* starting out as a sports reporter, then running the metro desk, and finally retiring as its long-standing managing editor. His contributions to the paper included expanding its arts coverage and adding a late edition on Sundays. He, along with a group of his colleagues, was the recipient of the prestigious Pulitzer Prize for an indepth analysis of the effects of gerrymandering in local elections. An avid football fan, Mr. Connelly spent his time out of the office cheering on his beloved 49ers. He was a long-standing Little League coach and worked at the local soup kitchen once a month. Friends and family gathered to say farewell to Mr. Connelly at St. Luke's Church in Modesto Thursday morning.

On Death Day each week, while Mitch edited the obituaries of legendary opera singers who'd lit up the stage at the San Francisco Opera, Caltech scientists who'd discovered cures for rare diseases, Stanford professors remembered for influencing thousands of young minds, he couldn't help feeling that he — Mitchell Connelly, age 47, newspaperman — had yet to leave his mark. It was too late to go back to school, that much he knew. But the literary magazine fit squarely within his wheelhouse. And it would mean he'd created something where nothing was before, not just carried a well-lit torch responsibly from predecessor to successor. Readers would type in a web address that was entirely new, read fresh content with a unique bent, and their lips would form smiles strictly because of him. And so he was pumped when he stepped onto the ship's gangway, even with his wife a stress case, his children utterly disengaged, and his in-laws on edge. Mitch felt like the dock was a portal into his new life and that when he came back to shore, great things lay ahead for him. He just needed to get over the hurdle of sharing his news with Elise. He mentally affirmed his plan to drop the bomb at the formal dinner — Elise had once said she couldn't resist him in a tux. And with her family around, she couldn't really throw a hissy fit. By the time they were alone again — many hours and glasses of champagne later — the initial shock would have dissipated and whatever tirade she'd been practicing in her head would hopefully be reduced to a slurred lecture.

He walked a few paces behind Elise as she made her way to their room. He felt a little nervous to engage with her at the moment. Since Freddy had announced he was staying in a suite, his wife had looked like she could spontaneously erupt, as though her body had been a dormant volcano all along. Mitch was happy for his brother-in-law. He had probably sprung for the suite to impress Natasha, who was clearly under some kind of delusion as to Freddy's situation. Or maybe he could afford it, which would mean he'd finally landed on his feet. That should please Elise, but that was not the vibe he was picking up from her. In fact, it seemed as though Freddy's larger room had the power to shrink theirs, as though size was purely a comparative thing. If he was honest, Elise hadn't seemed like herself in quite some time. It was another reason he wanted to tell her about his career decision on the boat. He hoped she would be relaxed, that her shoulders would drop from their perpetual hike, and that they would have sex that felt a little bit less assembly line. He wished women were less complicated, like men. Elise could drop just about any bomb on him after he had an orgasm and he'd just smile and say "no problem."

After Freddy and Natasha had left for the VIP check-in station (were those appletinis he saw being handed to them?), Elise had stalked off with an overloaded bag in the crook of her arm and moved wordlessly onto the ship, not even pausing to comment on the majesty of the boat's interior. He was speechless himself from the grandeur, so the two of them stood in the dazzling foyer not exchanging a word while his eyes squinted at a crystal chandelier that had to weigh three tons and hung the length of four stories on a red velvet rope. Around him, there was food, glorious food: patisseries, boulangeries, a pizzeria, and a stand just for egg rolls. It was a food court on steroids, reminiscent of being at Epcot with the kids when they were younger. Except here everything was free — well, not quite free but all-inclusive — and he wasn't the one footing the bill.

Mitch's stomach rumbled and he was tempted to make a stop at Fifty Knots, where New York–style pretzels rolled in dozens of different toppings hung in unlocked glass cases for the taking. But Elise was on a mission, and that mission seemed to be getting to their cabin as fast as possible. He dreaded hearing what she'd say the minute the door closed behind them. At least she couldn't rant for long. They were all due on Deck Two in an hour for a safety demonstration. Mitch didn't remember any of the *Love Boat* passengers being forced to listen to instructions on how to put on a life jacket just after boarding, but he supposed that was hardly the only unrealistic thing about the show. For starters, the overall attractiveness of the crew and passengers was way — and he meant *way* — overrated.

Finally they reached their room, which felt like a good half-mile walk from the elevators. The cruise was going to be amazing for his step count, Mitch thought, tapping at his wristband pedometer. "You know your phone counts your steps too," Rachel had told him in a snooty voice within minutes of her return home from campus in June. "I don't always walk around with it like you do," he'd retorted, but she didn't seem to grasp the dig. He saw Elise bend over to slide her key card into the metal plate. She'd bizarrely decided to purchase a hideous lanyard to house her ID — the card they would need to access their room, pay for any extras on board, and gain admission to the shows. Actually, she'd bought three of them as soon as they'd reached the ship's first convenience shop, cracking a joke about needing options to match her various outfits. There was nothing particularly sexy about a Paradise International family-oriented cruise, but Mitch didn't think they needed to wear ID passes around their necks like they were touring NASA.

"Can you hold the door for —" Mitch called out as he awkwardly wheeled two pieces of carry-on luggage. He had one in front of him and the other trailing behind because the hallways were too narrow for him to roll them at his sides. The preboarding email from Paradise International had said their checked luggage might not get to their rooms until after dinnertime so they should prepare hand luggage with whatever essentials were needed for the first day. Suggestions included a bathing suit, suntan lotion, and a sombrero. The first night's dinner had a Mexican theme. Mitch had patted himself on the back for having the best attitude in the Connelly household about the cruise, but he drew the line at costumes. He couldn't imagine what Elise had stuffed into her carry-on, which was busting at the seams. Probably the *Fiske Guide to Colleges,* the massive tome that Elise had dog-eared and sticky-noted the hell out of.

He heard the door slam shut before he got the rest of his sentence out. What had he done wrong? Should he have pretended to care more about Freddy's upgrade? Should he have gotten in the middle of the swipes that Annette and Elise were taking at each other? To what end? Nothing was going to change in the long run. Mother and daughter would still bicker; sister and brother would still resent each other. He was a reporter, not a psychologist, and this was supposed to be a vacation, not a family therapy session. When he got to the room he fumbled for the key card in his wallet, spilling out a few folded bills and a handful of business cards. What he could have used was a lanyard.

"This is positively lilliputian," Elise said when he finally entered. She was standing by the foot of the bed and, in her defense, if she stretched out her arms she could reach the window, the closet, the desk, the bathroom, and the front door. As if reading his mind, Elise extended her limbs to drive the point home, looking like she was playing Twister. "Wonder what Freddy's palace looks like."

"Our room isn't huge," Mitch agreed, silently congratulating himself for finding a woman who used words like "lilliputian" (and "herculean" and "philistine") in casual conversation. "But I don't think we'll be spending much time in it. Except at night. And then it'll be good that it's small." He winked at Elise, but she seemed to thoroughly miss the overture. Now Mitch was hating Freddy too, spoiling the mood with his braggadocio.

"Right. We have to go to that stupid emergency thing now anyway. Apparently they check you in and won't start the demonstration until everyone is there. Feels like the teacher is taking attendance."

Mitch rubbed the back of Elise's shoulders gently, trying subtly to push them down.

"We'll get it over with, then start having fun. Let's go to the casino after for a little bit. When's the last time we gambled?"

Mitch saw his wife's face light up momentarily but fade to black quickly when a loud buzzer sounded loudly in their cabin, three short but forceful blasts that could wake the dead.

"Good afternoon, passengers aboard the *Ocean Queen.* This is your cruise director, Julian, speaking. Please proceed now to the safety presentation so we can set sail and start the good times."

"I'm sure that alarm won't get annoying," Elise said, rolling her eyes in the same way Rachel was prone to do. But then she reached for his hand and smiled. "C'mon, let's go find out where the emergency exits are. You never know when we might need to jump off this thing."

"Ha," he said. "Let's try to stay optimistic."

"Fine," Elise said, tugging him down the hallway. "Let's discuss something more interesting than what to do if our ship hits an iceberg. How old could Natasha possibly be? I put the over-under at twenty-eight."

Mitch chuckled quietly. He couldn't believe it had taken his wife this long to bring it up. He wanted to put his money on under, but for the sake of his wife's sanity, he decided to go with over.

"Will Frederick Feldman and Natasha Kuznetsov please report to the Sunset

Lounge on Deck Two? I repeat, will passengers Frederick Feldman and Natasha Kuznetsov please report to the Sunset Lounge on Deck Two for the mandatory safety training? The ship cannot set sail until every passenger is accounted for."

The loudest collective groan imaginable sounded. The two missing passengers were the only thing keeping three thousand antsy people from their drinks, the pool, the casino, and, most tragically, the free food. So far, everyone had been gathered for fifteen minutes waiting, but it seemed more like an hour with so many options available the minute the boat left shore. For his part, Mitch was planning to hit the slots. He'd read that the games were rigged to make winners on the first day in order to entice people to return to the casino, where they'd give back their winnings and then some. Well — he wouldn't be fooled by that! Not everyone had spent as much time as he had on CruisingCentral.net, a blog run by some of the most enthusiastic cruisers imaginable.

He felt his stomach twisting into knots. Freddy wasn't his brother, but it was hard not to feel responsible when it was his party that was keeping the boat docked in the aptly named Dodge Island, a seedy cruise terminal adjacent to Miami. He looked over at his wife and kids. Rachel and Darius seemed to be the only two people delighted by the delay, their uncle's absence being the reason they could squeeze in extra time on their devices. But Elise. She looked like she could murder someone, her teeth bristling like sandpaper as they ground and her knee shaking violently. Annette had slipped sunglasses on, to avoid having to make eye contact with anyone. And his father-in-law? David Feldman rose from his folding chair with a fierceness that alarmed him.

"That's it," David roared. "I'm going up to drag his ass down here. The least he could do is show up for the goddamn safety presentation. I'm going to wring that no-goodnik's neck but good."

"David, David," Annette hissed, gently reaching for her husband's arm to guide him back to his seat. Mitch was surprised when she didn't give him a more powerful yank. His mother-in-law hated any kind of scene.

"Grandpa, sit down," Rachel yelped, looking up from her phone. "Let the boat people deal with this." His daughter looked painfully embarrassed and Mitch found himself delighting in the fact that neither he nor

Elise was the cause of her mortification for once.

"No, he should go get him," the man next to Mitch said. He was a rather large fellow, dressed in a Jimmy Buffett shirt and cargo shorts, with a dense thicket of arm hair. When Mitch looked down, he saw that his feet were clad in Tevas strapped over socks, which made him a hell of a lot less intimidating. "I could be in the Jacuzzi with a beer right now," the man said squarely in David's face.

"Ladies and gentlemen," came a voice from the podium. "Welcome aboard the *Ocean Queen.* I apologize that your trip is starting with this inconvenience. Let me introduce myself. I am Julian Masterino, your humble cruise director."

Mitch looked toward the stage, where a strikingly handsome, perfectly tanned man dressed in a full sailor suit stood. His black hair was gelled to withstand whatever ocean breezes came its way. Mitch had never thought much about what a cruise director would look like, but it wasn't quite this.

"I was waiting to show you my good-looking face and let you hear my charming accent — that's Brooklyn, New York, that I'm covering with a faux British inflection for those of you who couldn't tell — at tonight's fiesta, but given the situation, I figured I better come out of hiding. We've dispatched crew members to locate Mr. Feldman and Ms. Kuznetsov and in the meantime we've decided to go ahead and start the briefing without them. If the boat crashes, they are on their own unless one of you is kind enough to show them where we store the life buoys."

The room devolved in stitches and even Annette and Elise smiled. David, however, still looked grim, like he was ready to strangle the next person who crossed his path, which, considering his prolonged absence, was unlikely to be Freddy.

"And now, lucky cruisers, please direct your attention to the closest screen, where you will see a four-minute video on what to do if this boat goes *Titanic* on us. I promise it's entertaining. De Niro directed."

An animated film started and Mitch shut his eyes, trying to imagine how in the world his brother-in-law could manage to get away with acting like an unruly child. All Mitch felt when he woke up in the morning was the weight of his responsibilities, bearing down on him like a heavy barbell on his chest. He looked into the faces of his children and saw a running tally of how much they cost him. When he opened the chipped pantry doors to take out his coffee grinds each morning, he thought about how many thousands a desperately needed kitchen renovation would cost. Sitting at his desk at work, he worried how his pension was faring with the volatile stock market of late. But Freddy, forty-eight-year-old man that he was, was getting away with skipping a mandatory safety briefing with no consequences. What was this cruise director going to do to him? Ban him from the craps table? Quite unlikely. It was exactly a bozo like Freddy the cruise companies wanted in their casinos, ordering drinks at the bar and piling far too many chips on the pass line.

"Let's go," Elise said to him. Mitch hadn't even noticed the film had ended. "I desperately need a drink."

"Elise, did I hear you say you're going for a drink?" Annette piped in.

"Yes. Do you want to join?" Elise asked. Mitch was proud of her for being inclusive, though he assumed his wife just wanted a partner for Freddy-bashing and he'd never give as satisfying commentary as Annette would.

"No," Annette said. "Your father and I are going to get something to eat. I just wanted to tell you that we only signed up for the Doubly-Bubbly soft drink package. For alcoholic beverages, you're on your own."

"You're joking me," Elise said, her voice sharp and menacing. "I would have thought booze would be the first thing you'd spring for, considering you've tethered the eight of us on a boat together for five days."

Annette's face fell and even David's eyes widened in surprise.

Mitch forced his face into a smile.

"Elise, you're hilarious. But let's leave the joking to the cruise director." To Annette he added, "You know Elise. Her jokes don't always land."

THIRTEEN

Darius stopped in front of a massive neon green sign located in the aft portion of the boat's uppermost deck. He was, in theory, en route to the boat's sail-away party along with the other throngs of passengers. After that stupid safety show, the cruise director had announced that everyone was welcome to head to the pool decks at the top of the ship for a "rollicking good time" with DJ Mast-a-mind. Darius had audibly groaned. Was everything going to be one never-ending stream of boat puns?

He remembered his father taking him and Rachel out sailing a few times as a kid. It was a Saturday activity for them after his mother briefly went "on strike." Something about his father working on Sundays meaning that she never got any downtime. His father tried any number of activities that would get them out of the house for a few hours so their mom could rest. Mini golf proved too short of an excursion, real golf too long and too expensive, but sailing — that seemed to work. Darius actually really enjoyed it — it was the only reason he even picked up on the Mast-a-mind pun — but Rachel claimed she got nauseated on the boat. Darius was skeptical. She'd bring along a book and a bag of gummy worms and manage to work her way through both with no trouble, only complaining when her reading materials and sweets ran out. Nevertheless, the sailing excursions stopped, and it was on to bowling.

Darius was a little worried about his uncle Freddy and why he hadn't shown up earlier. Nobody else seemed to consider that something might have actually happened to him and Natasha, but Darius was picturing all manner of catastrophe: pirates sneaking onto the boat and holding them hostage; a personal crisis forcing them to dash off the boat without saying good-bye; or maybe a terrible fall down a back staircase for both of them. He wanted to voice these concerns to his mom or grandma, but they both seemed angry and not the least bit concerned. A small part of Darius wanted something bad to have happened to Freddy, just so the rest of his family would eat their words.

"Anything good?" came a voice from behind him. Darius whipped around, embarrassed for some reason, as if the person addressing him could read his mind. He came face-to-face with a girl who looked about his age. She was skinny, with long straight hair and black-plastic-framed glasses. Her T-shirt, tight and faded gray, said *Highland Debate Team.*

"Huh?" he managed in return, after he'd glanced around and determined there was no one else she could be speaking to.

"On the schedule," the girl said, pointing to the gigantic board in front of which Darius had stupidly been standing, blocking other people's view. "I can't see the list of activities."

Darius took a quick step back. The lit-up sign read TEEN SCENE in circular bulbs and had a detailed list of activities available in half-hour increments. He instinctively looked at his watch.

"Looks like we missed bingo," she said with a tone that even Darius picked up on as tongue-in-cheek.

"Darn. Hopefully it's not too late for shuffleboard," he responded.

"Shuffleboard conflicts with pinochle and I haven't quite decided which one I'm going to choose," the girl replied, tucking a

205

chunk of her hair behind her ear. Darius noticed her lobe was pierced at the top with a thin silver ring, which surprised him.

Is this banter? Darius wondered. He never spoke to any other teenagers that he hadn't known from the time he was two. The kids who remembered when he pooped his pants on the class trip and had to wait on the school bus with the driver while the rest of the children visited the Exploratorium. The neighborhood crew who teased him about his Halloween costume the year he went as mustard and his sister went as ketchup. Why had either of them let their mom talk them into that?

"The outdoor movie doesn't look that bad, actually," he said. "It says they're showing *The Hunger Games* at the teen pool at nine tonight." Darius looked down at his feet. He didn't want this girl to think he was asking her on a date.

"I have dinner with my family then," she said. "We signed up for the late seating at the fiesta. By the way, I'm Angelica."

"Nice to meet you," he said. Was he supposed to extend his hand? He felt an acute awkwardness. "So . . . I, um, I gotta go to the sail-away party. My sister is waiting for me." Darius turned to leave, although he didn't have the slightest clue which direc-

206

tion the party was in and gambled on right. Around him, rowdy clusters of people were heading every which way and he hoped he wasn't making a fool of himself by taking a wrong turn.

"Wait," she called after him. "What's your name?"

Darius wanted to bop himself on the head. Angelica had told him her name. He was so socially awkward he didn't give her his. To think he was congratulating himself on his "banter" a moment earlier. He lacked the basic conversational skills that most preschoolers had nailed. No wonder Marcy never looked his way, choosing instead to splay her heavenly body across Jesse's lap. Jesse, who never forgot to say his name when he met someone new, which was probably how he got the job at the skate shop instead of Darius.

"It's Darius," he muttered.

"See you around, Darius," Angelica said. "By the way, the sail-away party is that way." She lifted a skinny arm ringed by a dozen or so string bracelets, the kind he and Rachel used to make on the camp bus.

"Aren't you going?" he asked. The cruise director had said that was where everyone was meant to go and Darius hadn't really considered skipping it. He should try to be more like his uncle Freddy. Assuming he hadn't been mauled by wild animals or detained by pirates, he'd just opted out of the required programming.

"I'm going to take an SAT practice test in the room while everyone else is at the party."

Angelica didn't even look upset or embarrassed about it. She stated it matter-of-factly, as though it was perfectly normal to sit for a three-hour exam in a room by oneself within minutes of commencing a vacation.

"I'm supposed to be writing my college essay on this boat," Darius said.

"Cool. What are you going to write about?" Angelica asked, looping her thumbs into the back pockets of her jeans.

"I have absolutely no idea," Darius answered truthfully. "But if I don't write something, my mom will go apeshit."

"Perhaps DJ Mast-a-mind will inspire you at the party. Or his backup dancers, the Wave Girls. Picture the Spice Girls but with floaties. I saw them warming up on the sundeck. Prepare for a lot of gyrating."

"Maybe," Darius said, grinning. "I'll see you around." He walked off in the direction of the booming base sound, wondering how he hadn't realized he should follow the music moments earlier.

When he was back on land, he'd tell Marcy about the loser he'd met who took an SAT practice test instead of going to a party. He needed stories to tell her, experiences that set him apart. And if anything crazy had happened to Uncle Freddy, well, the upside was that it would make another juicy tale for Marcy. He imagined her wide green eyes, rimmed black like a cat's, trained on his face while he regaled her.

Darius stepped out in the blinding light, wishing he hadn't left his Ray-Bans in the room. He looked toward the DJ booth, which was set up on a platform between two enormous swimming pools that were connected via an interlocking, twisty water slide in primary colors. Mast-a-mind was blasting Justin Timberlake's "Can't Fight the Feeling" while a group of dancers in bikinis and sailor hats were cherry-picking the motleyest crew of passengers — people that had no business dancing in public — to join them in a revamped Electric Slide. Hundreds — no, maybe thousands — of chaises surrounded the water and weaving through them was like an unpleasant game of Tetris. Darius suddenly felt like a sardine trapped in a can filled with suntan lotion. For a brief second, he considered that

Angelica was probably wise to retreat to her room for a practice exam rather than brave this spectacle.

He tried to find his sister and scanned his eyes over the tops of heads, looking for her reddish ponytail emerging from the hole in the back of her obnoxious Stanford cap. Next to one of the numerous bars around the pool, Darius saw a line snaking all the way past the towel dispenser, literally an ATM of rough terry cloth, which terminated at the farthest visible chaise lounges, where the main bar was stationed. He headed off in that direction, thinking maybe he'd find Rachel there attempting to use her fake ID. Even though she'd barely spoken to him all summer, his sister was proud enough of the driver's license she'd managed to get her hands on at school, which rechristened her Lisa Simmons, age twenty-one, that she'd actually initiated a conversation with him one night when their parents were out to show it to him. He *was* impressed. Even Jesse didn't have one of those.

All summer long he'd thought about asking Rachel to get him one that he could flash around after work in front of Marcy. Of course Marcy would want one, and she'd have to go to him. But he'd still not worked up the courage to ask his sister. He suspected he might have better luck with Uncle Freddy. As little as he knew him, Freddy just seemed like the kind of guy who could deliver things, no questions asked. That is, if he ever surfaced again. Darius felt his insides flood with worry once more.

As he approached the line, he noticed that it wasn't in fact for the bar. People were queued up to reach a mysterious dispenser on the wall lined with metal handles. He turned to a random kid — a young boy in a Gryffindor T-shirt who looked about ten (certainly not a customer for the Sail-Away Sex on the Beach that the crew members were pushing big-time) — and asked what everyone was waiting for.

"Free ice cream," the boy said, his eyes lighting up. "This machine is open all day *and* all night. It has chocolate *and* vanilla. And you don't need *any* moncy. And they have cones!"

"That's awesome, dude," Darius said, smiling. "I'm going to get both flavors."

"Me too," the kid said. "You can cut me if you want."

"Thanks," Darius said, stepping in, but making sure the kid was ahead. He felt calm for the first moment since stepping on board, because now he had a plan. He could get through the trip by getting in this line over and over again, looking busy and purposeful, avoiding his family, specifically his mother. Her laissez-faire attitude about his college applications when she'd called to tell him about the cruise had proven to be short-lived. She announced to him at the airport, a moment after the plane touched down in Miami, that if he didn't write his college essay on the boat she was leaving him on it when it returned to shore.

"You're blocking the chocolate," came an angry voice a moment later. Darius looked behind him and came face-to-face with an overweight man double-fisting cones. "Move it," the man said, reaching one of his cones under the dispenser for a top-off.

"Sorry!" Darius jumped to the side. He looked back over the line with a bit more scrutiny. There was a lot of pushing and shoving, as if people were aware of historical evidence that the ice cream machine could shut down from overuse. He saw the exasperated expressions if someone took too long to fill their cone, noticed with shock the use of walkers to box people out. A middle-aged woman wearing a sweatshirt that said *I Have No Cruise Control* shouted, "Where's the free pizza? I was told there would be free pizza," when she reached the front of the line.

"This is the ice cream line, lady. Pizza is on Deck Five," shouted an agitated guy swiping neon zinc on his nose in a crooked stripe.

"Not so," said an elderly woman wielding a cane and a sun umbrella. "This is my seventeenth Paradise International cruise." She paused to point to a shiny gold pin in the shape of an anchor attached to her flowered sundress. "This means Anchor Society. Technically, I have access to a different ice cream machine with a shorter line on a different level. But I didn't want to miss the sail-away party. Anyway, the pizzeria is always on Deck Five. In between Shoe Plus Plus and the jewelry store."

Darius felt a pit forming in his stomach. He wouldn't have thought a boat would have stores beyond a vending machine where you could buy shampoo and a toothbrush. Would his mother dare go there in front of the whole family? Maybe this could be a good thing. Surely one of his grandparents or his dad would take notice of his mom's behavior, assuming she was willing to risk hitting the shops hard in front of them. That would take the pressure off of him to do something. Rachel had already shed him like a bad habit, barely nodding her head in agreement when he'd suggested

213

they meet at the party. And now she was nowhere to be found. In fact, Darius hadn't seen a single family member at the party. He decided to walk around a little, sick of roasting in the sun, wanting someone to talk to even if it was one of his parents. He gave his ice cream cone a big lick. It didn't compare to the mint chocolate chip at Sundaze, the shop where Marcy worked. He'd blown a good chunk of his lifeguard earnings on scoops.

He came upon Grandma Annette sitting in a shaded area, staring toward the water. DJ Mast-a-mind was announcing that everyone should start counting down from ten because the boat was ready to depart. Passengers crowded along the deck's railing to wave good-bye to the shore, even though all that was visible from the boat was the string of desolate industrial buildings surrounding the port. Grandma Annette didn't budge. It seemed like she couldn't even hear the DJ, even though his voice boomed through a speaker directly over her head. Darius moved in her direction and sat down on the chaise next to her.

"Hi, Grandma. Do you want to go over to the balcony with me?" Darius asked. Though she smiled at him, her eyes looked teary. Darius chewed nervously on the

214

paper wrapping his ice cream cone. There was something so terrifying about seeing a grown-up cry.

"Are you okay? What's wrong?" He'd heard his mom and grandma snipe at each other at the safety demo, but that didn't seem like anything out of the ordinary.

"Of course I'm fine, sweetheart. It's just old age. Loosens the tear ducts." His grandma chuckled and he joined in too. He was pretty sure she wasn't being literal. "Help me up. Let's go wave to these buildings and get on with it."

He extended a hand and she took it and together they walked with arms linked toward the balcony. At "one," a foghorn sounded and confetti rained on them, little threads of silver and gold attaching to his swirl of vanilla and chocolate. He tried not to see it as a sign of things to come for the rest of the trip.

FOURTEEN

Elise woke up to the first full day on the boat with a pounding headache. She reached her arm across the bed and felt the empty space beside her. Briefly she wondered where Mitch had gone until she spied a note propped up on the night table that read: "Went to gym. Meet at breakfast at 9 at Skipper's?"

She pressed her thumbs into her temples, as though she could massage the molecules of her hangover into a more diffuse form. The last time she'd had that many margaritas was in college and she'd spent the entire next day doing a repetitive loop from her bed to the communal toilet. She'd had no intention of getting drunk last night — in front of her kids, no less — but when she'd arrived at the reserved family table at the fiesta she'd had to face Natasha propped on Freddy's lap, feeding him chips and guacamole. The two of them were as carefree as ever, as if thousands of passengers hadn't been delayed from starting their vacation because of them.

To be fair, she was already aggravated before she made it to the Feldman table. From the moment she entered the dining room, Elise was overwhelmed by a sea of heads stretching in every direction. It was impossible to flag down a maître d', and her heels, a strappy pair that cost the same as four sessions with Darius's SAT tutor, were already blistering her heels. She couldn't remember feeling less special or, to put it in the words of the ship's brochure, less "pampered, catered to, and indulged." Even when Elise squinted she couldn't see the end of either side of the room, which was filled with hundreds of round and rectangular tables.

"Excuse me, do you know how we find our table?" Elise asked a woman who looked about her age dressed in a floral jumpsuit and wearing way too much eye shadow. "I thought there would be a host or at least some signage."

"You a virgin, hon?" the woman asked in a thick Southern drawl.

"Pardon?" Elise said, nearly stumbling backward.

"A cruise virgin, darlin'. Didn't mean to

217

startle you. I lost my V-card on a cruise to the Bahamas fifteen years ago and never looked back. Best way to travel. Anyway, I see my gang back there. Just push on through and you'll find your folks eventually."

Can't wait, Elise thought uncharitably. She had seen in the ship's brochure that there was an option for dining as a family or for random assignment, and at this moment she couldn't decide what she'd have preferred, eating with the Feldmans or rolling the dice with strangers.

Waiters continued to float through the room with military precision, radiating as much emotion as Buckingham Palace guards, and finally Elise spotted a hostess with a megaphone directing traffic. How she would have loved to grab that megaphone and point out Freddy. "This is the guy who didn't think it was important to show up to the safety demo," she would say. "This guy kept you from your cocktails!" She imagined a storm of tomatoes flying in his direction.

When she was finally led to the Feldman table, her parents and children weren't there yet, so it was just her, hovering while Freddy and Natasha played Tostito toss. Fortunately she quickly spotted Mitch, chatting animatedly with a family one table over. He'd left their cabin earlier to catch the tail end of American History trivia and she could see him thrusting his score sheet hotly, debating answers with another middle-aged man boasting the telltale dad bod. When Mitch noticed she'd arrived, he bid the other table good-bye and sat down next to Freddy — well, technically Freddy *and* Natasha, since she was presently stapled to his thighs as though he were Santa Claus. Mitch looked totally at ease with the arrangement, sipping his martini and telling Freddy and Natasha about an Abraham Lincoln question that had really stumped him. Elise didn't know why he was bothering with those two. She knew her husband couldn't possibly have missed it when Natasha botched a metaphor earlier. Complaining about the server at the lunch buffet counting how many cucumber slices she took, Natasha said, *He was watching me like I'm a hawk.* Mitch, passionate linguist and smug grammarian that he was, drank his coffee from a mug that said: *Let's Eat Grandpa! Let's Eat, Grandpa! Punctuation Saves Lives.* Elise flagged down the nearest waiter and ordered the specialty margarita, the Prickly Pear. Nothing could suit her mood more.

"So, Freddy, I hadn't realized you'd lost your hearing," she said when she caught her brother's eye. "Have you seen a doctor about getting a listening device?" She seized her drink by the stem and took a delicate sip, attempting to appear relaxed.

"What are you talking about?" Freddy asked. Natasha looked uncomfortable and Elise had to give her credit for picking up on where she was going before her brother did.

"Um, I was just curious because three thousand other people heard the siren go off telling everyone to attend the safety demonstration, but sadly you seemed to have been the only one who missed it. Which is why I'm concerned about your hearing." Elise saw Mitch shoot her a warning glance, but she chose to ignore it. Why would her husband try to silence her just to avoid conflict with Freddy and a virtual stranger? Honestly, she couldn't figure Mitch out lately, his head seemed so fixed in the clouds. Whenever he had that far-off look, it usually meant there was some big story brewing at the *Bee* that he wasn't ready to tell her about. She steeled herself for another series of weeks on end where he'd be living at the office.

"Elise," Mitch said, this time making it impossible for her to ignore him.

"I heard you," she hissed, redirecting her

attention to Freddy. She noted with pleasure that Natasha had slid off his lap and returned to her own seat. It felt good to make someone sweat.

"We didn't hear it," Natasha said earnestly. "The loudspeaker in our room is broken."

"You only have one?" Mitch asked. "I would have thought with your luxury suite there would be at least two." Elise was pleased to finally witness some cojones from Mitch (it was *fiesta* night, after all), but when she made eye contact with him, he seemed to be gently teasing them and not upset at all.

"Sorry we're late," Annette interrupted, sidling up to the table with, of all people, Darius. Elise was surprised to see her son and mother palling around the boat together. It was hard to imagine what they could possibly be discussing other than their common enemy, which had to be her.

"We ran into each other at the sail-away party and ended up walking around the ship together. Did you know the boat has a rock wall and a bumper car track?" Annette said.

"Hi, Uncle Freddy," Darius said enthusiastically, choosing a seat opposite him. "Glad you're okay."

Elise inhaled sharply through her nose,

trying to contain the boil inside her. Dr. Margaret said breathing exercises could be very effective. Of course, she was instructing Elise on how to relax her body when she felt the urge to shop coming on, but surely these same principles could be applied to maintaining self-control with her family. Trying as she did to draw more oxygen to her lungs, she still felt herself wondering: Could it really be she was the only one still upset about Freddy's absence? Everyone else had apparently moved on, scooping chip after chip into the blood-red salsa and marveling at the Mexican lanterns strung from the ceiling. Elise pulled another deep breath into her body, imagining that the air inflating her organs was helium instead of oxygen so she could drift away.

"Hi, Mom. Hi, Darius. Freddy and I were just discussing why he and Natasha were MIA before," Elise said.

"Their loudspeaker is broken," came Rachel's voice from behind, approaching their table with David at her side. Elise said a silent prayer that it wasn't *another* alliance forming. It was true she had Mitch if she needed a partner with whom to commiserate on the boat, but he seemed so distracted — or at least not attuned enough to pick up on the hundreds of tiny insults that were scattering like shards of broken glass.

Rachel was wearing a ruffled miniskirt in blue, a white tank top, and a cowboy hat. It didn't exactly scream Mexican, but considering Elise hadn't bothered to change out of her madras shorts and polo shirt, she was in no position to judge creativity.

"And how do you know that?" Elise asked, aghast when she observed that Rachel was standing a good four inches taller than usual. Normally they were neck and neck — Annette too — the three Feldman women stacking up at five foot three each, like dominoes. Elise looked down to assess the footwear that brought Rachel up to this newfound height: a ridiculous pair of black stilettos, rhinestoned things coiling around her ankles that looked more dominatrix than Stanford sophomore. Certainly Annette would notice and wonder why Elise let her dress like that — as if she had that kind of control over Rachel. Elise prepared herself for a little dig.

"Because he told me," Rachel said, apparently satisfied with Freddy's excuse. "I went to his room to thank him for the gift cards."

Elise's daughter plopped down in the open seat next to Natasha and complimented her dress, a blue halter that looked like it had been spray-painted on her body.

Despite Elise's tendency to buy just about anything of late (the two-hundred-foot expanding garden hose she'd picked up at Lowe's came to mind for some reason), even she wouldn't have parted with a dime for Rachel's cheap shoes or Natasha's trashy dress. Standing out in contrast to these two was Annette, who looked perfect as usual in a navy shift dress and cream cardigan draped over her shoulders. In a subtle nod to the evening's theme, she had put a single pink carnation in her hair. Elise pettily resisted the urge to issue a compliment.

"Thanks, honey," Natasha said to Rachel. "I love that color of nail polish you're wearing." Rachel beamed and within seconds the two girls, who couldn't be that far apart in age, were whispering to each other about the virtues of shellac manicures. Elise cringed reflexively.

"I guess this seat is for me," Elise said, noticing that all the other seats had already been occupied while she was brooding. She was in between her parents and across from Freddy, Natasha, and Rachel. Mitch and Darius were at the other end of the table, her husband studying the menu and her son staring off into space. When she saw her son glassy-eyed and unfocused it reminded her of no one so much as Freddy, and with her brother and son seated at the same table, it was impossible to avoid seeing the resemblance.

As if he could read her mind, Freddy addressed his nephew.

"What are you going to get, D-money?"

Darius smiled, oddly unfazed by being nicknamed within hours of a reunion with his estranged uncle. Freddy had that effect on people. They immediately felt close to him, like they shared history and inside jokes. He'd tease people and they'd immediately feel like they were in Freddy's inner circle, where gentle ribbing was the norm. She had the opposite effect, holding people at bay, from the mothers at her children's school when they were growing up to the sweet woman who had come to clean their house every Monday for the past twenty years. When Elise tried a little joshing, the other person's face would indicate just how ineffective she was at adjusting her tone correctly. "I was kidding," she'd all too often have to tack on.

Elise knew she wasn't just being her own worst critic. One of her medical school professors, during a third-year rotation in gastroenterology, had suggested she might want to focus on radiation. "Less patient facing," the professor had said, as though it was obvious to the both of them that this was a problem of hers. The only people she'd managed the most comfortable relationships with — other than her husband, whose conversational skills and relaxed demeanor more than made up for her deficits — were salespeople. The transactions were blissfully straightforward: *Would you like another size? Credit card or cash?* Elise knew when she chose to buy something, especially when she filled an entire cart, she was making the clerk happy, saying and doing all the right things. Salespeople never rolled their eyes like her kids or made her doubt herself like her parents. Even her friends made Elise tentative — their plastic smiles gave nothing away. Mitch was wonderful, but she couldn't very well follow him to the office each day like her mother followed her father. That kind of symbiotic relationship wasn't for her. She and Mitch had a solid marriage, but they had their own lives. In fact, it was a testament to how much independence they had that her husband had no idea the way she'd gotten their family up a creek without a paddle, how she swiped her credit card nearly as often as she blinked.

All of a sudden she felt her mother's elbow dig into her side. Elise looked up and saw

Annette had taken a spoon and was clanking it against a wineglass, oblivious to the fact that each time she made contact with the glass, her elbow collided with Elise's rib cage.

"I'd just like to make a toast and say how happy I am that we're all together for the week. It's not often that we —"

But she couldn't finish. A four-piece mariachi band, wielding guitars and clad in glitzy black-and-gold outfits and matching sombreros, had strolled into the dining room and set up shop right next to their table. Once the first chord was plucked, Annette's toast was drowned out.

It was just as well, thought Elise. She didn't have much interest in hearing a saccharine toast, a nod to all things Elise was dreading. She reached for the pitcher of margaritas, filling and refilling her cup like it was an empty shopping cart at Target. And that was what led her to wake up the next morning with a bowling ball in her skull, still feeling blinded by the blingy embroidery on the entertainers' vests. Had it been a dream, or was there a giant piñata unveiled at the night's end that had forced her to duck and cover?

Elise dragged herself out of bed and traversed the three small steps it required to reach the shower. If she needed to shave, Elise could actually prop her foot up on the bed from the shower stall if she left the door open. That image wasn't in the brochure. Neither was the interior of the closet, which had barely enough room for an American Girl to unpack. Rachel had loved those overpriced dolls when she was little, begging for Elise to join her on the floor to hash out all sorts of made-up scenarios: school, dance recital, new baby. Elise was a left brain and she recalled these pretend play sessions as pure torture. Now she would stand on her head if it meant spending time with her daughter.

Freshly scrubbed and dressed, and feeling a bit better, Elise set out to meet Mitch at the breakfast buffet. Skipper's was located on Deck Ten and was the largest buffet available on the ship. Darius had shown her a YouTube video of a similar meal on a rival cruise ship. Danishes, doughnuts, and fruits were piled to the high heavens, but still people were jockeying for position, balancing multiple plates on their arms like waiters. "I think they're trying to get to an omelet station," Darius had said, the two of them bent over his laptop in a rare moment of camaraderie a few days before embarkation. "This has to be staged," Elise had protested, but Darius claimed the video was authentic. It had more than one million views. Now she had the chance to see for herself if it was theater or reality.

From the moment she stepped off the elevator, the answer was apparent. The line — which resembled a mosh pit — reached to the place where the elevator doors parted. Boat staffers attempted to corral guests into rows demarcated by velvet ropes (the least glamorous use of velvet ropes imaginable), but it was pointless. Around her, people were shouting about saving spaces and cutting. A rumor had been spread that one of the waffle irons was broken. How would she ever find Mitch in this mess? She couldn't imagine her parents navigating this well either. It was her father who had instituted the policy at the hospital cafeteria that doctors and nurses in uniform shouldn't have to wait in line. Annette still chastised Elise for not having enough stations at the smorgasbord at Rachel's bat mitzvah. Apparently she'd seen four people looking bored while waiting for their Peking duck to get rolled into a pancake.

"Mom!" She heard Rachel's voice barreling toward her. "This is insane. Some guy yelled at me for taking the last slice of French toast and a waiter was bringing out a tray with another few hundred stacked."

"I know," Elise said. "I think we might need to camp outside tonight so we can be the first ones through the doors tomorrow."

Rachel chuckled and Elise felt her heart swell. She was making a connection with her daughter, the person who had spent the whole summer looking annoyed by her existence. If Elise asked Rachel what she wanted her to pick up from the supermarket, Rachel would take four prompts before responding. And when she did, it was only with a monosyllabic "gum." And that was when Elise was serving her! What if she ever tried to sit her down for a heart-to-heart? After seeing those stripper shoes last night, it occurred to Elise there might be some space for parenting that needed filling. Sometimes it was hard to remember Rachel needed guidance too, that she couldn't just raise her on autopilot while tending to Darius like a tree in need of daily pruning. She wondered if she should intervene about the long hours her daughter was putting in at her summer internship, because it took a real adult to see that her days of potential carefreeness were painfully numbered.

"Rach, what was that you said at dinner about Freddy giving you a gift card?" She had meant to get to the bottom of that last night, but with the flagrant notes of Cumbia music and the flash mob of flamenco dancers, not to mention the amnesiac effect of the margaritas, it had slipped her mind.

Rachel pulled out a card from her back pocket and showed it to Elise.

"It's a hundred-dollar gift card to use in the Game Zone," Rachel said, growing animated. It was nice to see that childish side of her daughter emerge, the one whose face used to light up at the mere mention of Chuck E. Cheese. "I already checked with Guest Services. I can transfer the money to use at the spa."

Elise tried to keep her face from falling, willing gravity to stop doing its job. Whereas a beat earlier she'd seen a glimpse of Rachel in pigtails, now she was imagining her doing keg stands while some horny upperclassmen held up her legs. Why did she have to go there so quickly? Couldn't she just picture her lovely daughter with cucumbers on her eyes and a mud mask on her face, making chitchat with the aesthetician about her skin care regimen?

"That was very nice of Freddy," Elise forced herself to say. "I presume he got one for Darius too?"

"Yep," Rachel said. "Of course, he already spent his. I saw him in the arcade last night after dinner with some girl."

"Really?" Elise asked. These children never ceased being mysteries. "He looked like he was falling asleep at dinner. And he's supposed to be working on his essay. Rachel — I need you to help me with this. Darius doesn't have your natural motivation and he could use your support. By the way, you kids shouldn't be too impressed with Freddy. He's obviously just showing off for Natalia."

"Natasha," Rachel said, setting in motion one of her more dramatic eye rolls.

"Whatever. You get the point. Now, if you'll excuse me, I have to find your father, fight my way through the running of the bulls to get a bagel, and then I'm going to lie down before bingo at eleven."

"You know there's a place where you can get a yogurt and there's no line, right?" Rachel asked. "Only difference is that you have to pay for it."

"Even better," Elise said and spun around on her heels. She'd catch up with Mitch later.

FIFTEEN

Annette sat with David on the ship's Grand Promenade, which was just a fancy name for what was essentially a strip mall with cafés and shops. Both of them were sipping lattes, David's a decaf because his hematologist said caffeine could impair the effects of his medications. Annette wouldn't let him have any once she heard that, even clearing out the dark chocolate from their cupboards and the coffee-flavored ice cream from the freezer. She watched him twenty-four/seven, her ally and closest friend, hoping that if she didn't take her eyes off of him, nothing bad could happen. People didn't vanish into thin air; ergo, if she never stopped looking after him, David would go nowhere. It was magical thinking, but it was working for her on most days.

"What's on tap for today?" David asked her. He looked tired. The dark circles under his eyes and greenish tinge to his skin made

Annette feel anxious, but she reminded herself for the millionth time that the doctors had approved this trip. Several had said it would be good for him, not just in raising his spirits but in actually slowing the process of the cancer cells multiplying inside him. Apparently there was cold, hard evidence that time with loved ones could be more powerful than any medicine compounded in a pharmacy. It wasn't the reason they'd gone on the trip — Annette had decided on it before they'd learned that. Spending time with her children and grandchildren was the goal. Getting to see four Broadway-caliber shows in one week while on board? Another perk. But now she supposedly had another benefit, a far more legitimate one, even though she was dubious about those claims. She was a skeptic, like her husband. It was one of the many reasons they got along so well. They both had a "Don't pee on my leg and tell me it's raining" attitude and they never attempted to bullshit the other.

She and David had scrimped and saved so much during their younger years, trusting that they could finally enjoy their coffers in their old age when time would suddenly materialize as a vast resource and responsibilities would shrink. How foolish they were to take their health for granted, assuming that as the years progressed they would remain robust and virile, the very picture of the strapping grandparents shown in life insurance commercials. But instead of their financial obligations winnowing to a predictable stream of monthly payments, David's medications were costing a bloody fortune and Annette was spending hours on the phone dealing with their insurance company, thrilled if they recouped even just half the cost. She'd spent decades submitting other people's bills to insurance providers but hadn't ever really experienced the acute pain of dealing with these faceless conglomerates that were ceaselessly creative in finding reasons for rejecting claims. And now she had the added pleasure of dealing with the large pharmaceutical companies too because David had been accepted into a clinical trial. Not having to sit on the phone asking questions of their pharma rep, Sherri, for a week? That was perhaps the absolute best perk of going away.

"*Ocean Queen* passengers, may I have your attention, please? This is Sir Julian, your noble cruise director, speaking. Thank you to all those who danced your hearts out at the salsa competition last night. Family bingo will start in a half hour in the Lobster

Lounge on Deck Five. In the meantime, if you're near the shopping promenade, all fine jewelry at the Golden Nugget will be marked down twenty percent for the next three hours. Time to get your sweetheart a little something special."

"I'm getting awfully tired of those announcements," Annette said to David. They'd already heard from Julian three times that morning. Once at dawn to warn them about rough seas ahead, then at breakfast to advise queuing up early for the illusionist show, and now this latest — like they were in a bargain basement and not on what was supposed to be a luxury liner.

"Think Freddy's intercom is actually broken?" David asked her.

Annette shrugged. It was so beside the point.

"Elise was really put out about it," she said. "Speaking of, is that her over there? I think I see her trying on a necklace."

David squinted to follow her gaze.

"Looks like it," he said, doing that thing David always did when he talked about Elise, which was letting just the faintest hint of disappointment — or maybe it was better described as a lack of understanding — creep into his voice. How badly David had wanted to expand his practice with Elise:

Feldman & Feldman: Obstetrics, Gynecology, and Reproductive Endocrinology, the one-stop shop for women from Mill Basin to Syosset. But we don't always get what we want, Annette thought, wishing her husband could grasp that.

"She's happy," Annette said. "I think so, at least. She certainly never calls me to tell me otherwise."

David nodded, with maybe a dash of sympathy, though Annette doubted he felt even a fraction of her emptiness and pain. His parents, humorless Polish immigrants, had faithfully raised four boys in the Bronx until they each reached the age of eighteen, when they were turned out on the stoop. She, on the other hand, had the closest of relationships with her mother, Eleanor, for whom Elise was named. They were more like friends, doing each other's hair, gossiping about what the neighbors were wearing. When Eleanor died at such a young age — while Annette was pregnant with Elise — she took it as a sign when she birthed a baby girl. This would be the continuation of a beautiful friendship, only now Annette would be the elder of the pair.

But Elise and she had never really bonded and it was truly impossible to pinpoint the blame. It could be that Annette wasn't the mother that Eleanor had been, a Jewish whirling dervish who made killer gefilte fish and bargain hunted with sharpshooter precision to put Annette in the finest clothing. Or perhaps it was because Elise was naturally reserved and the distance between them was a product of her daughter's unique DNA, which might as well have stood for Do Not Approach. Annette thought often of a sign a friend of hers had framed in the guest room of her country house: FRIENDS WELCOME, RELATIVES BY APPOINTMENT.

Freddy was in fine spirits at dinner the prior evening, which Annette had to assume was thanks to Natasha's spandex dress rather than on account of family time. Still, he'd accepted the trip, and that wasn't necessarily a given when she'd called him. They were "estranged" for the most part, a word that stuck in her craw every time she said it out loud. Because it wasn't really that they were *strangers* to each other, rather it was the "strange" part of "estranged" that got her. It *was* strange to Annette how she and her son had got to this place where he never came home to visit and she didn't really understand what he did for a living or how he spent his time. Oh, he'd hurt her all right. But that was years ago, even though

Annette could still feel the pain like a fresh bee sting.

It was the day she'd driven all the way to Vermont in a snowstorm to pack up Freddy's things from college. Yes, she was angry as all hell that he'd gotten himself expelled. After everything she and David had done for that kid — the tutors, the exorbitant tuition they paid for a subpar private college — he repaid them by throwing it back in their faces. But still, she hadn't let go of that optimism, even when she walked up the five flights of stairs to Freddy's dorm room, dragging the empty suitcases behind her after her last-ditch effort to negotiate with the dean. They would figure out next steps together. Eventually their son would turn around. But what did she hear when she stood outside his room? Her son, speaking to his roommate, not even bothering to lower his voice.

"So what are you gonna do now?" the kid asked. He was another privileged underachiever like Freddy, a bratty boy named Jay they all called Jack-O for some reason.

"My mom is taking me home today," Freddy said. His voice, normally muffled like he was speaking into a paper bag, came barreling toward her loud and clear. "She's such a fucking bitch I don't know how I'm

239

going to stand moving back in with her. My dad's a total dick too."

Annette had dropped the bags she was carrying, the two empty vessels thudding against the linoleum of the landing. Freddy must have heard the noise because he opened the door right away.

"Hey, Mom," he said, though it was obvious he didn't suspect she'd overheard a thing.

She could barely make eye contact with him the rest of the day, feeling so nauseated that she clutched her gut like it had an open wound. Mentally, she made a list of all the things she'd done for Freddy: the choo-choo trains of meat she spiraled into his toddler mouth, the waiting in line for hours to get him Air Jordans, the testing him on his Spanish vocab instead of relaxing in front of the television. *Tocar* — to touch. *Nadar* — to swim. *Bailar* — to dance. She was still certain she could pass a high school–level Spanish exam. If that's what a bitch does — give so much of herself to a child that there is barely a sliver left for her husband and other child — then Annette would be damned. Still, he was just a kid when he said it. Maybe it was to impress his roommate. Or because he was nineteen and had shit for brains, like all teenagers whose

240

parents have coddled them.

"Do you think I ignored Elise because I was too focused on Freddy?" Annette now asked David, who looked like he'd perked up a bit since they sat down. She wondered if he'd secretly swapped his decaf for regular when she was dropping in her Splenda packets. She'd have to watch him even more carefully.

"I think we did the best we could," David said. "You were an excellent mother to both of our children."

Were? Were! He'd used the past tense, corroborating what she'd suspected. That her role as mother was done, finito, kaput. She was dead weight, the appendix of organs, the VCR of home electronics.

"Look over there," David said, pointing toward the Golden Nugget. "Looks like Elise found a lot of things she liked."

Annette glanced over and saw her daughter carrying at least four small shopping bags with gold ribbons dangling from the handles.

"Huh. Mitch must be doing better than we thought," she said.

David put down his coffee cup and took Annette's hand in his own. She felt the tremor but pretended it was his heartbeat. It had a similar rhythm.

"By the way, I think it's daddy issues," David said.

"What?"

"Natasha and Freddy," he said.

"Oh." Annette sipped her coffee, which was already cold. "I assumed green card."

SIXTEEN

Freddy crossed the living room of his suite and stood next to where Natasha was sitting at the dining table, munching on a platter of fruit that had been delivered moments earlier. Platinum-status guests were entitled to three daily amenities and so far they'd received a bottle of champagne with a plate of chocolate-covered strawberries; a tower of French macaroons; and now this, a decadent fruit platter where trios of honeydew, watermelon, and cantaloupe slices were arranged into the shape of sailboats. Based on the conversation last night at the fiesta dinner, Freddy was fairly certain his and Natasha's accommodations were more than a cut above everyone else's. Rachel showed everyone a bruise on her thigh from banging into the knob on the bathroom door. David said he and Annette had to walk around the room single file. Meanwhile, Freddy and Natasha's suite was

243

spread on two levels with a spiral staircase and an outdoor balcony large enough to hold a small cocktail party.

"What do you mean, she seemed weird?" Freddy asked Natasha, who had recently returned to the room after a visit to the Grand Promenade, where she'd hoped to find a new bathing suit. After meeting the Feldman clan, she was apparently rethinking the swimwear that she'd packed, bikinis with less material than the inside pocket of Freddy's jeans.

"I mean, I saw your sister at some jewelry store and I was about to say hi, but she just had this really furtive look. For some reason, I stood there watching her shop, and she must have given over ten different cards to pay. She bought a bunch of stuff and was given a different shopping bag for each one, but I saw her sit down at Fifty-Five Flavors — the frozen yogurt place — and consolidate everything into one bag. She was, like, cramming it all in."

Freddy sat down next to Natasha and plucked off the sail from one of the fruit boats.

"Is that so strange? Don't a lot of people try to carry everything in one bag?" He really didn't know, considering the last time he'd gone shopping was for Natasha's fancy bracelet. Everything else he bought on Amazon, even though the cardboard box waste troubled him, though not enough to make him willing to browse actual stores.

Natasha propped her feet up on the chair and wrapped her arms around her shins. She looked like a little ball when she did that, an accordion in its closed position. He wanted to expand her, show her range to his family, so they left the boat knowing she was fluent in three languages and visited sick children in the hospital once a month.

"Just trust me, it was weird," Natasha said. "You said yourself that you barely know Elise anymore, so why are you so surprised?"

"I'm not. Or I guess I am. I don't know." He replaced the triangular piece of cantaloupe in its original spot on the platter, feeling his appetite waning. "She seemed normal at bingo."

"Yes, but I asked her what she did in the morning after breakfast and she said she read a book on the sundeck. Didn't say a word about the jewelry store."

"That's not weird. That's just Elise trying to show she's an intellectual. Trust me. She wants to be superior to everyone. At least me and you, anyway. She'd rather say she was reading than admit she was doing something as commonplace as buying a necklace." He felt that familiar aggravation well up inside him when he thought about his family, like his insides were microwave popcorn bursting through the bag. Of course his girlfriend couldn't see the reason Elise had fibbed about her morning. She suspected something sinister or deceptive, when it was plain old haughtiness.

"If you say so. I didn't press her on what she was reading or anything," Natasha conceded. "I think I'm going to hit the gym. What are your plans for the rest of the day?"

"I called the kids' room and Darius picked up. He and I are going to try the rock wall together. I'm swinging by his cabin in a few minutes to pick him up."

"All right. I'll see you at dinner later. I can't wait for this boat to arrive in Sint Maarten tomorrow. Feeling claustrophobic," she said, slipping out of her blouse and into a sports bra.

"I wouldn't mention that around my family," Freddy cautioned. "I'm pretty certain our suite could hold all of their cabins combined."

Natasha leaned down and kissed him and he found himself peeking down the valley of her sports bra.

"Stop worrying so much about what I will

and won't say. That goes for you too." She patted his cheek before stripping out of her jeans and into leggings with tantalizing mesh panels.

He nodded, knowing she was right but well aware it would be nearly impossible for him to heed her advice.

"Speaking of the fearsome Feldmans, do you think they actually believe that our intercom is broken?" he asked, knowing from the way Natasha looked up at him from her shoelaces that she was getting annoyed.

"It *is* broken," she said, popping in her earbuds. He heard the blare of the pop music she exercised to seeping out through the thin space between her lobe and the headphones.

"One of them anyway," Freddy said louder.

"Well, they don't have to know we were in the shower when the announcement came on, Freddy. That speaker is broken. The technician said so. You want to have your mom and sister come test it out?" She didn't wait for an answer, spryly standing up and heading out the door without so much as a wave.

Freddy felt light on his feet as he made his

way down the fourteen flights of stairs to the floor where Darius's cabin was located. Taking the elevators was proving a super-human feat. Even with two elevator banks on board with eight lifts apiece, it was still at least a five-minute wait for one, and all too often when the doors slid open there wasn't space for even a stick figure to squeeze in. He hated to think what the situation would be by the end of the week, after the free food practically thrown at them stretched them into caricature versions of themselves, swollen and bloated in all the wrong places.

Spending time with his nephew was finally something he was looking forward to on the cruise. He'd hoped for Rachel when he called, not because he would rather be with her than Darius, but because the two of them had some unsettled business to attend to. He had signed off on a letter from the court that said he'd oversee Rachel's fifty hours of community service, and he had yet to check in on her progress. But Darius said he had no idea where his sister was and Freddy thought he detected a note of irritation in his voice.

"Let's you and I do the rock wall, okay?" Freddy had asked spontaneously. "I can be at your room in about twenty minutes."

"Sure," Darius said almost immediately. He got the feeling Darius would love to try many of the cool features on the boat — the bumper cars, the surf pool, the paintball obstacle course — but felt lame going it alone.

Freddy walked briskly down the narrow hallway, noting how much closer together the doors were on this floor than on his. After a lengthy walk in the aft direction, he reached the kids' room. Through the door Freddy heard muffled voices that quieted after he rapped on the door. He assumed it was his nephew flipping off the TV, but when the door swung open, he came face-to-face with his sister.

"Elise," he said, hoping his voice didn't convey disappointment. "What are you doing here? Are you going rock climbing with us?" His sister had been a great athlete once upon a time — cocaptain of their high school tennis team, if he remembered correctly — and he could imagine that she'd be rather nimble on the rock wall. Probably much more so than him, though they'd both be terrible compared to Darius, who had the simple fact of youth on his side, limbs that didn't get arthritic in the rain, and a limber back that allowed him to go from sitting to standing without missing a beat.

"No, and neither is Darius," she said sharply and Freddy wondered if she had any idea how much she sounded like their mother, so shrill and inflexible, determined to have things her way.

"Mom, I can work on it later," Darius protested.

Freddy peered over Elise's shoulder, since she was standing sentry in the doorway, and saw his nephew seated on the corner of a twin bed, a baseball cap pulled low over his face. Freddy couldn't see his eyes, but it sounded like he'd either been or was about to start crying. He remembered a few of the occasions when his parents brought him to tears long after it was socially acceptable for a child to cry, how he'd overwork his throat muscles to keep the lump at bay and bite down on his bottom lip to stop it from quivering. Once was when Annette called him a lazy sack of you-know-what after his math teacher complained for the umpteenth time about him not turning in assignments. Another time it was because his father said he couldn't go to the Allman Brothers concert with his friends because he had come home from the mall smelling like cigarette smoke.

Elise spun around to address Darius.

"You've been putting this essay off for the

entire summer. There are seven essay topics to choose from on the common application. Surely you can come up with *something.*" She turned back to face Freddy. "I'm sorry to crush your plans to go rock climbing, but Darius is way behind on his work and needs to focus now."

Darius gaped at him with a helpless expression that his mother did not see. It made Freddy pity him, but he was also just so grateful that he himself was no longer a child, puppeteered by a clueless parent.

"Maybe I could help?" Freddy asked. He was about to say that he'd taken several writing courses at the Aspen Institute through their Aspen Words program but stopped himself. In fact, the professor had singled out a creative writing piece he'd done, about a young woman who learns at age thirty that her parents are in the witness protection program, as an example of excellent plotting for the entire class. But he wasn't quite ready to uncork his life in that way, to reveal something about himself that would unleash a flurry of questions from Elise.

"No," Elise said, at the same time that Darius said, "Sure." Their monosyllabic answers collided like a car crash.

"No, thank you," Elise repeated and

Darius shrugged his shoulders limply. "We're going to hammer this out together until it's time to go down for dinner. Tonight is the around-the-world buffet," she added in a lighter tone, perhaps hoping that the opportunity to get corn arepas, chicken lo mein, and lamb vindaloo in one meal would make Darius any less put out about being crammed into his cabin with his mother to float essay ideas when the sun was shining brightly and there were at least fifty activities going on that were preferable to brainstorming.

Freddy looked past Elise again, wondering if he was perhaps missing another part of the room, a corner around which a generous living area revealed itself. But no, Darius and Rachel's room really was that small. There wasn't even a window out of which to gaze at the sprawling ocean that he and Natasha had been taking for granted. And with Rachel and Darius not caring to tidy up, the entire floor was littered with clothing and towels, so Freddy couldn't even tell if it had the plush carpeting of his suite or, as he suspected, cheap parquet. No wonder his niece wasn't hanging around. Freddy wondered if Elise's room was equally tiny but couldn't imagine asking to see it without sounding like a complete ass-hole.

"Okay, then I'll catch you later, D," Freddy said. "Elise," he added with a solemn nod, knowing the formality made him sound like he was concluding a busi-ness meeting and not bidding adieu to the girl with whom he used to take bubble baths well into grade school until it got weird.

"By the way, what'd you do this morning? Before bingo." He addressed his sister.

She seemed to flush a little before saying, "Oh, nothing. Relaxed. Went to the pool for a bit. Why? I mean, what'd you do?"

"Not much," Freddy said, suddenly feel-ing that Natasha was onto something. "See you guys later."

Freddy stepped back into the hallway and headed to the spa level to find Natasha. Huffing up the stairs to the sports club, he couldn't stop thinking about his poor nephew, trapped in that minuscule box with his uptight mother who was intent on draw-ing words from her son's mouth onto the computer screen, as if writing an essay was just a matter of transcription and force of sheer will. Freddy noticed his knees were suddenly weak. Watching Elise seem so disappointed by Darius felt like a fresh as-sault on his own childhood. Or maybe it was just that he was an out-of-shape old man who had stupidly rejected his girl-friend's dogged requests to join her at the track at the Aspen rec center. Halfway to the spa, Freddy gave up on the stairs and headed toward the nearest bank of elevators.

He was standing quietly, mulling his sister's attitude and his nephew's look of desperation, when all of a sudden a group of teenage boys who looked like the stoners that operated the ski lifts on Ajax began to gaze in his direction. Freddy looked down at the floor, considering the range of possible reasons why any group of people stare: His fly was open; they had seen him with Natasha and were hoping for another glimpse of her; mistaken identity. The boys were whispering to each other, looking back at him, and then whispering again. He saw them all laughing and shoving this one particular kid until they pushed him forward so that he was a mere inch from Freddy's face.

"Are you Freddy Feldman?" the boy asked while his friends all cackled like it was the funniest thing they'd ever heard.

"Yes," he said tentatively. It was then he noticed the embroidered bong on the boy's T-shirt.

"Dude, you're a rock star. Can we, like, get high with you tomorrow? There is supposed to be some sick ganja on the islands. You can get a hookup right on the pier. You would know that, of course."

"How do you know who I am?" Freddy asked, lowering his voice and gesturing with his hand for the boys to do the same.

A different kid stepped forward, with unruly dreads spilling out from a trucker hat.

"Dude, you're on the cover of *High Times*. Don't you know that? They said you have a fifty-million-dollar pot empire. How'd you do it, man?"

Freddy's eyes widened. The article wasn't supposed to come out for another week. And he'd never said a word about how much his business was worth. The reporter, who had looked no more than seventeen years old and barely took notes, had asked how he got his start in the business, what his favorite variety to smoke was, and to expound on the future of edibles. Freddy had opined on the environmental impact of the pot business and shared his views on legalization while the reporter gazed at him with admiration and awe. They'd never once broached the topic of how much money he had. Freddy wanted to pound his forehead

255

with the palm of his hand for being so naive. Natasha had told him he should hire a publicist to help guide him through the interview and liaise with the reporter, but he'd scoffed, saying this wasn't a *Dateline* exposé. At the end of the interview, he'd driven the kid to the train station, stopping off on the way for ice cream at the famous Paradise Bakery. Freddy had treated.

"I gotta go," he stammered, taking a few steps away from the group. He needed to read this article, fast, in the privacy of his room. The Wi-Fi on board had been spotty, but Freddy would storm into the central command station to get a fast connection if necessary.

"You gotta get high with us, man," another boy pleaded, but Freddy had already started flying down the hallway back toward the steps. "Weird guy," he heard someone utter.

He practically ran the entire length of the boat to get to his suite, arriving in a full pant. The door was propped open with a housekeeping cart.

"Discúlpeme, por favor. Necesito privacidad ahora mismo. Lo siento mucho." Freddy's Spanish was fluent now from conversing with the workers who tended diligently to his plants. Ironic that the Spanish now flowed from his tongue like a native lan-

guage when as a student he couldn't grasp a verb conjugation to save his life. He remembered his mother's anguished face while she tested him, the look of disbelief at his incompetence washing her in a grayish shadow. He was the classic student of life, simply unable to learn things unless they had a practical application. Unfortunately his parents had walked out of the movie of his life a long time ago and so they had no idea that a foreign language, writing, and especially math no longer gave him trouble. He could calculate the yield of each new grow house he acquired in his sleep. He could compare same-store sales month over month without even a computer.

"Yo voy a salir ahora mismo, Señor Feld-man," the housekeeper said and slipped outside with her cart. *"Voy a regresar más tarde con uno plato bonito con vegetales y caviar."*

Freddy dropped into the desk chair, his knee shaking. He brought his laptop to life, following a complicated set of instructions to tap into the ship's Wi-Fi, which included a thirty-digit alphanumerical string that looked like a nuclear code. He really should tell his niece and nephew about the complimentary Wi-Fi in the suites, since they must be suffering without it. Connectivity to the internet was certainly Natasha's biggest concern before she got on board, and since they'd set sail, she'd been updating her Instagram every hour with new pictures: glistening postworkout, at shuffleboard, smoking hot in her halter dress at the fiesta night sandwiched between two sombreroed waiters. Freddy typed "High Times" into Google and clicked over to their website and was greeted — no, petrified — by the sight of his own face. They had doctored the photo they took of him by superimposing a huge green marijuana leaf on the bottom half of his face, with a blingy dollar sign at the tip of each point. The headline read, in font large enough for the sight-impaired (or the very stoned), MARIJUANA'S MEGAMILLIONAIRE FREDDY FELDMAN ROCKS THE POT WORLD.

It was *not* what he was expecting. It was not what he wanted, not remotely. When the editor from *High Times* called him and asked if he would like to be interviewed for a profile, Freddy's first response had been no way. He wasn't looking for fame or glory. If anything, attracting the attention of the government or mainstream media was the last thing that would be good for his business. He operated on the up-and-up, but could he swear that all the workers in his

grow houses were legal? He hadn't personally checked every one of their papers. Was
he certain that every one of his transactions
was one hundred percent kosher? Many of
his deals were signed with Native American
farmers and which rule of law applied
wasn't always black-and-white. Then that
kid reporter showed up, looking at Freddy
like he held the answers to every one of life's
complicated questions in his brain, and he
found himself opening up in volcanic fashion. He and the reporter even smoked
together — Freddy rarely did that anymore,
but he thought it was important to convey a
belief in his product — and within an hour
Freddy forgot about the little tape recorder
set on the coffee table in his apartment log-
ging every word he said.

He put a cold can of Sprite to his forehead
and clicked on the link.

Frederick Feldman didn't plan to make a
fortune in the drug world. And when he
was sitting in a jail cell in Rikers Island,
wondering which of his "derelict" friends
would have the money to bail him out, he
hardly thought there was any future for
him at all.

Born to a traditional family on Long
Island, his father a well-regarded obstetri-

cian and his mother an office manager and homemaker, Freddy Feldman knew from a young age that he was made in a different mold than the rest of his family. His sister, Elise, attended a top medical school and graduated as valedictorian from their local public school. Meanwhile, Freddy was suspended so many times from school that his parents actually considered military school for him. He was, by his own account, a terrible student and a troublemaker.

"I just didn't care about school," he said. "The teachers were all annoying."

Freddy paused, thinking about Ms. Liness, his tenth-grade chemistry teacher. She was amazing. Funny, patient, and with a soft spot for him — even after his beaker shattered because he'd been dared by one of his buddies to add baking soda to the mixture they were cooking. Ms. Liness was anything but annoying. While she'd been forced to give him a C in the class — he hadn't helped her in that department after refusing to memorize even a fraction of the periodic table — she'd insisted on putting an insert into his report card detailing his many contributions to the class and his natural gift for science. Unfortunately his biology

260

and physics teachers didn't feel the same way.

Now forty-eight, Feldman speaks like a man half his age. His home, around which he toured *High Times* cameramen, is a modest attached condo about fifteen minutes' drive to the base of Buttermilk Mountain and to his biggest commercial venture, Mary Jane Market. It is not the home where one would expect to find the owner of more than a million square feet of grow houses, fifteen retail boutiques, and a majority stake in an overseas edibles distributor.

"I don't care about stuff really," he said. "My parents were into accumulating. They had to have nice cars and a fancy house. I'm wired differently, I guess. And they just never got me or what I was about." Feldman described his parents as "uptight" and "perpetually disappointed" in him.

Freddy could no longer stomach reading the article. It was too startling to see his words regurgitated. He sounded like a spoiled brat, not like a child who came from a loving home where his parents literally gave him everything. Of course he'd said a host of other things, he was sure of it. That

261

his mom was an amazing baker and that he used her recipe when he sold pot brownies in college. That his father took him to science museums when he was little, which piqued his interest in chemistry and agriculture. But somehow he just knew that the reporter hadn't captured those details, even in the later paragraphs. He forced himself to scan the rest of the article, a staggering five pages, which detailed the arc of his career. The convict he met in jail who told him about the opportunities in Colorado, his first investment (which tanked), getting a bank loan by pretending he was farming lavender, and so on and so forth.

He shut his laptop and lay down on the bed, waiting for Natasha to return. She'd read the article and make him feel better, putting salve on his wound like always. Nobody read *High Times* anyway, other than the die-hard legalization folks and the aging stoners. There was zero chance of any Feldman coming across this. But still . . .

He didn't like the things he'd said. There was no need for him to bring his family into the article at all. His upbringing was cookie-cutter upper middle class and, if anything, sickeningly privileged, and he should have steered the conversation to the present. He could finagle the best financing from bank directors and arrange cutthroat rates from his bong manufacturers in China, but he couldn't control a conversation with an acne-smeared intern whose jeans hung low around his ratty boxers? And besides, what was he complaining about? There were children in the most unfortunate of circumstances, with abusive parents or worse. His parents had grounded him often and their screaming could wake the dead, but he usually deserved it. His was hardly a sob story.

Freddy checked his watch. Two hours until the family reconvened for another group dinner. Fourteen hours until he could disembark in Sint Maarten and enjoy some time alone with Natasha. The boat was massive, like fifty circus tents combined, with just as much psychedelic distraction, but still he felt his family's judgment as clearly as if he were in a claustrophobic confessional booth with all of them. Things would be better on land, in the open air. He'd get through the around-the-world buffet tonight by imagining taking Natasha's hand and crossing the gangway bright and early tomorrow morning.

SEVENTEEN

"Okay, let's go through the questions one by one," Elise said, sitting with her legs folded in an uncomfortable crisscross applesauce on Darius's bed. Rachel had once shamed her for saying "Indian-style" — you'd think Elise had personally scalped someone — but ever since then she'd been firmly reconditioned into the more politically correct, nursery school terminology.

She tapped the stapled copy of the common application nervously with the eraser side of her pencil. In this bleak room without even a window, and with the mildly nauseating lull of the ocean, where would she and Darius find inspiration for a plan of attack for his essay? Elise tried to mask her feelings, but even she got hives from these ridiculously open-ended essay suggestions.

Think of a time you solved a difficult

problem and explain what you learned from it.

If you could have dinner with any three people, living, dead, or imagined, who would they be?

Describe an activity in which you feel so engaged that you simply lose track of time.

Sure, Elise had a ready answer for that last one, but it's not like shopping would make for a suitable college essay. And Darius's all-consuming activity was thinking about that trampy-looking girl in his grade, Marcy something-or-other. Yeah, she knew about his obsession. The way her son asked his friend Jesse "who all was going to the movies" and then waited with bated breath to see if he named Marcy. The way he turned around to have one more look at her before driving off with Elise, back before he had his license and she was still his on-call chauffeur. Oh, and she'd checked his email and gone through his entire search history on Google. It was what a responsible mother did and she didn't have two licks of regret about it. She appreciated that Darius was too guileless to clear his browser history. There were at least some perks to having a child who wasn't two steps ahead of you.

Back to the questions, she thought, looking down at the paper once again. There were seven different "prompts" and none of them were particularly inspiring. Elise gave her head a strong shake, reminding herself that she wasn't the one on trial, needing to cobble together enough positive qualities and persuasive reasons why College X should admit her. This was Darius's problem and she was simply stewarding him along, a combination proofreader and taskmaster.

"Anything jumping out at you?" she asked her son, who was sitting with his back to her at the desk, ostensibly to type up their ideas on the laptop. When she'd arrived at his room, he was lacing up sneakers, announcing without a trace of compunction that he needed to postpone their brainstorming session because Freddy had invited him to go rock climbing. What did her son think — that she was so desperate for the family to bond that she wouldn't mind if he put her off so he could hang with his uncle? Maybe if her brother was a different sort of person, the kind who would give Darius the much-needed swift kick his bum needed, she'd have acquiesced. But Freddy

266

was exactly the wrong influence around her son during this time — the boy who never grew up counseling the boy who still had a chance. Freddy honestly looked like a washed-up rock star with his silly hair, string bracelets, and vintage tees, though Darius probably thought it was cool. She could just imagine the conversation between the two of them, roasting her like a pig on a spit, giddy in their self-righteousness about being "laid-back." So when her brother came to the door, she had no choice but to swiftly dismiss him. Her plan for the day was to solidify an essay choice for Darius and offer him some direction, and then head straight to her parents' cabin to ask for the money.

It was going to be a lot to tackle in one day, she thought, thumbing the necklace she'd purchased earlier. She had had every intention of abstaining while on board the ship. Frankly she'd never expected there to be any opportunity to part with money once they set sail. But her daughter was embarrassed by her very existence, her son looked upon her as a maternal albatross, and her parents were on their own island — and, damn it, that crescent charm on the twenty-four-karat chain had looked so dainty and elegant and was just the pick-me-up she needed. Besides, she was mere hours away from solving her financial crisis.

"The first one," Darius said, his voice muffled. Ever since he was a baby, when Darius was tired, he'd chewed on things. It started with his thumb, until the doctor made them put some terrible-tasting ointment on it to discourage the sucking. Elise remembered the screwed-up face Darius would make when his delicious thumb disappointed him so. Undeterred, he moved on to a weathered lamb blankie, then pen caps, and now the strings of his hoodie sweatshirts. Was there an essay there? Something about adaptability?

"Okay!" Elise said a bit too enthusiastically. "What was the problem and what was your solution?" She rocked herself to standing on her knees, primed to tackle the six hundred and fifty words this beast required.

"Huh? I thought that was the one with the dinner guests," he mumbled.

Elise dived forward and swiveled Darius around to face her.

"Mom!" he yelled, having been thrown nearly off the seat by her force. "Calm down. I just got confused for a second."

"Darius, you need to focus. This is your future. If you don't get this application done, you won't go to college, which means you'll have about zero decent job opportunities. Is that what you want? To do nothing with your life?" She'd been hoping to avoid this didactic tack, having assumed that, stuck on the boat without his iPhone and no-good posse (yes, she knew that word!), Darius would buckle easily under her pressure. She didn't want to have to guilt Darius by talking about how much she and Mitch had put into raising him or to bring in Freddy as an example of what happens if a person doesn't focus from a young age. But her son was giving her little choice.

"But *you* didn't —" Darius started to say, but she noticed him catching the sentence in midair.

"I didn't what?" she said, wanting and not wanting to know what her son thought of her. She dug her nails into the mattress.

"You didn't read all the essay options yet. I'm pretty sure there's another one about how I'd want to change the world."

Elise unclenched her fists. Could that have been all he wanted to say? She didn't think so. The air felt thick suddenly, a stew of unfinished thoughts clogging the atmosphere. She wanted desperately to crack a window, but the kids were in an interior cabin.

"Right," she said briskly. "I didn't think

269

the world question was the right one for us. I mean for you. Speaking of the world, are you looking forward to the buffet tonight? I heard the sushi is arranged on a gigantic block of ice in the shape of a Shinto temple. And one thousand macaroons are stacked in the shape of the Eiffel Tower."

"Cool," Darius said, with about as much eagerness as a person sitting in the dentist's chair awaiting a root canal. She remembered taking Rachel and Darius to Epcot when they were in grade school, how they'd tugged at her hands to pull her toward the wonders of France, China, and Mexico. In Japan, Darius had convinced her to buy him a set of metal chopsticks that he repurposed as ninja swords. Rachel had looked so cute in her pink Mickey fez that they got at the Moroccan bazaar, proudly wearing the wool cap even though it was sweltering — Disney tickets were much cheaper in the summertime. As kids, Freddy and Elise had the luxury of going over Christmas, when the lines were long but the weather was mild and breezy. Well, so what, Elise had thought at the time. Sweating it out builds character. She'd let them stay up way past their bedtime so they could enjoy the fireworks show and swing back into France for a late-night crepe. There could be no greater joy than this, she had thought, taking in her children's sleepy faces, oversugared and over-stimulated so they looked nearly comatose. Mitch had taken her hand later in the hotel room and together they'd stood looking down at their best work, nearly moved to tears by the rhythm of their children's soft breathing and the way Darius, who always slept like a starfish, had his arm splayed across Rachel's stomach.

Ten years later, another world showcase, and things couldn't be more different. Her daughter was walking around with gluten-free faux-nola bars from Whole Foods because she'd heard from some undisclosed source that "cruise food is nasty" and her son couldn't muster up enthusiasm about anything on the boat other than spending time with his uncle. Had she too changed this much in the past decade, becoming a jaded, seen-it-all, done-it-all person? Was that why she was on a constant shopping spree, because she needed newness to invigorate her tired spirit? She made a mental note to email Dr. Margaret. If things were that simple, perhaps she could just dye her hair and become vegan and problem solved.

"Well, even if you think it's lame, try to put a smile on your face. Remember

Grandma and Grandpa are paying for this and I'd like them to believe you're actually enjoying it."

Elise wondered if he realized that what she was saying could apply equally to her, that she was officially the pot and not the kettle, though it was doubtful since Darius rarely seemed to consider anyone but himself. A symptom of teenitis, Elise hoped, and not a lifelong personality flaw. She shouldn't have freaked out at her mom about the beverage package or rolled her eyes during charades or taken a nap during the nighttime comedian's hokey act. Mitch was doing a much better job of faking it than she was, jumping up and down when he won twenty dollars at cash bingo, signing the family up for karaoke (which everyone refused — not only her), and complimenting the sloppy Joes at the lunch buffet while the rest of the family forked the ground beef with disdain.

"I got it, Mom," Darius said, and she had that awful feeling all over again, that she was as unwelcome in her son's life as another zit. God, his skin looked awful, she thought now inopportunely. She really ought to bring him back to the dermatologist, but she didn't want to trample on his self-esteem. He had to be bothered by it, though — his cheeks were so pockmarked he looked like a connect-the-dots drawing.

Elise glanced at her watch. She wanted to make sure she located her parents before dinner. Mitch had gone off to use the golf simulator for a few hours with a couple of men he'd met at lunch (imagine getting chummy that easily with perfect strangers!) so she knew she wouldn't stumble into him.

"You know what, Darius? Why don't you try to write two or three paragraphs on your own and I'll read it later? I think I'm cramping your creativity."

Elise rose quickly and left the room before she had to see the relieved expression on her son's face and hear his deep exhalation, ejecting their commingled air from his body. She wondered how many paces down the hall she'd make it before he snapped his laptop shut. She'd only made it three cabin doors down, but she could swear she heard the numbskull guffaw of the dad on *Family Guy* coming from the kids' room. She shook off the itchy scarf of her disappointment and took the stairs the five flights up to her parents' cabin.

"Mom? Dad?" Elise rapped gently on their door a few times but nobody answered. Her parents had said they were going to lie down after lunch in order to rest up for the Gala Around the Globe, the formal title for the evening's *fress*-fest. They were aging, Annette and David. Elise could see it in the bluish veins that ran just below the surface of their skin, the liver spots that could no longer be mistaken for freckles, and the curves of their spines that made it seem they were about to pick something up from the floor. They even walked differently, cautious and slow, always braced for a fall like they were roller-skating for the first time. They seemed to have aged about two decades since retirement, idleness sending the message to the brain that it ought to just shut down entirely. Should she suggest that the two of them pick up a hobby together? It didn't have to be something active, like tennis or golf, but maybe bridge. When Elise dropped Darius off at the community center for basketball or to swim, she passed room after room filled with elderly foursomes gathered around card tables, fluorescent lighting bouncing off the silver hair. Her mother played mah-jongg already, but that seemed to be the domain of the ladies. It didn't have to be a game at all. They could take up something entirely out of their wheelhouse: bird-watching, gardening, anything that would reignite their neural

274

pathways and spring some life into their brittle bones.

Her parents had been so worried for her after she quit medical school, concerned that she'd wither. It seemed to Elise that it was an eventuality for everyone and really just a question of when. Fortunately for her, raising Rachel and Darius kept her on her toes like a prima ballerina. At least it had until recently, when her role converted to backup dancer. Seeing her parents descend into old age was causing Elise to reflect on her own trajectory. After so many days of repetitive behavior — grocery shopping, driving carpool, preparing dinner — it had been easy to feel that she was standing still and not on a moving walkway. She pictured the entrance to Bloomingdale's at the Palisades Mall. The automatic doors from the parking garage opened onto the young, contemporary section with the hot designers and bright colors. She used to shop there, choosing wacky prints and daring higher hemlines. When did she make the decision to bypass that department and head straight for the A-line dresses and sensible pumps? Did it happen overnight or had it been gradual? There was the day she had been embarrassed to go to a friend's birthday luncheon in a one-shoulder pink blouse and had run inside the house to change. And the time when Rachel taught her how to snap a picture of her back with her phone and she'd suddenly noticed dimples of cellulite that she had no way of dating. It didn't matter when the total eclipse of her youth occurred. She could hardly remember what it felt like to be spry and energetic. It only came upon her in unexpected bouts of déjà vu, like when she heard a certain song on the radio or threw on her old Columbia Med School sweatpants.

"Excuse me, did you lose your room key?" came a sudden voice.

Elise whirled around and saw a short, brown-skinned woman wheeling a housekeeping cart. Her name tag read *Abeba, Papua New Guinea.* All of the staff on board wore name tags that stated their country of origin. Nobody was from America or even western Europe. It was mostly East Asia and Africa represented. She wondered what they must think of all these travelers, fretting about getting priority use of the ice-skating rink or front-row seats for the nighttime entertainment. Frivolous concerns for frivolous people, and she was maybe among the worst of the lot with her buy, buy, buy mentality.

"Yes, yes. Thank you so much." Elise leaned down to read the name again. "Abeba."

She didn't think twice about entering her parents' room without permission, much like she used to barge into their master bedroom as a child. Occasionally the door would be locked and by the time she was a teenager she knew what that was about. They had lived alone now for decades, but Elise wondered if their door was ever metaphorically locked anymore. She followed Abeba into the room, expecting to find her parents napping, explaining why they didn't come to the door.

She felt oddly small standing in her parents' cabin, the echoes of entering their private sphere as a child more poignant than she expected. The cruise was reinforcing how fluid her life was at this point: She was a child and a parent and neither role felt totally second skin. The labels were fungible, especially for her and Mitch, the only ones in the group sandwiched between generations — serving both roles simultaneously, feeling powerless in each position. They were the bread, the peanut butter, and the jelly, and it was exhausting.

"Need more towels?" Abeba asked.

Elise's mind wandered to the place where

she thought Papua New Guinea lay on a map. Far, far away from whatever radar blip their boat was now on the Atlantic Ocean, and far from any of the boat's likely destinations.

"Do you have children?" Elise nonsensically answered the housekeeper.

"Excuse me?" Abeba asked, handing Elise a stack of fresh-from-the-industrial-dryer towels.

"Do you have kids? Like me. I have a girl and a boy. They are on the boat too," Elise said, expanding on her question.

"I do. I have three," the housekeeper said quietly, and Elise regretted asking. Abeba's face shadowed as undoubtedly the faces of her babies came in front of her eyes. Elise saw a pink string tied around her wrist, worn and nubby, but strong enough that it could withstand a thousand showers without falling off. "I have three daughters. They are eight, six, and four. I haven't seen them in almost two years." Abeba's eyes brightened. "But I get break in four months and I see them."

"In time for Christmas," Elise said, smiling warmly.

"Oh, no, the holiday time is the most busy on the boat. I see them after. In the new year."

Elise blushed. That teacher of hers in medical school had been right. She never knew the right thing to say to people.

"Where is your family now?" Abeba asked. "This boat have everything for the lucky children."

Elise shook her head wanly and looked around her parents' empty room.

"I have no idea where my children or my parents are. Thank you for the towels."

Abeba nodded and walked off with her cart toward a neighboring cabin and Elise stood alone in her parents' room. She suspected Abeba was thinking that if she could have her family so close to her, she wouldn't let them out of her sight. But it's not that easy, Elise would have protested.

She opened the closet doors and saw the neat row of her mother's sundresses pressed against her father's khakis. The colors of her father's button-downs coordinated with her mother's wardrobe, every sundress having a corresponding men's dress shirt. Elise wondered if that could possibly have been intentional, or if her parents were just that uniquely in sync. She cringed thinking how much she was keeping from Mitch. They were metaphorically light-years away from matching sweaters.

Hanging at the end of the rod under a

protective layer of plastic, Elise saw a silver dress of her mother's that triggered an irritating memory. It was from the time Elise flew home for her cousin Sonia's wedding. It had been especially difficult for Elise to find something for the occasion. In order to spy on her children, Elise had signed up to serve hot lunch at their school, which had led to an unfortunate weight gain. This was back in the days before gluten was a thing and the PTA micromanaged the nutritional content of every dish served. Her children would float through the school kitchen, looking down at their trays or deep in conversation with their friends, and she'd be lucky if either of them even mustered a sign of recognition as she slopped mac and cheese onto their plates. After the lunch rush, Elise would fix herself a plate, tending to the comfort foods whose high salt and fat content elevated her dampened spirits, and she gained ten pounds before the school year was done.

Cousin Sonia's June wedding was a black-tie affair at the Pierre Hotel (*Can you believe how much your uncle Harvey is spending?* asked Annette about twenty times), and Mitch and Elise decamped to her parents' house, where it was an easy commute to the festivities. After days of searching, Elise finally found a gray satin dress at Ann Taylor that minimized her billboard of an ass and had enough beading on the torso to distract from her bulbous stomach. Mitch more than made up for what she was lacking, looking especially dapper in his getup (her ink-fingered husband wasn't one for tuxes normally). Moments before they were set to leave for the wedding, Elise, in search of lipstick, went downstairs and found Annette struggling with a bracelet clasp at the kitchen counter.

"Elise, I need help with this," she sputtered. "I can't find your father anywhere."

David, with his nimble surgeon's hands, used to be expert at things like threading needles for detached buttons and fastening intricate locks.

"Sure," Elise said, moving closer to her mother, who smelled of hair spray and perfume, an Annette cocktail that she suspected she'd be able to summon long after her mother was gone.

"Thanks, honey," Annette said, looking up at her daughter with gratitude crinkled in the corners of her eyes, which lasted all of two seconds. Quickly her face morphed into a menacing squint. "You've got to change," she said urgently, eyeballing Elise's gray dress with utter dismay. "We are twins."

"Mom, what are you talking about? Your dress is silver. Mine is gray. And who cares? They look nothing alike." Elise ran through the differences in her head: different hemline, sleeves versus strapless, lace instead of satin. Three major elements, she thought triumphantly, since Mitch always said it was important to put descriptions in triplicate. His rhetoric would often spawn a discussion over whether there should be a comma in front of the "and" between the second and third item in a list (the *Bee* was a no-comma place, whereas the Language Arts Department at Sacramento High was adamant about the comma, much to Mitch's chagrin).

"What else did you pack?" Annette asked, the unlatched diamond tennis bracelet now resting on a cellophane-wrapped plate of noodle kugel from dinner the night before.

"I flew across the country for this wedding with a carry-on and one garment bag. You have an entire closet full of gowns and cocktail dresses. Which one of us do you think should change? Assuming anyone needs to change at all, which of course we don't," Elise said. She remembered meeting Mitch's gaze. He'd come into the kitchen holding his bow tie, the last piece of his ensemble, hoping, like Annette had been, for someone to help finish his dressing. Life would be so much easier if people could be totally self-sufficient, Elise had thought. A world with eight billion uncomplicated tiny islands, each wholly self-sustaining. In the end, Elise *had* changed, into a dress of her mother's — a black silk column dress that was admittedly nicer and more expensive than anything Elise owned at the time, but which didn't do her hips any favors.

Elise moved to quickly shut the closet doors, when a wall-mounted safe inside the closet caught her eye. Without thinking, she entered the code her family used for everything from the home alarm system to the petty cash box at her father's medical office. As a child she had loved to look at her mother's jewelry. It wasn't an extravagant collection, but to a young Elise the gems had seemed as big as rocks, their colors more vibrant than anything inside a Crayola box. In particular, she loved trying on Annette's sparkling engagement ring, shaped like a pear, which made it look even bigger than it was. "Spready," Annette had told her once when she was playing dress-up with it. "Pears are very spready," which apparently meant the cut showed its size mainly on the surface instead of in depth. Elise now wondered if people too could be described as "spready." It was a rather apt adjective for the vacuous mothers Elise contended with back home.

Elise looked down at her own ring from Mitch, a half-karat round that had cost her husband a quarter of what his internship paid him the year he proposed, and thought about Annette's reaction when she first showed it to her. "Well, I suppose it's a nice starter ring," she had said, appraising the color and clarity of the diamond by the light of their living room window. Elise had never upgraded or thought to change it. Even with shopping as her modus operandi, the ring had sentimental value and she'd only taken it off twice in her life — before checking in to the hospital to give birth to Rachel and Darius. Besides, her fingers were squat, shaped like baby carrots, and a larger ring wouldn't be flattering.

She had now entered the familiar code onto the safe's keypad, but the lock didn't click open. Strange, thought Elise. If she were to need to enter her parents' house, would the alarm code she grew up with also no longer work? The notion was surprisingly off-putting.

She shut the cabinet doors, annoyed that her parents weren't in their cabin. How many chances would she have to get them alone on the trip? She noticed the boat's daily schedule, the *Deep Blue Digest,* on one of the nightstands and saw that "Makeup Techniques with Mary" was circled. So that was where her mother was. And her father had trotted along to hold Annette's pocketbook while she climbed into the tall cosmetics chair to get a new face. As Elise turned to leave, a glowing light from the bathroom caught her eye. She peeked inside and saw a line of pill bottles on the countertop, big ones slapped with overlapping labels that clearly held more important things than prescription-strength Dramamine. There had to be at least ten of them lined up neatly next to twin toothbrushes and a bottle of saline solution. Elise felt the inside of her stomach turn to sludge. So that was what this trip was about. Her mother was sick. It had been so out of character for Annette to want to celebrate her birthday in a big way that Elise should have known something was up.

She felt the hurt even before the panic, a too-hot beverage sliding painfully down her esophagus. Why hadn't anyone told her? Was it because her mother was married to a doctor, a retired one who had the time to monitor her care and take her to appointments? Perhaps. Elise would just be a nagging voice with nothing to add aside from the fragments she remembered from her medical textbooks that had zero practical application. Especially considering how geographically far away Elise had positioned herself from her parents. Nobody but she knew that Mitch had had an equally attractive offer all those years ago from the *Hartford Courant.* And that it was Elise who had made a point of talking about the California climate being so refreshing and had been the first to call a real estate broker on the West Coast. The guilt stung.

"Anyway, I think we should see what the kids want to do tomorrow. I'd like to just walk around the little town and maybe have lunch off the boat. We don't need to sign up for any of the excursions until later tonight. I doubt Freddy will join us." Elise heard her mother's voice coming from down the hall. She quickly jumped out of the bathroom before she had a chance to read the labels on any of the pill bottles.

"Sounds fine. Maybe I'll even do the nine-hole golf course if it's not too h—" David started to respond.

"Elise, what are you doing here?" Annette said, eyeing her suspiciously from the door frame.

"Nothing. I just wanted to talk to you guys

alone. And the housekeeping lady let me in. I thought you were resting. Can we talk?"

Annette set down a large shopping bag on the bed, labeled — as Elise had predicted — *Makeup by Mary.* Elise felt a swirling urge to peek inside the bag and to check the *Deep Blue Digest* for Mary's hours. Annette was radiant. Her skin looked practically airbrushed and the green in her eyes shone even brighter thanks to Mary's use of copper eye shadow. Elise realized how much unused beauty knowledge she had squirreled away, all those years of storing tips from Annette. Green and orange were opposite each other on the color wheel, and therefore made an excellent eye color/shadow pairing. For a sick person, she was ravishing.

"Of course," her mother said and her father gestured toward their tiny balcony. Outside, they sat on chaises and stared for a moment at the water. It looked like an endless sheet of steel blue tinfoil, shiny and crinkly and reflective of the sun in the most miraculous ways. Elise wondered if there were people on board with minds uncluttered enough to appreciate the vast beauty around them. And, if so, Elise wondered what it would be like to be one of those

people even for just a few precious moments.

"What's up?" her father asked, seeming to
grow impatient. His face bore the same
expression as when a woman's cervix
wouldn't dilate past seven, no matter how
much Misoprostol he administered.

"So, Mom, Dad, I've got some exciting
news that I want to talk to you both about."

And, just like that, the spigot was open.
Elise detailed her business plans, finding
her brain remarkably nimble. She was spewing statistics about the number of diabetics
in the United States, how food manufacturers were going to want to get in on the action, the way apps and medicine were an
inevitable marriage. She got so fired up
herself that by the time she got to the only
number that really mattered, how much she
needed to borrow from her parents, Elise
had convinced herself that Dia-Beat was
actually happening.

"Basically, what I need is fifty thousand
dollars to get this off the ground. And with
Darius starting college next year, we just
don't have it."

Annette and David exchanged uncomfortable looks. This wasn't what Elise had
expected. In her mind, broad smiles broke
across their faces, and her father all but

reached into his back pocket to hand over his wallet.

"What does Mitch say about all this?" David asked, looking, if Elise was seeing correctly, extremely tired. The boat had rocked erratically all night, like the sea was in a terrible fight with itself, only to calm down into the still blanket it was at this moment. Based on the chatter around the boat, for some cruisers the motion had lulled them into a trance-like sleep, while for others it meant tossing and turning all night. Elise had hit the bed like a lead balloon, but that was more on account of the margaritas than the motion of the ocean. So perhaps her father was just in the didn't-sleep-well camp. If only Elise had known, she might have waited to ask for the money. She and Freddy used to be afraid to ask David for anything if he'd pulled an all-nighter at the hospital.

"He doesn't know." She watched surprise, then worry, spread across the senior Feldmans' faces. They were probably thinking she and Mitch were getting a divorce. With all the disappointment Freddy had caused, her parents couldn't really take another blow. It made her resent her brother even more, the fact that she always had to be yin when she wanted to go yang.

"The reason Mitch doesn't know is that he *can't* know. Because of his job at the *Bee*." Elise expanded. "There are too many conflicts of interest. Which is why I can't get a bank loan either. Our finances are totally commingled and he'd know right away." She gave herself an imaginary pat on the back for adding in that spontaneous detail.

"Elise, your father and I need to talk about this before we can commit. I'm sure you understand," Annette said, smoothing out the linen of her capri pants, which had no wrinkles needing smoothing.

Elise didn't understand. Her parents could spend a bloody fortune to bring the entire family onto a cruise ship for a week of overeating and mediocre sightseeing, but they couldn't seed her business? Something that could change the course of her life and help sick people! It was incredible how quickly she was growing indignant over a fictitious scenario. Because what if it had been true? All that really mattered was that her parents weren't willing to help. They didn't believe in her anymore. She forced herself to take a Dr. Margaret breath. In through the nose, out through the mouth. She simply couldn't let her anger show. Not if she had a prayer of getting the money.

No, Elise needed to play the long con.

"Of course. I expected that. The only issue, though, is the patent. I know I'm ahead of the competition in terms of my software development, but others will catch up quickly. You know how this market is." Naturally her parents had *no* idea how the app market was. They had AOL email addresses. Assholes Online, her kids called it.

"Let's discuss this later," her father said firmly and Elise blanched at his tone.

"Sure. I'm going to go get ready for the around-the-world party. Can't wait to see that sushi ice sculpture." Elise managed to deliver the last bit without a trace of sarcasm. She got up from the chaise and headed inside, hoping to peek into the bathroom for another glance at those pill bottles. But her father slipped in before she could.

On the other side of the cabin door, Elise searched up and down for Abeba's face. She needed someone to remind her how lucky she was to have her family close, but the hallway was abandoned. Elise headed for the casino, where she thought Freddy and Natasha might be. She descended the grand, circular stairway, following the ding-a-ling-a-ling of three cherries lining up on slots and the swoosh of tokens collecting in plastic buckets. She said a silent prayer that of all the addictions that could have befallen her, it wasn't this. The scene in the casino was dismal, like at one of the budget hotels on the Las Vegas Strip. There was nothing sadder than the sight of an oxygen tank parked next to a slot machine, and so far Elise had seen three.

She scanned the psychedelic space, looking from the craps tables to the blackjack high-tops to the roulette wheels, but didn't spot her brother. Disheartened, she bought a vodka martini off a waitress in a sequined cropped blazer and took an unladylike swig. She was really rattled by her parents' hesitation about lending her the money. What a miscalculation to have assumed they would be thrilled. Instead they had hemmed and hawed, silently telegraphing each other not to commit to anything without a private discussion. Oh, yes, she had noticed the side-eye.

She supposed it had been unrealistic to expect them to fork over an immense sum of money without thinking it over. There was parity to be considered. While it was only a loan, what would Freddy think if he caught wind of it? And even though it wasn't likely he would ever find out, clearly it would take a toll on Annette and David's collective conscience. She ought to tell Freddy about the pill bottles. There wasn't much he or she could do, considering their mother was keeping her illness a secret, but Elise would certainly be upset if Freddy had been the one to find out and not told her. The problem was, she wasn't even sure what there was to tell.

It was possible things weren't as bad as she first suspected. Annette had participated in Zumba twice since embarkation, joined the fiesta night conga line, and found three mah-jongg pickup games, where her concentration was so sharp she'd won more than fifty dollars off her competitors — ladies from the Scarsdale canasta league. Elise ran through the encyclopedia of possible diseases that could necessitate so many pills. Annette's hair was fuller and glossier than ever, so Elise ruled out cancer. Her skin glowed like she'd just stepped out of the spa, so the liver wasn't a likely trouble spot. The heart. It had to be something cardiovascular. Her mother was a rubber band ball of anxiety, who got worked up if she couldn't find a parking spot or the brisket didn't brown evenly. The heart was a muscle, and Annette had flexed and squeezed the hell out of it for too many decades. Those pill bottles must contain blood thinners, beta-blockers, statins, and whatever else was necessary to keep her ticker from giving out.

Still, even if it was something manageable, Freddy should know about it. When they were little kids riding in the back of the family Buick, poking, prodding, and kicking each other until one of them cried for help, Annette was prone to dramatically announcing that one day she and David would be gone and all they'd have was each other. It didn't stop the name-calling, but it did curb the physical attacks. Come to think of it, why hadn't she or Mitch ever repeated the same to Rachel and Darius the second they heard the first cry of "he/she touched/ruined/broke my phone/sweatshirt/racket"? Guilt worked, better than any form of grounding. Mitch was Catholic, for crying out loud. His mother loved to kiss the cross around her neck and talk about the eventual day her kids would bury her. To think Annette thought she had nothing in common with Marie Connelly!

Elise did one last three-hundred-sixty-degree twirl around the casino floor. Satisfied that Freddy wasn't there, she set her drink down on a cocktail table and decided to check the teen arcade, where her brother was just as likely to be sitting on one of those pretend motorcycles, racing against a ten-year-old.

But as she headed for the stairs, she spotted someone that looked a lot like Natasha, pulling the lever on a giant "Price Is Right" wheel and laughing like she'd just heard the best joke in her life. The arrow must have lined up on a big prize because Natasha — yes, it was definitely her in the platform slides and jeans skirt — started jumping up and down. A man in a white naval uniform, tassels on the shoulders and gold buttons gleaming even from a distance, gave Natasha a high five and a more-than-amigos shoulder squeeze. The guy was tan, muscular, and rugged and basically Freddy's physical opposite in every way.

Hmph. Elise stalked over to Natasha, finding herself suddenly overcome with a protective force that she'd thought she could only muster for her children.

"Where's Freddy?" she asked, tapping Natasha's shoulder from behind.

"Elise, I didn't see you were here," Natasha said, clearly startled. "Freddy's working in the room. This is the captain of the boat, John McPherson."

"Pleasure to meet you," said the captain in a sportscaster's deep baritone. "I've been having a lovely time with Ms. Kuznetsov in

295

the casino. I'm about to show her the bridge, if you'd like to join us."

"The bridge is where the captain steers the ship," Natasha said to Elise.

"I knew that," Elise said, even though she didn't. "I think I'll pass. I need to find my brother. What's your cabin number?" To the captain she added, "My brother is Ms. Kuznetsov's boyfriend." Captain John seemed unfazed by the revelation.

Natasha glared at her.

"He's on a very important conference call," Natasha said. "I don't think it's a great time to go up there."

Conference call! Freddy! My God, how stupid did this woman think she was? His last gig that Elise was aware of was hawking juicers. She'd only bought one because she felt sorry for him. Come to think of it, where was that thing?

"Fine. I'll wait for dinner," Elise said, casting an "I'm watching you" stare at Natasha before she turned away.

Elise gave her watch a quick glance. Two hours until dinner, where she'd be forced to gush over the moo goo gai pan, pickled herring, and baklava so that nobody realized anything was wrong. Tomorrow morning was their first disembarkation. She planned to call Michelle Shapiro and beg one last time for a lifeline. If she needed to photograph herself sitting in a lifeboat begging for mercy, so be it. Some people did better with visuals.

EIGHTEEN

Mitch was about to tackle the twelfth hole at Augusta National when he remembered why he didn't play golf. He had a bad back, an inflamed rotator cuff, and stiff hips, all of which were activated the moment he took his first drive. After an hour trying to suppress his winces, he bid adieu to the other guys in the golf simulator — a periodontist from New Jersey, a contractor from Ohio, and a schoolteacher from the Bronx — and went back to his room to take a monster dose of Advil and lie down.

They all wished him luck as he took off, because he hadn't been able to resist talking about his professional plans. There was something about the four of them wielding nine irons that made these perfect strangers feel like lifelong friends, and within minutes of exchanging pleasantries he was running projected numbers with Joseph Lichter, who taught AP calculus in a rough neighborhood. Joe had pointed out a couple of flaws in the assumptions he'd made in his business model, which Mitch had pulled up on his phone, and it seemed he needed an extra thirty thousand in start-up capital if he was going to be able to keep the website afloat before the ad revenue kicked in.

Rubbing his aching shoulder, Mitch lay in bed with his laptop. He'd hoped Elise would be there. It had been so long since they'd had a midafternoon quickie. The last time was when he had been promoted to managing editor. His predecessor had had a debilitating stroke and twenty-four hours later Mitch was named the highest-ranking employee on the editorial side of the *Bee.* He'd driven home and found Elise in the kitchen making chicken cutlets, her hands slicked with egg yolk. In the adjacent den, Darius and Rachel were doing homework with the TV on.

"Come upstairs," he'd said to Elise, surprising her enough to make her drop a slab of raw chicken into the sink. He had pulled her by the tails of her apron, locked the door to their bedroom, and made love to his wife in a way reminiscent of the first few years of their marriage. He loved thinking back to that day, almost as much for the way he and Elise had celebrated as for the cause célèbre. Now with just one more year before they became "empty nesters" — though he took exception to the negative connotation of that phrasing — Mitch couldn't begin to comprehend why Elise was so broken up about it. The freedom to enjoy each other anew, to rule their household once again, it was a future condition with enough mass to more than fill the void created by the absence of dirty socks on the floor and empty orange juice containers on the counter.

Regrettably, he had found that Elise was not in their room and his text messaging didn't work on the boat. Instead he was scrolling through his emails, which were mostly work related, closing matters he had to attend to. One email caught his eye and caused him to jolt up in bed. It was a Google alert. The subject was Frederick Feldman. Years ago, he'd set up a web alert for every member of the Connelly and Feldman families. It wasn't as stalkerish as it sounded. All journalists set notification alarms for the things they cared about: stories related to their beats, favorite sports teams, companies in which they held stock, and, naturally, family members. The Feldmans rarely appeared. Until recently, the only articles bearing the Feldman name were about unique deliveries David had performed (quintuplets in a snowstorm; a singleton on an airplane). More often, he came across articles about his youngest brother, Mikey, who was a little too familiar with the holding pen at the local precinct in downtown Chicago, where he lived. Mikey was a regular in the Crimes & Misdemeanors column of the *Chicago Sun-Times.* But Freddy? Never had Mitch seen his name before.

Mitch opened the email, convinced it was going to be about a different Frederick Feldman. The article was from *High Times.* Mitch hadn't seen a physical copy of the dope rag in decades, not since it used to be distributed for free on campus, and he had no idea it was still around. The headline forced him into a goggle-eyed gape. Multimillionaire? Pot world? Freddy? This was the person who lamented the prior evening that the resident manager wasn't dealing with the roaches in his condo. The same guy who once asked Mitch for seven hundred dollars in secret so he could pay back a bookie. Had it been that long since Mitch had wired the money to a Western Union in Colorado? Come to think of it, he'd had to bring Darius along because Rachel and Elise were at a birthday party, and if memory served him correctly Darius had been wearing his Little League uniform. He remembered the teller saying, "Good luck, slugger," and Darius just staring back blankly.

He read on with urgency. If the article was to be believed, his slacker brother-in-law, the underdog for whom Mitch had always had a soft spot, was halfway to being a hundred-millionaire. Well, that certainly explained his high-roller situation on the *Ocean Queen.* And his smoke show of a girlfriend. Elise clearly had *no* idea. Nor did anyone else in the Feldman family.

A selfish thought popped into Mitch's head. What if Freddy became a seed investor in his literary journal? He clearly had the money and it would lend his brother-in-law the legitimacy he possibly desired. "Publishing investor" certainly had a more elevated ring to it than "pot magnate." But Elise. Was there any chance she would approve? His wife wasn't one to put her hand out for anything, especially not charity from her brother. He shrugged off the momentary high. *High.* What Mitch wouldn't do for a toke right about now . . .

The article delved into Freddy's upbringing and Mitch almost glossed over it, familiar with the Feldman family roots, until he noticed the pull quotes: "Uptight . . . demanding . . . materialistic . . . goody-two-shoes sister." He had to make sure nobody ever found out about this article. Obviously Annette and Elise didn't read *High Times,* but there was the possibility that the Associated Press would reprint it. The legalization of marijuana in Colorado and other states was a popular news story and the pot business was a burgeoning sector of the economy. The idea that a college dropout (actually an ejectee, even more salacious) could amass tens of millions of dollars from some marijuana farming and a few retail stores was staggering. Hell, if he was still at the *Bee,* he'd want to write about it. Mitch would have to use his connections to get the online version of the article scraped of the Feldman family commentary. What was his brother-in-law thinking saying those things? It must have been the work of a wily reporter. Mitch knew all too well that a skilled journalist could pull confessions from a reticent interview subject with a few simple tricks. He himself had done it many times, aware of the collateral damage but needing to do his job.

It was almost time for dinner, but Mitch didn't feel the least bit hungry. Now he had two secrets from his wife: quitting the *Bee* and the Freddy affair. Where *was* Elise? Mitch wondered again. And where the hell were his kids? They'd been practically MIA since the boat set sail. He had seen Darius earlier in the day playing foosball with an Asian girl, but when he'd waved at him, his son had pretended not to see. Or maybe he really hadn't seen him. It was impossible to tell with teenagers. They always had the same vacant look in their eyes. Rachel was hardly any better. The curly-haired princess he used to bounce on his knee was now bored by everything, consistently seeming a low level of pissed off.

Mitch got up from the bed and reached for another Advil. His bad shoulder was now the least of his concerns. Rubbing his temples, he ran through his mental Rolodex. Who did he know who could connect him to an editor at *High Times*? Maybe the new kid who'd just joined the *Bee* from the *Denver Post*. It was a good place to start. He combed through his emails and tried to find the newbie's contact information.

NINETEEN

1700 hours. 200 miles to A. C. Wathey Pier, Sint Maarten.

Julian looked at himself in the mirror before heading out the door. In his slim-fitting sports jacket and expertly tailored gray slacks, he looked — in his own estimation — rather good. Young, professional, maybe even hot. He was glad he'd let his trainer Aldo back into his life. After a tough breakup that involved multiple long emails explaining why he simply didn't have the time to work on his biceps and draw out the six-pack Aldo claimed was lurking beneath the shallow layer of soft flesh on his torso, Julian had decided to give the gym routine another go. And it seemed to be paying off. Certainly Roger thought so, attacking him more than usual. Their sex life waxed and waned with no apparent rhythm. Could it possibly be tied inversely to the girth of his waistline? Doubtful, since Julian was the more shallow of the pair. Once his middle sister, after too many daiquiris, had said he had the depth of a kiddie pool.

Tonight was the boat's around-the-world gala, a signature dinner on all *Ocean Queen* cruises that took gluttony to the next level. Forty different countries were represented and many of the guests seemed hell-bent on sampling from at least thirty of them. It wasn't normally his favorite night on the boat. Instead of getting on stage to introduce a show or warm up the audience before the comedian came on, he was meant to flit around the room making small talk with the tables. He'd have to be a chameleon all night, ready to talk hunting with the Southerners, football with the Texans, finance with the New Yorkers.

But tonight was different.

He was truly looking forward to stepping into the Grand Ballroom and gliding among the tables, slowly making his way toward one in particular. Two dozen of the most attractive gay men Julian had laid eyes on in a long time were on board the ship, an affinity group out of Los Angeles called Buoys II Men. They were, collectively, the best thing to happen to a Speedo since Ryan Lochte. And for some reason, every one of them had wanted to get a picture with him on the first night following the cabaret show. Julian had to admit that his bawdy jokes had been spot-on at the late show. He reassured himself that Roger wouldn't mind. They were both gay men, flooded with hormones pent up from years of hiding who they were, and it didn't really matter where they got their appetite. As long as they came home to each other for dinner. They were fully committed to one another. He just couldn't figure why Roger was so desperate to make it official.

Julian *was* admittedly jaded about marriage and family, it was true. The boat did that to him — to everyone who worked on board for more than a few years. You couldn't help feeling depressed by the married folks knotted for too many years, sentenced to travel everywhere together like salt and pepper shakers. On the first night or two, Julian might see the conversation flowing as they clinked glasses and toasted the week ahead. But by the third or fourth night, the chemistry seemed about as bubbly as the soda from the always broken tap in the staff lounge. Because there was only so much that a chocolate fountain, the premium beverage package, and the rhythmic waves could do for a marriage that had run its course. And don't get him started on the kids — whiny brats, most of them.

An email from Roger popped up on his laptop as he was about to leave his cabin. The subject line: Miss me? The body of the email read: Hope you're having fun! xoxo, R. As if Julian had time for fun when he was at sea. With three thousand passengers milling about, clawing their way into buffet lines and demanding the utmost in service and entertainment, and he marionetting it all with his clipboard, megaphone, and walkie-talkie, free time was a laugh. This particular moment was probably the worst of all. He was already running late to the dinner and needed to run a sound check with the World Vibrations band. Why couldn't his partner realize how much damn work it took to run things on the ship?

"These are the Feldmans," Lindsay whispered in Julian's ear after consulting her seating chart. "Grandma's b-day. She's Annette. Two are VIP. Rest are regs." He nodded and his assistant discreetly slipped away.

"And how are we all doing this evening?" Julian asked the Feldman family, who were seated at a round table, poking at the lingering food on their plates.

They didn't look overly enthusiastic, unlike the other tables he'd visited. The evening had overall proved a success. World Vibrations got a good chunk of the guests onto the dance floor and the ice sculpture had serendipitously fallen to the ground during the African drum circle so barely anyone heard the crash. Buoys II Men, as Julian had predicted, had been delighted when he came over to their table to greet them and had insisted he join them in a shot of tequila. As he licked the salt from the rim of the glass, he caught a glimpse of a tall man in a velvet blazer who looked quite a bit like Roger carefully dipping strawberries into the chocolate fondue. Julian blinked hard twice and he was gone. No more alcohol on the job for him.

"Oh, just fine," said the older woman. Birthday grandma. "Lovely evening."

"What are everyone's plans for tomorrow when we reach Sint Maarten?" Julian asked. It was an easy entry point of conversation, especially on the night before the first disembarkation. This was when everyone was anxious to get off the boat and didn't realize yet the hassle of the onshore excursions — the piling into vans, the interminable queues, the overpriced nature of everything. By the next night, everybody would be grumbling about the same thing: *Two hundred dollars for a thirty-minute snorkel? Seventy-five dollars for a tour of a maritime museum the size of a walk-in closet?* It was as predictable as the seasickness.

Julian looked at the teenage boy. *Gimme something I can work with, kid.*

"I dunno," Darius said, woodpeckering a chopstick. "I guess the parasailing."

"We're doing the downtown tour by van," Annette said, pointing at herself and the older man at her side. Julian wondered if he should tell them how painfully boring the driving tour of the island was. Sometimes letting guests in on boat secrets was very effective, because most people liked to feel like insiders, but other times it backfired completely and it was like filling in the customer complaint forms for them.

"I told you I may just stay on the boat," the gentleman said to his wife.

"And you?" he said, turning to the middle-aged woman, who was in the midst of yanking the chopstick out of the teenage boy's mouth. "Stop it," he heard the kid snap.

"Oh, I'm just going to walk around a little on my own. Get a feel for the place," she said, tucking her hair behind an ear nervously.

Julian turned next to the man at her side, who was topping off his wineglass with the

310

bottle chilling in the ice bucket. It was the cheap swill, the boat's "signature" chardonnay, but still known to get the job done.

"How about you, sir?"

"I'm going swimming with the dolphins with my daughter," he said, breaking into a broad smile as he looked at the teenage girl across from him.

"Actually, Dad, I decided to sign up for stand-up paddleboard lessons. Forgot to tell you," she said, popping a piece of sushi into her mouth. "I want the cardio." The father looked crushed. Julian wished Roger were here to witness all this domestic bliss.

"And you?" Julian addressed the platinum blonde who was busy taking pouty selfies.

"I'm going to do the sunrise yoga on the beach." She reapplied lip gloss and clicked another selfie.

"You are? I thought we were spending the day together." A different middle-aged man, scruffy and dressed in a T-shirt and unbuttoned flannel, looked at her with disappointment. "I guess I'm deep-sea fishing by myself, then."

"Wow. Looks like everyone is headed in different directions. Lots of exciting plans," Julian said. "You will all have a lot of catching up to do at tomorrow night's black-tie dinner." He waved to the family and set off

311

for the neighboring table. One hundred and thirty-two more tables to greet, Julian thought, signaling to Lindsay to cross off the Feldman family from his diagram.

"You must be the Taylor family from Minneapolis," Julian said, approaching the next group and putting a friendly hand on the shoulder of the man seated at the end of the table. "Tell me, what's everyone planning to do tomorrow?"

A little girl about six years old piped in with her plans to go banana boat riding and Julian regaled her with a tale of him losing his bathing suit when he fell off a banana boat. The table loved it. "More stories," the little girl begged. "Tell us more stories."

This was so much easier than thinking about pesky Roger.

TWENTY

Darius's plans changed by the time they reached Sint Maarten.

Some time ago, Marcy had posted a picture of herself parasailing in Jamaica. Okay, fine, he knew exactly when she'd done it — last April, with her two sisters, and Marcy had been wearing a neon green bikini. When he saw it on the list of excursions, Darius had immediately decided that was what he would do. Then when he got back home and was back with the group, he'd casually bring up parasailing, pretending that he didn't remember Marcy had ever done it, and surely she'd chime in with her own experience. And just like that, they'd have a "thing."

But he was late in signing up, as he was in everything in his life, and the parasailing was sold out. Downcast, he walked into the teen lounge after the around-the-world dinner with his mind made up to just stay on

313

the boat the next day. He didn't dare ask Rachel to join her in the stand-up paddle class. For one thing, if he was anything on a paddleboard like the way he was on a skateboard, Rachel would mercilessly tease him. Secondly, if she'd wanted him there, she would have asked him to join. He'd given her lots of openings, following her around like a shadow, whenever he could even find her on the boat. She'd been a slippery eel and Darius couldn't understand why. The boat seemed entirely lacking in the stuck-up overachievers she normally rolled with. Those kids were probably all saving orphans or building huts, like Rachel had done over spring break. He'd hoped once she got into Stanford the pole might come out of her ass, but so far it seemed firmly wedged in.

"Whaddya doing tomorrow?" came a familiar voice when Darius was sitting on a white leather couch in the arcade, nursing a flat Coke. He looked up and saw Angelica, this time wearing a Highland chess team T-shirt tucked into a pair of bell-bottoms. Under an illustration of a knight, the shirt read:

Five, Six, Seven, Eight
First You Check and Then You Mate!

"Um, not sure," Darius said. He dropped the straw he'd been grinding with his teeth. Supposedly his habit of chewing on things was a nervous tic that he would outgrow, at least according to their pediatrician. And Darius was pretty sure the doctor's instructions were for his mother to ignore it, not yank out objects from his mouth. "I wanted to parasail, but it's sold out."

"Come with me, then. I'm going to take the snorkel class. The rest of my family is going to the aquarium, which is so dumb. We live in Maryland, near one of the best aquariums in the world. I guess they really like fish."

Darius hadn't considered where she was from. Highland sounded like a town that could be anywhere, from Michigan to New Hampshire or Nebraska. And Angelica, with her chess and debate team shirts, was the sort of teenager that existed in every high school. Darius couldn't begin to imagine why she took even the slightest interest in him. She must be very lonely. Maybe she thought he didn't realize she was a dork back home. The nerdy kids in overnight camp were like that, always trying to reinvent themselves for four weeks and praying nobody from back home outed them as losers.

"No more practice SATs for you, then?"

"Nope. I got a 1550 on the last one so my parents decided to let me out of my cage." Without asking, Angelica sat down next to Darius on the couch and grabbed the Coke from his hand. "Flat!" she said, wincing after taking a sip.

"Your cage?" he asked, bewildered by her sharing his beverage.

"I shouldn't complain really," Angelica said. "My parents aren't terrible. I guess they just don't want me working behind the counter at a dry cleaner's for the rest of my life."

Darius laughed. "Ugh, can you imagine?" He literally couldn't. When he was a kid he used to love to go along with his dad to pick up the dry cleaning. He found the rotating rack and the metal pole with the hook used to get the clothes down endlessly fascinating. But now? He'd be miserable working in one of those places, hot and smelly and customers complaining about their clothing getting damaged. That was about ten rungs below working in the lifeguard chair, where at least he got sunshine and could ogle girls in bikinis.

"I can, actually. My parents own a dry cleaning store. They are really proud of their business, but like — they want me to be a rocket scientist or something. I work there every day after school. I get my homework done while I'm there and then I'm free to just chill out when I get home."

Darius couldn't look at her. He was such an ass having assumed she'd been joking. But how could she be on a trip like this? he wondered. He knew it was costing his grandparents a pretty penny. His mother had made him thank them each, like, a dozen times already.

As if reading his mind, Angelica said, "My uncle is paying for this trip. He's my mom's sister's husband. They love to show off. He's got a huge electronics exporting business in Beijing. My family never takes vacations. My parents can't close the dry cleaner's and the only people who work there are my mom and dad and me and my brother."

"Who's working there now?" Darius asked.

"My cousin on my dad's side of the family. But my parents are freaking out about it. I had to train him on the register for, like, five days before he figured it out."

Darius nodded.

"So, you wanted to know about my 'cage'?" Angelica asked, putting "cage" in air quotes. "When my parents first moved to this country — I was six and my mom

317

was pregnant with my brother — their first landlord suggested that they play Scrabble to help them learn the language. I learned right alongside them and I guess I was pretty good at it, you know, for an immigrant kid. I'll never forget, the landlord said to my parents, pointing at me: *This one is smart. She could end up at Harvard.*"

Darius recalled a memory. When he was in middle school, he had a Harvard T-shirt that Grandpa David had bought him after he'd delivered a lecture at their medical school. It was super soft and came down to his knees and he loved to wear it around the house on weekends. Rachel, who'd been given a Harvard notebook and was walking around the house with it everywhere, scribbling mysterious notes that she'd cover up if anyone walked by, had been quick to point out to their parents that the shirt was the closest Darius would ever come to Harvard. "Maybe Grandpa will give a lecture at Hartford and get you a more appropriate shirt," she had said. Darius didn't even know what that was supposed to mean, but he was certain it was an insult. And his parents hadn't done anything more than say, "Rachel," in their cautionary voices.

Later that night, Darius had stolen the notebook out of Rachel's room while she was sleeping and looked inside. All he found were lists of her homework assignments and he wondered why she went to such effort to shade them from view. At the time Rachel had been in tenth grade and he was in eighth. She was as opaque as a paper lunch bag and he felt like cellophane. Or so it had seemed to him until he cracked open her notebook. Then he realized she was just desperate to appear like she had secrets worth guarding.

"So then what happened?" Darius asked Angelica.

"My mom said, what is Harvard? And the landlord — this old white guy named Terry McDougall who I don't think even went to college — proceeds to explain to my parents that if you go to Harvard, you will be rich and your life will be perfect. You should have seen my dad's eyes. They looked like golf balls. I have no idea what they did after that — whether they asked friends for advice or went to our pastor or maybe even looked up Harvard in the library — but after that they were on me nonstop. Piano practice, chess team, debate, gymnastics, learning more languages. I became this kid they programmed like a microwave. She-will-go-to-Harvard-no-matter-what," Angelica said in a robotic voice.

"What about your brother?" Darius asked.

Angelica's eyes glazed over and she blinked twice quickly.

"Theo's severely learning disabled. He goes to a special school. So it's all on me, Angelica Harvard Lee, to get the family out of Chinatown." She reached over and took another pull of Coke from his straw. He must have looked at her wild-eyed because she said, "Oh, the germs? You have no idea the things I've come into contact with at the cleaner's. Let's just say people come in needing some very personal stains removed. I guess I've just become numb to it."

"So you think you'll get into Harvard?" he asked.

"Well, I'm an immigrant with near-perfect SATs, I work a part-time job every day, and I'm captain of the debate, chess, and field hockey teams at my school. So, I'd say I have a fifty-fifty shot." She gave a wry smile.

"What do you mean? You're perfect. I mean, you sound perfect for a place like Harvard."

"Who knows? There are a million other kids just like me, except maybe they do everything I do but they're blind or their parents are in jail. That's a real thing, trust me. I read this article about how colleges love to admit kids whose parents are incarcerated."

"Or maybe they're blind *and* their parents are incarcerated. Oh, and they started a school for Tanzanian refugees," Darius said.

"I don't think Tanzania has refugees. But yes, the perfect applicant would be a kid who started a school for Tanzanian refugees who are blind and their parents are incarcerated," Angelica said, throwing her head back with a maniacal laugh that shook her bun loose. "That's pretty much who my guidance counselor tells me I'm up against."

"Sounds like mine. Does she also hide behind the cafeteria making out with the assistant principal?"

"No, mine sneaks cigarettes in the faculty lounge with the gym teacher, Mr. Nostril. That's really his name."

"Ours is Mr. Strong — that's just what he makes us call him," Darius said, but suddenly he felt a weight returning to his shoulders. Marcy flirted openly with Mr. Strong, asking him to time her sprints or for tips on how to stretch her calves. She joked about how the gym teacher totally wanted her and Darius would think, *Well, you do lead him on.* Nobody dared say it out loud, though he couldn't imagine Jesse wasn't thinking the same thing. Marcy was one of those girls that nobody called out on stuff.

"You okay?" Angelica asked and Darius fretted about how totally incapable he was of maintaining a poker face.

"Yep, fine. I think I'll do the snorkeling with you. Will you come with me to sign up? I'm not sure where to go," he lied, looking down at his untied shoelaces, yellow and loosely looped through his checkered Vans.

"Sure," she said, pulling him up to stand. He was surprised by Angelica's forwardness, drinking from his straw, touching him. "But you need to tell me at least something about yourself after I just gave you my autobiography."

Darius jammed his thumbs into his back pockets. Where to start? His bitchy sister giving him the slip? His shopaholic mother? Or maybe his wayward uncle? Then there was finding his grandmother inexplicably weepy at the sail-away party.

"My mom has, like, a crazy shopping problem. I saw, like, hundreds of bags in our attic and she doesn't know that I found them."

"That's about your mom. Tell me about *you*," Angelica said, *superciliously.* Of all the SAT vocab words, that was his favorite for no particular reason.

Darius groaned. This girl was worse than the common application.

TWENTY-ONE

Natasha had been upside down for three minutes already, but still she felt all her energy pulling her down. She was supposed to invert her feelings by performing Sirsasana, but even with the blood rushing to her head and her lips swollen stiff, she was still pissed at Freddy.

She rolled gracefully out of her pose and took a big gulp of kombucha. She was doing yoga amidst about a hundred other women and a group of delightfully cute gay men, all from the boat. She recognized some of them from the fitness room on board and gave them pleasant nods. Natasha was a yoga fanatic and held a teaching certificate that she never used, preferring the act of massage and finding the pay better too. But still, she knew she stood out in the class as one of the best. She saw others take notice of her perfect Bakasana and the way she effortlessly transitioned in Vinyasa without even breaking the rhythm of her breathing. She could stay in this class forever, where nobody looked at her like they thought she was a clueless little girl. People came up to her during the break to ask her for pointers. If only her boyfriend would follow suit.

She had told him at least a dozen times not to grant the interview to *High Times* without hiring a publicist first. How did she know? First of all, basic common sense. Second of all, her friend from the St. Regis, Lucy, who worked as a concierge, was a former daytime television actress. At one time she had a pretty good gig on *All My Children* playing somebody-or-other's mistress and there were no immediate plans to kill her off by a poisoned martini. Lucy gave an interview (her first ever) to *Soap Opera Digest,* where she accidentally spilled the beans on how the show's season would end and also made a few badly timed jokes that made her seem, incorrectly, like she was a gun enthusiast. Her contract was shredded faster than the cheddar at Taco Bell, which was why Natasha was certain that Freddy shouldn't go into the interview without some coaching and a third party present to help steer the conversation. But did he listen to her? Nope. He'd all but patted her on the head when she suggested it.

And then, after the fallout, did he come apologizing to her after the article was published, outing his financial status (with surprising accuracy) and blazing with all those terrible quotes about his family? No, he did not. Instead, he came bounding into the gym and actually pressed pause on the treadmill while she was running at seven miles per hour, nearly causing her to fall flat on her face. He ranted about the reporter and the editor and blamed everyone but himself. And instead of saying he regretted the things he'd said about his family, he just kept repeating over and over that he hoped they'd never see the article. Maybe it went without saying he was remorseful. Natasha sure hoped so.

Her frustration with Freddy aside, she still wanted all of the Feldmans to take her more seriously. David had hardly spoken to her, other than to randomly ask if she'd be interested in participating in a study related to early detection of ovarian cancer that supposedly his former colleague was conducting. She was pretty sure it was his fairly inelegant way of determining her age, since he made a point of saying that the study subjects had to be between the ages of twenty-two and twenty-nine. Annette had barely looked in her direction for more than

326

two seconds, instead either focusing on her compact mirror or staring off forlornly into space as if waiting for someone to ask her what was wrong.

And what about Elise, with her haughty protectiveness of Freddy when she came upon her chatting with the boat captain? Freddy's sister clearly thought she'd stumbled upon some illicit scene and had a visceral reaction of outrage on her brother's behalf, as if it was her place to suddenly look out for her brother when she never had before. Natasha could have cleared up the whole matter easily — suite guests were entitled to a meet and greet with the captain at the time of their choosing and Natasha had scheduled this appointment in advance of boarding with the concierge (officially called their "wish granter") who was assigned to manage their stay. Freddy, at the last minute, had bailed and she'd gone off to meet Captain John by herself. He was a charming guy and very handsome. He was also happily married and delighted in showing Natasha about four dozen photographs of his children. Of course the endless iPhone slideshow had occurred before Elise had stumbled onto the scene, acting like she'd found them in flagrante delicto. And Natasha had felt like it would make everything worse if she clarified why she was hanging with the captain. She certainly hadn't missed Elise's face when Freddy announced he had upgraded rooms.

Rachel was nice enough at least. They had really hit it off in Aspen a few months earlier and she'd been hoping to re-create their camaraderie on board. Freddy's niece was probably the only one in the group who thought she had anything valuable to say, even though they hadn't really delved past the Kardashians and the wonder of dry shampoo yet. Darius was a cute kid — reminded her a bit of her own younger brother. When she bid good-bye to everyone this morning before setting off on the yoga van, she saw him walking off in a different direction with a cute girl about his age, both of them carrying towels from the boat. She couldn't help herself — she'd darted over to fix his hair and pick a flaky remnant of morning croissant off his T-shirt. Darius had given her an embarrassed but appreciative grin.

That left Mitch, who didn't seem half bad, though when she'd bumped into him in the espresso bar the prior evening he'd been writing the strangest things on a napkin:

The Unwrinkled Raisin

"What's that?" she asked, surprising him. He looked up at her in alarm, like she'd caught him watching porn, and quickly obscured the list with his palm.

"It's nothing," he said, putting the napkin into his back pocket. "I was just . . . just . . . it's a long story. Want to sit down?" He pulled out a chair for her and, reluctantly, she took it. With the way Elise had looked at her in the casino, she could only imagine how she'd feel about Natasha having coffee with her husband. Especially because that evening Natasha was dressed, even in her own estimation, rather scantily. Their suite had free laundry service, but all of her sensible leggings and exercise shirts had been terribly shrunk in the industrial dryers. Perhaps she'd invest in a sweatshirt, even if it said *Ocean Queen* across the back. She had the *Happy Birthday, Annette* hoodie, in which she was tempted to hide out, wrapping up her exposed skin with the soft fleece, but she wouldn't risk upsetting Freddy's mother all over again. Not to mention that she couldn't possibly commit the same crime against fashion twice in one week.

"Why not?" she said, sitting down across from Mitch and taking a sip of her skim cappuccino. "The coffee is terrible on this boat, isn't it?"

"The worst," Mitch agreed. "The food in general has been pretty unbearable. I should have stayed away from the sushi, but I'm a sucker for a spicy tuna roll."

"Freddy and I go to Matsuhisa all the time. You know, Nobu's place?" Natasha said. "Like, sometimes three times a week. My mercury level is so high I could probably be a thermometer."

It wasn't her place to elaborate on how the two of them could afford to eat at such an expensive restaurant regularly. This was Freddy's family and his business, but she was starting to feel his instincts weren't as great as she might have thought when they first started dating and just the sight of his spreadsheets and land maps impressed her.

"Anyway, I think I'll head to bed," Natasha said. "Good luck with your list." She saw Mitch's lower jaw open, as though he was about to explain, but then he just gave her a friendly wave good-bye.

"Did Elise get anything good, by the way? At the Golden Nugget. I saw her shopping this morning, and she seemed to clean up pretty well." Natasha had turned back toward Mitch, innocently taking another sip of her cappuccino.

"Huh?" Mitch said. He was already reaching for the napkin in his pocket. "I have no idea what she bought."

Natasha reflected now on Mitch's reaction last night: best described as utterly unfazed. Perhaps she was wrong about Elise. But she was not wrong about Freddy and the fact that he should have used a publicist, or at least had her sit in on the interview. She knew *some* things.

The yoga teacher announced the break was over. Natasha wiped the sweat from her brow and assumed tree pose. It was a calming position that would resettle her insides after the inversion. She needed to get a hell of a lot more zen before she got back on board and had to put on a freaking gown for the black-tie dinner, which she already knew was going to be a mentally taxing evening. The Feldmans certainly were an impenetrable bunch, a family of hard-shelled turtles, and it was tiresome to be around a group of people who so clearly wanted to be left to their own devices but also needed to be liked and respected by everyone.

331

Table conversation the prior evening had been stilted and forced, and so Natasha had decided to venture into neutral territory by asking everyone what they thought of their food. Boy, did that make the Feldmans come alive! Annette's fish was too dry, David's steak overcooked, Elise's chicken rubbery, Freddy's salad wilted, Rachel's bread (because that was all she was willing to try) was stale, Darius's cheesecake was moldy, and even Mitch chimed in, complaining that his scotch was watered down. The group of them had transitioned from awkward silence to an animated dialogue in seconds. Natasha had never heard a group of people so capable of analyzing whether the bread crumbs on the mac and cheese tartlets were over-salted. Tonight's nine-course dinner was sure to be a doozy, but at least there'd be dialogue.

Before departure, Freddy had tentatively decided to tell his family about his business on the last night of the trip, but with the *High Times* article out there, she doubted that was still in the cards. If he announced he was one of the largest pot producers and retailers in the United States, who wouldn't go right back to their room to Google him? So it looked like the best Natasha could hope for was that they might add the weather to the fascinating repertoire of dinner conversation, since she simply couldn't take listening to Annette ask again how the boat staff could have the nerve to serve such lumpy mashed potatoes. Natasha had half a mind to fill out a comment card apologizing on the Feldmans' behalf.

As if reading her mind, Julian, the cruise director, came into Natasha's sight line. He was nearly incognito in the back row of the class, his face shaded by a neon green visor. She waved at him spontaneously. Julian waved back with a smile.

When the class was over he walked toward her with a boat-issue royal blue towel slung over his shoulder.

"Rosalie is the best teacher on board. She used to have her own studio in Los Angeles before we stole her," Julian said. "Did you enjoy the class?"

"Loved it," Natasha said. She studied his kindly face. He didn't seem to place her with the rest of the Feldmans, at least not obviously. "I'm going to take her full-day in St. Lucia when we dock there."

"How are you enjoying the trip so far?" Julian asked.

"Um, it's great. I love the boat. The magician at teatime was amazing. And the gym is really nice. I love that there's a Peloton."

She tried to think of other positive things to say. If she complimented the food, she wondered if it would sound disingenuous. Or was it worse not to say anything at all about the meals, considering what a big part of the cruising experience they were?

"You getting enough to eat? Rubber chicken doesn't seem like your thing," Julian asked.

Phew. Natasha relaxed.

"I sweet-talked one of the line cooks at Docksiders into making me green juices every morning," she said. "So I've been getting by."

"I'm on my way to a decent coffee shop on the island if you want to join me," Julian said. "We can talk sun salutations. Or not."

Natasha thought about it briefly. She'd love to go with Julian and have a break from any Feldman-related business for the next few hours. But she knew her place was back on the boat, calming Freddy, shoveling him out of this mess.

"Wish I could," she said. "But I'll walk you there."

TWENTY-TWO

Elise stepped off the boat and sucked the fresh air into her lungs. All that recycled air clearly hadn't been good for her or anyone else in her family. Instead of her parents quickly acquiescing to her request, they'd frozen. Mitch was as distracted as ever, scribbling notes for work on scraps of paper every time she turned around. So much for him not seeming to care about being absent from the *Bee*. And her kids, if it was possible, looked even more glazed than normal. It was amazing how a boat so big could still feel suffocating. The way everyone was desperate to get off, it was as though they'd been crammed in a stalled elevator for the past forty-eight hours.

She hadn't signed up for any of the excursions because all of them required getting piled into a van and shuttling somewhere else as a group, and she was sick of feeling like herded cattle. What Elise needed was some time alone, even if it meant she'd be wandering aimlessly around Philipsburg, Sint Maarten, for eight hours before the boat set sail for St. Lucia. She had almost decided to leave her wallet in the cabin safe. It would be healthier for her to cut this leather limb of hers loose for the day, but in the end she decided it wouldn't be prudent to wander around a strange place without identification and some emergency money.

Her plan was to find a café with dependable Wi-Fi and contact Dr. Margaret. She desperately needed to vent. The only problem was that an hour would hardly be enough time to cover the latest developments: her mother being sick, Freddy pretending to be a baller, Mitch the most distracted she'd ever seen him in his life, Darius's college essay word count still at zero, and even reliable Rachel dressing like one of the cabaret performers from the adults-only show.

She stood outside on the pier for a moment staring at the gigantic moorings tethering the *Ocean Queen* to land. The boat rocked gently to and fro in the calm waters of the Caribbean but remained anchored to within three feet of the dock. It made her think of her children and the way they must see her, as the rope tethering them to home when their place was really on the open sea.

She turned her back on the vessel and headed away from the water. Around the port there was a smattering of touristy shops peddling seashell picture frames, beaded jewelry, magnets in the shapes of flip-flops and sand toys, and Sint Maarten spirit gear. The vibe around the port was very Bob Marley, steel drums pulsing somewhere in the distance and dreadlocks a popular local style, but even she knew he was from Jamaica, not here. Elise soldiered past the stores where salespeople stood in the doorway beckoning her with offers, pretending like the coffee shop she saw in the distance had ions that were pulling at the metallic strips on her credit cards. She made it, and opened the doors to a charming, though unair-conditioned, bakery with a sign advertising Wi-Fi at the rate of five dollars per hour. Well, not everything could be free, Elise reasoned, and she couldn't expect to spend an entire day off the boat without parting with any money. She pulled out her wallet, noticing that the stitching was already coming loose.

Elise ordered a bran muffin and an iced coffee and found a seat at a small table in the back. She pulled her laptop from her beach bag. Dr. Margaret wasn't on call twenty-four/seven, but Elise sent her an urgent email requesting a live chat session for sometime during the day. It was only nine in the morning, and therefore too early to reach her banker — the other desperate call she needed to make — so she decided to take a stab at drafting the opening paragraph for Darius's essay. She hadn't been able to sleep well last night and while she tossed and turned she had thought about the essay prompts, trying to channel Darius, or at least the plausible thoughts of any given teenager.

The essay topic that stood out to her the most was the one about the people she'd like to have over for a dinner party. Mealtime in the Connelly household was a sacred thing. Before Rachel left for college, it had been the only part of the day where the four of them were together for longer than a ten-minute burst, and there was something about the chewing and the passing of dishes that relaxed everybody. For a long time, if Elise had been asked which three people she'd like to share a meal with, she'd have picked Mitch, Rachel, and Darius. Now she wasn't so sure. Was she really that desperate to watch her kids pound away at their phones? Did she really need to hear Mitch utter his perfunctory "delicious," his adjective of choice no matter what she made? She considered alternatives: the medical school professor who thought she was personality challenged, so he could see that she'd done all right in the end, or Michelle Shapiro, to show her banker that what she lacked in financial management skills she more than made up for with her chicken française. And then Freddy came into her mind. They had shared thousands of meals together as children but hadn't sat down at the same table to eat consistently until this trip. She wouldn't mind having him to herself, to find out what the hell he'd been up to for the past decade and check if he was genuinely okay, though she was probably too late to be of any help to him. And that was when it hit her. If she were to write an essay where she could choose any three people to have at her dinner table, she'd pick the people who she'd had the opportunity to help in the past but hadn't done so. To make amends. Freddy would top that list.

Of course the theme of recompense wouldn't remotely work for a teenage boy — certainly not hers. She chuckled at the implausibility and then Googled "teenage icons" and started jotting down ideas. Some famous downhill skier whose legs had been amputated below the knee came up. She decided that should definitely be one of Darius's picks.

"This seat taken?" came a familiar voice. Elise looked up to find the cruise director standing over her, carrying a tray overflowing with dishes: oatmeal, a croissant, juice, and a fruit salad — not a ringing endorsement for the ship's cuisine. He was wearing spandex and a tank top instead of his white uniform and it had taken a moment for Elise to place him from the night before.

"No, no," Elise said, moving her beach bag off the empty chair opposite her. She looked around the tiny café and saw it was the only empty seat. How thoughtless of her to prop her bag on it like it was a person. Is that how elevated she was treating possessions these days? She'd be sure to mention that to Dr. Margaret, who had already responded that she could Skype at noon. Elise would have to go back to the boat for that, which wasn't a big deal. There was only so long she could loiter in this restaurant or stroll through downtown Philipsburg, which according to a map posted outside, was about three streets long. She couldn't imagine what the heck her parents would see on the van tour.

"Thanks," he said, placing his tray on the table. "You're from the boat, yes?"

"Guilty," Elise said, flattered he recognized her out of three thousand passengers. Then she remembered the lanyard around her neck with the cruise line printed on it.

"I'm Julian, the cruise director. You might not recognize me without my megaphone."

"I know who you are," Elise protested.

"Get a workout in this morning?"

"Yes. Just took a fabulous yoga class. You ought to try the three p.m. if there's still space. Have you been enjoying the trip so far?" Julian added three Splendas to his oatmeal. She remembered testing artificial sweeteners on rats during her first summer internship in medical school and recording all the negative effects, but she decided not to caution him. Score one point for having EQ!

"Oh, yes," Elise said brightly. "It's incredible." But something in her eyes must have conveyed the opposite.

"You can tell me the truth," Julian said. "I won't take offense. Honestly, you'd be doing me a favor by giving me some constructive criticism."

Elise considered Julian. He had gentle eyes, which he focused on her exclusively. She couldn't recall the last time anyone had

341

looked at her like that — without seeing everything else in the background or mentally running through their to-do list. Sure, sometimes Mitch trained his gaze on her this intently, but that was only when he had certain intentions. From what Elise could size up about Julian, there was no chance he had those same thoughts about her.

"The cruise ship is great. I had my doubts about how three thousand people could be fed and two thousand cabins could be cleaned and one thousand people could be corralled into a conga line, and yet, you manage to pull it off with aplomb." Elise was proud of herself for being so gracious and for not letting her foul mood pervade their interaction. It certainly wasn't the cruise director's fault she was in the seventh circle of hell. And Julian, with his earnest face, tidy gelled hair, and double dimples, was hardly the punching bag she had in mind.

"Well, I don't do it alone. We have thirteen hundred in crew. If the guests don't properly line up to conga, I blow a special foghorn and it's all hands on deck until they do," Julian said, giving her a wink.

"Have you worked on the boat long?" Elise asked. Julian looked like he was about her age. She couldn't remember the last conversation she'd had with a contemporary that didn't revolve around the children. She was sick of the logistics: where to park for the SATs and what time to pick up from the winter dance and what the going rate was for a calculus tutor.

"Almost eleven years," Julian said. "I started out as a concierge. It was an easy way to see the world. Moved my way up the ladder and here I am now, master of ceremonies." He looked mildly self-conscious and Elise had the urge to speak out of turn. She wanted to tell Julian that it was nobody's business what he chose to do with his life. She wondered if he had parents who were disappointed in him, who'd hoped their seafaring son would become a marine biologist instead of the judge of a blindfolded pie-eating contest, which was on tomorrow's schedule. But she held herself back, realizing she was probably just projecting. Come to think of it, Julian didn't actually seem embarrassed.

"Anyway," Julian said, collecting his empty cup of oatmeal and piling the rest of his food into a to-go bag, "it was nice to talk to you." He produced a card from his wallet. It read, *Julian Masterino, Cruise Director, the* Ocean Queen, *Paradise International,* and underneath, in smaller italic font, it said,

343

Where Everyone Is Treated Like Royalty.
"You too," she said, sad to see him go so quickly. "I really am having a fabulous time. You're doing a marvelous job."

"You're on with family, aren't you?" Julian asked.

"What gave it away?" Elise asked.

"A sixth sense," he said. He pulled mirrored sunglasses from his pocket but hesitated briefly. For a moment she thought he would sit back down and continue their conversation. Julian looked like he had something on his mind. But why would he choose to confide in her, a woman he didn't know, who had chosen to be alone in a random café instead of being with her family? "I like your necklace, by the way," he added.

Elise's hands floated to her collarbone. "Thanks," she whispered, the shame of her splurge at the Golden Nugget lodging in her throat.

When Julian was gone, Elise reached for her cell phone and dialed Michelle Shapiro's office number. After four rings, voice mail took over. Elise left a breezy message asking for a call back. She flipped open her laptop again to take a crack at Darius's essay. She'd never let him submit her words — what a terrible example that would set

— but it wouldn't be cheating if she just drafted an example of an essay for inspiration, right?

She decided to fortify herself with another snack and looked up at the menu printed on a mirror behind the counter. Underneath the specials, written in white chalk, someone had added in bright pink: *It's Satur-Yay . . . Have dessert!* Until then Elise hadn't realized it was even a weekend. Of course Michelle hadn't picked up the phone. And she certainly wouldn't be calling her back until Monday. Because of the vacation, Elise was completely losing track of the days of the week. The feeling of being unmoored to a schedule was startling. Was this what it would be like when she no longer had a child living at home? Normally, she could tell the day of the week just by the things Darius had strewn around the house: gym clothes on Tuesdays and Thursdays, electric guitar for practice on Mondays, skateboard in the foyer on weekends. Plus his unzipped backpack, which he always left with crumpled papers spewing all over the couch in their den, meant Monday through Friday. She thought about Dia-Beat. It was pure fantasy that she could start a tech-pharma business at this point in her life, but she'd need to do something regimented once

Darius left for college. Otherwise she'd go crazy, living in a world where Mondays felt like Thursdays, which weren't that much different from Sundays.

She looked back at her computer screen and felt a wave of writer's block, which triggered a sympathy for Darius she hadn't yet experienced. Rattled by her inability to come up with even a decent first sentence, she gathered her things and dropped them into her tote bag, wondering if it was too late to perhaps join Mitch on his dolphin adventure. She'd picked up on how disappointed he was when Rachel bailed on him and stupidly hadn't offered to go in her place. For so long she had prioritized her children and, because her husband was such a mellow, understanding man, she'd relegated him to the bottom of the totem pole, knowing that he'd forgive her if she made Darius's favorite chicken dish instead of his or skipped the *Bee*'s holiday party because she was chaperoning Rachel's high school dance. Now that it was going to be just the two of them soon, she hoped she had been right in her estimation of Mitch. He was a complacent person by nature, never eyeing a neighbor's new golf clubs with envy or complaining when it rained on his day off. And while life was about to dramatically change for her as the primary caregiver, for Mitch things would roll along at mostly the same clip. Busy as a *bee,* he'd joke when he walked in the door and she asked him how his day was.

Elise looked out the window of the café and saw a cloud in the shape of a heart. It was positioned over the cruise ship docked next to theirs, an even bigger and flashier boat named *Jewel of the Sea,* its bow painted with gigantic rubies, emeralds, and sapphires. She shifted her gaze to the portion of sky above the *Ocean Queen.* It was cloudless, just a wash of blue, and so if Elise was hoping for a sign of encouragement, she was out of luck.

"Can you hear me?" Dr. Margaret shouted. The audio component of FaceTime was working, but the video had yet to connect. Elise was nervous. She and Dr. Margaret had never shared this level of intimacy before. There was a barrier of anonymity that was about to be broken when they saw each other's faces. Another thing for which she could be judged. She'd fixed up her hair in advance of the call and swapped her white T-shirt for a more vibrant turquoise.

"Yes," Elise shouted back at her unnecessarily. "I'm here, Dr. Margaret." Elise had the laptop propped on a pillow in her lap, because despite everything rational she'd learned in medical school, she still couldn't imagine it was a good thing for a hot battery to sit on her ovaries. She chastised her kids every time she saw them holding the cell phone to their ear instead of using earbuds. Sometimes she awoke in a cold sweat from a dream where she saw Rachel crisscrossing the length of the Stanford campus with the phone to her ear. That's when she could sleep at all. Since menopause, her uterus had descended on her bladder like a lead balloon, and she barely got through a REM cycle without popping out of bed.

Dr. Margaret's face appeared suddenly and Elise was startled by her appearance. She looked so normal. Pretty, really. A middle-aged woman with a severe auburn bob and a straight row of bangs, rimless glasses, and shimmery pink lipstick said, in a placid tone, "Hello, Elise." She had excellent teeth. Elise wondered where her patterned blouse was from. She had no idea where the doctor lived, but she was guessing, based on her smart haircut and fashion choices, it was somewhere coastal and warm. Elise glanced at her own face, a tiny rectangle in the upper-left-hand corner of the screen. Somewhere, wherever Dr. Margaret was, she was seeing the screen in reverse. Elise's face magnified and her own in miniature.

"Thanks for doing this with me. My computer is on the fritz so I need to use FaceTime for our session," she continued. Dr. Margaret was seated at a desk, behind which was a full bookcase, the kind that looked scholarly and not just a landing place for objets d'art. Elise removed the air quotes around "doctor" in her mind — Margaret was for real. Looking back, it was insane that just a few months earlier Elise had considered digging out her medical school textbooks and refreshing herself on addiction theory. Just as pediatricians shouldn't treat their own children, it would have been totally irresponsible for Elise to attempt to cure herself. Besides, as her father was always quick to point out, she had never actually earned her M.D., let alone developed any specialty in psychiatry.

"How's it been going on the trip? Have you practiced the breathing we discussed?"

Elise appreciated that Dr. Margaret didn't dive right in with the obvious question: Have you shopped? She had a gentle way about her. Elise's former professor would have given her high marks for bedside manner. She ought to ask Dr. Margaret for advice on how to handle Darius. There had to be a less aggressive way she could badger her son about his essay. After her failed attempt in the coffee shop to put anything decent together, she was committed to being less pushy. It wasn't so easy to put pen to paper. Hell, it was partially why she'd gone to medical school. The political science and history majors were always writing papers, and there was no question she'd rather be in the lab filling pipettes than scrambling for words. Mitch's ability to channel his thoughts so eloquently into the written word had been part of his mystique. Come to think of it, why the hell was he not the one managing Darius's essay?

"Five counts in, ten counts out," Elise said, demonstrating now with a deep inhalation.

"And is it helping?" the doctor asked.

Elise looped her thumb through the chain of her necklace and angled it toward the camera's eye.

"I see," Dr. Margaret said, but she did a remarkably good job at masking her disappointment. What a skill it was to have the face of an actor, unlike Elise, who found it nearly impossible to smile at the family meals. "Well, you couldn't imagine you wouldn't face setbacks in beating this. Especially considering you are in an unfamiliar setting, surrounded by family, which can be stressful."

"My banker won't extend another line of credit to me. Darius may not be able to go to college next year. I asked my parents for money and they didn't exactly jump at the chance to give it to me," Elise said.

"You were honest with them?" Margaret asked.

"Not exactly." Elise decided not to get into the particulars. There was no need to explain the depths of her machination, not when she and Margaret were face-to-face. She'd save Dia-Beat for a typing session.

The boat foghorn suddenly sounded, the three short blasts used for nonemergency notifications.

"What in heaven's name was that?" Dr. Margaret asked, removing her glasses. She had lovely dark blue eyes and Elise admired the way she'd shaded them in plum tones. In the background Elise saw picture frames scattered throughout the bookcase, pictures of teenage boys skiing and surfing. Margaret was about Elise's age. Could they, would they, be able to become friends? Elise resisted the urge to ask her where she was based, though she wondered if maybe Margaret had been in California all along, that the website she'd used to find a therapist had actually paired patient and doctor by the proximity of their routers.

"Hang on, I need to listen to the announcement," Elise said.

"Good afternoon, cruisers. For those of you not out on excursion, we have a special treat," barreled a husky voice through the boat's intercom. "We are discounting all swimwear at the Beach Hut by twenty percent for one hour only. Who needs a new bikini?"

"Elise," Margaret cautioned, having heard the announcement, "you don't need this. You are in control. Not the salespeople, not the store, not the clothing. You say you're losing control of everything in your life. That your children don't listen to you. Take charge now. Have agency for your actions."

"It's hard," Elise said, starting to weep in front of her new friend. She'd never once cried during a previous session, but somehow seeing Margaret made her situation more tangible. The doctor was becoming another person she felt like she was letting down. "I have to end the session early, Dr. Margaret. I'm not feeling very well."

"Elise, stay with me. We still have twenty more minutes to talk. How are the children enjoying the boat?"

"Oh, I don't know. They don't really speak to me. Darius seems to have made a friend. Rachel is distant. Nice to everyone but me, pretty much."

"And your parents?"

"The same, though I suppose I should tell you that my mother is sick. I was in their room — it's a long story — and I saw all these pill bottles. I'm not supposed to know. At least I know what this cruise is all about."

"Well, I think you can forgive yourself the necklace incident. You have a lot on your plate. People say it's good to switch venues when you're planning a big change — in your case, returning to a normal relationship with money and shopping — but you're not at a peaceful rehabilitation facility. You've relocated but taken all your daily stresses with you. I think we should revisit our discussion about a stay at an addiction center. There are many in Northern California. With all those wineries . . ."

"Do you live in Northern California?" Elise asked, a little too excited.

"It doesn't matter where I live, Elise. But no, I do not."

Elise's face fell. She was embarrassed, but not as much as she was disappointed.

"Dr. Margaret, I really don't feel well. I'm

not going to the store, I promise. I just need to reschedule the rest of our call. I'm so sorry." Elise clicked the red button on the FaceTime icon before Dr. Margaret could protest further, watching the pixels of her face compress until there was nothing to see but Elise's home screen — a picture of Darius and Rachel at the beach from a lifetime ago. She closed the laptop and curled up in a fetal position. If her parents didn't come around within the next twenty-four hours, she was going to come clean to Mitch. Maybe he could work something out with his publisher, like an advance on his salary or a loan directly to Darius. She was running out of options and the window in which she could keep her secrets to herself was shrinking.

TWENTY-THREE

Rachel learned very quickly that she had terrible balance. One hour into the stand-up paddle lesson and she'd barely been upright for longer than twenty seconds. All the middle-aged women who were in the class with her shot up on their boards, paddling confidently so far toward the horizon that they became tiny blips in Rachel's view.

Who knew SUP (stand-up paddleboard) was such a craze among the mommy set? She shuddered at the memory of her mother trying strippercise a while back, the (thankfully) quick-passing fitness fad that swept through Sacramento. The SUP instructor was a hot guy in his twenties with a thick Australian accent named Nick. He took Rachel's hand so she could plant her knees on the board, which was the starter position, and then pulled her waist up to standing. All she felt under his touch were the pillows of flesh on her hips. Nick didn't seem to mind. In fact, she thought he might be holding on to her a little more than necessary.

"Don't worry, love," he said encouragingly when she couldn't move the oar from her right side to her left without falling. "It's not your fault. A lot of the cruise people can't keep their balance because their equilibrium is off from the rocking." Rachel doubted that was true. She had always been clumsy, tripping over tennis balls at practice and unable to jump rope to save her life. Her mother had been a fine athlete once upon a time, but all she'd inherited from her were those damn wide hips.

"I've got to do this," Rachel said, determined to keep up with the old ladies spreading white foam in their wake. She squeezed her abs for better control. Her spin teacher said the core was the nerve center of the body, but maybe it was time to stop taking the bulk of her advice from a woman whose sole goal in life was to consistently maintain eighty rotations per minute while doing arm curls. "I'm good now," she said, paddling hard three times on the right.

"All right, darling, you got it," Nick said, and he swam off to help a ten-year-old kid.

But Rachel didn't have it. When she tried to switch to paddling on the left, her body refused to play along and she fell sideways off the board and crashed into a rocky part of the ocean floor, scraping her left thigh badly. I'm outta here, she thought, tugging her board by its handle to shore and leaving it in a pile for Nick to load onto the van. Cold, wet, and freckled with sand, she walked into a hotel on the beach and pretended to be a guest. She figured the bellman would get her a cab and prayed it wouldn't cost more than she had in her wallet.

She missed Austin terribly, especially in that moment. Unlike the boy-men on campus who took her for pizza and then insisted on going dutch, Austin was a real grown-up who made reservations and had a bank account. They had only been dating for a month at this point, but she felt differently about him than anyone else she'd ever been with. He was so much wiser than her past boyfriends, who belched their way through Sunday night football and thought they were cool as hell because they vaped. Austin was the kind of guy who read *The New Yorker* for fun. He watched foreign films and seemed to genuinely like them. On the weekends, he wore skinny jeans and soft T-shirts, though at work he never deviated from classic gray trousers and an array of finely made button-down shirts, usually with a subtle check pattern.

She and Austin hadn't communicated since she'd boarded the boat and it was killing her. Her parents had been clear that they were not to sign up for the forty-dollar-per-day internet package. Rachel knew it wasn't just about the money. If their devices worked, both she and Darius would be largely checked out. Her parents' desperation to connect with them was palpable. Her father nearly cried when she announced she didn't want to see the dolphins! As if they weren't spending enough time together already.

Rachel had rather erroneously thought not speaking to Austin for a few days wouldn't be that big of a deal. The relationship was in its nascent stage and she had believed it could be a good thing for Austin to miss her a little bit. After all, they were both spoiled, seeing each other at the law firm every day. But as the days at sea dragged on, Rachel was finding the lack of communication excruciating. Austin had been on a similar boat and he had told her she would be so occupied with the meals, shows, and nonstop activities that he would barely cross her mind. Apparently on his cruise, Austin had come in second place in a *Jeopardy!*-like game show. Rachel loved all the random knowledge he had tucked under that thick head of hair. She didn't like to think about him taking one of these trips, though. Austin had done the cruise thing only once before, with his wife.

It wasn't as bad as it sounded. Austin was still technically married, but he was in the (very) early stages of a divorce. Jenny, his wife (oh, how Rachel hated that word and wanted desperately to plant an *e* and an *x* in front of it), was not making things easy. While Austin made a good living as a seventh-year associate at the law firm where Rachel was interning, there wasn't much to fight over. Still, to hear Austin tell it, Jenny wouldn't be satisfied until she possessed all of his belongings, right down to his underwear. Thank goodness there were no children.

Rachel wasn't the cause of their split. Austin was already living in a rented apartment above a bicycle shop when Rachel started her internship. She was assigned to paralegal on a case he was working on and was utterly clueless, which led to a lot of her knocking on his door, feeling foolish and asking for help. One night she stayed at the office very late, well past the time when the evening janitors plowed through the halls with their industrial-strength Lysol, to help

Austin sort through a sky-high pile of documents that needed sticky notes. A large part of her job, it turned out, involved Post-its. When they finally finished and walked outside together, she blurted out that she was hungry. They walked to a diner and ordered eggs and fries and tuna sandwiches, comfort foods that didn't spell romance in the slightest. But something was there. Even though it was nearly midnight when they finished their dinner, when the waitress asked if they wanted dessert, they both said yes simultaneously.

A week later, there was a Post-it peeking out from under her keyboard. It said, "I like you." She knew Austin's handwriting as well as her own, having combed through his notes for the past month, loving the way he never dotted his *i*'s or crossed his *t*'s. It was rather irreverent, for a lawyer.

When they first kissed, Rachel still didn't think it would lead anywhere serious. Austin was thirty-two. She was nineteen. The specter of her parents' disapproval appeared to her as waves crashing against the shore, relentless and perpetual. But she did it anyway, started seeing Austin. They met after work at his apartment and, on the weekends, she told her parents she was going to see friends, but really she would pile into his car and they would do day trips to go hiking on the Palomarin Trail and wine tasting in Sonoma. Austin looked painfully uncomfortable when she pulled out her fake ID at the first winery. They needed fewer reminders of how pitifully young she was, and he had to call her Lisa the whole time to match her fake identity. Natasha and Freddy had a good thing going — she had seen that firsthand when she visited them in Aspen. But it was hard to miss the sniggering from her grandparents and her mother about their age gap, like it was this vast gulf that was illegal to cross. She couldn't even imagine their reaction if they found out she was treading similar ground.

She told herself that she would keep the relationship light. He was still married, after all, and she was due back in school before Labor Day. It was hard to picture Austin coming to see her on campus, bunking up with her and her roommate, squeezed into an extra-long twin bed with a paper-thin mattress. But try as she did to keep the attachment at bay, Austin had invaded her brain. Her feelings for him were almost like air pollution, if pollution was a good thing, because it was everywhere and couldn't be cleared. She loved ruminating on him, picturing his prematurely gray hair, hearing

361

the legalese roll off his tongue. *Habeas corpus. Certiorari. Lis pendens.* It was as good as dirty talk.

It was proving impossible for her to be around her family, listening to white noise about flaky Dover sole and what time the roller-skating rink converted to bumper cars, when all she wanted to do was replay conversations she'd had with Austin. Thank goodness she'd been smart enough to print out his emails so she could read them over at night. She hid them in her toiletries bag, where Darius would never peek (*the disgusted face he made when a tampon once fell out of her backpack!*), although he had been awfully put out about how much time she was spending in the bathroom. How many times had she reread the line: You seem so much older than your age . . . I feel like I can really talk to you. Whenever she could, Rachel disappeared on the ship, looking for nooks and crannies of quiet where she could fantasize about her boyfriend. Yes, he was her *boyfriend,* even if they hadn't taken the label maker out of the supply closet yet. He said he needed to take things slowly. Not for nothing, he was her superior at the law firm and they couldn't go public about their relationship until her internship was over. Just as important, if Jenny were to find out that her soon-to-be-ex was dating a college coed, the optics would be brutal. So the whole relationship was shrouded in secrecy two times over, and Rachel felt like a pot about to boil over.

She knew all too well that Freddy could keep a secret and so she planned to tell him about Austin as soon as she got him alone. Honestly, she just wanted to have a reason to say her boyfriend's name out loud, over and over. But so far it had been impossible to pin him down. Freddy seemed weirdly interested in Darius, which surprised her, since her little brother was the most one-dimensional, unmotivated character around. The kid couldn't even compose a simple college essay and Rachel was sick of hearing her mother nag him about it. She was tempted to write the damn thing for him and let him pass the work off as his own. Anything to muzzle their mom.

Once she scanned herself back onto the boat, Rachel headed toward the adults-only roof deck, where the towel crew, a nimble group of Ghanians, already knew her by name. She liked a particular chair at the end of the mile-long row, where she could quietly imagine her future with Austin without the distraction of the sunscreen-basted pool crowd who were drunk by noon and loved to join any choreographed dance. But, en route, she had an epiphany that necessitated a detour: a pit stop at her parents' cabin, where the internet was suddenly a magnetic force field pulling at her feet. She would ask any one of the numerous sycophantic crew members to unlock the cabin, claiming she'd misplaced her room key. Then she'd locate the paper with the Wi-Fi password on it — she'd heard her father tell her mother that he'd left it on their night table — and dash off a sweet but not overly desperate email to Austin. It was now or never, because today was the only day she was assured both her parents were off the boat. She'd seen them disembark.

Her parents' cabin was on the seventh deck of the boat, unlike the one she shared with Darius on the second level, where the roar of the engines could be heard day and night. The moment she stepped off the elevator, Rachel sensed the vomit.

Since she'd been a child, the stench of throw up had made Rachel retch herself. She'd had numerous embarrassing episodes in grade school throwing up in the cafeteria moments after another kid upchucked. The boat had been off-and-on rocky, but so far she'd been feeling fine, unlike whoever was puking on the seventh floor. She didn't envy the housekeeping staff. Darius had made some offhand comment to her, like, "What happened to your seasickness?" using finger quotes around "seasickness," but she had no idea what he was talking about.

Despite the noxious odor, Rachel was determined to contact Austin, so she soldiered on toward her parents' room. Unfortunately, this was the first time she didn't see any crew members passing through the halls who could offer her entry.

Rachel slumped against the wall opposite her parents' cabin and pressed her nose against her T-shirt to dull the odor. If the boat wasn't the size of a small city, she would con her way into getting a room key at Guest Services, but the walk alone to the other end of the boat was daunting. She was tracking something like eighteen thousand steps a day, not that it was helping to whittle down her physique. Austin said he loved her curves, but they'd yet to have sex with the lights on.

Rachel closed her eyes and tried to summon their last encounter, regrettably in a hotel room. Austin was paranoid that Jenny had eyes on his rental, so he'd booked a modest room at the Hyatt. They'd classed the experience up by ordering champagne from room service and playing some background jazz through Austin's iPhone.

Suddenly, her mother's voice broke through Rachel's reverie. It was the last thing in the world she wanted to hear while she was picturing herself strewn on a bed with Austin, who was bringing parts of her body to life she hadn't previously known could have sensation.

"Yes, I'm here, Dr. Margaret," Elise was saying, speaking in a deliberate manner, rather loudly.

Dr. Margaret? Was somebody ill? Rachel wondered. And, if so, what kind of doctor went by their first name besides the pediatrician? The doctor she and Darius went to back home was named Dr. Greg. He was a passionless man, who when they were younger read out a list of questions from a notebook, like, "Can you tie your shoes?" "Do you know your letters?" "Have you made new friends?" before unceremoniously concluding the conversation with, "Now go pee in a cup."

Rachel had told Elise recently that she didn't want to see Dr. Greg anymore. It was embarrassing going into his office with the giant whales painted on the walls and sitting among the crying toddlers duking it out over the toy abacus. Elise had had Rachel's files moved over to the primary care physician she used, a tiny Indian woman named Dr. Rahal, after an awkward chat about how Rachel should feel comfortable asking Dr. Rahal anything and that it wouldn't get repeated to her (read: a prescription for birth control pills). Could her mother's call have to do with Darius? Rachel had a sudden flight of panic that something could be wrong with her little brother. Darius had been dodgy about something he was keeping on their shared night table in the cabin. Could it have been medication? She had thought it was his gnarly mouth guard. Rachel cursed herself for ever thinking unkind thoughts about him, resenting the attention Freddy was showering on him. Now she wanted to hug him tightly, let him know she'd give him a kidney, a lung, any organ he needed.

Rachel pressed her ear to the door of the cabin.

"Have you practiced the breathing we discussed?" Rachel heard Dr. Margaret ask. This wasn't what Rachel had been expecting. Was her mother about to meditate over the phone? Typically her parents scoffed at the New Agey types back home.

A short man with a curlicue mustache and dressed in uniform appeared, barreling down the hall with a stack of *Deep Blue*

367

*Digest*s that he was slipping under cabin doors. Seeing Rachel with her ear up against the door, he asked her if she needed assistance. Rachel put her fingers to her lips to quiet him and he moved past her with a simple shrug of his shoulders.

She must have been standing at her parents' door for nearly fifteen minutes before her mother ended the call. Rachel got enough of the broad strokes, though. Dr. Margaret wasn't a pediatrician. She was a shrink . . . her mother's shrink. And Rachel was not the only one on board with a secret, and suddenly hers didn't seem quite so terrible. Instead of feeling relieved, though, she felt worse, an ugly anxiety working its way from the top of her head down to her toes.

By the time she reached the elevators, Rachel had made a list of everything she'd gleaned from the call and that was now wrong with her life:

1. Her mother had a shopping addiction.
2. Her brother wasn't going to be able to go to college.
3. Her grandmother was sick.
4. Her mother thought she was a bitch.
5. She never got to email Austin.

TWENTY-FOUR

The Feldmans cleaned up nicely. After a day of being scattered to the winds, they reunited promptly at six thirty in their finest attire, gowns for the ladies, penguin suits for the men.

Darius's bow tie was choking him and his cummerbund kept riding up, but Angelica told him he looked super fine. They had had a great day together snorkeling. Neither of them could keep their masks on properly, and so they ended up laughing through most of the session while everyone else was oohing and aahing about the spectacular yellowtail damselfish and the glasseye snappers. When they were stripping out of their wetsuits, Darius mentioned to Angelica that he had no idea how to tie his bow tie for the party that evening and she offered to help him out.

"Come by my room on the way to dinner," she said. "I'll tie it in two seconds."

"You know how to do that?" Darius said, a bit in awe. She had a 1600 chess rating (that was even higher than Sacramento High School's own Miss Perfect, Caroline Shapiro), she was a competitive volleyball player, and now he was learning she could tie a bow tie in seconds.

"I work at a dry cleaner, silly," she said, laughing. "You should see me sew a button. I bet I hold a record time."

"I'd like to see that," he said, watching as Angelica tossed her wetsuit to the side and slipped a white, gauzy summer dress over her bathing suit. She was still wet and it clung to her body, translucent in choice places.

"Maybe tomorrow. If we're too bored at the teen scrapbooking class I'll give you a full demonstration of my tailoring skills."

"It's a date," Darius said, and Angelica didn't blanch. He still couldn't fathom why this girl wanted to spend time with him. Either she was utterly bored or she was experimenting with a bad-boy phase, considering Darius had been pretty up-front with her about the myriad ways in which his high school performance differed from hers.

When he was back on the boat later in the day, he found Rachel in their room looking agitated and chewing her nails feverishly.

"What's wrong? Stand-up paddle not all it's cracked up to be?" he asked.

"Shut up," she said, which was a standard response for Rachel, but somehow this time it sounded more sad than cruel.

"Never mind." Lying down on his bed, he pulled out a worn copy of *On the Road* and pretended to read.

Rachel rose suddenly and sat down at the combination desk-vanity under the television. He saw her reflection in the tabletop mirror, worried eyes that were unaware they were being watched.

"So living home with Mom and Dad kinda sucks, right?" Rachel said in a cautious tone. Darius felt himself tense up. This was the longest sentence his sister had said to him in months besides "Could you please pass the salt?"

"I guess," Darius said. "I don't really have much of a choice. Next summer you could probably stay on campus."

"Yeah, maybe. But they're weird, right? Mom and Dad. Mom especially, I think."

Darius watched her closely in the mirror. Did she know about the attic? He couldn't figure out where this was coming from. Maybe Rachel was testing him, sussing out what he knew. He'd never been good under pressure and had no idea how to proceed. He wished his sister would just open the door if she knew something and he'd gladly walk through it.

"Yeah. So weird. I wish she'd leave me alone about my essay. I'd write it if she'd just back off."

Rachel swiveled around and he lost his window into her feelings.

"What *are* you going to write about?"

"Maybe this trip," Darius said, mostly kidding.

"Dysfunctional family reunites on cruise ship," Rachel said with a hearty laugh. "I fear that may not be enough to get you into college, little bro. We might not be loving this trip, but I'm afraid people have it far worse than us."

Rachel's demeanor was relaxing. She walked over to the closet and pulled out a silver dress.

"Last time I wore this dress was to prom with Michael Sedgwick. Remember him? I heard he sued UCLA because his fraternity hazed him so badly." She went into the bathroom before Darius could respond and exited with the dress hanging on her loosely. "Wherever and whenever you end up in college, don't do anything stupid like that, okay?"

372

Wherever and whenever? He didn't even bother answering.

"Zip me up, 'kay? I'm going to try to sneak into the casino before the dinner starts."

Darius obliged, finding the act of zipping his sister's dress a welcome invitation into her personal space. They were back together: ketchup and mustard. True, she didn't ask him to join her in the casino, but this was the most natural conversation the two of them had had in ages and he could enjoy it without looking for more. He even managed to put his mother's issues out of his mind while he fumbled his way into the tuxedo. How he would like to put this very outfit on and drive by Marcy's house to pick her up before prom. She would probably wear something tight, definitely black, with a high slit up the leg. He'd give her a corsage that she'd roll her eyes at but still slip on her wrist, secretly happy that he hadn't broken with tradition.

Darius went into the bathroom to give himself a once-over before heading to Angelica's room. He remembered seeing a sample of cologne next to the Q-tips and lotions. The boat was all about samples. Of course everything was for sale in larger scale on the shopping concourse. Lord only knew how many bottles of Sun-Fun Body Cream and Beach Bod Perfume Spray his mother had already purchased. He picked up the tiny spray bottle and was fiddling with the nozzle when it dropped into Rachel's makeup bag. Darius reached inside to fish it out and touched what felt like a stack of paper folded many times over. He knew he shouldn't, but he pulled it out, telling himself that he just wanted to make sure his sister was okay. She had been acting awfully strange moments earlier and this could be a clue.

Darius unfolded the papers carefully, trying to remember the way the creases went so Rachel wouldn't know he'd snooped. He sat down on the toilet and started with the one on top.

You're so beautiful . . . I can't get you out of my mind . . . Jenny never made me this happy . . . Once the divorce is . . . Careful at work . . . You seem so much older than . . .

Oh, shit. He read on, sifting through the papers quickly.

Rachel was dating someone at work. Someone married. Someone older. Named Austin. What a douche name. Darius shuddered. He wanted to unknow this information. He wanted to unknow so many things, actually. It would feel so good to take an eraser to his mind and wipe it clean like a blackboard. At least he knew why his sister had acted so evasive all summer and why she was putting in such long hours at the office.

Darius put the papers back where he'd found them and headed for Angelica's room, palming his bow tie with sweaty hands. He considered bringing along Kerouac as a prop, to pretend he planned to read it at dinner if he was bored. But it was silly to carry it around all night and Angelica, with all her brainpower, would probably quiz him on it. She was sharing a room with her grandmother in a cabin located four decks above Darius's room. He thudded his way down the hallway in his dress shoes and took the stairs two at a time, his bow tie now crumpled into a ball.

He knocked rhythmically on her door with a *dun-dun-dun-dun-dun . . . dun-dun!* Angelica answered and Darius nearly fell backward when he saw her. He wasn't sure what he'd been expecting, maybe another debate or chess team T-shirt tucked into a skirt, but Angelica had transformed herself for the evening completely. She was wearing a strapless shiny purple dress and heels that brought her to Darius's chin. He was used to her barely reaching his shoulder.

"Holy shit," he said when he stepped into her room, because his mouth had run away from his brain.

"You like?" she asked, doing a quick twirl. He noticed black eyeliner rimming her brown eyes and the lip gloss that made her mouth look wet.

"Yes. Did you borrow that from the dry cleaner's?" He didn't intend to be hurtful, but he had always wondered if that sort of thing happened. Angelica widened her eyes dramatically, pretending to be scandalized.

"That's actually against the dry cleaning code of ethics," she said. "In our business, it's basically on par with murder. I got this at Forever 21 last year when they were doing their prom sale."

Darius looked past Angelica and saw a tiny old Asian woman slumped into a wheelchair. She had a black beaded scarf draped over her outfit to obscure the fact that she had not otherwise gone black tie for the evening.

"That's Grandma," Angelica said, following his gaze. She started speaking to the woman in Chinese, presumably talking about him, because the woman started addressing him.

"I don't speak Chinese," Darius said to Angelica, feeling helpless.

"It's Mandarin. Not Chinese. But don't worry about Grandma. She was saying that you are very handsome."

"No, she wasn't," Darius said. He might not understand Mandarin, but he could tell from the way the old lady twisted her face and raised her pointer finger at him menacingly that she most definitely had not called him handsome.

"Fine," Angelica said, walking over to her grandmother and resting her hands on her shoulders, which seemed to relax the woman. "She told you not to get me pregnant and ruin my life, because I have a big future ahead of me."

Darius felt heat rush to his face in a sudden volcanic eruption.

"Relax!" Angelica said, obviously seeing his crimson shading. "She's nuts. And just wants the best for me."

"Yes, yes. Harvard. I know all about it," Darius said, running a jittery hand through his hair. He mustered the courage to flash Grandma a thumbs-up to reassure her that there was no chance of him impregnating anyone on this ship.

"Now let me see that," Angelica said,

touching his hand and loosening his grasp on the bow tie with her fingers. "Easy." He ducked down a bit so she could wrap the tie around his neck and Darius noticed her cleavage, minimal but there nonetheless, protruding into his sight line and demanding attention. There were leg men and ass men (Jesse was definitely the latter and he had all sorts of crude names to refer to girls' behinds: booty, bedunkedonk, can, caboose, and tail-feather, to name a few), but he, Darius Connelly, was decidedly a breast man.

True to her word, Angelica had fixed up his tie in seconds and she was now standing back from him to admire her handiwork.

"Looking suave," she said, making a peace sign.

"Thanks," Darius said, poking his head into the bathroom to see his reflection. He looked passable, definitely nothing approximating suave. But when he squinted hard, his acne pockmarks disappeared, and that took him a little closer to handsome. "Want to go down together?"

"Yes," Angelica said brightly. "If you don't mind wheeling Grandma and waiting forever for the handicapped elevator. But first I want to check my email. I applied for a few scholarships and need to make sure everything is copacetic."

"You have internet in here?" Darius asked, wide-eyed.

"Yep. My uncle is a really big spender." She must have repeated the same in Mandarin to her grandma because the old lady nodded vigorously and made the universal hand signal for money.

"Can I check my email after you?" Darius asked. What he really wanted was to see all the text messages he'd missed, but he hadn't bothered to bring his phone, which was impotent without the internet. Email would have to do.

"Sure," Angelica said, plopping down on the bed. She tapped away at the keys and Darius stood awkwardly, feeling too tall, too white, too useless. Now he wished he had brought the book.

"All good," Angelica chirped, gesturing for him to sit next to her. "Your turn."

Darius took the computer and logged into his account. He had about a dozen emails from the school about registering for classes, new policies about leaving campus during the day, and a refresher on the antibullying policy. He ignored them all. Scrolling down, he saw one email from Jesse with the subject line sup. He clicked it open, but it was blank inside. Darius responded nada and hit send.

They communicated like Neanderthals. Below Jesse's email he saw an email from mcl777@gmail.com. His pulse raced. M.C.L. . . . those could be Marcy's initials. He was pretty sure her middle name was Christine. Marcy Christine Lungstrom, emailing him! This was a first. He clicked on the email, but nothing happened. He pressed harder, jamming his index finger into the mouse pad.

"You okay?" Angelica asked.

"It's not opening," Darius said, hearing the way it came out as an accusation, as if it was Angelica's fault that he couldn't find out what Marcy had written to him. Assuming it *was* Marcy.

"Yeah, the internet is pretty crappy. I was emailing my chess coach the other day and had written out this whole long question for him about the Italian opening and then the internet crapped out and I lost everything."

Chess coach . . . how could Angelica possibly compare the importance of rooks and pawns with a communiqué from Marcy Lungstrom, goddess incarnate? Out of aggravation, he yanked at his bow tie but stopped short of undoing it.

"Hey, you're ruining my handiwork," Angelica protested.

"Sorry. Do you think we could just wait

here for a few minutes and see if the internet comes back?" Darius asked. Angelica translated the question for her grandma, who decisively said no with a vigorous head shake.

Darius was beside himself. He hadn't even seen what Marcy had written in the subject line. Was it "Hey"? He thought it might have been. Or was it the more suggestive "Hi there"? He was ninety-nine percent sure it started with an *H*. What if it was "Help" and she needed him for something important?

"Grandma doesn't want to miss a minute of the party tonight," Angelica said. "Sorry."

Darius moved the laptop back onto the desk, looking at it forlornly as he left the room with Angelica at his side and Grandma rolling ahead in front.

The cocktail hour was in the Starboard Ballroom. Guests would have one hour to drink and mingle before being scattered to smaller ballrooms for the sit-down portion of the evening. The ballroom had been transformed completely from its prior use the night before, when a combination magic and light show had taken place after dinner. Twinkling lights were strung from the ceiling and votive candles and faux flowers sat on every tabletop. A large banner read: MAY ALL YOUR FANTA-SEAS COME TRUE.

"This is gorgeous," Angelica said, her eyes widening.

"I see my people," Darius said, pointing ahead. "Maybe I'll see you later. My family is in the Horizon Room for the dinner. You're in Tide, right?"

Angelica nodded and Darius waved to her grandma, who gave him an "I'm watching you" stare for a good-bye. She may have been topping ninety and confined to a wheelchair, but she was fierce.

He strode over to his family, who were gathered near a crudité model of the *Ocean Queen.* Grandma Annette was bent over it, inspecting the architecture of the foundation, which was made of stacks of raw onion rounds. It *was* incredible, there could be no denying that, and it felt almost criminal to wrestle a red pepper from the water slide replica or take a celery stalk from the oval arrangement that made up the jogging track.

"Could you get me a drink from the bar?" Darius whispered in Rachel's ear. Normally loath to ask her for a favor, he felt tonight was not one on which he could stand on ceremony. She agreed rather easily and came back a few minutes later carrying two "ginger ales," which she mouthed to him were actually vodkas mixed with Pepsi, hence the goldish color that made them pass for Canada Dry.

Darius looked at his mother. He still hadn't had the chance to do much investigating into the shopping situation, or to speak with Freddy about it. Tonight she was wearing a dress he didn't recognize, a light pink lace, but that didn't mean anything. It wouldn't be weird for her to buy something new to wear on the boat, or maybe it was an old outfit and he just didn't remember it. Until he'd found all those bags in the attic, Darius had never paid a lick of attention to his mother's clothing. She could have had fifty pairs of shoes or five, for all he knew.

Grandma Annette gave him a big hug and made a fuss over how handsome he looked. Ever since they'd gone on that walk together the first day, she'd been treating him extra lovingly. When she bit into her Mexican chocolate cake at the around-the-world feast, she'd singled him out as the only one at the table who just had to try it. Was it that easy, Darius wondered, to satisfy his grandmother? If he'd known that, maybe he would have picked up the phone every now and then to check in. He was embarrassed by how little thought he gave her or

Grandpa David. Even Jesse had a monthly brunch date with his grandparents, but they lived in Modesto.

Freddy, no surprise, was not in a tuxedo, but in an unexpected nod to the evening's formality, he had gelled his longish hair into a tighter-than-usual man-bun. Natasha was a boob man's delight, resplendent — overflowing, frankly — in a gold sequined dress that pushed the bookends of her rib cage even closer together.

His father gave him a series of staccato pats on the back. Mitch seemed overly excited, like someone who had had too many cups of coffee and had no place to burn off his extra energy. Darius observed him ask everyone about their adventures off the boat but then barely have the patience to listen to their answers. At one point, he swept his mother into a quasi-twirl-dip that might have had something to do with the background music but could have just been totally random. Darius cringed at the awkwardness, but when he looked over at Rachel, she seemed oddly enchanted by the whole thing, a heck of a lot more relaxed than she'd seemed in their room earlier. Maybe she'd won at the slots or the "ginger ale" was already working its magic.

His father suggested they ask someone to

take their picture. He was big on documenting family time and was known to make
hapless strangers do ten or more retakes
until he was satisfied it was *Bee* photojour-
nalism quality.

"I'll take it," Darius offered. He hated being in pictures. His forced smile was hideous
— too much teeth and an unexplained need
to widen his eyes. But if he tried a serious
face, he looked like a future serial killer in a
yearbook photo.

"No," Mitch said. "We all need to be in it
tonight. This is a special occasion and I
want to have a memory of it."

Huh? Rachel was right. Something was
off and the weirdness didn't stop with their
mother. Their dad was never this sappy.

"Let's do it later when we're at the table,
Mitch," Grandma Annette said. "I want to
touch up my makeup in the ladies' room
first. You'll come with me, Elise. I happen
to have an extra tube of lipstick in my purse
in a good color for you. I'm surprised you
always choose that same nude one."

Darius saw his mother grimace.

Waiters flitted around with trays and while
the parentals and grandparentals sampled
the nibbles, Rachel and Darius gave each
other knowing glances as they avoided food
altogether to concentrate on their bever-

ages. His father flagged down a server and requested glasses of champagne for the grown-ups and sparkling cider for the "kiddies." Couldn't his dad let the waitress deduce that he was a minor on her own by looking at his raging acne and bulbous Adam's apple?

"Bring your finest bottle. Please bill it to my expense account, cabin 7732," Mitch added inexplicably. Darius saw his mother give his father a "What the hell are you doing?" look that he chose to ignore. Darius, only because he was standing next to her, heard his grandma mutter to his grandpa that he was only allowed a single sip of the champagne, which was bizarre because his grandfather was many things — stern, didactic, a die-hard Rangers fan — but he was *not* an alcoholic. Natasha said, "Ooh, champers, great!" and slipped an arm through Freddy's.

While the server went off to retrieve the bubbly, there was some idle chatter about everybody's excursions, but Darius could barely concentrate. He heard something about the tour van breaking down at a gas station from his grandma and then his uncle mentioned a thirty-pound grouper that broke somebody's line — but all he could really focus on were the initials M.C.L. and getting back to a computer. He wondered if he could ask Angelica for her room key and slip away during dinner. He saw her from across the room gathered with her family. She was imitating something that involved a lot of hip shaking and shimmying (which he hoped wasn't the image of him sidling out of the wetsuit) and everyone in her party was laughing hysterically.

The waitress reappeared with the champagne and his father took the bottle from her hands and poured everyone a healthy serving that brought fizz down the sides of the glasses. Darius accepted his sparkling cider gingerly.

Grandpa David started to say that he'd visited the hospital on the ship — *it's like a miniature version of Beth Israel* — and spoke to the chief resident about protocol. Darius felt his stomach burbling. Just the talk of a mass virus spreading on board made him queasy. He couldn't handle being quarantined, not when he needed to collect interesting stories about the cruise to tell Marcy. Not when he urgently needed a strong Wi-Fi connection.

"Fascinating, David. Just fascinating," Mitch said. "Now, you might be wondering why I ordered the champagne when I'm typically a Guinness guy. I happen to have a big announcement and I wanted to share it with all of you. We are so rarely together, after all."

Darius noticed his grandma shake her head at no one in particular, as if she was thinking, *Well, whose fault is that?* His mom gaped at his dad with a confused look that made it clear she wasn't in on whatever news was forthcoming. Rachel was sucking vigorously through her straw and barely looked up.

"Anyway, before I say anything, I want everyone to know I've given this a great deal of thought."

Darius was reminded of a recent school assembly when a quiet boy he'd known since kindergarten had taken the mic — it was the first time Freddy could recall hearing his voice — and announced he was going to become a girl. *I, Ben Nordeman,* the boy said in a voice that grew more confident by the syllable, *will now be known as Bianca.* And then he said something that echoed what Darius's dad had just said . . . *I've given this a lot of thought.* He was pretty sure his father was going in a different direction.

"I've worked at the *Bee* since finishing journalism school. Twenty-two years. I started as the local politics reporter, then moved up to national affairs, then deputy editor, and then what I am today — or was, rather — managing editor."

Was? Now he had everyone's attention.

"I've been satisfied by my career and it has provided for my family, but I felt I needed a change. I resigned my post two weeks ago and will be launching an online literary journal with a focus on satire. Only thing missing is a name. I thought we could all raise a glass to this new phase."

Natasha squealed. Freddy looked uncomfortable. Rachel finally looked up from her drink. Darius jammed his hands into the pockets of his tux because he needed to do something.

"Mitch, are you serious?" Elise said. "You didn't think to consult your wife about a thing like this before you announce it in front of all these people!" She slammed down her glass hard and Darius was surprised when it didn't shatter. He didn't think her "these people" would sit too well with his grandparents.

"I honestly had made up my mind, Elise. And we're in a good place now. I thought it would be more exciting to make the announcement on the trip, in front of the kids and your parents. Don't you remember your parents used to treat us to dinner once a week at that fancy Italian place on the Upper West Side when we were both in grad school — the one that was next to the dry cleaner's that reeked of bleach?"

Darius took offense on behalf of Angelica with the dry cleaning dig. No way her family's store, Harvard Cleaners, stank.

"What the hell does that have to do with you announcing you've quit your job in public?" Elise barked, and Darius had to agree — he failed to see the connection.

"Just that your parents have helped us out along the way and it seemed right they should be here," he said.

"Thank you, Mitch," Grandma Annette said, dabbing at her eyes with a cocktail napkin. Damn, this woman was in need of some loving, thought Darius. Every little overture made her mawkish (another dreaded SAT word). "And, Elise, now you can tell Mitch about your business plan. Since he's not going to be at the *Bee* anymore! We felt awkward about lending you so much money with all this need for secrecy." She clasped her hands together gleefully.

His mother went ashen. Darius pictured the attic. Somehow he just knew it was all related.

"What business plan?" Mitch said. Now it was his father's turn to look confused and hurt. "You're borrowing money from your parents?"

"It's nothing," Elise said swiftly. "I'll tell you later. Let's toast you now!"

Well, that was a quick about-face, Darius thought.

"No, tell me now," Mitch said gruffly.

The tension was steak-knife-cuttable. Darius ditched his straw and took a large gulp of his drink. He missed his friends, especially Jesse. He missed Marcy, who was so achingly beautiful. He missed Angelica too, whom he'd temporarily lost in the crowd.

A waiter came by with mini tarts and all the Feldmans instantly seized up. They were, true to form, well behaved in public. As Grandma Annette liked to say, "It's always better to steal a scene than to cause one." Freddy took a tartlet off the tray and popped it into his mouth. Rachel reached for one as well. It was the first boat-issued food item that Darius could recall seeing his sister eat. The inside of her suitcase was jam-packed with Kind Bars and boxes of raisins, as though she expected a shipwreck.

"Don't!" Freddy said suddenly, with his mouth full. He knocked Rachel's hand away from her mouth. "I think these have sesame in them."

391

"Really?" Rachel said, trying to speak with her tongue out. She started wiping her mouth frantically with a napkin.

"Why are you telling her not to eat that?" Elise asked, turning abruptly to face Freddy.

"Because she's allergic to sesame seeds," Freddy said, clearly not understanding the question.

"But she only developed her sensitivity to sesame seeds three years ago. It happened to her after she got a terrible flu in high school and her immune system totally broke down and reconfigured."

Darius looked from Freddy to Rachel and back again, watching as they attempted to hatch some type of coherent response telepathically. It was the same communication he would have with Jesse when either of their mothers interrogated them about where they'd been.

"Yes, how *do* you know that?" Mitch said, also agitated. Darius had always thought it was his mother who had the bigger issue with Freddy and his dad just kind of played along. But his father was definitely not loving the idea that Freddy and Rachel were on intimate, allergy-awareness terms.

"Doth my thongue look swollen?" Rachel asked. She stuck it out like a frog. "I feel like ith gething bigger. Ith thingling. Someone pleath look at ith."

"Why don't I go find the waiter or someone who can tell us if there were sesame seeds in the recipe or not?" Natasha asked sensibly and left without waiting for an answer.

"I'll come with you," Freddy said, dashing off behind her.

"What business plan?" Mitch repeated.

"Let's discuss it after we know if Rachel is okay," Elise said firmly.

"She's fine. Right, David?" Grandma Annette said rather strongly. "Elise, didn't you tell me the worst thing that happens to her is that she gets a rash? It's not anaphylactic."

"Ith not anathylathic *yet,*" Rachel said, barely able to speak coherently with her lips puckered and her tongue protruding.

Grandpa David took a large gulp from his champagne glass like he was gunning it in beer pong.

"David," Grandma Annette exclaimed, forcibly taking the glass out of her husband's hand. "You cannot be having this much alcohol."

"I'll do whatever I damn please," David said, which shocked Darius. He'd never heard his grandfather raise his voice to his grandma.

"Elise, I'm sorry that I didn't tell you sooner about leaving the *Bee,*" his dad persisted, ignoring Rachel. "I honestly thought you'd be excited for me to pursue my dreams. Can we please go back to why you asked your parents for money?"

"Which, by the way, we may not be able to lend you at this time," Grandpa David said, attempting to pry the champagne from Grandma Annette's grasp. "Notwithstanding what your mother said about the secrecy making us uncomfortable."

Darius looked at Rachel and she looked back at him, panic-stricken. Maybe with forces united they could have prevented the current mess.

"If you need money, by the way, you should probably ask your brother for it," Mitch said sharply. "He's a millionaire."

"What?" Elise said, looking on the verge of fainting.

"It's true. Your brother is the most successful drug dealer around."

"Don't speak such nonsense about our son," Grandpa David said reproachfully. "Besides, Elise wouldn't need money from us anyway if she'd stayed in medical school. Or if you had a better-paying job."

"Are you seriously bringing that up now?" Mitch asked, bewilderment seeming to overtake his anger.

Around them, a crowd had started to form. Inopportunely, the jazz trio went on break, as if to encourage eavesdropping.

"Yes, I am," David said defiantly.

"You're being a real jerk, you know that?" Mitch said.

David set down his drained champagne glass, raised both his arms like he was in retreat, then shook his head and jammed his shoulder into Mitch as he moved to step past him.

Darius's father went to push back, but Grandpa David ducked quickly, which meant that Mitch's open palm landed directly on his nose. Grandpa David yelped in pain. A drop of bright red blood streamed down his chin and landed on the white of his tuxedo shirt. Rachel and Elise screamed in unison.

"He's not well!" Annette shouted at Mitch. "What's wrong with you?"

And that was exactly when Freddy and Natasha reappeared.

"Mom? Elise? What the hell is going on?" Freddy asked, stumbling. "Dad, are you okay?" He dabbed at his father's nose with a napkin. Between Grandma Annette's wailing, Rachel's tongue scrubbing, and Grandpa David's bloody nose, they must have used up a hundred Paradise International cocktail napkins.

Natasha looked utterly petrified. As the only one without a branch on this crazy family tree, she was free to simply walk away. But Darius watched her grab ice out of Rachel's fake soda and divide it between two paper napkins while the rest of the family just stood gaping.

TWENTY-FIVE

When the gurneys had been dismissed and all the other boat guests relocated, the Feldmans sat in a circle in silence. David's nose had stopped bleeding. Mitch said his shoulder felt better. Rachel's lips didn't swell up. Everybody had stopped crying for the time being. The cruise director had fled the scene of the crime.

Annette was feeling so many emotions it was hard for her to discern which one was the most overriding. There was shock about learning Freddy was a millionaire, and in the drug world, no less. There was anxiety about Elise, since clearly the cockamamie diabetes app she'd told them about was a fiction, covering up something much worse. Disappointment toward her son-in-law for not realizing he should have consulted with his wife before making a gigantic career change. Concern about Rachel, who she suspected was hiding more than her relationship with Freddy. Compassion for Darius, who seemed the most innocent of the lot, though couldn't he just write his damn essay already? Worry that she might have outed David's illness when he'd been so perfectly clear about his wishes to keep it a private matter. Embarrassment in front of that handsome cruise director and all the other passengers, who had stared at them like they were a bunch of wild animals thrown into a cage together for the first time. And guilt, of course, because she was the one who'd engineered this whole trip, who put her family into a crucible and lit the burner.

She had been so foolish to insist on the cruise. Instead of bringing them closer together, they were in a worse position than when they started. The status quo had not needed tampering with. She and Elise spoke once a week. Facebook allowed them to see that Freddy was alive and healthy. The grandchildren called for her birthday and knew enough to thank her for the gifts she sent them. David probably would have been better off at home. The doctor who said a trip might do him good clearly didn't realize she was throwing him into a tempest. His weekly radiation appointment was more soothing than the *Ocean Queen.*

Annette knew she should be the first one to speak. She was still the team captain, even if she desperately wanted to abdicate the role.

"Well, this evening certainly didn't go as planned," she finally said.

Mitch crossed his arms across his chest. Elise was nervously tying and untying the lace ribbon on her dress.

"It's okay, Mom," Freddy said, putting a hand on hers. His touch sent a shiver down her spine. The last time she'd felt his open palm, it had been soft and bare. He'd probably been a boy no older than thirteen and she was still forcing him to hold hands when they crossed the street. Now his hands were rough, with hair on the knuckles, and so much bigger than hers. "I should probably explain some things."

"Let me do it," Rachel said, looking at her uncle. Freddy nodded for her to go ahead. Her granddaughter looked like a human Pandora's box.

"I went to visit Freddy last spring when I said I was in Guatemala." She spoke in a sprint, as if she couldn't free herself of the admission fast enough.

"She was the best house guest," Natasha interjected.

"She wasn't supposed to be a house *guest.*

She was supposed to be *building* houses," Mitch snapped.

Natasha pretended not to hear him. "You should be proud of Rachel. She was also quite the hostess to us."

"Hostess?" Elise asked Freddy. "You went to visit Rachel at Stanford and didn't think to tell us? We live an hour away — I'd have thought you might have told us if you were in the area, considering we haven't laid eyes on you in — I don't know — three or four years."

"Well, it was sort of last —" Freddy started to say, throwing an exasperated "How could you?" look at Natasha.

"Uncle Freddy, it's fine," Rachel said, putting her hand on his arm. "Thanks for helping me, but I need to come clean. I got arrested in April and Freddy bailed me out."

"Arrested?" This Annette simply couldn't believe. Freddy was some kind of superstar drug dealer and now her granddaughter was in trouble with the law? She longed for the days when the worst she thought of all the Feldmans was that they were distant and self-involved. "Was there some kind of protest on campus?" Annette remembered her roommate at George Washington University going from one sit-in to another. Sometimes it was civil rights; other times, the women's movement. There was always the risk of arrest and Annette just couldn't ever bring herself to join in, no matter how strongly she believed in the causes. To defend her family, she would chain herself to a fence or face a wrecking ball, but for people she didn't know, whose problems were real but remote, she didn't have that kind of courage. Maybe Rachel did.

"No, it was nothing like that," Rachel said, taking another gigantic slurp of her soda.

I really ought to review table manners with that child, Annette found herself thinking despite the tumult.

"I had a little too much to drink and got into it with a police officer. Well, it was campus security, but apparently they have arresting power."

" 'Got into it'?" Mitch prodded.

Natasha giggled out of nowhere.

"Something funny about this?" David said to her. He was sweating and his fists were still clenched. Annette had to get him out of here. This was too much stress for him to take. But she knew it would be difficult to extricate him with all of these truths about their family being laid bare. They still hadn't gotten to the matter of Elise being broke or Freddy's supposed millions.

"Natasha is laughing because of what hap-

401

pened," Rachel explained. "There was this thing called a Porn Party on campus, which sounds worse than it is. You just dress up in a ridiculous outfit, something sexy. I got this idea to make a skirt out of balloons only. And then, I guess I had a little too much Tito's, and I went over to this campus security guard and asked him to pop my balloons."

"Rachel!" Elise gasped.

"That was it?" David asked. "They arrested you for that?" David had always hated law enforcement and was known to scuffle with the security guards at the hospital over what he felt were overly tedious searches at the metal detector.

"Well, when he said no, I tried to take his handcuffs. He brought me down to the local precinct and Freddy bailed me out. There are more details, but those are the broad strokes. And I'm really, really sorry about it. I knew you would freak out and be so disappointed in me and I just couldn't face calling you." She put her head in her hands and dropped it between her knees.

"Rachel, your father and I will discuss this privately and address it with you later," Elise said. Annette was proud of her daughter for managing to keep her cool. She'd never had that kind of composure when it came to

Freddy. Maybe that spared Elise from being called a "fucking bitch" behind closed doors.

"That's right, Rachel. We need time to digest this," Mitch said. "Elise, can you please explain why you said we have no money? I was under the impression we were far from broke," Mitch said.

Annette watched the panic spread across her son-in-law's face. This new development was surely going to impede his professional plans. Timing was never Elise's strong suit. She quit medical school a beat before Annette and David's twentieth anniversary party, which had brought on a string of irritating questions all night long.

"And what does all of this have to do with you starting a business?" Mitch continued.

"I'd like to understand that myself," David said.

"Me too," Freddy said quietly.

"Kids, why don't you go to your cabin," Elise said. "Or to the teen lounge. I think there's a silent disco tonight after the dinner."

"OMG, I've been dying to try a silent disco," Natasha said. "Look at these pics of the girls from work at Cloud Nine." Natasha started to pull up images on her phone.

"Will you please put away that *fakakta* thing?" Annette said. "You're worse than the teenagers."

"Mom!" Freddy said, putting a protective arm around Natasha, who looked like she was about to burst into tears.

"That's because the kids don't have the Wi-Fi plan," Mitch explained to no one in particular. "Trust me, they'd be on them incessantly if they did."

"Why are we talking about phones?" David said. "I want to understand why my daughter has no money." He lowered his voice dramatically. "I would also like to understand how — and why — my son is involved in the illegal drug world."

"Legal," Natasha and Freddy said at the same time.

"Kids, you need to leave," Elise repeated.

"You keep telling me to act like an adult, Mom," Darius said, speaking up for the first time. "There is obviously something serious going on and I'd like to know what it's about. You can't send us off to some kids' dance party and think we're going to forget what we heard." Annette saw the determination in his face and wondered what he already knew.

"Fine. Just fine. You want to stay, you can stay. Listen, I'm not proud of it," Elise said, speaking slowly, her voice in a timid staccato, "but I've developed something of a shopping problem. It started small. A new dress, some shoes. A set of dishes. But things spiraled out of control rather quickly."

"I went to the attic," Darius said quietly. "I found your stash."

"I heard you on the phone with your therapist," Rachel added.

"Why am I the last one to know anything that is happening under my roof?" Mitch demanded.

"I wouldn't start if I were you," Elise said, raising her voice. "You left your job without telling me. You announced your plans in front of my family so I couldn't object or disapprove. Well, I don't care what they hear anymore. You shouldn't have quit without consulting me. If you had told me your plans, perhaps I would have shared my situation and told you why you couldn't leave the *Bee* now."

"You're shifting blame, Elise," Annette said, instantly regretting her interjection. She ought to be a silent spectator, but it was just so excruciating to sit back and watch her children say and do all of the wrong things. Perhaps that was what her husband had felt all these years about their daughter's choices, like a steaming pot that can't keep its lid.

"Stay out of it," everyone seemed to say to her at once. Fine, she'd quiet down. Who was she anyway, except the reason all these people even existed?

"You shouldn't lecture anyone on keeping secrets, by the way," Elise said. "I saw all the meds in your room. I know why we're on this cruise even if you don't want us to know."

Before Annette had a chance to formulate an answer, Freddy interrupted.

"Mom isn't sick, Elise. Dad is."

"What?" Elise's question came out as a squeaky gasp. Annette watched her daughter process the information. Not only had she been wrong about who was sick, her brother was more plugged in than she was.

"Why do you say that?" David asked Freddy, obviously unwilling to let go of the charade.

"Your mouth sores. Your eyebrows. The way you've been walking," Freddy said. "Should I go on?"

"Is it true, Dad?" Elise said.

"It's true," David said matter-of-factly. To Freddy, he asked, "How do you know all those things?"

"I suppose that brings us to yet another

family secret, which Mitch alluded to ear-
lier. I've built a largish business in Colorado.
I own marijuana farms and retail stores.
Many of our customers are on chemo and
the pot really helps ease the side effects.
Dad — if you wanted — I could help you
find the right strain." He then turned to
Mitch. "How did you know?"

"It's best we discuss that later," Mitch said
firmly and it seemed Freddy caught his
meaning. Annette could hardly guess what
there was left to say that couldn't be said in
present company.

Before any further conversation could
ensue, a lone waitress appeared with a trolley of desserts.

"Excuse me, ladies and gentlemen," came
an accented voice from behind a massive
cheesecake with a triangular wedge missing.
"Your cruise director, Mr. Julian, has asked
me to bring you a selection of sweets since
you are missing tonight's feast. Can I offer
anyone a piece of cake? Perhaps you like
chocolate mousse?"

All eyes gladly redirected their focus to
the dessert cart, where the mousse, a glossy
brown foam, jiggled in a gleaming silver
bowl. Partially carved cakes, the shortest
one ten inches tall, tempted in carrot,
cheese, chocolate chip, raspberry truffle,

and pistachio fluff. Descriptions were scrawled in neat handwriting on tented cards. Annette fantasized that if they each took something and focused on spooning bite after bite, then all the ugliness of the past half hour could dissolve as easily as the sugar on their tongues.

"I'm allergic to sesame," Rachel said to the waitress. "Do you have anything you're positive has no sesame in it?"

The waitress, a hearty woman with a white blond chignon, seemed excited by the question. Annette squinted to read her name tag: *Ekaterina, Ukraine.*

"I'm very glad you asked, miss. Our specialty is the baked Alaska. No sesame — I prepare fresh for you. It is a delight for the eyes. Perhaps you have seen our baked Alaska presentation on the YouTube?"

Annette saw Darius smirk.

"We have not," Annette said. "Please tell us."

Ekaterina looked as though she didn't fancy herself up to the task. Whether it was a question of her English language skills or the sheer weight of describing the rapture that was supposed to be the baked Alaska, Annette wasn't sure.

"Oh, it is spectacular. We do a parade. Our biggest baked Alaska — it goes on the float,

I think you say — is three meters tall," she said.

Meters, not feet. It was just one of the many differences between the staff and the guests. There was kind of an *Upstairs Downstairs* thing happening on the boat. Annette had gone for a stroll the other night after David had fallen asleep again before nine. The medicine made him so tired, as though it was preparing her in stages for what life would be like without him. She'd made her way below deck to where the staff cabins were located and all she saw was merriment — waiters playing cards, dancers twirling with the croupiers, engineers building houses of cards with tented *Deep Blue Digest*s. Annette had stood out of sight for as long as she could, tucked behind the open door of a supply closet filled with barf bags, wondering if things really wcre better below deck.

A common theme among the crew — almost a universal truth — was that they were far away from their families. There were the occasional husband-wife pairings (porter/cleaner or bartender/waitress), but most of the workers were oceans away from their families, sending money home, breaking their backs to provide their children and spouses with schooling and clothing. But still when Annette came upon them, they were smiling and laughing. She wondered if it was easier for them to be distant, shielded from the daily insults of family by miles of ocean.

"For you, though, I have a small sample. But don't worry, it is enough for you to share. On the *Ocean Queen,* we do everything big." Ekaterina smiled and reached under the trolley, where a tablecloth was obscuring a mini refrigerator. For the next few minutes, the Feldmans watched in silence as the ceremony of the baked Alaska unfolded. A thin layer of pound cake was pressed into a pan and topped with four generous scoops of vanilla ice cream. A meringue with remarkable adhesion (Annette could never get the egg whites to peak when she beat them) was then draped on top like a cloak. Finally, Ekaterina poured a generous amount of rum around the perimeter of the plate.

"And now, the magic moment," she said, reaching for matches. She struck a match against the book in one graceful swoop. Annette struggled sometimes with the flimsy matches from restaurants, but these looked long and sturdy, oversized like everything else on board. Ekaterina touched the flame to the alcohol pooling around the dessert and, voila, a blue ring of fire was formed. The flames worked their way up the meringue, toasting its edges to golden brown. The smell was evocative and Darius said, "Rach, this is like toasting marshmallows at Camp Lackawanna."

Lackawanna was the overnight camp on the East Coast that the Connelly kids went to for five years straight, where they learned to sculpt jugs on potter's wheels, windsurf, pitch a tent, and all manner of skills practical and impractical. In a gesture of generosity, Annette and David had offered to pay for their grandchildren to attend. Freddy and Elise had been to a similar camp, Camp Topanga, which had since been disbanded over ugly rumors about the camp director fraternizing with the female counselors. Annette didn't want her grandchildren to miss out on the camping experience, which had been so formative for Elise and Freddy. It was on the clay courts of Topanga that Elise had mastered her tennis serve and in the nature center where Freddy had developed his fondness for the outdoors. (He'd lasted four whole summers at the camp until he was kicked out after being caught with a clove cigarette.) Not only did she wish her grandchildren to experience camp life, she didn't want to sit out when all of her friends discussed what to send in the care packages and mock complained about the *schlep* to the boonies for visiting day. Now she thought about all that camp tuition money that would have accrued interest, carving a sizable dent into David's medical expenses. She shook off the thought. There was no sense living life planning for doomsday. And besides, apparently her grandchildren were skilled in marshmallow toasting. Could she really put a price on that?

She looked back at the flaming dessert. The white of the meringue was starting to blacken, but the fire was still going strong.

"Excuse me, are we supposed to blow out the fire or wait until it burns out?" Annette asked Ekaterina, but she was already out of earshot, rolling the trolley out of the ballroom toward the galley.

"You're supposed to blow it out," Elise said firmly. "I've made baked Alaska before."

Really? thought Annette. Anytime she'd been in the Connelly house, the closest Elise came to baking was slicing from a premade cookie dough roll. Even her meals left something to be desired. She'd have thought her daughter might have invested in a cooking class after all these years of phoning it in.

"No, you haven't," Rachel said, confirming Annette's suspicions. But now her annoyance shifted to Rachel. Her granddaughter still hadn't passed into that stage of adulthood where she realized that her parents sometimes did things when the kids weren't around and that didn't revolve around them. It reminded Annette of how both of her kids thought their teachers slept in school until Elise's fourth-grade teacher brought her daughter to work one day and blew everyone's minds. She would love to discuss this with Elise, but her daughter could be so prickly about how she raised her children, as though she and Annette were on different teams.

"I don't think so," David said. "You're supposed to let the alcohol burn out and the flame will extinguish on its own."

Annette looked at her husband. He was a man of science, but then again, Elise claimed to have made this dessert before.

"Blow it out," Elise said again, this time more urgently. "The whole thing is burning."

"No, your father's right," Annette said. "If we had to blow it out, Ekaterina would have told us to. And she just left."

"Who?" Darius asked.

"Ekaterina. The waitress who brought the

dessert," Annette said. She eyed the dessert with growing concern. The flames weren't growing taller, but they showed no signs of subsiding either. And the meringue had gone from golden brown to crispy black. Still, David usually knew what he was talking about. Why trust Elise? She wasn't in her right mind.

"You're going to burn the ship down," Elise said, standing up from her chair and leaning over the baked Alaska, lips puckered and ready to blow.

"Do it, Mom," Rachel said. "I want to try it before nothing's left."

"Why? You don't even eat anymore. Is it because of Austin?" Darius said.

"Who's Austin?" Mitch asked, his eyes moving between his children.

"Rachel's married boyfriend," Darius said.

"You are the worst, Darius," Rachel said. "Just so you know, Mom spent all your college money. So you're probably going to have to come work for me one day. Bet you wish you'd known that before you ratted me out."

"Guys. The dessert is really smoking now," Natasha said. "Like, more than I think it's supposed to." Her doe eyes were washed with concern. She was so Bambi-like it was ridiculous.

"The alcohol needs to burn off," David repeated, like he was telling a nurse to back the hell off with her IV bag. "If you blow it out, it will taste like straight Bacardi."

"This is ridiculous," Elise said. Like she was blowing out the candles on a birthday cake, she moved her head in a dramatic circle and blew hard to beat back the flames. But then, before anyone could push it aside, a lock of hair escaped from her bun.

"Owwwwwwwwwwwwwwwwwww!" Elise let out a virulent shriek. "Help me! Help me! *Help!*"

For a few seconds, nobody moved while they tried to grasp what was happening. Then the smell, noxious and forceful, made it obvious. Elise's hair was on fire, her reddish locks singeing and crisping. Freddy jumped up first, dumping his water glass on Elise's head. It helped, and a reassuring fizz sounded. But then Elise shrieked again and it was obvious her hair was still smoldering.

Freddy grabbed Rachel's glass and flung it at Elise.

"No!" Rachel screamed, but it was too late. Elise's hair sizzled and the smell grew even more lethal. "That's vodka! I'm so sorry." Rachel began to cry.

Natasha appeared with a large pitcher of water (when had she even run off to get it?

Annette wondered) and poured the whole thing on Elise's head in one quick motion. The stench of burning hair finally began to subside.

Annette watched as Elise slowly lifted her hand and brought it to her head. In patent disbelief, she grasped at the clumps of her hair, assessing the damage while biting down hard on her bottom lip.

"Elise —" she started to say, wanting to comfort her daughter. She knew her hairdresser Antonio could work magic on anybody, and there was no doubt if Elise was willing to make the trip, Antonio could fashion a flattering bob out of the remains. Truthfully, Annette had always thought Elise should cut her hair shorter. So maybe this was a blessing. "If you want, I can ask Anto—"

"I. Am. Going. To. My. Cabin," Elise said and nobody dared to convince her otherwise. She turned her back on the group and headed toward the exit, her fist still grasping a clump of her sopping wet hair. Mitch, dutiful, followed quickly behind.

When they were gone, Freddy, Natasha, David, Rachel, and Darius all looked to Annette for instruction. They only treated her like the matriarch when convenient. She rubbed both her eyes, even though she knew it would drag the coal of her eyeliner toward her temples. It was rare she was this tired.

"What are you all waiting for?" Annette finally said. "Time for bed." She honestly didn't want to hear another word out of any of them. The following day she was turning seventy. Surely nobody had thought to bring her a gift. So she would give herself a present: a deep and dreamless night's sleep, compliments of another one of David's Valium.

TWENTY-SIX

2300 hours. 120 miles from St. Lucia.

Julian had a monster migraine. Soon after he turned forty, the debilitating headaches began. He had assumed the worst, a brain tumor. For a few weeks he avoided seeing a doctor because he couldn't face having his worst fears confirmed. But Roger made him go after he found him sitting in a corner of their bathroom in a pool of his own vomit. They went to the neurologist together, holding hands in the waiting room even though both of their palms were clammy, and Roger left his side only when the radiation tech forced him outside.

"Migraines," the doctor said, after an excruciating wait for the results. "Your MRI and CT were clean. It all makes sense. The vomiting. The waves in your vision."

Julian and Roger exhaled, a collective breath that ruffled the papers on the doctor's desk.

418

"It's not a tumor," Roger said in Arnold Schwarzenegger's voice from *Kindergarten Cop* and they all started laughing, though it couldn't be the first time the neurologist had heard the joke.

"But I've never had them before," Julian said. "How could they just start out of nowhere?"

The doctor, a white-haired fellow whose bookcases were lined with pictures of grandchildren, smiled kindly.

"You've just had a big birthday, haven't you?"

Julian didn't answer. It was rhetorical anyway. The doctor had his chart right in front of him.

"Forty is not unheard of for the onset of migraines. In fact, some new literature is showing that more and more men are having their first episode in middle age," he explained. "Happy birthday."

In that moment, even though Julian had been grateful to Roger for forcing him to make the appointment with the best neurologist in Miami-Dade County and taking off work to accompany him, now he wished his boyfriend was not sitting there listening to the doctor talk about Julian getting old.

Roger was nine years Julian's senior. He had thinning hair and a back that creaked.

By contrast, Julian's head of hair was shampoo-commercial-worthy and he bounded up and down the steps on the cruise ships without so much as a touch of charley horse, no matter how many times a day he did it. Julian loved being the younger partner. He had exclusively dated older men. And while turning forty in no way narrowed the age gap between them, somehow it bookended them both in middle age. He didn't want Roger to see him that way, as a man on a collision course with fifty, someone who developed a medical condition simply because of the number of rings in his trunk.

Julian had left the doctor's office immensely relieved that he was tumor free but still with a nagging feeling. What would come next? Perhaps a soft penis that no amount of coaxing or dirty movies could bring to a salute? Cellulite that was defenseless against the Total Body machine at which he prayed every morning?

"Cheer up," Roger said when they reached their Volvo in the parking lot. "You could be dying. Instead you're just old like me."

The migraines always started with the same symptom, a stiffness at the base of his skull. The thin gold chain Julian wore around his neck would take on the feeling of an albatross. He knew one was coming before the black-tie gala when he struggled to put on his bow tie. He took his medication immediately and hoped to be spared the worst of the symptoms, since this was the biggest night on the cruise. But the moment he walked into the cocktail hour and the jazz trio sounded like toddlers with tambourines, he knew it was going to be a difficult night. Maybe Roger was right and he should find a job that he could leave behind in the evenings. A job where he wasn't literally trapped.

And then the fiasco with the Feldman family happened. He wasn't surprised it was one of the most vanilla-looking families on board causing all the commotion. It always happened like that. The motorcycle gangs would embark in their leather and chains, inked with dragons and flames on their massive biceps, and he wouldn't hear a peep out of them the whole time. Not a noise complaint or a scuffle in the casino. Sometimes those guys were the surprise hit of the amateur comedy night. The bachelorette squads would cross the gangway giggling loudly, already drunk on Red Bull and vodka and life, and then the next day he'd see them all fast asleep at the pool, because they were young, overworked professionals who above everything else were just tired. But the families, the multigenerational clusters of slow-moving grandparents and fast-talking teenagers, of middle-aged parents getting crushed on both ends, they were always the source of drama. They were the ones for whom the Caribbean cruise was a trip, not a vacation.

He made his way down the hallway toward his room, stepping over a chorus girl from the late-night adults-only show making out with a busboy she'd ignore the next day. Normally he'd tell them to take it inside somewhere. Same with the line cooks who were smoking Turkish cigarettes while playing cards, ashing right into the carpet. But tonight Julian couldn't be bothered. He needed to get to his room, lie in the dark, and wait for the migraine to subside. Above everything, he needed silence. His room was at the end of the hallway. He had one of the better cabins, with a small sitting area and a queen-size bed he loved to lie in on the diagonal. Roger was a cover-stealer and tosser-turner, so Julian relished his evenings in bed alone.

When he opened the door, Julian saw a small pool of light in the corner shedding from the desk lamp. In the desk chair sat Roger.

"Ahh!" Julian yelped in fright. "What are you doing here?"

"Surprise," Roger said. He rose from his chair and looked like he was coming to give Julian a hug, but stopped himself short.

"You're not well," Roger said. "You have a migraine."

"Yes," Julian said, moving into the room and sinking onto the bed. "How can you tell?"

"C'mon, Julian. I know when you need to pee." He joined Julian on the bed and took his hand. Roger wore a Dolphins string bracelet that Julian teased him about. *Just because I love football doesn't mean I can't love you,* Roger would say back every time. *Don't be so stereotypical.*

"What are you doing here, Roger? How did you plan this? And why did you wait so long to tell me you were here?" Julian's head felt like an aquarium, questions swimming in circles like bettas. "And who is watching Takai?"

"My sister has him. I've been having the best time watching you work without you knowing. It's like *Undercover Boss,* except it's 'Undercover Boyfriend.' Also, I'm technically not Roger. I booked the trip under the name Carlos Rodriguez and listed my occupation as traveling urinal salesman.

Figured I'd have some fun with it. I thought you might have said something when you were reviewing the manifest, but it didn't get your attention."

Julian attempted a smile.

"That is hardly the strangest occupation I've come across. But nice effort," he said. "I still want to know why you're here." Roger's coming on the boat felt like an invasion of Julian's territory, even if his boyfriend intended it as a loving gesture. It was a sign that Roger didn't take his work seriously, if he thought he could show up like this. Julian would never just appear at the Dolphins offices and expect Roger to drop everything, even though he had promised to bring him into the locker room before a game at least just once.

"Actually, this isn't the time to discuss this. And not because of my headache. You might think it's cute that you showed up here under an assumed name and snuck into my room —"

Roger put up a hand.

"I did not sneak," he said. "I found Lindsay and she let me in. Though I have to say I met the head chef when I was in your office and he had literally zero recognition when I introduced myself to him, and he said he's worked with you for the past six years. Do you ever talk about me?"

"I like to keep my personal life personal. Sue me. Let's say what this is really about, Rog. I shut down the marriage conversation the night before I left. I'm skittish. But do you have any idea what I see on the boat day in and day out? Tired couples desperate to revive their lifeless marriages. Families that can't stand each other, trying to pretend otherwise, but, trust me, by the third or fourth day the jig is up. I trust you saw the little explosion tonight. The gloves come off even earlier if the seas are rough. You need to believe me that making it official, slapping on a label, is not all it's cracked up to be."

Julian's vision suddenly zigzagged, as happened from time to time during his attacks, and he saw Roger as fractured, his face a million different planes.

"I'm sorry. I knew it was a risk, but every time I try to talk to you about it you say you're leaving for a —"

"Listen, I have stuff to deal with," Julian said abruptly. "Don't wait up for me." He stood up, even though his vision was still shot, everything around him wavy and with a halo effect. He left the room and let the door slam shut behind him, the sound like an icepick to his skull.

Julian wasn't sure where to go when he left the room, but he knew he needed distraction and darkness. His first choice would have been the yoga room, which was usually free in the evenings and smelled like aromatherapy oils, but he remembered that it was booked by the Seattle chapter of Claustrophobics Anonymous for a private event. The CA folks had been coming on board for a while now, as part of an experimental immersive therapy. Julian didn't think it was working too well because he still had to reserve a private elevator for them and open the breakfast buffet an hour early for their exclusive use.

Deck Three had an Irish-style pub called the Salty Anchor that was always kept dim, lit indirectly by the neon beer signs behind the counter. If he kept his back to it, Julian could be safe from the light, which was kryptonite to his migraines. Unlike everything else on the ship, carnivalesque and flashy, the Salty Anchor was intentionally mellow, serving as an escape room for people who needed time away from the action or their traveling companions. It was the perfect spot to nurse, or chug (no judgment from Julian), a drink in peace. He wasn't supposed to drink when he took his headache meds, so he planned to order a tea, find a small table in a corner, and wait for relief. He was friendly with Jimmy, the bartender, who wouldn't give him any guff for skipping out on a pint. If things were quiet, Jimmy might keep him company. Jimmy was straighter than a ruler, but he had a chiseled jaw, long floppy hair, and a sexy Cockney accent, so Julian was willing to overlook his disappointing preference for women.

It must have been Roger that he'd seen out of the corner of his eye at the chocolate fountain. He still couldn't believe his boyfriend — partner, whatever — had booked himself on the *Ocean Queen* under an assumed name. It was true they often played little tricks on each other. Roger once put a picture of Julian as a pimply teenager with Coke-bottle glasses on the JumboTron at a Dolphins home game. Julian, knowing Roger had a major phobia of insects, once convinced him that their apartment had bedbugs and didn't confess it was a joke until half of their clothing had been sealed in plastic bags. But this latest didn't feel like April Fool's one-upmanship. This felt like an ambush. Julian had often deflected conversations about their future by saying he was leaving soon for a cruise. So Roger had brought the discussion to sea, where the closest thing Julian had to a getaway route was to sign up for the daily Escape-the-Room challenge at eleven.

"Well, well, if it isn't our fearless cruise director," Jimmy said when Julian entered the Salty Anchor. "I heard there was a little episode at cocktails. The medi guys were pissed because they were in the middle of a Ping-Pong tournament when they got buzzed."

"Nothing I couldn't handle," Julian said and looked around for an empty seat. Tonight the place was jam-packed with guests, rumpled in their formal wear but not ready to call it a night. Bow ties were discarded and French twists were set free and everyone seemed to be speaking two notches above the appropriate decibel level. Julian almost turned to leave but realized that any place he sought out was going to be mobbed after the formal evening. He plopped himself in an empty chair near the bar's front entrance.

"Tea, please. Herbal," he mouthed to Jimmy, who nodded his understanding.

A waitress he didn't recognize set the mug and a box of assorted teas down in front of him a moment later. The cruise ship had many long-standing employees: Jimmy, the barkeep from central casting; Oxana, the cabaret dancer who claimed she wouldn't retire until her boobs were too saggy to hold up her pineapple bra; and Ralphie, the head of security on the casino floor, a tough guy who could spot a card counter with one eye closed. But the rest of them: the bellmen, the greeters, the shop clerks, the maintenance guys, and the Purell pumpers, they were like a revolving door of cast members. Julian formed few attachments because just as soon as he developed an inside joke with the maître d' at the Italian restaurant or the gym manager learned which treadmill he preferred to use, they were gone. When the boat's senior hairdresser went all Sweeney Todd on him last year, lopping off two inches instead of two centimeters (measurements were a constant source of confusion because the staff hailed from both the metric and imperial systems), Julian barely had time to give him the stink eye before he announced his return to Sri Lanka.

Julian liked it just fine this way. He was never, ever lonely, because you simply couldn't be when you were surrounded by thousands of people with whom making small talk was your occupation. But he didn't bother with close entanglements. Which was why Roger was totally overreacting about the head chef not knowing about him. Roger just didn't get boat life. It wasn't like at the Dolphins, where the same group of lawyers and accountants went to eat the same salads and turkey sandwiches in the cafeteria every day, sitting at the same table and complaining about the same annoying coworkers three tables over. Maybe that was why Roger wanted to come on board, to observe firsthand this major part of Julian's life.

"Excuse me," came a timid voice just as he was taking his first sip of tea. Julian looked up and saw Mrs. Feldman of the Fighting Feldmans. He couldn't suppress a groan, but she didn't seem to hear it over the din.

"I just wanted to say how sorry I am about the commotion earlier. I feel terrible if it made things difficult for you." Whereas earlier Mrs. Feldman had looked rather attractive for an older woman, like one of those regal-bearing matriarchs on cable TV, now she appeared drained and haggard. If it was possible to age a decade in an hour, Mrs. Feldman had done so.

"It's fine," Julian said, hoping to sound reassuring. "These incidents aren't as uncommon as you'd think."

"Really?" Annette said, a glimpse of hopefulness spreading across the planes of her anguished face. "We really aren't the types of people to cause a scene. We're . . . We're . . . I don't know." Her voice caught.

Julian smiled. "The boat brings out the best and worst in people. It's a lot of togetherness." He thought of Roger. Was he still sitting on his bed, waiting? Or had he gone to find wherever Julian was secreting himself?

Julian considered if being at sea together for the first time would bring out the best or the worst for him and Roger once their initial scuffle subsided and Julian was headache free. He tried to lighten his own mood with a favorite, if not a bit tired, joke among the crew: *If the boat's a-rocking, don't come a-knocking.* It would be uniquely intimate to be with Roger in his cabin, the private sphere that many a chorus boy had intimated they would gladly enter. He may not have advertised Roger to the crew, like the women who bored everyone with endless cell phone pictures of their families back home, but he did something far more important. He'd resisted the temptation that hung in every particle of air, that moved with every hip sway, that dripped like sweat

431

off the beautiful bodies. The *Ocean Queen* was a gay man's delight, but Julian had only looked, never touched.

"It's okay," Julian said and pushed out the chair opposite him. "Want to sit down?" Mrs. Feldman looked like a woman who really wished she could trade her heels for Keds right about now.

"Are you sure?" she asked, but she sat down before he could answer.

"Want to talk about it?" he asked.

He was rarely curious about the passengers. When you saw so many different walks of life routinely, each bizarre situation you encountered became less intriguing. He'd seen body piercings in places he'd thought biologically impregnable, love hexagons that made your basic love triangle milquetoast, and family situations that Jerry Springer wouldn't put on his couch. But the drug revelation with the Feldmans, the fact that the Jewish Pablo Escobar might be on board, now *that* got his attention.

Mrs. Feldman raised her eyebrows and her forehead creased with a dozen horizontal ravines. The lines gave her face a softness and a sense of character. Julian had already frozen the muscles in his forehead and around his eyes so that his skin was as smooth as the inside of a seashell. The only benefit of his migraines was that his Botox was now covered by insurance. He wondered, looking at Mrs. Feldman, why he was so afraid to get older.

"Not really," she said. "I wouldn't even know where to start."

A flash of light cut through the space between Julian and Mrs. Feldman and he winced, dropping the sugar packet he was fidgeting with right into the hot liquid.

"Are you okay?" she asked.

"Yes. I get migraines," he managed.

"You poor thing. I can't imagine it's easy to have a migraine with all this mayhem around you. You should go lie down in your cabin."

"I can't," he said. "I mean, I can. But I don't want to. It's complicated."

She smiled warmly and Julian noticed an endearing smudge of pink lipstick on her teeth. "I think you've seen that I'm rather familiar with complicated. No judgments," she said and began to laugh, almost hysterically.

"What's so funny?" Julian scrutinized Mrs. Feldman. She looked kind of crazy, if he was being honest.

"Oh, it's just that my kids would say that I'm the most judgmental person they know. So if they heard me say 'no judgments' to

433

you, they'd have a fit."

"You seem very nice, Mrs. Feldman. I'm sorry your family is giving you a hard time." He could see how much it meant to her when he said their family drama was nothing he hadn't seen before, so he took the opportunity to reassure her again that a few punches and shoves were practically commonplace on the *Ocean Queen.*

"So why is it that you can't go back to your cabin?" Annette asked. She'd admonished him not to call her Mrs. Feldman. *As if I don't feel old enough,* she had said, which struck a chord.

"My partner, Roger, surprised me by coming on the ship. He was waiting for me in the room."

"And that's a bad thing?" Annette asked.

"Not bad per se. It's just that this boat has always only belonged to me and it's uncomfortable to have him in my space. We've been together for three years. We have a dog, share an apartment, the same friends. Roger wants us to get married and I just can't see the need for the label. I'm a witness to all these people who come on board to celebrate the life cycle events: anniversaries, birthdays, retirements. And they are under so much pressure to maximize the fun and make sure everyone they've brought along is happy. But you know who is always having the best time? The people who, when I ask them why they decided to take a cruise, just look at me and say, 'Because we felt like it.' No special occasion, no reason for forcing a good time. I'm not sure Roger gets that. He wants a label. Like those personalized shirts you see the groups wearing around the boat, especially on the first day. It's like he wants us to have *I'm with him* T-shirts with arrows pointing at each other."

"I understand," Annette said. "Regrettably, I'm one of those people who tried to force the togetherness. And the owner of a personalized sweatshirt. I was instructing my children and grandchildren: You will make memories together and you will like it. You can see how well it's working out for us. But I have to tell you, forced or not forced, label or no label, I like having people that are bound to me in some way. The older you get, the lonelier life becomes."

Her voice quavered and Julian motioned for Jimmy to bring her a hot drink.

"I'm turning seventy tomorrow and I get to have all of my closest relatives around me. Yes, I have friends. Many of them. And they love to get together for parties and be there when times are good. But for them,

435

and for me too, family will always come first, especially if and when — pardon my French — the shit hits the fan. The ladies I have lunch with might make me laugh more than my own children. They certainly laugh at my jokes more. The nurses and doctors I used to work with — I was the office manager in my husband's medical office — respected me a heck of a lot more than my grandchildren do. Although I seem to be making some headway with my grandson. But what can I say? I'd rather be around my family, even if they don't think I'm particularly funny or clever or interesting. Even if it's obligation that brought us all together, I'm glad we're here. Having a family brings obligation. There's no doubt about it. But through fulfilling obligation, I think can come great joy."

She took a grateful sip of the hot water with lemon that was set before her and continued.

"It's kind of like the sky. You know how there are so many stars on a clear night that you can't begin to count them? The people who make up our worlds — the friends, the coworkers, the ones we pass on the street who smile at us — they are those stars. They brighten our lives. But there are nights when it's so cloudy that you can't see any stars.

Our family members are the stars we can call on to shine when we need a little light. And they have no choice but to turn on, even if they are far away, even if they would rather be doing other things." She paused for a beat, squeezing more lemon into her mug. "Do I sound wise or just crazy? As you get older, it's hard to tell."

"Definitely not crazy. Have a very happy birthday, Annette. You deserve it," Julian said, rising from his seat. "I'm suddenly feeling very tired and like I need to go back to my room."

She gave him a warm smile and dismissed him with the wave of a liver-spotted hand.

TWENTY-SEVEN

"How do you know about Austin, you little weasel?" Rachel demanded when she and Darius were back in their cabin. "I can't believe you would spy on me."

"I'm sorry," Darius blurted out. "I shouldn't have said anything in front of Mom and Dad. But your papers fell out of your bag when I was getting ready. It's not exactly like there's a lot of room to move around this place."

"Well, you didn't have to read them." Rachel pouted. "I would never do that to you. If I found your personal things, I would put them back exactly where I found them and try my very best not to read a thing." Rachel found herself getting more upset with her brother as she yelled at him, because every bit of what she was saying was true. She wouldn't snoop on him. Darius *was* sneakier. Rachel remembered that even as a child, her little brother loved spy kits. He was always trying to take her fingerprints and installing toy cameras in the hallways that could see around the corner. *Creepy.*

"That's because you don't care about me in the slightest. If I leave my email open on the kitchen computer, you X out of it without even glancing. That's how little interest you have in me."

Rachel felt her ears burning, like what was supposed to happen when people talk *behind* your back. But Darius was speaking right to her face, telling her what he thought of her. That she was selfish. A shit sibling. She racked her brain for a rebuttal.

"Remember when you were five and Mom was backing out of the garage while you were riding your bike in the driveway? I ran and pulled you out of the way, even though I could have gotten hit too."

"Rachel, that was forever ago. And what does that prove? That you didn't want me dead? I agree with that. You would prefer that I stay alive. But have you asked me once what's going on with me? About school. My friends. My college search. Nada. It's fine, by the way. I'm totally used to it."

Rachel bit down, pressing her top teeth into a blister on her bottom lip. She always did that when she was thinking hard. Austin

439

had noticed it. He loved to tease her about her habits: everything from the complicated Starbucks orders to her weird need to wash her hands before they had sex. What were Darius's habits that she should have picked up on? People who care about each other know their quirks and mannerisms. Her brother chewed with his mouth open exclusively. He cut his toenails over the toilet and then never flushed. But those were both negative! She was also pretty sure he had gotten himself fired from his lifeguard job, but that was another bad thing. Ah, she had something! When they sat down in the den to watch TV, he always asked her what she wanted to watch, even if he got to the remote first. And another thing! He was really clever at naming things. He christened their goldfish Fishtopher, the ficus in the living room Plantricia, their father's black Honda the Accordian.

"It doesn't matter now. I'm going to the arcade," Darius said, flinging off his bow tie and unbuttoning his top button. "There's no way I can fall asleep. Not after that crazy dinner-slash-hair-burning-slash-everyone-in-our-family-is-screwed-up."

"I do know something about you," Rachel said quietly. "You like that girl on the boat.

The one who always wears the school shirts."

"Her name's Angelica. And I don't *like* her. She's just someone to hang out with on the trip. She's way too smart for me anyway," Darius said.

Rachel felt a surge of irritation course through her. She blamed her parents for making her brother feel so bad about himself. Their mother nagged him from morning until night about his work, always quick to throw in a "When I was in medical school I studied until three a.m. regularly," or, "This vocab list is a fraction of what we had to memorize in chemistry." Their father wasn't much better. He seemed to have forgotten what it was like to be a kid. Dinner conversation centered on the articles he was editing — the modernization of the sewage system in Sacramento; why the opera house couldn't hold on to a director for longer than a year's tenure — and he would have a look of patent disappointment when Darius couldn't respond with anything intelligible. At least she knew to say something innocuous like, "That'll make a great piece," or, "Can't wait to read it when it's done." She partially admired Darius for caring so little that he didn't bother to concoct a phony response, but more so she

441

fretted about his cluelessness. *See that, little brother! I do worry about you.*

"You *are* smart, Darius. You know Mrs. Hatcher, the history teacher? I ran into her at the nail salon last weekend. I had her for American history in ninth. She actually told me you have an amazing memory and are the only person in class who can keep the timeline of the Civil War straight." She realized that she hadn't shared that compliment with Darius. But it wasn't out of malice. Her entire brain felt invaded by Austin. It was hard enough to clear space to remember to take her birth control pill or register for fall semester classes.

"I do know all the presidents in order and what states they are from," Darius said, with one part pride and two parts embarrassment. "So what kind of trouble do you think you're going to be in with Mom and Dad? I can't believe you got arrested. Miss Perfect in the slammer."

Rachel shrugged. Weirdly enough, she didn't really care. A large part of her was relieved that everything was out in the open. Two other girls had gotten arrested alongside her the night of the Porn Party and they'd both called their parents to ask for a bailout. Only she had been too afraid, hence the emergency call to Freddy. And her parents finding out about Austin? If there was any chance of a real relationship with him, he couldn't stay a secret forever. Her parents would certainly punish her for the alcohol infraction and the run-in with the police, and they'd raise hell about her dating a married man, but she knew that deep down the thing that would bother them the most was her clandestine kinship with Freddy. They wouldn't admit it, but she knew.

"I'm back at school in a week," she said. "I can't really imagine what they can do to me other than cut back on the monthly allowance I get. Though it seems our family is broke anyway." She attempted a wry smile.

"Do you think I'm going to end up at one of those colleges that advertise on the radio?" Darius asked. He had curled up on his bed, balled into a miniature version of himself. Rachel saw something in his expression that made her cower. He thought she had the answers. He still believed she knew if there were monsters lurking under his bed.

"No, no, no. Grandma and Grandpa will help. Or you'll take out loans. I will write you the best damn college essay on earth and the scholarships will pour in. I promise," she said. "Are you still going to hit the arcade tonight?"

"Yes, but I need to swing by Angelica's room first. They have Wi-Fi and there's something I need to check."

Wi-Fi?! She could email Austin!

"Can I come?" she asked meekly. He nodded yes. For the first time in a long time, she followed Darius and not the other way around.

TWENTY-EIGHT

As eager as he was to finally read Marcy's email, Darius walked slowly toward Angelica's room, enjoying the feeling of his older sister following his lead.

"We need to tap quietly on the door," Darius said. "Her grandmother is pretty scary. She only speaks Mandarin, but I can tell she doesn't like me."

Rachel nodded. He felt bad about outing her to his parents — it had certainly not been his intention at the evening's outset — but he had the feeling that with all the drama unfolding between the adults, his sister might come away relatively unscathed. He really needed to be careful about loose lips when he drank.

They made their way into a cramped elevator, where a group of women wearing *Bride Squad* sashes over their dresses were singing "Sweet Caroline" at the top of their lungs. The bride, whose name, according to her crown, was actually Caroline, had streaks of mascara down her cheeks and kept saying over and over again, "I love you guys. I love you guys." Rachel gave Darius a look of amusement and he wondered how long it had been since she'd eyed him in that way, telepathically connecting with him over shared disapproval of other people. It was the way she used to look at him when their great-aunt Marcia squeezed their cheeks like they were Pillsbury Doughchildren.

Angelica didn't look surprised when she opened the cabin door for them. She had changed out of her purple dress and into sweatpants and yet another Highlawn T-shirt. This one said *Yearbook Committee*. Her hair was loosely braided and she had a Coke bottle in her hand.

"We didn't wake you," Darius said. "Good."

"You okay? I caught a little bit of your family's hissy fit before the cruise director booted us all."

"We're okay," Rachel responded. "I'm Darius's sister. It's nice to meet you."

"Angelica," she said, extending her hand. "Are you guys here for me or my Wi-Fi? Never mind. Don't answer. I know." She ushered them inside and brought a finger to

446

her lips.

In the far twin bed, orchestral snores came from a body that, underneath the bounty of covers, looked no bigger than a child's.

"Grandma is a very loud sleeper," Angelica said. "My eyeballs are ready to fall out of their sockets from exhaustion."

She took her laptop into the deserted hallway, empty but for a few room service trays with half-eaten burgers and ketchuped fries awaiting collection from the ground. The three of them sat in a row, Darius in the middle, and Angelica booted up the computer and entered the necessary codes to beam them to civilization.

"Who first?" Angelica asked, lifting the laptop from her legs.

Rachel looked at Darius, knowing that because Angelica was his friend, it was up to him to choose.

"Go for it, Rachel," he said and Angelica handed her the computer. His sister's fingers tap-danced with lightning speed. She was clearly on a mission.

"He wrote me," she said out loud, sounding like a lovesick child, even though that was so not her style. Rachel's smile filled her whole face and Darius watched as she read silently, noticing how gradually the corners of her mouth came back down and her teeth fell out of view.

"Are you okay?" he asked.

"It's fine," she said. "Just some legal stuff."

But Darius saw that she wasn't fine. She was doing that thing where she rolled her eyes around to stop them from watering.

"Take this," she said and handed the computer over to Darius. "I'm going to head back to our cabin and find something to watch on TV. Thanks for the Wi-Fi." Rachel disappeared down the hallway.

He logged into his own account, hoping that Angelica didn't see his email address: SkataBoy666. It was so painfully dumb that he couldn't remember ever being so short of brain cells as to think that was a cool name. He looked over at her out of the corner of his eye. She was picking at a cuticle on her thumb, not paying him much attention.

"Do you want privacy?" Angelica asked when she noticed him looking her way.

"Um," Darius muttered, not sure how to respond. It was her computer, after all. Her Wi-Fi. It didn't seem right that he should ask her to relocate. Not that it was all that comfortable in the hallway. With the sea rocking gently beneath them, the geometric pattern of the carpet was increasingly nauseating to look at.

"It's fine," she said, getting to her feet. "I was in the middle of an SAT II chemistry practice test."

Darius scrolled through his emails furiously, not finding the one from Marcy. Had he dreamed the entire thing? He felt numb at the thought. Maybe everything was a dream: His uncle, loaded from selling pot. His mother, a shopaholic who'd bankrupted the family. His grandpa, the doctor who he'd always believed could fix anything, sick with something he couldn't cure. It wasn't that bad imagining that the past six months of his life had been one long, dizzying dream. He wanted Marcy to be real but nothing else. Except for maybe Rachel treating him like a fellow human. That was nice.

But then he found it, sandwiched between an ad for the new Bad Religion single and a welcome-back message from the school principal. He clicked it open and immediately his heart sank. It wasn't just to him. It was to all the kids they hung out with and some email addresses he didn't recognize. Apparently Marcy had lost her phone and needed everyone to send their numbers. The subject line *was* Help, but it wasn't the damsel-in-distress-seeking-his-services note he'd been pining for. It wasn't even the "How's the cruise?" or "I have another band for you" email he'd been wishing so hard for that his brain actually hurt. Absence hadn't made her heart grow fonder. He was just number twelve on a list of thirty people (yes, he'd counted) whose number Marcy needed.

"All set?" Angelica asked. Darius looked down and saw that he'd shut the laptop, which he didn't even remember doing.

"Yep," he said. "Thanks a lot for letting me use it."

"No problem. You know, my grandma's snoring just took a turn for the worse and the people in the cabin next door seem to be having a crazy sex party so there's no way I'm going to be able to sleep. Do you want to maybe walk around a little? I heard there's a jail on the boat. For real. It's on the lowest deck. We could try to sneak in and see it."

Darius stood up quickly. He needed zero convincing.

"That sounds awesome."

The jail, a.k.a. the brig, wasn't so much a metal-barred room with inmates in black-and-white-striped jumpsuits as three adjacent conference rooms with a table each and a locked door with a keypad entry. And the guard wasn't a tough guy patrolling the corridor with a menacing baton, but a non-threatening, white-haired old-timer with his head down on a desk, taking a nap.

"I guess this is it," Angelica said in a whisper. Darius wasn't scared per se, but there was a big sign that said NO UNAUTHORIZED ENTRY on the door that Angelica had brazenly ignored. He marveled at her cool, the sheer unexpectedness of it.

They tiptoed past the first two "cells," both empty. The third was occupied. A goateed middle-aged man in a collared Izod was sitting in a corner of the room, tapping his fingers against the wall. He had bright white tennis shoes on. He could have been any given teacher at Darius's school. As if reading his mind, Angelica said, "This guy looks like my advanced calc teacher, Mr. Taylor." The inmate made eye contact with them and Angelica quickly put her finger to her lips to signal him not to wake the guard. He caught her drift.

"What do you think he did?" Darius whispered.

"Broke the dress code? He's not in a tux," Angelica suggested.

"Hmm. I bet he's like Walter White. Nerd by day, meth dealer by night," Darius posited. "He was probably cooking in his cabin." He thought about Freddy. Maybe his uncle would have told Darius what he was up to if they'd ever gotten any time alone, but his mother had made certain that never happened. Nevertheless, Darius had a cool, rich uncle dealing drugs. Now, *that* was a story for Marcy.

The inmate could apparently hear them through the glass. He signaled that they were way off the mark, miming something that involved a lot of spastic body movements.

"He punched the craps dealer after he didn't get a seven for four rolls," the guard said, suddenly very much awake.

Darius and Angelica jumped back, afraid they were going to be in big trouble.

"I wasn't sleeping, by the way. My left sinus is clogged and I needed to drain it to the right. That's why I had my head down."

"Um, okay," Angelica stammered. To Darius, she mouthed, "TMI."

"If you kids want to see something a bit more interesting than the jail, you should check out the morgue." The guard gave them a dodgy smile. He was missing two teeth, and the rest were yellowed and crooked, planted nearly perpendicular to each other.

"Like, for dead people?" Darius asked.

"I guess it makes sense," Angelica said.

"They can't just throw the bodies overboard and I suppose most people on the boat don't want their loved ones buried on some remote island. Though that would be lovelier than my family's plot in Queens right next to the interstate."

"You know where you're getting buried?" Darius was aghast.

"Oh, yeah. Grandma is very into death. She saved up for us to get into a high-end Chinese cemetery and we all had to go visit after she bought it. She was psyched about the cherry blossoms and the wide lanes — that's in between the rows of graves — but I was like, what the hell, we are going to be sucking car exhaust for the rest of our lives."

"Well, you'll be dead. So you won't be sucking anything," Darius said.

"You kids want to see the morgue or not?" the guard asked, taking a swig from a mug that said *You Nail Them. I Jail Them.*

They nodded.

"It's at the other end of this hallway behind two sets of doors. The second door has a sign that says 'Safety Equipment' but trust me, that's the morgue."

"Any, um, occupants?" Angelica asked. Darius couldn't tell if she was hoping for the guard's answer to be yes or no.

"You'll have to find out," he said and lit

up a cigar.

"I'm allergic to smoke," the Walter White look-alike called from his cell, pounding on the glass. The guard paid him no mind.

"Should we?" Darius asked Angelica. They had moved away from the brig and were standing in a small, dark corridor with only a few floor lights casting a glow on their shoes. Angelica was so tiny next to him without her heels. She didn't have much in the boob department, but there was a definite femininity that came from her long hair and heart-shaped mouth.

"Let's do it," she said and reached for his hand. Together they walked, hands clasped, down a quiet hallway that was, in contrast to every other place on the boat, eerily quiet. Darius willed his palm not to sweat and considered pulling it away momentarily to wipe it on his pants, but didn't want Angelica to be offended.

"I see the double doors," she said, pointing with her free hand. She pushed open the first door, which wasn't locked, and immediately they both felt the chill.

"Take this," Darius said, slipping out of his black tuxedo jacket and draping it over her shoulders. He was a narrow guy, but three Angelicas could have fit under it.

He opened the second door and they

stepped into a room that felt and looked like a meat locker. Four metal caskets were against a wall with drawer-like openings at the end. Thick, squared-off handles were centered on each door and there were no locks. Darius got a strong sense of déjà vu from the time he stumbled into his family's attic and found his mother's stash, the overwhelming feeling of being somewhere he didn't belong.

"Think anyone's inside?" Angelica asked him.

"We could look," Darius said, eyeing the handles.

"Or we could not. And get the hell out of here and get ice cream."

Darius was relieved. He didn't want to appear chicken in front of Angelica, who was proving to be far more brazen than he, but he also didn't feel like capping off what was an extremely difficult night by looking at a bluish, rotting corpse stuffed in a metal box. Between dead flesh and mint chocolate chip, he would choose the latter.

"Ta ma de!" Angelica exclaimed, grabbing his elbow tightly.

"Sorry, I thought I heard someone coming," she said. "I curse in Chinese. Comes from so many hours at the dry cleaner's. My dad has a real potty mouth."

"Ta ma de," Darius said, attempting to copy her.

"Not bad. We'll work on your accent later," she said, suppressing a laugh.

"Agreed. Let's get ice cream." They rushed out and dashed up four flights of stairs until they were above sea level, in the land of the living and the non-criminally-sanctioned. The ice cream dispenser in the teen lounge had its usual crowd around it and Darius took a seat in an empty butterfly chair. Angelica propped herself on a beanbag next to him.

"You okay?" Angelica asked. "That was spooky."

Darius had his head cradled in his hands.

"The morgue really freaked me out. I don't know why. Or maybe I do. My grandfather has cancer. I think it's serious. And there was this kid in my high school who killed himself over the summer. Nobody even knows why. All I can think about is how happy I am to be alive. I can see and smell the ocean. I can be with my family. I know that sounds really corny."

"I hate to go all guidance counselor on you, Darius, but that would make a great college essay. You know how there's that open-ended question on the common app? Everyone thinks that's the worst one because, I mean, how self-absorbed or pretentious do you have to be to be, like — oh, the other questions aren't good enough for me, I need to do my own thing. But this, Darius, this is good. You write an essay — hell, you could even do it in a list form — about all the reasons you're happy to be alive. You could talk about being here. Or maybe say you were at a funeral or something, so they don't think you're some kind of freak sneaking into morgues, and the funeral made you think about everything you want to do with your life. It's genius."

"That's actually a pretty good idea," he said, meaning it. It was the first essay topic that didn't make his fingers cramp and his mind block before he even sat down to type.

"I'll read it over for you if you want," Angelica offered.

"Maybe," he said. It would depend on what he put on his list. Climbing Kilimanjaro. Learn sweep picking on the guitar. These were things he wasn't embarrassed about wanting for himself. Others, well, he wasn't even sure he knew what else he would say. Closeness with his sister. A kiss from Marcy, maybe. At least now, for the first time, when he thought about the blank computer screen, he felt excitement instead of nausea.

"What'd you write about?" Darius said, uncomfortable with this much attention on him.

"Nice pivot," she said. "I chose the question where you write about something difficult you did that you're very proud of."

"Which was . . . ?" Darius asked. Everything Angelica did seemed difficult. Debate team, chess team, cross-country, working after school, keeping straight As, honors everything.

She tugged at the drawstring of her sweatpants.

"Not trying to be all depressing or anything, but I wrote about teaching my disabled brother how to use the cash register at the store. My parents really didn't think he could do it. They were worried he'd give customers the wrong change or not be able to keep the claim tickets in order. And in our business, those tickets are like the holy grail. For whatever reason, I was sure he could do it. Sometimes I would see him doing the craziest math in his head and it was like he only did it when I was around. I felt like I saw something in him everyone else was missing. So I trained him. It took about two months, but he's the best cashier you'll ever meet. All the customers love him and he came up with this color-coding system

458

for the rush orders that is a lifesaver. So I wrote about that."

"Wow," Darius said. He hated that after all she'd described, the best he could muster was a monosyllabic response. Sometimes his tongue was as tied as a shoelace and he pictured reaching into his mouth and just giving it a good yank. The right words had to be inside him, lying in wait.

"Walk me back to my room, okay? I'm getting tired. Screw the ice cream. I don't want to get fat on this trip, anyway."

"You could hardly be fat. You look great." He immediately reddened and made an effort to look anywhere but at her.

"Thanks," she said calmly, but the corners of her mouth were turned up like apostrophes.

They walked the six flights to her cabin in silence, Darius's brain already at work compiling a list of things he wanted to say in his college essay. *To get to know my grandparents better . . . to fall in love . . . to learn how cell phones work . . .*

"Strange night," Angelica said when they reached her door.

"My family ruined the biggest night on the ship. We visited a jail and a morgue. I would say that's an understatement."

"Fun, though. In a weird way," Angelica

459

added. She took out her key card from her pocket and clicked open the door. "I'll see ya tomorrow maybe. What are you signed up for?"

They were arriving in St. Lucia in the early morning. Darius had signed up for a rock-climbing excursion that he was already thinking of skipping.

"Some climbing thing. Not sure if it'll be cool or not." He wanted to leave the door open for Angelica to invite him to join her again. It was so much less boring to have company, and while some sort of wall had broken down between him and Rachel, he couldn't count on finding the same warmth the next day.

"I'm going fishing with my dad," Angelica said. Darius tried not to look disappointed.

"Have fun. Hope you catch a big one," he said, perhaps a bit too enthusiastically, like he wanted nothing more than for Angelica to hook a thirty-pound flounder.

"Well, good night," she said. "I'm gonna stick in earplugs to drown out Grandma." She gave him a wistful look and closed the door behind her.

For a long moment he just stood outside her door, listening to the sounds of her shutting down for the evening. The tap turning on and off, drawers opened and shut. He pictured Angelica, her small frame moving about the room, maybe on tiptoe so as not to wake her grandma. And then the door flung open unexpectedly and Angelica saw that he hadn't moved from his spot. She was holding his tuxedo jacket.

"Wanted to give this back to you," she said, extending her hand. "Were you just coming back for it?" She probably knew he hadn't budged.

"Yeah, thanks."

She stepped into the hallway and closed the door behind her gently. Darius reached for the jacket, or for her waist, he didn't know. Her chin tilted up as his tilted down, their movements mirror opposites, kissing the natural conclusion. Openmouthed, a lot of tongue twisting. It lasted ten seconds, or was it ten minutes, Darius couldn't guess. He didn't know who pulled back first. Just that it was over suddenly and they were facing each other. Darius didn't know what Angelica was thinking, but he knew that he didn't want to look away or down at the floor. He wanted her to know that he was happy about what just happened.

"Good night for real now," she said softly.

"Hey, one more thing," he said, and Angelica held the door open. "What did one ocean say to the other?"

461

"Nothing. It just waved," Angelica said and made a little smirk.

"You really do know everything, don't you?" he said, cocking his head to the side.

"I guess I do. Sweet dreams, Darius," she said and stepped back into the room. He managed to wait until the door was closed for the big, dumb grin to spread across his face.

TWENTY-NINE

Mitch couldn't remember ever feeling so conflicted in his life. The entire walk back to the cabin from the ballroom, he felt himself pulsing with anger toward his wife. How could she be so duplicitous? How could she be so careless? They had worked hard and been cautious since day one so they could provide a proper education for their children, four years at a private college with room and board all taken care of. They wanted Rachel and Darius to graduate and not be ridden with debt and worry, so they could follow their dreams, whether that meant the Peace Corps or Wall Street. Elise had gone and trashed that plan all by herself, going to great lengths to cover her tracks, and he was finding out about it only now that he'd left his job and Darius was less than a year from graduation.

Another side of him felt sympathy beginning to flood through his veins, pumping blood to his heart in waves of compassion. How broken and lost must his wife have been to have spiraled this low? And how scared must she have been about fixing the mess? It made him want to cradle her and let her have a good cry on his shoulder, not chastise her and make her feel even worse. Besides, she was minus half a head of hair now. It made the notion of yelling at her, at least now, downright cruel. Still. How would he ever trust her again?

They had barely taken two steps into the room when Elise started speaking.

"Before you start, I know I've created a huge mess. I don't know how I'm going to fix it. I don't know if I can. But I'm relieved it's finally out in the open." She had walked across the room and sat down in the single armchair in the corner, avoiding looking in any of the mirrors. The curtains had been drawn while they were out and the room was dark except for two small pools of light coming from the night table lamps.

"Are you okay?" he asked, taking a seat on the edge of the bed. He glanced around the room and saw no shopping bags or extravagant purchases. Nothing that would suggest what had been happening right under his nose.

"I'm okay. I mean, clinically, I guess I'm

not okay. I have an addiction. Gosh, I've never really said the *A* word out loud before. Even to my shrink."

"Yeah, what was that Rachel said about a therapist?" For some reason, this wounded Mitch even more than learning about the shopping and the bonfire of their savings. He was supposed to be the person that Elise could turn to at any time. He pictured them lying next to each other in bed, both of their noses in open books, when the closed book was *their* story. He was guilty too of keeping secrets. He'd buried his unhappiness at the *Bee* for too long. And set off on a new path without consulting Elise. But still, her secret was bigger. It was infinitely more destructive. He was steaming all over again. He needed a shrink. Not that they had money for one. How the hell was Elise paying whatever astronomical hourly fee therapy had to be costing in their upscale neighborhood? Was buying a ten-pack of therapy sessions no different from a new pair of sunglasses for her?

"Yes. Dr. Margaret. It's an online thing. She's actually pretty amazing," Elise said.

"Well, what does Dr. Margaret say about the fact that you've squandered all our money on purses and shoes?" His tone was as calloused as a heel, fitting, since that was what he felt like.

"Can you just give me a freaking minute?" Elise said, tugging at her hair for sympathy. She was processing a lot of new information quickly, all of it bad. But so was he. Their daughter had been in jail. Freddy had a life they knew nothing about. David had cancer.

"Fine. Take all the time you need. Better yet, call Dr. Margaret," he snapped.

"She listens to me, Mitch. She tries to figure out how this happened. She doesn't think I'm a vapid person who all of a sudden developed a burning desire for designer labels." Elise hit the "she" hard, as though this Dr. Margaret was his foil. They were supposed to be each other's voices of reason, confidants, and best friends. He wondered when that had stopped for them, if it was as recently as the start of Elise's shopping spree or if their splintering had deeper roots.

"Well, sounds like she's not helping too much, considering you announced that we're bankrupt tonight," Mitch retorted.

"You're not blameless either, Mitch. What was that bull about you wanting to tell my family at the same time as me because they used to buy us fancy dinners? You waited to tell us all at once in case I was going to stop you. You figured by telling my parents at the same time as me then I couldn't derail your plans."

It was true-*ish*. He had been a coward.

"I wouldn't have stopped you from changing lanes, Mitch. Why would you think that about me?" Elise looked genuinely hurt.

"I'm sorry," he said, which was true, but wasn't much of an explanation. It occurred to him suddenly that his marriage had hit some kind of fork in the road — a subtle one — and he and Elise had gone in different directions. The roads were so closely parallel that neither of them seemed to have realized they weren't in the same car anymore. Something shifted in the room. The awareness and acceptance that both of them had crossed lines was cooling the tension.

"I can't believe I hit your dad." Mitch actually found himself smiling and pretty soon Elise was chuckling.

"Yeah, I never really pictured our family coming to blows. I thought we Feldmans preferred a more passive-aggressive form of combat. I still can't believe I just assumed it was my mom that was sick, not my dad. Goes to show what I know. I just don't understand people. Not my parents, not Freddy, definitely not the kids. I feel like I speak family as a second language. Do you ever feel that way?" Elise asked him.

"All the time. That should be a mandatory part of the school curriculum: FSL. It's not like my side is any better. Don't you remember last year when my sister wouldn't hang any ornaments on the tree that my mother gave her because she was pissed my mom said her gravy was lumpy at Thanksgiving?"

"Yes, but this is different. That's petty stuff. With my family I just constantly feel that there's this elephant in the room. There's so much we're not saying and so much we're not sharing. Like we can have all these meals together for days and not actually have a clue what's going on in anyone's actual life. Honestly, what have we even talked about at the meals? Whether the croissants were being recycled day to day. If anyone was going to participate in 'Cupcake Wars.' Meanwhile, Freddy was calculating his pot money, my dad was hiding an illness, Rachel was thinking about her secret boyfriend, and Darius — who even knows with that kid what is going on?"

Mitch hopped up from the bed, energy springing to his extremities.

"That's it! Elise, you just did it. My journal! I'm going to call it *The Elephant*. All these observations about life and the weird interactions we have every day — it can all boil down to there being an elephant in the room. Something we're not saying. An awkwardness we all feel but choose to ignore."

"Glad my family's craziness and pain have inspired you," Elise said, but she didn't sound angry. In fact, she was grinning.

"It *is* a silver lining." He squeezed Elise's shoulders. "On a grimmer note, what are we going to do about Rachel? I don't know if I'm more upset that she is running around wearing a balloon skirt, has a married boyfriend, or has been keeping her relationship with Freddy from us."

"How did you know about Freddy and the whole pot thing? Don't tell me you've also been taking trips to Aspen without my knowledge."

"Elise, don't start with me about secrets. I came across an article about him," Mitch said truthfully. There was no more space for lies at this point. "It was just yesterday."

"Show me," Elise said. She fished reading glasses from her purse.

Mitch took a deep breath and pulled up the article on his laptop, because what choice did he have? The headline remained the same. In fact, it almost seemed like they had increased the font size. And Mitch didn't remember having seen the money sacks that had been Photoshopped into Freddy's hands.

Elise took the computer onto her lap and started reading. Her jaw went slack and it looked like she wasn't breathing. Mitch read over her shoulder, shuddering. When she got to the middle of the article, having clicked through to the second page, Mitch let out a massive sigh of relief. It was gone! His buddy had come through for him. There was no mention of Freddy's upbringing at all! No Feldman family references whatsoever.

"Wow. This is really insane," Elise said. "Freddy really made something of himself. I mean, he's selling drugs, but I guess it's legal. It's kind of fitting actually. He was always good at making money when we were little. I did the dishes and took out the trash and got three dollars a week. Freddy arbitraged Garbage Pail Kids and sold candy bars that our mom bought in bulk before Halloween and made at least five times what I did. He's clever. I never really gave him credit for it. None of us did."

"So you're okay with it?" Mitch asked in disbelief.

"Honestly, it's a lot to take in. The brother I thought was living hand to mouth, scrap-

470

ing together a living working as a part-time barista or something, could buy and sell us a hundred times over. Explains Natasha, at least. I'm happy for him, though. Better that than both Feldman children are broke, right?" Elise put the laptop down and walked over to the mirror. Mitch watched her reflection as she took in the state of her hair. The left side of her shoulder-length waves was singed up to the ear. The other side was still nicely coiffed and fell in smooth ripples. It looked, like it sometimes did under dimmed lighting, like it was on fire. He thought not to make that observation to Elise. Perhaps she noticed it too. It was an elephant.

"I'm hideous," his wife observed. "I'm going to have to cut the other side to match and I need the longer-length hair to minimize my double chin. That's what Paulo told me." Paulo had been Elise's hairdresser for as long as Mitch could remember. Like the shrink, Paulo was another person in Elise's orbit whom she could apparently confide in.

"You're beautiful, Elise." Mitch went to stand beside her and they looked at each other's reflections thoughtfully. He cupped her chin, an intimate, tender gesture that he wouldn't have done if he was facing her.

She put her head on his shoulder and they continued to stay like that, side by side, shoulder to shoulder.

He put an arm around her waist and twisted her into him. They were kissing in a way they hadn't done in years, almost like the mirror was magic and wiped away the decades. Elise was light in his arms, as though he could feel her emptiness. It was something he wanted to fill. He led her to the bed. She seemed open in this moment, cut at the seams, and he seized his chance to enter. They could fight tomorrow.

When they were done, Elise didn't jump out of bed to wash off her makeup or brush her teeth. She lay curled with her head on his chest, which rose and fell with his breathing.

"Was that better than shopping?" he asked, lightly tracing her ear with his index finger. She didn't answer, just gave him a gentle swat. "Too soon?" he asked.

"Too soon. But you are funny. And your journal, *The Elephant,* is going to be wonderful. We may be back eating canned soup for a while and homeschooling Darius for college, but at least we'll have something entertaining to read."

"We're going to figure things out, Elise. We'll go work for Freddy."

"Still too soon, Mitch."

They both laughed, harder than was called for, but it gave them another release they desperately needed.

THIRTY

David had avoided taking the Valium prescribed by his primary physician. He toted the pills with him wherever he went because Annette insisted, but he had yet to break the seal on the bottle. Sometimes, when he failed to mask his anxiety, Annette would urge him to take a pill and he'd lie and say he'd done so. He'd heard too many stories of patients getting hooked on narcotics over the years. What would often start as a valid prescription for back pain written for the most responsible patient could turn into a life-threatening heroin addiction. When he reluctantly gave new mothers Percocet after a cesarean, he would urge them to take it only if absolutely necessary and to flush any remaining pills down the toilet or dispose of them safely. For regular deliveries, he would prescribe narcotics only if the patient had a level-three laceration or higher. That was how strongly David felt about avoiding opioids, painkillers, narcotics, and the like. But after tonight's fiasco, he went straight to his cabin, secreted himself in the bathroom, and went for a single ten-milligram Valium.

He tightened his grip around the white cap and prepared his strength to break the initial seal. His hands weren't what they used to be, when he could wield scalpels and needles like Edward Scissorhands, and he hated thinking about the amount of concentration and effort it took to do a simple task. But when he went to loosen the top, it slid off easily. He wondered if one of the crew had pilfered his stash. These pills, relatively cheap in America, often went for more than five dollars a pop in impoverished countries.

"You okay in there?" Annette called out. "Stomach feeling all right?" She was so nervous around him it was making David crazy. Her intentions were pure, but her hovering made his skin feel like a layer he was desperate to shed.

For decades they'd been equals, true partners. Annette respected the work he did and he knew she was an indispensable part of running the practice. But now . . . he was like a child in her eyes. She managed his diet, his vitals, his emotions, and even his damn bowel movements. Some of the medications in his regimen were known to constipate; others could make his stool loose. As such, he had to give a report to Annette every time he went to the bathroom, calling out, "hard one" . . . "watery" . . . "sizable." They were light-years from that hormonal newlywed stage, and they were well past that chunk of middle age where they were reliably intimate once a week, but this was truly a new low. He was one step above Annette coming in to change his diaper.

"David, did you hear me? I just want to know how you're feeling."

Annette. He looked back down at the Valium bottle in his hand with the broken seal. That was who must have helped herself to a few pills. He counted out the little white tablets, neatly arranging them in rows of five. Two were missing from a thirty-day supply. That wasn't terrible. For the first time, instead of focusing on how much Annette's angst was bugging him, he took a one-hundred-eighty-degree turn and considered his wife's emotional state in a vacuum — without the attendant reverberations back to him. He softened considerably, regretting all the times he'd all but barked, "I'm fine," after she'd inquired. He was the one who was sick, so it had somewhat irritated him the extent to which Annette was looking and acting like she was in more pain than he was. It occurred to him, in a sudden epiphany manifested in rows of white pills, that she could be more afraid to be left alone than he was of dying.

"I feel good," he said now, gently. "Just getting ready for bed."

He held a pill in his hand and thought briefly before putting it under his tongue. There was no shame in seeking a little relaxation. If nothing else, it would help him get to sleep. There was so much to discuss after the night's fiasco that it was daunting to find a place to begin. How to prioritize the drama, the shocks, the revelations. He imagined Annette felt the same way.

Should they tackle Elise's bankruptcy first and her baloney story about starting an app? Or should they address their granddaughter's criminal record and secret boyfriend? Or, perhaps most painfully, should they start with how their estranged son had managed to build a vast business and hadn't told them a thing about it? Last, but not least, there was the fact that for the first time in history, their family had resorted to physical violence. He lifted his tongue and placed the pill underneath, feeling the graininess as it dissolved with his saliva. It was so much smoother and less effortful than the grass he'd smoked in college a few times. With that came a lingering smell, a burning in the lungs, so much paraphernalia needed. He knew enough, from watching a multipart series on CNN, that dope wasn't just rolled into paper or smoked from a pen cap anymore. There were candies, vapes, pot balls that looked like breakfast cereal. He remembered watching in fear, thinking how easily a kid could go off to school high from ingesting Cocoa Puffs look-alikes. He was, in reality, rather curious to ask Freddy about his affairs.

David stepped out of the bathroom and found Annette in her dressing robe, an unopened novel on her lap. So they were going to improvise the motions of a regular evening.

"David, I know we have a lot to talk about, but I don't think tonight is the night. I would rather you get a good night's sleep. I'm wired, but I'll just read." She lifted the book in the air. He noticed it was upside down.

"I'm fine, Annette. And I don't want you stewing over everything alone either. I have cancer, not dementia. I can process these things and discuss them with you. I want to." He pictured the broken seal of the

Valium bottle. "I care about how you're feeling."

Annette put her book to the side and said, "Did you know that I once heard Freddy call me a fucking bitch and after that I just could never look at him the same?"

David nodded. "You said something about him calling you a name when you were helping him pack up his dorm."

"It hurt so much because here was this kid — this problem kid — for whom we did everything. You slaved at work, on call at night, on weekends. I drove Freddy to school every day because he could never make the bus on time. Then all those textbooks and homework assignments he'd forget and I'd be driving all over town while he tried to remember if he left it at the diner, the mall, or a friend's house. The Spanish tutoring and the math flash cards and all that effort. And then how I begged the dean to let him stay, embarrassing myself, groveling. And then what did I hear? That my son, who I did everything for, thinks I'm a fucking bitch. I'd say it was a knife to my heart, but it really felt more like a sword to my brain. Because more than feeling hurt in the emotional sense, I was so utterly confused that he couldn't see how much I loved him and all that I did for him.

And looking back on that day, I'm still sad, but I've come to see that the parent-child give-and-take isn't like the Secret Santa we used to do at your office, where everyone gets a present and a certain dollar amount is agreed upon. It's more a straight-up Santa Claus situation, where this one guy works his tail off to deliver bags of presents in the snow and, if he's lucky, he gets a plate of cookies. And that, as bad as it sounds, is just the natural order of things. Freddy never had children so he hasn't gotten to see it firsthand, which is a shame because I think he would have more empathy for us, but Elise sure does now. She has her chance to know what it's like to do so much for people and get so little in return. But it's only so little in a transactional sense. Because what we get from our children and grandchildren — the tingly feeling when they hug us, the symphony of their high-pitched squeals, the gratification of their successes — it's worth a thousand times what we give. And besides, we put them on this earth to make us happy. They didn't choose it."

David sat down next to Annette and put an arm around her shoulders. They'd spoken often of their children, especially when the kids were younger and living at home, but rarely on such a meta level. He and Annette had agonized over Freddy's future and whether Elise was happy with the path she'd chosen. They had talked about the groups of friends their children surrounded themselves with and whether Mitch was the right guy for Elise. They had largely followed Spock and hoped for the best. But they'd never done the airplane view before, discussing why they had become parents or what kind of parents they wanted to be. It wasn't done in their generation, these navel-gazing, soul-searching types of talks, the kind he was sure Mitch and Elise had, maybe in front of some nonsense feelings doctor.

It was David's natural instinct to play devil's advocate, but he honestly agreed with everything Annette said and he told her so.

"What should we do about Elise? I was thinking we could take out a mortgage on the house," he said. It had been such a point of pride the day he and Annette finally paid off their mortgage. Never did it occur to him that he might take a step backward. But it went without saying, he thought, that they would help see her through this. They were parents of parents, which only multiplied their responsibility.

"Yes. That's an option," Annette said. "I will call Jeff Simpson at the bank when we get back home and see what he says."

"Where are we tomorrow again? St. Croix?" David asked. "Maybe you can do it from there."

"St. Kitts, I think. Or maybe St. Thomas. All these islands look the same, don't they? Beach, conch fritters, a place to get hair braided. Oh, and some water sport we're too old for."

"Sightseeing wasn't the point of the trip," David said. "I was actually thinking of trying the kayaking tomorrow. Would you want to do it with me?"

"You sure you're up to it?" Annette asked.

"Totally. And I think it's good tomorrow's not a day at sea. We could all use some time in the fresh air to clear our heads. Hard to believe the trip is almost over."

"I know. It went fast. Or maybe slow. I'm not even sure. Needless to say it was not our typical week. I can't believe how much time had passed since we were all together. And clearly the intermittent phone calls weren't cutting it. I think on my last call with Elise we discussed gel manicures versus regular manicures. Oh, gosh, I think I told her definitely to do the gel even though it costs three times as much. Little did I know she was headed to debtor's prison."

"You couldn't have known, Annette. The blame isn't ours. Should we have maybe tried to keep more tabs on the kids? Perhaps. But they *are* grown-ups and it's a fine line. They knew, even Freddy, that our door was always open."

"I hope so," Annette said, but she didn't look convinced. David wanted to continue to reassure his wife, but his eyes were getting so incredibly heavy, like little paperweights had been attached to his lids. He stood up to get into his pajamas and felt a soreness in his back that was getting difficult to ignore. He tried to move smoothly, but Annette was on to him.

"You're in pain," she said and for once he didn't argue, just nodded.

"I'll feel better in the morning," he said, which was more of an aspiration than a statement. Within minutes of his head hitting the pillow, David fell into a dreamless sleep and was utterly confused when the sound of the ship's bugle roused him some hours later.

"What time is it?" he asked Annette, who was punching numbers into the calculator on her iPad, which was glowing in the dark. He didn't even know she knew how to use that machine. It had been a gift from the women she played mah-jongg with for her seventieth and she'd complained about it the minute she came home with it. *Steve Jobs became a billionaire because of this thing?*

"Shush, there's an important announcement," Annette said, waving him off.

David heard the cruise director's voice through the intercom.

"Ladies and gentlemen, I repeat, this is your cruise director speaking. I regret that I have some bad news about our planned visit to St. Lucia today."

"I thought it was St. Croix," David whispered to Annette.

"We need to hear this, David," Annette said, putting a finger to her lips.

"Unfortunately, we received word overnight from the CDC that there has been an outbreak of a mosquito-borne virus on the island of St. Lucia. Common symptoms of Fermentalisminutia include extreme diarrhea, rash, and fever. More extreme cases can lead to lack of sexual function, infertility, and, I am not making this up, excessive body hair growth, particularly in the nasal area. So, as I'm sure you can understand, our boat will not be making its scheduled stop in St. Lucia. If you all wanted extreme

484

diarrhea, you would have booked yourselves on one of our competitors' cruise lines. Kidding, of course. Don't tell them I said that! I'm sure you're disappointed with this development, but rest assured my staff has worked through the night to create an itinerary of special and never-before-done activities that will leave you happy about the outbreak of Fermenta-whatever-it's-called. New schedules were slipped under your doors early this morning. Any questions, feel free to reach out to my staff or you can find me at the Festive pool participating in the belly flop contest at eleven hundred hours. Signing off for now. Thank you for your understanding."

"This boat is a circus," David said. He had no tolerance for things like belly flop competitions. For decades, he delivered two or three babies a day. A year ago he was guest lecturing at Stony Brook Medical School. Now he was an out-of-work doctor, constantly surrounded by other doctors telling him what to do, and the highlight of his day was going to be watching a belly flop competition.

"Let me grab the schedule from the door," Annette said. She had her hair already set in rollers and the overnight mask she applied once a week had dried to a flaky crust.

485

Incredible that with all the hullabaloo the previous night, Annette hadn't deviated from her routine. His wife was committed to growing old gracefully, that was for certain. He knew Elise found her mother silly with all the self-care and anti-aging strategies, treating her body like a laboratory. Annette and Elise could no more relate over their varying commitment to beautification and preservation than he could relate to Mitch, leaving a perfectly respectable and decently paying job to follow his dream of creating a humor magazine that wouldn't even exist in print.

"What were you doing on your iPad, by the way?" David asked.

"I was just running some numbers. We need to figure out how we're going to lend Elise and Mitch the money and still be able to cover all of your medications."

"Annette, it's your birthday. I understand you're anxious, but trust me, our problems will still be there when we get home. Try to enjoy today. It's the last full day." He took the schedule from her hands. "Look. There's something called 'How Well Do You Know Your Family?' this afternoon. Let's round up everyone and do it."

"You're serious?" Annette asked him as she started the laborious task of unfastening her rollers.

"Maybe," he said. "First let's eat breakfast. We'll see who we run into at the buffet. You'll be ready to go soon, birthday girl?"

"I'm hardly a girl," Annette said.

"To me you are," he said and reached out his hand.

THIRTY-ONE

Freddy slept through the announcement that the ship wouldn't be stopping at port. He slept through breakfast and through the extra morning rounds of bingo, the belly flop competition, and the free stacks of chips being handed out in the casino. Freddy finally woke to the sound of violent retching. It was coming, he realized slowly, from inside his cabin.

"Tash?" he called out, confused because a glance at the alarm clock showed it was after eleven. She was supposed to be doing another marathon yoga session at some sanctuary onshore. He had told her that he'd join her there later in the day, which he hadn't really meant, but it seemed to make her happy.

"You really could use the relaxation," she had told him when they returned to their suite after the night's debacle. "I'll even do a beginner class with you."

After everything that had come tumbling out that night, it didn't seem like he was the Feldman most in need of Ashtanga. He hadn't been positive that his father was sick before last night, but he'd been pretty suspicious. Then when Elise mentioned all the drugs she'd seen in their room, he was certain.

A few of his buddies in Aspen had lost parents in recent years. Freddy wasn't sure how he would process such a loss, not that he should be thinking in these terms just yet. His father had non-Hodgkin's lymphoma and that was all he knew so far. Nothing about his chances or his treatment or what else lay ahead. And that was pretty much on par with everything else about the Feldman/Connelly crew. Freddy was on the outside. The surprising thing was that Elise was also on the wrong side of the fence. They were all outsiders in a way, slices of a pie with only a pin dot in the center connecting them.

"Natasha? Is that you?" Freddy called again, and when she didn't answer, he climbed out of bed and looked inside the master bath. Their cabin had three bathrooms, which felt excessive, even given the ridiculous price he was paying for what was basically the nicest room at a floating carnival. He found his girlfriend hunched over the toilet, the tip of her ponytail dangling inside the bowl just above the waterline.

"Oh, my God, are you okay?" He dropped down next to her.

Natasha shifted to sitting on her backside, her head slumped against the toilet paper holder. She was ashen, the space beneath her eyes hollowed out in dark shadow.

"I'm scared I have Fermentalisminutia," she moaned, wiping the corners of her mouth with the back of her hand.

"What are you talking about?" Freddy asked, wondering if Natasha was having delusions.

"You slept through the whole thing," Natasha said weakly, forcing herself back to her knees, clearly anticipating another wave of nausea. "There's some disease from mosquitoes on the island we were supposed to visit today and I think I have it. The cruise director made an announcement this morning while you were out cold."

"But we didn't get off the boat there," Freddy said, putting a hand on Natasha's bare back, which was slicked with sweat.

"Mosquitoes fly, Freddy! What if one flew onto the boat and bit me?" She started to examine her arms and legs in panic.

Freddy looked closely at his girlfriend. He hadn't thought it was possible for her to look unsexy. Now she was nearly grotesque. Her skin was pale with a grayish pallor. There was dried vomit on her negligee and her hair was coated in grease. And still he wanted to cradle her, to kiss away her discomfort.

"I don't think bugs can live on the open water. Like, I don't think mosquitoes would be on the boat." He'd heard that once. Maybe in biology class, when everyone thought he wasn't listening. "Do you itch anywhere?"

"I itch everywhere. Since the cruise director made that announcement my entire body feels like one giant bug bite."

Freddy knew that was psychosomatic, but he didn't want to delegitimize anything Natasha was saying, especially seeing her curled in the fetal position looking like an extra in a horror movie.

"Do you think you can stand up? I can wash you off and help you into bed." Freddy reached out a hand to her and she took it. Feebly, she stepped out of her nightgown and he ran the water in the shower until it felt just right. Realizing there was no way he could clean her without getting himself soaked, he pulled off his boxers and went inside the stall with her. It was quite a bit different from the last time they'd showered together, just a few days earlier, when they missed the safety briefing. Well, that was okay, he thought, as he squeezed shampoo from the mini bottle and worked it into a lather in Natasha's hair. A real relationship wasn't just sex and making other guys jealous, it was wiping away vomit and reassuring the other person that they didn't have whatever the hell that bizarre virus was.

After he was satisfied that her hair was clean, he took the bar of soap from the tray and massaged it over her skin, starting with her shoulders and working his way down to her toes. It recalled the times when his mother dipped a washcloth into an ice bath to cool his body when he had a fever.

Color was returning to Natasha's cheeks, possibly from the hot water, but either way she was looking more like herself. Freddy turned the water off and wrapped her in a fluffy towel. This was quite the role reversal. Normally Natasha took care of him. She tenderly unknotted his neck when he talked about business and counseled him about how to manage his family. She was the one who told him to have a publicist present for the *High Times* interview, advice he'd regrettably ignored.

"Let's put you in bed. I bet you'll fall back asleep and hopefully that was the worst of it," he said.

Natasha nodded as he patted her dry and slipped one of his baggy T-shirts over her head. He squeezed the wetness from her hair and gathered it into a bun, reaching for one of the hair elastics that were lying all over their cabin, much like they were in his condo in Aspen. *Their* condo. He lifted the covers and Natasha collapsed onto the bed. With a weak hand, she gestured toward the phone on the bedside table. The message light was on.

"Don't worry about that. I'll listen to it. You just rest."

She needed no extra prodding and within minutes her breathing took on the soft, even rhythm of sleep. Freddy dialed in for the messages.

"Hi, Freddy, it's Mom. Last full day on the boat and I was hoping we could all meet after lunch in the Starboard Ballroom for the game show this afternoon. Um, thanks, 'bye."

His mother's voice tremored like a mild earthquake. She was trying to right the ship before they all went their different ways tomorrow. Freddy climbed into bed next to Natasha with his iPad, planning to look up

493

that cockamamie mosquito illness she had mentioned, but first he went back to read the *High Times* article again.

Now that the cat was out of the bag, it was only a matter of time before every member of his family Googled him, and he wanted to prepare a fulsome defense. There were a lot of Frederick Feldmans in the world, but not quite so many would pop up when you added "marijuana" and "millionaire" to the search string. He still wasn't sure how Mitch had discovered the article. Freddy wasn't angry with his brother-in-law, just confused. His livelihood wasn't a secret per se. He read through the introductory paragraphs, which gave the gestalt picture. Maybe his family would stop there, too stunned to read on. But no, of course they wouldn't. They would read every damn word, as he would do if the situation were reversed. Chewing on his bottom lip, he continued reading the article, feeling his stomach rolling as he approached the parts about his family.

But they were gone! Lifted from the article as if they'd been written in disappearing ink. Freddy waited to rejoice, fearing the editor had simply rejiggered the piece, moving the part about his family to the end. But he got through the entire article with bated breath and there was no mention of his parents or his sister. He wanted to shake Natasha awake to tell her. Maybe she'd had something to do with the disappearance of his damning words. But no, she would have told him, knowing how upset he was last night when he went to sleep. It was a mystery.

He looked back at his girlfriend, sleeping peacefully. Her cheeks retained their flush and her body was cool to the touch, so he felt comfortable leaving her alone in the room for a few minutes. There were people he needed to see.

"Uncle Freddy," Rachel said, answering the door with a bag of chips in one hand and a crumpled tissue in the other. It looked like she had been crying.

"Hi, Rach. I wanted to check if you were doing okay. I'm guessing not," he said, gesturing toward her eyes.

"It's Austin, the guy I've been seeing. He waited until I was on the cruise to send me a 'Let's not rush things' email that doesn't quite tell me we're finished but also gives me, like, zero confidence that we have a future together."

"You're in purgatory," Freddy said, draping an arm around Rachel's back. He pictured Natasha suddenly, curled up in bed, wondering if she ever felt that way about him. She never asked to have "the talk," nor did she drop hints about wanting to get more serious — at least none that were overt enough for an obtuse guy like him to pick up on. But he couldn't imagine she enjoyed their amorphous status. Yes, they had moved in together, but Freddy still never called if he was going out for a boys' night nor did they celebrate anniversaries in the manner of people moving toward a particular destination.

"Guys suck," Freddy said and Rachel acquiesced by propping her head on his shoulder. "How you feeling about the stuff with your parents? I was upset to hear about your mom. I can't imagine how difficult it must be for you and Darius."

"Yeah. I feel worse for Darius because this could really screw him for college. But in a way, I'm also relieved. Mom had been acting weird all summer and I thought maybe it was just me being paranoid about what I was hiding, but deep down I guess I knew something was off. One night I saw her sniffing Darius's pillow, like he was dead or something. I think she's pretty whacked."

An unexpected emptiness welled inside Freddy. As much as he felt sorry for his sister, there was a pang of envy as well. If Natasha were to leave him, he'd be crushed, but would he open up her shampoo bottles to breathe in her familiar scent? Probably not. That was the behavior of a lovesick teenager. And, apparently, of a parent.

"I'm going to try to talk to your parents about going easy on you with the police bit and secretly visiting me. I'll tell them I invited you to come. As for the arrest, maybe we'll concoct something about it being a sorority dare."

"But I'm not in a sorority," Rachel said earnestly.

"Well, of course not," Freddy said in a drawn-out, dramatic tone. "You would *never* have thought to follow through with rushing a sorority after you saw the unsafe and silly antics they were putting you up to." Freddy gave her a wink. He had so much more practice than his niece in such machinations.

Darius surprised them both by bounding into the room wearing a goofy grin.

"Oh, hey," Darius said. "I didn't know anyone was in here. I was going to work a little on my essay before we have to go to the game show thing."

"You seem awfully happy about writing," Freddy said. "At least that'll cheer your

497

mom and dad up."

"What? Uh, no. I'm not. I mean, I had a good idea. Someone gave me a good idea. It doesn't matter," Darius stammered.

Freddy exchanged looks with Rachel. He took in Darius, floppy hair draped over his eyes, hands jammed into the pockets of his oversized sweatshirt, that blank but kind expression he always wore on his face. Freddy knew what he needed to do, or rather, he realized what he very much wanted to do.

"See you both later. I need to check on Natasha. She wasn't feeling well earlier." He kissed Rachel on the top of her head and offered up his fist for Darius to bump. "I need to talk to you later, buddy."

Natasha was sitting up in bed when he reentered, scrolling through her phone.

"I feel so much better," she said the minute he shut the door behind him.

"That's a relief. No Fermentalism, then, I guess."

"It's Fermentalisminutia. And no, it seems I've been spared. I listened to your mom's message about the game show. I can go for sure."

Freddy sat down next to Natasha on the bed and took the phone out of her hands. Her cell phone obsession was one way in

498

which their age difference could not be ignored.

"I've been thinking about Darius's college. I'm going to offer to pay for it. And I'm going to lend Elise and Mitch whatever they need to pay off their debts. And I'm going to help my parents too. It sounds like Dad's medical bills are out of control."

He looked at Natasha, waiting for her to throw her arms around him, oh-my-hero-style. Instead she got up from the bed and pulled a water from the minifridge.

"You know, Freddy, it won't be that simple to swoop in and fix everything." She took a few sips. "Your family is still adjusting to all this new information. For years they thought you were the black sheep, as you say, and now they find out you're a highly successful businessman. Even though it's good news —"

Freddy felt himself stiffening. He heard the air quotes around the "good news."

"— it's going to take them some time to process. Your sister has thought for the past thirty years that she was the one who had her stuff together and you were some clown without two nickels to rub together. Now she's in trouble and you're going to be everyone's savior. Your parents are going to have to grapple with the fact that you kept all this from them for a long time, not to mention that parents are supposed to provide for their children and not the other way around. I just don't want you to be disappointed when you go all Daddy Warbucks on them and they aren't jumping for joy. And that's without us even getting into the source of your wealth."

Freddy looked at Natasha incredulously. She'd certainly regained her strength. He might have preferred it when she was vomiting in the toilet and needed his assistance to stand upright. Still he had a nagging feeling she might be right. But what about satisfying his own impulses? For the first time since amassing a fortune, he had a clear direction of what he wanted to do with the money.

"Just don't go out guns blazing. That's all I'm saying. It's wonderful that you want to help. But nothing is as straightforward as it seems; meaning, helping others is also a way to help yourself. And that won't be lost on anyone either."

He avoided looking at Natasha. Surely she hadn't forgotten what he'd said before they departed for the trip. That he wanted to be damn sure that every single Feldman and Connelly realized he had left Freddy the Fuckup in the dust. But that had been anger and insecurity talking. Now things were different. His motivations were pure. He was as certain of that as he was that his father should really try his Blackberry Kush for his aches and his White Stripe to regain his appetite. Freddy had seen the way his father had pushed around the food on his plate all week like a child avoiding the Brussels sprouts. His best budtender, Richie, famous from Vail to Denver, could roll a superjoint that would pack a one-two punch for his father.

"Maybe you're right," Freddy said, because suddenly he didn't have the strength to debate something to which he'd already set his mind. He would speak to everyone in his family tonight, the last night of the trip and his mother's actual birthday. It was kismet that the excursions had been canceled.

Freddy and Natasha walked into the Starboard Ballroom at precisely five minutes to three, expecting to find a few scattered families waiting to play the silly game show. Instead, the ballroom was jam-packed with competing clans strategizing in football huddles.

"There's your mom," Natasha said, pointing to Annette in the far corner of the room.

Next to her, David was reclined in a chair with a rolled-up magazine in his hand, impervious to the competitive spirit flowing through the air vents. Freddy couldn't blame his father. It was rather hard to imagine the Feldmans having a fighting chance at "How Well Do You Know Your Family?"

They made their way over. Up close, he saw a single bandage across David's nose. Freddy offered his mother a kiss on the cheek and surprised his father with a hug. He was in charge now, the mature son who had been the only one of the three grown men in their group not to have been involved in the previous night's bar fight.

Next arrived Darius and Rachel, looking chummier than he'd ever seen them. Rachel seemed to have pulled herself together and Darius had the self-satisfied air of someone who'd finally gotten lucky. They plopped down on chairs next to their grandparents and Rachel asked how her grandfather was feeling. Freddy could see the annoyance spread across David's face. This was clearly what he'd been hoping to avoid. Having everyone fawn all over him, making him feel like the patient instead of the doctor.

A moment later Elise and Mitch trickled in. They appeared to be speaking to each other, which was a relief. Elise was wearing a baseball cap to cover up the wreckage from the hair flambé. Freddy zeroed in on Mitch. There was something forced about his brother-in-law's gait. His right arm was swinging freely but his left was stiff. His dad must have really given Mitch a good slugging. Freddy was impressed.

He watched Mitch and David eyeball each other sideways and then both of them mustered a grumbled apology simultaneously. His father said something about the side effects of his medication and Mitch muttered an excuse about his nerves, and it seemed enough to momentarily pacify the both of them. Freddy was fairly certain there was no long-standing animus between those two. Everyone loved Mitch. He had the personality of a Little League coach. And instead of feeling jealous that Mitch possessed that je ne sais quoi, good-guy quality, Freddy was filled with a feeling of contentedness. His sister needed a guy like that. She deserved it.

Annette reached into her bag and pulled out muffins wrapped in paper napkins.

"From the breakfast buffet. I have two blueberry, three banana bran, and one chocolate chip. Any takers? I figured you'd want to have a little snack at this time of day."

"Grandma, there's a massive table with food set up in the back," Rachel said, cuing up her infamous eye roll. "Besides, those muffins probably have, like, eight hundred calories each."

Freddy leaned over to whisper in Rachel's ear: "He's not worth the dieting, Rach."

She grabbed the single chocolate chip muffin and took a huge, obviously pleasurable bite.

"All right, families," boomed the cruise director from the stage, where a surprisingly realistic game show set had been erected. "Welcome to 'How Well Do You Know Your Family?' which I promise will be more entertaining than dolphin watching or scuba diving on St. Lucia. To get you all warmed up, we're going to start off with a few lightning rounds of 'Family Feud,' which I'm sure you're all familiar with. You have received schedules indicating when your family will be called up to play. The winning clan will take home a whopping thousand-dollar gift certificate to be used toward any Paradise International cruise taken within the next year."

The crowd burst out in applause while Mitch said, "Is that for the winner or the loser?" Elise shushed him while suppressing a grin.

"And for a special surprise, something I've never done before, I will be competing in the game as well with my family. I'd like everyone to give a wave to the handsome guy up front looking painfully embarrassed right now. Say, 'Hi, Roger,' everyone." The crowd obeyed, echoing, "Hi, Roger" in the half-asleep tones of children greeting a teacher at arrival in the morning. "And since we're a family of two and you all look way too fierce for us to face alone, I've asked my assistant, Lindsay, and the boat captain to round out our team. Let's hope we don't hit any rough waters for the next hour because I am not letting Captain John leave until we've had our turn."

"We're up in the third round," Annette said. "Who wants to go first for our team?"

Freddy put up his hand.

"All right, Freddy it is." His mother wrote down his name and then numbered the rest of them. Natasha was listed last, but at least she was included.

They sat around the table picking at muffins while Julian announced the first category: Places You Are Most Likely to Fart. The cruise was so terribly lowbrow that it was almost campy cool, like a horror movie with such gruesome effects that you find yourself laughing. Two families took the stage and made their best guesses: in bed, in the shower, on an airplane.

"I'd say the car," Freddy said, turning to Natasha. "Tash! Are you okay?"

His girlfriend had her head dropped between her knees and was throwing up again. When she looked up, her bottom lip was quivering.

"I'll get napkins. Stay put," Freddy stammered. "Dad, you need to help Natasha. She threw up this morning and we thought she was doing better. She's worried she has that mosquito virus."

David sprang into action, rising from his chair and touching the back of his hand to Natasha's forehead.

"Forget the napkins. Darius — go run in the kitchen and ask for a dish towel and wet it with ice water. We need to cool her off and get her to your cabin without anyone noticing she's sick."

Elise had jumped up as well. She put two fingers to Natasha's neck and checked her watch. Freddy saw that his sister was playing the role she was born for: caretaker, which could take many forms.

"Why can't anyone on the boat see that she's sick?" Mitch asked.

"Because if any of the crew notices, they'll quarantine her in the boat hospital. And trust me, we don't want her there. She's much better off with me taking care of her. And Elise," he added.

"*Is* she contagious?" Rachel asked.

"You can't catch this," David said, patting Natasha on the head.

"Are you sure?" Natasha asked weakly. "I looked up Fermentalisminutia and the CDC says they don't know how it's spread yet. Freddy — I knew it was ridiculous that bugs can't live on a boat." Before she could ream him further, her head dropped and another wave of vomit hit the ground.

"Where is Darius with that dish towel?" David groused, looking around.

"He probably ran into his new girlfriend, Angelica," Rachel said.

"Not now, Rachel," Elise snapped. "Dad, let's just get Natasha to her room and we'll deal with everything there. Mitch, grab an arm. Dad, you must have your medical bag in your room." David nodded.

Freddy recalled that as children their father never went anywhere without his trusty black leather doctor kit. Elise would bring her plastic Fisher-Price version and together they would listen to the heartbeat and take the temperature of any willing patient, which was usually him.

Mitch slipped an arm through Natasha's and Freddy took the other one. They brought her to her feet and slipped out of the room without calling attention to themselves. For someone who probably weighed no more than a hundred and five pounds, Natasha was awfully cumbersome — Freddy found himself panting by the time they reached the elevator. Why did he never join his girlfriend at the gym? And what the hell were they going to do if she *had* contracted some terrible sickness? Finally they reached the door to the cabin and Freddy passed his half of Natasha's weight on to Rachel so he could grab his key card. When he pushed open the door, he heard a collective gasp.

"Holy crap." His sister's voice sounded first. "You really are rich."

THIRTY-TWO

Darius and Rachel walked into the breakfast buffet for the last time. The crowd was slightly thinner than usual. Disembarkation times were scattered based on airport connections and final destinations, and the Connelly children actually found an open table.

Rachel filled her plate with pastries: two mini croissants, a Danish, and a blueberry muffin. Darius was happy to see her eating again. He didn't know what happened with Austin, but ever since she'd checked her email on Angelica's computer, she was back to consuming a normal caloric intake. Maybe even larger than normal.

Although his sister was dressed and ready for breakfast earlier than he was that morning, she'd sat back down on her bed and leafed through the Paradise International magazine. She hadn't announced her intention to wait for him, but it was definitely a shift in behavior. He didn't even mind when she made fun of his Thrasher T-shirt and complained that he was taking too long in the bathroom.

"Do you see Mom or Dad anywhere?" Darius asked, scanning the crowd. Rachel looked up from her half-eaten muffin.

"No. And I don't want to either. Now that Mom has relaxed about her hair bonfire, she and Dad will be ready to skewer me. They're so pissed at each other that the best way to deflect will be to focus on something they agree on — that I deserve to be grounded for the rest of my life. Can college-age kids get grounded?" Darius assumed the question was rhetorical.

"What about Grandma and Grandpa? We should probably say good-bye to them, right?" Darius asked, moving his scrambled eggs around aimlessly.

"Grandpa told me they're in Departure Group Six, whatever that means. I think their flight to New York is much later than our flight home. But he said Mom and Grandma made some arrangements for all of us to meet up in front of Peace O'Pizza at noon to say good-bye. Freddy and Natasha should be there too, assuming she's feeling better."

"Got it," Darius said, distracted by the

crowds. It was so hard to find anyone with all these people milling about.

Darius felt really sorry for Grandma Annette. The day before had been her actual birthday and the family was in tatters. Sure, they had reached a détente (he listened in his Cold War history elective), but it had a forced quality to it. He couldn't stop picturing his grandmother's face when he'd found her alone on the pool deck the first day. He wondered if there was anything he could do to make her happy. Maybe he would tell her about the kiss. It was hard to keep it inside and it wasn't like he could go back home and tell Jesse, who would make fun of him mercilessly for stopping at first base. Then he would demand to see a photo, and if Darius was willing to share the one selfie he'd snapped of him and Angelica in the arcade, Jesse would goad him about her glasses and debate team T-shirt. Grandma Annette wouldn't tease. She would just be ecstatic that someone was voluntarily confiding in her.

"Anyone else you might want to say goodbye to?" Rachel asked, giving him a kick under the table. He looked up at her and she was smiling in a smug, know-it-all way.

"What? No," Darius said. "I'm excited to go home. This has been a little too much family time for my taste."

"Uh-huh. I just wondered if maybe you were looking for Angelica? You haven't taken a bite of your breakfast and you keep looking around the room. So I was just thinking you might be —" She raised a croissant at him accusingly.

"I'm not anything," he snapped, but of course his sister was totally right. Angelica's family had booked a private room for their last dinner and the Feldmans/Connellys had scrounged with room service after Natasha had taken ill, so he hadn't seen her since the kiss. It was his first one if he discounted all the sloppy misfires during Seven Minutes in Heaven at the middle school parties. He reviewed what he knew about Angelica: She went to a school called Highland, worked at Harvard Cleaners, and had a rich uncle. Even though she had the fairly common last name of Lee, he felt confident he could track her down on social media. He had already crafted a nonembarrassing reason to reach out to her: sending her a draft of his college essay. It was already half-done.

"Chill out. You read my private emails so it's not exactly like you're in a position to be upset with me for a little prying," Rachel said.

"I'm sorry about ratting you out," Darius

said. He looked down at his eggs, dicing them into smaller pieces. "I actually really like hanging out with you. I hope you're not mad."

"Awww, little brother. You're sweet. Why don't you come visit me at school this fall? After you turn in your applications. We can celebrate. I know a bunch of places that don't card. Or maybe I'll hook you up with a fake ID." She winked at him.

"That would be amazing. Although I'm still not sure I'm even going to be doing applications. Well, maybe for that school on Route 18 that teaches air-conditioning repair."

"I think the tuition thing will work out. If you have to take a gap year, that'll just give you more time to visit me. Since you're not eating anything, want to try the Ferris wheel on the sundeck? I flirted with one of the Sports Center dudes and he gave me a VIP pass so we don't have to wait in another dreadful line."

Darius shoveled in a bite of toast and grabbed his hoodie. The last ride he and Rachel went on together was It's a Small World. She had made fun of him for asking where the kangaroos were in Austria.

"Sweet," he said and did one last sweep

for Angelica as he followed his sister out the door.

THIRTY-THREE

"I guess this is good-bye," David said, reaching out an arm to put a hand on Freddy's shoulder. He put his other arm around Elise's waist. He hadn't held his two children at once since the year Annette got it into her head that they should send out holiday cards. Elise and Freddy had each climbed on a knee, giggling, and the photographer had snapped a candid picture while they were getting themselves properly sorted. Annette didn't like the way she looked in the picture — apparently her hair had gone flat with all the tumult of tucking and retucking Freddy's button-down and adjusting Elise's bow, but David loved it. It captured the Feldmans in a rare moment of pure joy. He displayed it in his office, but for the holiday card Annette chose a more formal pose, everyone with Say Cheese smiles and ample hair volume.

The Feldmans and Connellys were gathered in a holding pen where mountains of luggage waited to be sorted. After splitting two pies at Peace O'Pizza, they had made their way to the departure zone together even though they were scheduled to disembark at different times. The cruise was officially over.

"Thank you so much for taking care of me last night," Natasha said to him. She really did look better. Her eyes were bright and she had attacked the pizza with gusto.

"Of course," David said. "Elise was a big help too." He nuzzled the top of his daughter's head.

"Sorry your birthday didn't work out the way you wanted," Freddy said, looking at Annette. "I feel bad we didn't get to have our last family dinner together. I know the crew goes all out for birthdays."

"Trust me, I didn't need a cake with sparklers and thirty sailors serenading me," Annette said. "I want to thank you all for coming on this trip. I know how busy everyone is."

"We should be thanking you and David," Mitch said. "We never get to be away together like this and it was wonderful." Everyone nodded and echoed a chorus of thank-you-so-muches.

David wondered if Mitch meant a word of

it. If any of them did. He looked poignantly at his wife. Had the vacation accomplished half of what she'd hoped for? She looked exhausted, but she didn't appear unhappy. She was doing her Annette thing: fussing about, checking to make sure her suitcases had the proper tags, distributing snacks for everyone to take with them as they went their separate ways.

"Elise, you guys better get going," Annette said, looking at her watch. "The first bus to the airport leaves in twenty minutes."

"You're right," Elise said. "Rachel and Darius, get your stuff together." The kids were already far gone. With the boat docked in the States, their devices were back in action. "Put those cell phones away and help with the bags."

"Feel good, Grandpa," Rachel said, standing on tiptoe to kiss him on the cheek. "And don't worry about me. I realize the jail/balloon-skirt story wasn't what you wanted to hear, but I promise I'm okay. You just take care of yourself, and when you're better, come visit me in school."

"You could come visit him," Annette said. Her suggestion came out abrasively.

"She's a busy girl, Annette. It's okay. I will visit you when I'm better, sweetheart," David said. "And you too." He patted

Darius on the head.

"Well, he might be more motivated to come to the East Coast now," Annette said and winked at Darius. David had no idea what that was supposed to mean.

"I will," Darius said and hugged both David and Annette.

"It was really nice to be together," Elise said. "This is definitely the most excitement I've had in a while." She attempted a feeble laugh.

Nobody really answered her. Elise's statement hung in the air awkwardly, everyone imagining the depths of her troubles.

"Don't miss the bus," David said, and he beckoned for Elise and Mitch to give him a hug. He had made clear he didn't wish to discuss his illness and he appreciated that the children were following his wishes. They enveloped Annette, and it was their four heads bowed together for maybe the first time ever.

The Connellys and Feldmans bid goodbye to each other, calling out a round robin of "Thanks again," "Have a safe flight," and "Love you" until they were out of earshot.

"I think I'll go settle the bill at Guest Services," David said, turning to his son. "I know you're off the boat in the next wave so I think we should part ways here. Natasha — let us know how you're feeling. Freddy — what can I say? You've always been full of surprises."

"I try," Freddy said, with a sheepish grin. "Actually, I don't try. It just happens."

"We love you, Freddy," Annette said.

"Love you too, Mom. And Dad."

The three of them exchanged another round of hugs, and then brought Natasha into the fold.

"Maybe we'll see you soon," Freddy added.

"I bet we will," David said, smiling.

■ ■ ■ ■

PART III
TERRA FIRMA

■ ■ ■ ■

One Year Later

THIRTY-FOUR

We're getting into the rental car so I gotta go. Lunch next week?? Elise texted.

Absolutely, Lynn responded. Maybe at the farmers' market. Have fun!

Elise clutched the phone in her hand and smiled. She looked at Mitch, who was still totally absorbed in his iPad. On the screen was the latest issue of *The Elephant* and Mitch had spent the whole flight rereading articles and making notes in a leather-bound notebook, a gift from Rachel and Darius for Father's Day. He looked up at her and said, "You look happy."

"I am," she responded. "I really like Lynn. We're going to have lunch next week when I'm back. And then we're going to try hot yoga together. Natasha said it's life changing and she really missed doing it last year."

The Wellspring Treatment Center, in-patient program, had been a godsend to

Elise for many reasons. She'd resisted full-time care for weeks after returning from the cruise, insisting that thrice-weekly therapy (in person, although she still held Dr. Margaret in high regard) would be sufficient. But by mid-September, it became obvious she needed more intensive management. Having her secret out had perversely made her more cavalier about her habits, and she would brazenly leave bags around the house and announce with almost no compunction when she was off to the mall. She falsely assumed that having the sympathy of her family meant they would cut her some slack. By October, Mitch had sat her down after dinner with the Wellspring brochure.

"Your mother found the place," he said, offering no explanation as to when they'd been in contact. Elise wasn't mad. Actually, she was touched. She got a fuzzy feeling thinking about Mitch and Annette exchanging emails. Two people connected strictly because of *her*. Doing something for *her*. She had been caregiving for so long, managing everyone else's lives as the family's personal secretary, that to have other people tending to her well-being was more gratifying than she'd have imagined. It was just one of the many ways the dynamics of the Feldman family were shifting, not that Elise

524

saw it coming at the time.

David was gone.

Four months after the cruise, his health took a turn for the worse. The nasty weather in the Northeast combined with his ravaged immune system led to a brutal case of pneumonia. He was hospitalized for nearly a month, but his body wouldn't respond to any of the medications. Surrounded by Annette, Elise, and Freddy, David Feldman passed at two in the morning. He was made to feel as little pain as possible, though he was lucid until the bitter end. Everyone had a chance to say good-bye; though, as Elise suspected with all final partings, there was an ocean left unsaid.

Her father's funeral and the week of shiva were Elise's first time away from Wellspring. She, Freddy, Annette, and the children sat hunched on backless stools in a circle in the Feldman living room, receiving condolences from neighbors and chanting prayers with the rabbi, their tight ring forming a scaffolding. After the seventh day of mourning and the customary walk around the block to signify the end of shiva, Elise went directly back to Wellspring. She wanted to stick around to help her mother, but Annette insisted. "You have a family to take care of," she said. "A mother must always be strong and healthy."

The treatment center was in Palo Alto and Rachel came to visit most weekends. Elise ended up spending twelve weeks there. The work to repair her mind and soul was harder than she expected and her counselor, a kind young woman named Dania who had successfully battled anorexia, warned her that the addiction would always be a part of her. There wasn't a cure. There was just *better.* The best part about her time in treatment was the friends she made, most of all Lynn, who was ten years younger than Elise and a recent divorcée with no children. She was the kind of person who if Elise had met her before Wellspring, she would have dismissed as someone with whom she had nothing in common. But it turned out emptiness was a theme that could be shared, and it was a more meaningful entry point for a friendship than hailing from the same demographic. Fortunately Lynn lived not far from Elise, and since they were supposed to stay away from stores as much as possible, it was nice to have someone to go out with to eat lunch and try new activities that didn't involve consumerism. Hence the hot yoga, and the cooking class, and the long hikes they took together in Alpine Canyon.

"Can you navigate?" Mitch asked. He had

a terrible sense of direction and guiding him through lefts and rights and roundabout exits was another one of Elise's never-ending jobs. Not that she would complain about it. After many marital counseling sessions, she and Mitch were well on the way toward repairing the damage to their relationship caused by her secrets. Genuine trust between them felt within grasp.

"Sure. Let me just put Freddy's address into Waze." Elise tooled around on her phone. "It says it's an eighteen-minute drive. It's so gorgeous here. We should have visited him ages ago. Rachel had the right idea."

She looked out the window over the aspen trees to the mountaintops, which were still snowcapped even though it was August.

"We'll come back next winter so we can ski," Mitch said. "By then the baby will actually be doing something."

It turned out Natasha didn't have Fermentalisminutia. She was pregnant. About five weeks at the time of the cruise, although neither she nor Freddy had any inkling. The only person who had known was David, who had taken one look at Natasha and known with absolute certainty that she wasn't seasick, nor did she have a mosquito-borne virus. What was making Natasha's GI tract feisty was none other than his future grandchild. He hadn't breathed a word, not even to Annette, until his suspicions were confirmed three weeks after the cruise with a joyous phone call from Freddy. It was an unspoken source of pain that David would never have the chance to meet his third grandchild, who also happened to be his namesake.

"You never liked the baby phase," Elise teased Mitch. "I still remember when we brought Rachel home from the NICU and you asked me when she was going to get interesting. If I had birthed mini adults, we probably would have had four or five children."

"I can't help it. Babies are boring. They just lie there and poop and spit up and everyone oohs and aahs, but they are really quite terrible. Everyone is just afraid to admit it. Maybe I'll write about that for *The Elephant*."

"That could be funny. Although maybe wait awhile so Freddy and Natasha don't think we're talking about Davie. I still cannot believe Freddy has a kid. And a baby girl, no less," Elise said. "You need to bear right at the next exit."

"I bet Freddy will actually be a great dad to a little girl. Rachel worships him. And he's really quite good to Natasha," Mitch said. "Think they'll get married?"

"Who knows with them? My mother would certainly like it. Actually, she's kind of calmed down. You know how people are supposed to get crazier as they get older? I think she might be going in the opposite direction. I always assumed if my dad died before her she'd totally fall apart or go totally batshit. But she's actually mellowed. Though I don't want to say any more on the subject and potentially jinx it." She watched as Mitch scratched at his chin, which he always did when contemplating another possible article.

"Annette's already been out here for a month, huh?" Mitch asked.

"Yes. Apparently the dry air is amazing for her arthritis. And she loves visiting the baby as much as possible. Between you and me, I don't think the pot hurts either, not that she's officially admitted to using any. But I'm pretty sure Natasha swapped out her Bengay for cannabis lotion."

Mitch chuckled.

"She's even talking about putting the Great Neck house on the market. I guess it's too big without my dad. Or just too many memories."

Elise eyed the gift she'd chosen for the

baby, propped in the backseat. It wasn't easy to find something when she was prohibited from nonessential shopping. For the shiva, Annette had wanted to display old pictures of David and she'd asked Elise for help locating them in the attic. While they were up there, Elise had come across a stack of Dr. Seuss books Freddy used to read to her when she was little. She had chosen a stack of her favorites and brought them home to California, then decoupaged an old trunk with lovely floral paper and placed the books inside, with *Oh, the Places You'll Go!* on top.

She'd also included a small velvet box. Inside was the crescent moon necklace she'd bought herself on the cruise, something for Davie to wear when she got older. It was the one that nice cruise director had complimented. She hadn't thought about him in months. Julian, she thought was his name. She remembered how desperate she had been for him to keep her company in the coffee shop in St. Kitts. Or was it Sint Maarten? She could hardly remember. Now she had actual friends. Lynn was only one of the women she'd connected with at the addiction center. There was Kathryn, a retired schoolteacher, and Abigail, a freelance chef. These women were enriching

Elise's life and making it bearable that Darius was going all the way to the University of Maryland next fall. The choice seemed random to almost everyone but her and Mitch, who knew that after Darius got home from the cruise, he had done an exhaustive internet search on Maryland, trying to locate a place called Harvard Cleaners. Puppy love was so magical and adorably unrealistic that Elise and Mitch were happy just to watch it from the sidelines. Apparently in his Googling he'd come across U of M and gotten hooked. Thanks to a killer personal essay and a loan from Freddy — Elise and Mitch had refused an outright gift — Darius was headed there next fall.

"Can't believe it's been a year since the cruise. It was kind of fun, looking back on it," Elise remarked. "I never thought I would participate in a pie-eating contest or a conga line or an eighties roller-skating party, let alone within one week." She pointed out the windshield. "Go straight for another five miles and we should arrive at Freddy's."

She double-checked that she was following the GPS correctly and saw Lynn had sent another text: Don't forget to send me a picture of the baby! Elise responded, I won't, adding a newborn emoji with a thumbs-up.

Darius had patiently schooled her in emojis and she was quite enjoying using them. To Rachel, she would text: How is your day going? and insert a stack of books. One time, feeling brazen from two glasses of chardonnay, she wrote to Rachel: Miss you . . . Hope you're not wearing any 🐛 anymore!

"And if we hadn't gone on the trip, we wouldn't even know the mother of our new niece," Mitch said. "What time do Rachel and Darius get in?"

"Their flight lands at five p.m. so we should all be able to have dinner together. I can't believe he said he didn't want to leave work early to fly with us. Can this be our same child? Though I figure it has something to do with that girl Hannah in his grade. God forbid he should have three less hours in her presence." Darius had moved on from Marcy, briefly fixated on a barista in town named JoJo (Elise had never seen their child quite so caffeinated), and then moved on to a girl he met at his summer job named Hannah, who — as far as Elise could see — had no visible piercings or tattoos. From her snooping, Elise knew that Darius was still in touch with Angelica, but it was platonic. Even though he was moving to her state in a few weeks to start freshman year, she was heading north to start her own college journey. At Yale.

"Rachel told me she'd like to bring her boyfriend home for brunch one weekend this fall," Mitch said. "Apparently his parents visited in the spring and they took them out for dinner. Jed seems like a good guy. I was worried after that Austin broke her heart that she wouldn't rebound so easily."

Elise smarted a little that Rachel spoke to her father more than her about matters of the heart, but she tried not to show it. Rachel wasn't really a daddy's girl per se, and she certainly wasn't a mama's girl. She was just her own girl, much like Elise had been.

"That would be great," she said flatly, and she saw it pass by in front of her face. Another elephant. She knew Mitch saw it too.

"This is it." Elise pointed to a sign for an apartment complex that read THE PINES. "Look, they're waiting for us." She pointed ahead and saw Annette, Freddy, and Natasha standing outside by the building's front entrance with a hot pink baby stroller over which they were all bent, mesmerized. As their car approached, they started waving and Freddy reached into the bassinet to lift Davie.

"She's so cute," Elise squealed and unbuckled before Mitch had even slowed down. "I need to get my hands on that kid."

THIRTY-FIVE

Annette pulled the veal roast from the oven and set it down on a wire cooling rack. It had browned beautifully and the natural juices pooled in the pan, which would make excellent gravy. She hadn't made a meal for the whole family in at least a decade, and even though she was working in an unfamiliar kitchen a fraction of the size of her own, with a hodgepodge of shoddy pots and pans, it felt good. The sting was that it wasn't her entire family she was cooking for. David — her soul, her better half, her partner — was gone. In his place was Davie. A *fakakta* name for a little girl, but the overture was so grand and surprising that Annette kept her mouth sealed shut.

From the living room, she could hear the tinny cries of the baby and everyone fussing over her, making suggestions of what could be wrong: wetness, gas, hunger. "She's a baby," Annette wanted to say. "They cry."

But she kept mum. It was instinct to try to solve a child's problems and there was no sense in interfering. In fact, what she ought to say was that the new parents should prepare for a lifetime of this: trying to smooth out the wrinkles of Davie's life.

Things were going well so far. Annette always had a bit of apprehension when the family gathered, but after surviving the cruise, she was more confident about their ability to coexist in close quarters. And the baby helped tremendously. A single coo could soften any rough edge.

She was staying at a hotel about four blocks away from Freddy's place in one of the residential time-share units. No check-out date had been decided upon yet. Annette appreciated the proximity to Davie. She was needed to babysit every Tuesday while her parents went on "date night" and she was on call for whenever Natasha's work schedule necessitated coverage. Freddy had arranged for Elise and Mitch and the kids to stay in a friend's condo that was vacant for the week of their visit. Annette suspected that Freddy had actually rented the apartment for them on VRBO, because it was just too perfect for a family of four and too close to Freddy's place, but she didn't press him and, as far as she knew, neither did Elise.

536

Annette had been pleased to see Darius and Rachel arriving in stitches, giggling about some episode that occurred on the airplane that nobody else could follow. When she had Darius alone for a moment, she asked if he still kept in touch with the girl from the boat. He said yes, they emailed and texted, but were just going to be friends. Rachel had a boyfriend — Elise had told her on the phone — but so far nobody but Darius had met him. "He's cool," was all Darius would say, and Annette realized she would just need to wait. Rachel was still a young girl. There was ample time before she ought to settle down and take on the responsibilities of family. Both her grandchildren seemed like more mature versions of their boat selves. She ought to remark on that to Elise — remind her daughter what a fine job she was doing with those two.

Elise looked like a different person than she had on the boat. It was like a twenty-pound weight had been lifted from her shoulders. She was less snippy and less anxious, and she didn't scoff when Annette suggested to Elise that she try a smidge of her skin-tightening serum around the eyes. A few times Annette had spied Mitch putting a thoughtful hand on Elise's back or the two of them exchanging a quick peck.

There was really no greater happiness than seeing a child settled into a happy marriage, and Annette and David had both remarked that Elise and Freddy had succeeded in that department. True, Freddy wasn't married, but he and Natasha were clearly devoted to each other. It was just such a shame that David never got to hold his third grandchild — a little girl with almond-shaped eyes just like his that neither of them would ever have predicted would be born.

"Dinner's almost ready," Annette called out and she heard an appreciative chorus of "great" echo back.

"Need help setting the table, Grandma?" Rachel asked, surprising Annette in the kitchen.

"I'm fine, sweetheart. Just go be with the family. I'll take care of everything."

Rachel nodded and retreated and within moments Annette heard her and Darius devolve into laughter again, still rehashing that same plane story. At the same time, Elise was explaining to Natasha the importance of a well-packed diaper bag while Natasha snapped endless photos of Davie. At least she had finally stopped taking selfies. Her entire focus, phonewise, had shifted to documenting Davie's every move. The infant even had her own Instagram feed:

@BabyDavie. Mitch was busy telling Freddy about how *The Elephant* was going. She heard Freddy thank Mitch for something, but couldn't hear what it was, only Mitch's response: "No problem. That's what family is for."

The roast was at its prime and the potatoes were crisped. She really ought to transfer everything onto serving platters. But instead she took a seat at the counter stool and tightened her favorite (and only) personalized sweatshirt around her, letting the chatter from the den float into the kitchen in a satisfying waft.

"Mom, you should be outside with everyone else," Elise said, startling her with a warm hand on her shoulder. "I have to get started on your birthday cake." She wasn't used to her daughter fiddling in the kitchen. So much had happened in the past year. Big and small moments, the most sorrowful and the most joyful. Time didn't stand still for anyone.

Another year.

Another birthday.

She looked up, willing David into the tableau for a moment. Then she stepped aside and let Elise have at the kitchen.

ACKNOWLEDGMENTS

So many talented and kind people helped make this book a reality, and I appreciate the chance to pay them a debt of gratitude here.

My editor, Kerry Donovan, is wise, encouraging, and thoughtful. She always "gets" my vision (and my jokes)! Best of all, she suffers my "little changes" with a smile. Stefanie Lieberman is my rock and my friend, and luckily also the star agent who works tirelessly on my behalf. Fareeda Bullert is a marketing whiz who never ceases to amaze me with her creativity and dedication. Lauren Burnstein and Tara O'Connor are a crackerjack pair of publicists who do the hard work of bragging about my work so I don't have to. Adam Auerbach has done it again with another gorgeous cover. Sheila Moody takes copyediting to a whole new level, and I thank her for expertly tidying up all the places where I was sloppy. Kathleen Carter, I really appreciate that you deal with my million emails and never stop trying to bring attention to my books. Thanks also to Leigh Abramson, Cristina Alger, Sarah Blumenstock, Jamie Brenner, Lauren Smith Brody, Georgia Clark, Fiona Davis, Abby Fabiaschi, Talia Katz Friedman, Emily Giffin, Alissa Grad, Shoshanna Gruss, Charlotte Houghteling, Brenda Janowitz, Pam Jenoff, Robin Kall, Jill Kargman, Jenny O'Regan, Amy Poeppel, Susie Orman Schnall, Allison Winn Scotch, Maureen Sherry, Hamilton South, Molly Steinblatt, Jennifer Weiner, Stanley Zabar, Randy Zuckerberg, Tanya Zuckerbrot, and so many others who have been supportive in one way or another.

Andrea Katz of Great Thoughts' Great Readers was a superb beta reader, and many of her suggestions made this into a better book. Jennifer Millstone was another star early reader, who made many insightful comments and also filled in my Aspen knowledge gaps with rapid-fire text responses.

My mom is a great editor and an even better cheerleader. My entire extended family has been with me on this journey, supporting me, loving me, fetching me wine, and listening to me complain about basically everything. You guys are the best.

William, you are the stuff dreams are made of. I couldn't love you more.

To the best kids on the planet: Charlie, Lila, and Sam. There is no greater joy than being your mom. You make me proud and happy every day, even when you refused to go to the kids' camp on our cruise.

I must pay homage to the late David Foster Wallace, whose seminal essay "A Supposedly Fun Thing I'll Never Do Again" served as a great source of inspiration for me, in both its brilliant writing and its dazzling insights into the world of cruising. Michael Ian Black, Dan Saltzstein, Joyce Wadler, Kate Silver, and Mark Bittman have all written on the subject as well, and their tales of cruising regaled me, inspired me, and reaffirmed my belief that cruising brings out the best and worst in people. In the fictional realm, I particularly loved the approaches of Maria Semple, Jonathan Evison, and Ruth Ware, all brilliant writers who took cruising to places I didn't expect — and I don't mean literally Antarctica, Alaska, and the North Sea.

Finally, to my readers: I wouldn't have a job if it weren't for you. Thank you for reading my work, sharing your feedback, and keeping fiction alive.

ABOUT THE AUTHOR

Elyssa Friedland is the acclaimed author of *The Intermission* and *Love and Miss Communication*. Elyssa is a graduate of Yale University and Columbia Law School and lives with her husband and three children in New York City.

CONNECT ONLINE
instagram.com/elyssafriedland
elyssafriedland.com
facebook.com/authorelyssafriedland
twitter.com/ElyssaFriedland

The employees of Thorndike Press hope you have enjoyed this Large Print book. All our Thorndike, Wheeler, and Kennebec Large Print titles are designed for easy reading, and all our books are made to last. Other Thorndike Press Large Print books are available at your library, through selected bookstores, or directly from us.

For information about titles, please call:
(800) 223-1244

or visit our website at:
gale.com/thorndike

To share your comments, please write:

Publisher
Thorndike Press
10 Water St., Suite 310
Waterville, ME 04901